COURTNEY MILAN

Unclaimed

HQN™

Recycling programs for this product may not exist in your area.

ISBN-13: 978-0-373-77603-0

UNCLAIMED

Copyright © 2011 by Courtney Milan

www.HQNBooks.com

Printed in U.S.A.

Dear Reader,

I've always wanted to write a rock-star hero. Unfortunately, I write historical romances, and that means no burning guitars, no long, unkempt hair. I had pretty much chalked that one up to "lost causes" for good. Then I started thinking about the sorts of things that would be popular in the nineteenth century. Sure, they wouldn't go for Bon Jovi. But there were popular men back then—men like Beau Brummel or Lord Byron. Once you venture into early Victorian times, you can imagine what would prove popular: Novelists. Prince Albert. Books on public morality....

Which is why my Victorian-era rock star is Sir Mark Turner, who wrote a book on chastity. Mark is more than a little embarrassed by his popularity. And unlike modern celebrities, he can't fall back on "sex, drugs and rock 'n' roll." He doesn't do drugs. Rock 'n' roll hasn't been invented yet. And as for sex...well, you'll have to read the book to find out.

I thought you might enjoy a membership card to his most embarrassing fan club for kicks.

Courtney

Male Chastity Brigade Membership Card

1. I solemnly agree that I will strictly adhere to the teachings of *A Gentleman's Practical Guide to Chastity*, and venerate its author, Sir Mark Turner.
2. I solemnly agree to uphold the solemnity of the M.C.B., and to assist my Brothers in Chastity as they resist Temptation.
3. I solemnly agree that I will not engage in flirtatious or otherwise lascivious conduct, as such leads to Peril.

_____
(name of member)

_____
date

Once again, an army went into making this book as strong as it could be. Tessa, Amy and Leigh all helped with brainstorming. Kristin Nelson, my amazing agent, and the rest of the agency staff, Sara, Anita and Lindsay, smoothed the way on a thousand counts. My editor, Margo Lipschultz, tirelessly worked to make this the best book it could be, and didn't flinch too much when I said the hero was a virgin. Thanks to Libby Sternberg, for copyediting above and beyond the call of duty. The team at Harlequin produced my favorite cover yet.

The Vanettes helped with cover copy. The Pixies, Destination Debut and the Loop that Must Not Be Named helped with sanity. Franzeca Drouin, as always, saved me more times than I could count. Elyssa Papa holds a special place in my heart for catching a mistake that would have been very embarrassing, and Kim Castillo made my life easy in a thousand other ways. And my husband didn't complain (much) when I went to England without him.

Last but not least, I owe a debt of gratitude to those who helped with the research for this book. Lorraine Pratten and Sue Wilson at Shepton Mallet's Tourist Information and Heritage Centre answered numerous questions. I relied extensively on Fred Davies and Alan Stones's accounts of historical Shepton Mallet, and would never have found Friar's Oven without the walking guide from the Mendip Ramblers. Thanks!

Unclaimed

For Wathel. Who was always my sister,
even when she was very, very far away.

CHAPTER ONE

London
June, 1841

SIR MARK TURNER did not look like any virgin that Jessica had ever seen before.

Perhaps, she mused, it was because he was surrounded by women.

The uneven glass of the taproom window obscured the tableau unfolding across the street. Not that she would have been able to see anything, even had she been standing in the muck of the road. After all, it had taken less than a minute for the mob to form. The instant Sir Mark had come out the door across the way, a carriage had come to an abrupt halt. A pair of young ladies had spilled out, tugged along by an eager chaperone. Two elderly matrons, strolling along the gangway, had laid eyes on him a few moments later and darted in front of a cart with surprising speed.

The oldest woman now had one clawed hand on the cuff of his greatcoat and the other on her cane—and she was merely the most aggressive of his hangers-on. Sir Mark was thronged on all sides by women…and the occasional man, sporting one of those ridiculous blue rose cockades on his hat. Jessica could see nothing of him through the crowd but the gray of his coat and a glint of golden hair. Still, she could imagine him flashing that famous smile reproduced in woodcuts in all the newspapers: a confident, winning grin, as if he were aware that he was the most sought-after bachelor in London.

Jessica had no desire to join the throng around Sir Mark. She had no autograph book to wave at him, and the likes of her wouldn't have been welcomed in any event.

Sir Mark handled the crowd well. He didn't bask in the attention, as the men of Jessica's acquaintance might have done. Neither did he shrink from the pressing women. Instead, he ordered them about with an air of gentle command—signing the little books with a pencil he produced from a pocket, shaking hands—all the while making his way inexorably toward the street corner, where a carriage stood.

When Jessica thought of virgins, she imagined youths plagued by red spots or youngsters who wore thick spectacles and spoke with a stammer. She didn't think of blond men with clean-shaven, angular faces. She certainly didn't imagine tall fellows whose smiles lit up the dark, rainy street. It all went to show: Jessica knew nothing of virgins.

Hardly a surprise. She'd not spoken to a single one, not in all her years in London.

Beside her, George Weston let out a snort. "Look at him," he scoffed. "He's acting like a damned jackanapes—parading up and down the street as if he owned the place."

Jessica traced her finger against the window. In point of fact, Sir Mark's brother, newly the Duke of Parford, *did* own half the buildings on the street. It would annoy Weston if she corrected him, and so for a moment, she considered doing so.

But then, Sir Mark's presence was irritation enough. Some days, it seemed as if every society paper in London sent out a new issue every time he sneezed. Not much of an exaggeration. How many times had she passed post-boys waving scandal sheets, headlines a half-page high declaring: *Sir Mark: Threatened by Illness?*

"He must think," Weston continued, "that just because his brother is a duke—" he spat those words "—and the Queen has shown him a little favor, that he can caper about, displacing everyone who stands as his better. Did you know they're considering him for Commissioner?"

Jessica slanted him another glance. No; no need to rile the man. He could work himself into a lather without any help from her, and for now, she still needed him.

"He's never had to try for anything," Weston groused. "It just falls in his lap. And here I've been running myself ragged, trying to put myself forward. Lefevre's spot was practically *promised* to me. But no—now it's Turner's for the asking."

Sir Mark reached his carriage. He smiled to one and all. Even inside the taproom, Jessica could hear the cries of disappointment as a footman closed the carriage door.

"I don't understand how he became such a darling of London society," Weston vented. "Would you believe that they've tapped him for the office not because he has any administrative experience, but because they wish to increase public approval? Why everyone cares about *him,* I can't understand. He's unwilling to engage in even the most time-honored gentlemanly pursuits."

By which Weston undoubtedly meant drinking and wenching.

"He wrote a book." Jessica pressed her hands against her skirt. Understatement served her purposes better than truth. "It has enjoyed a run of some little popularity."

"Don't start on the bloody *Gentleman's Guide,*" Weston growled. "And don't mention the bloody MCB, either. That man is a *plague* on my house."

Before Sir Mark's conveyance could spirit

him away, the footmen had to politely clear the crowd from in front of the horses. The carriage was closed, but through a window on the side that faced her, Jessica could see Sir Mark's silhouette. He removed his hat and bowed his head. It was a posture halfway between despair and exhaustion.

So. All those smiles and handshakes were false. Good. A man who put on one false front would put on another, and if all his vaunted moral superiority was an act, it would make Jessica's work very, very easy. Besides, if Sir Mark despaired over a little thing like a mob determined to pay him adulation, he deserved what was coming to him. One paid a price for popularity.

And Sir Mark's book had been very popular indeed. The Queen had read it, and had knighted its author for his contribution to popular morality. Thereafter, his work had been read in all the favored salons in London. Every Sunday sermon quoted passages from the *Gentleman's Guide*. Why, just last month, a diminutive version had been printed, so that women could carry his words about in their skirt pockets—or in intimate compartments sewn into their petticoats for just that purpose.

There was something rather ironic, Jessica thought, about proper young ladies carrying *A Gentleman's Practical Guide to Chastity* as near to their naked thighs as they could manage.

But women were not his only devotees. Some days, it seemed as if half the men of London had joined that benighted organization of his followers. They were everywhere on the streets these days, with their blue cockades and their supposedly secret hand signals. Sir Mark had done the impossible. He'd made chastity *popular.*

Beside her, Weston watched with narrowed eyes as the carriage finally started up. The coachman flicked his whip, and the conveyance moved slowly through the gathered crowd. He shook his head and turned to consider Jessica. It was only in her imagination that his eyes left a rancid, oily film behind.

"I don't suppose you asked me here just so I could talk about the insufferable Mark Turner." His eyes fell to her bosom in idle, lecherous speculation. "I told you you'd miss me, Jess. Come. Tell me about this…this *proposition* of yours."

He took her arm; she gritted her teeth at the touch of his fingers and managed not to flinch.

She hated that appellation. *Jess* sounded like a falcon's leash, as if she were captured and hooded and possessed by him. She'd hated it ever since she realized she *had* been pinioned—tamed, taught commands and trotted out on the occasions when he needed to make use of her. But she had hardly been in a position to object to his use of it.

Someday. Someday soon. It was not a promise she made as he led her to the table in the back room. It was a last breath of hope, whispered into darkness.

Jessica sat in the chair that Weston pulled up for her.

Six months ago, she'd sent him on his way. She'd thought she would never have to see him again. If her plan succeeded now, she would not have to. She would be free from Weston and London…and this life in its entirety.

Weston took his seat at the head of the table. Jessica stared across at him. She had never loved him, but for a while, he had been tolerable. Neither generous nor overly demanding. He had kept her safe and clothed. She hadn't needed to pretend too hard; he'd not wanted her false protestations of affection.

"Well, Jess," Weston said. "Shall I ring for tea?"

At the words, her hands clenched around the sticky wood of the taproom table. She could feel each of her breaths, sharp inside her lungs. They labored in the cavern of her breast, as if she were climbing to the top of a tower. For just an instant, she felt as if she *had* ascended some great height—as if this man was a small, distant specimen, viewed from on high. Reality seemed very far away.

What she managed to say was: "No tea."

"Oh." He glanced at her sidelong. "Ha. Right.

I'd forgotten entirely. You're not still put out over *that,* are you?"

She had always thought that the life of a courtesan would take its toll slowly over time. That she might tolerate it for at least a decade to come, before her beauty slowly faded into age.

But no. Six months ago, her life had become unbearable over the course of one cup of tea. She didn't respond, and he sighed, slouching in his chair.

"Well, then. What is it you want?" he asked.

What she wanted sounded so simple. When she went outside, she wanted to feel the sunlight against her face.

She hadn't realized how bad matters had become until the first sunny day of spring had arrived. She'd gone outdoors—had been chivied outside, in fact, by a friend—to promenade in the park. She had felt nothing—not inside her, nor out. She hadn't felt cold. She hadn't felt warm. And when the spring sun had hit her face, it had been nothing but pale light.

This man had made her into dark gray stone, from the surface of her skin to the center of her soul. No nerves. No hopes. No *future.*

"I didn't come here to tell you what I want," she said firmly.

She wanted never again to have to fill another man's bed, telling falsehoods with her body until her mind could no longer track her own desires. She wanted to rid herself of the murk and the mire that had filled her. This life had bound her as effectively as if she were a falcon tied by a leather shackle, and she wanted to be free.

She steepled her fingers. "You've offered a reward to the woman who seduces Sir Mark Turner."

These words had an immediate effect. Weston sucked his breath in. "How did you know that was me? I thought I kept that quiet." He looked at her. "It's supposed to be *quiet*. It's no good if I ruin the man at the expense of my own reputation."

She shrugged. "A little research. There's not much secrecy among courtesans."

"I shouldn't have bothered. A reward of three hundred pounds, and the finest whores in all of London have failed. Don't tell me *you're* thinking of taking him on, Jess."

She met his gaze without flinching.

"You *are* thinking of it." Weston's lip curled. "Of course you are. You're between protectors. Honestly, Jess. If you're that desperate for funds, I'll take you back."

After what he'd done to her six months ago, the offer should have made her skin crawl. As it was, the proposition felt like nothing more than the cold gray of shadow.

She should have yearned for justice. She should have wanted revenge. She should, at a minimum, have wanted to extract something from him, of a size and shape to fill the desolate wasteland of nothingness he'd left inside her.

But she'd learned years ago that there was no justice, not for a woman like her. There was no way to crawl backward, to unravel the harms that had been done. There were only small, timid paths to be found through tangled underbrush. If you were lucky, you might hit upon one and escape the dark forest.

"It happens," she said, "that I have something none of those other women had."

Weston rubbed his chin. "Well, what is it?"

Desperation, she thought.

But what she said was, "Information. Sir Mark is returning to his boyhood home for the summer—a small market town called Shepton Mallet. I gather he wants to escape the adoring throngs for a period. He'll be away from his loving public. Staying, not in his brother's mansion, packed with servants, but in an isolated house, with only a few villagers to come by and take care of his needs."

"That's not precisely a secret."

"With nobody watching him, he'll have the opportunity to stray from his righteous path. He wouldn't dare, here in London—he's the center of everyone's attention. Out there…?" She trailed off suggestively. "At a very minimum, I should like the chance to try."

"If you know I made the offer, you know the rules. Seduce him. It needs to be believable—I've tried to ruin him with false accounts already, so you'll have to prove it by getting his ring. Tell the entire *ton* your experience through the gossip sheets and destroy Sir Mark's good reputation. Do all that, and you'll get your money."

Jessica tapped her lips. "I will be investing far more than an evening's work. He'll have to think me available. Not good enough to marry, but genteel enough that I'd make good...company. I'll be hiring a house in the country. Retaining servants." It would stretch her last reserves to the breaking point. If this failed, she would have no choice but to find another protector. She stared flatly at the table in front of her. "If I do it, I want three thousand."

Enough to purchase a small home in the country in a tiny village where nobody knew her. Enough to have morning after morning to herself, to lift her face to the sun. They said time healed all wounds. Jessica prayed it was so, that one day she might feel more than this impossible emptiness.

Weston clapped his hands. "So. The vicar's daughter has learned to bargain. Admit it, Jess. I *made* you who you are. You owe me."

She *did* owe him. He had made her, twice over. But there was no point in dreaming of a revenge that would never come. Right now, she just wanted to survive. "Three thousand," she repeated coolly.

"One thousand pounds," he countered. "Ruin Sir Mark, and I'll consider it a bargain at the price."

She'd be damned if she agreed. But then, she was already damned. The only question was whether she'd get full value for her soul.

"Fifteen hundred," she told him, "and not one penny less."

"Agreed." He held out his hand, as if he honestly expected her to shake it.

For one brief second, she imagined grabbing hold of the fireplace poker, not too distant, and smashing it into his arm. Hard. He would fall to his knees… The imagined jolt of the impact shook her from her reverie. "Agreed, then," she said, pushing to her feet.

Still, she didn't shake his hand.

CHAPTER TWO

Shepton Mallet
Two weeks later

PEACE. AT LAST.

Sir Mark Turner had walked all the way from the small house on the northern edge of Shepton Mallet into the very center of town, without attracting any more attention than any other newcomer who might make his way to Market Place in the early morning. He'd received a few nods, a few long stares. But there had been no choking crowds, no cries of recognition. No men had followed him, aghast that he walked about without an honor guard twelve-strong.

He'd wanted distance and anonymity to think about the proposal he'd received, to join the Commission on the Poor Laws. Here he'd found it.

He stood in the midst of the market, unmolested. Tomorrow, the rectangular pavement would be filled with butchers and cheesemongers. Today, it was blissfully quiet: only a few individuals could be seen.

Mark had grown up in Shepton Mallet. He knew the history of this square—a mix of the new, the old and the downright ancient. The public house, off to the side of the market, had been built centuries before Mark had been born. An elderly woman had taken shelter from the early-morning sun under the stone arches of the structure that marked the center of the square. Market Cross was a haphazard combination: half gothic spires, half hexagonal stone gazebo. Its tallest tower was topped by a cross. It stood alone in a sea of cobblestones, as if it were the confused, lost nephew of the stone church that stood on the corner.

In the two decades since Mark had left it, the town had changed. People he dimly remembered from childhood had grown older. He'd walked past a building on the way here that had once been a bustling wool mill; now, it was nothing but a burned-out shell. But those minor alterations only underscored how slow change was in arriving. Shepton Mallet was very distant from the frenetic hustle of London. There was no hurry here. Even the sheep he'd encountered on his walk seemed to bleat at a slower rate than the livestock in London.

A few people stood on the edges of the square, conversing. From here, he could not make out individual words—just the rough lilt of Somerset farm country, a rise and fall that, from a distance, sounded like...home.

He hadn't been back in more than twenty years. Long enough to lose the accent himself, long enough that his tongue felt too fast, too sharp in his mouth, an unwelcome, foreign invader in this familiar place. London sped along at the frenzied pace of steam and piston; Shepton Mallet strolled, like cows returning from the field at the end of a long summer day.

If anyone heard his name, they might recall his mother. They might even conjure up an image of his father, which was more than Mark himself could bring to mind. Perhaps they would also remember Mark: a thin, pale child, who'd accompanied his mother on her charitable missions. They wouldn't think of Sir Mark Turner, knighted by Victoria's hand, author of *A Gentleman's Practical Guide to Chastity.* They wouldn't see a shining beacon of saintly virtue.

Thanks be to God. He'd escaped.

He turned slowly. It was early on a Thursday morning, but the market was exactly how he remembered it. The ancient stalls of the marketplace—rough, broad-wood benches—were no doubt still in use because in all the centuries of their service, nobody had ever considered replacing them. They were even called by their old name here: the Shambles. Doubtless, they'd seen as many centuries of service as the public house.

Mark smiled. With all this aging history around him, not one person would care who he was in the present.

"Sir Mark Turner?"

Mark whirled around. He'd never met the man who stood at his back, one hand raised in tentative greeting. He was a plump fellow, dressed in clergyman's black, with a stiff white clerical collar to match.

The man dropped his raised hand. "I'm Alexander Lewis—the rector of the Church of St. Peter and St. Paul. Don't look so startled. I've been expecting you ever since news got out that your brother the duke had purchased the old Tamish house."

It *wasn't* the old Tamish house; it was the old Turner house. But then, this fellow was one of the few things that was new to Shepton Mallet. As the rector, no doubt he concerned himself with comings and goings. His curiosity was natural. He wasn't the harbinger of a sudden throng. Mark relaxed slightly.

"I'd heard of your family from my predecessor," the man was saying. "Welcome back to Shepton Mallet."

So he was to be the prodigal, returning after decades of desertion. Even better. "The town's almost exactly as I recall," Mark said. "But surely you can tell me. What is the latest news?"

As Mark had suspected, Lewis needed little encouragement to begin talking. In minutes, he'd produced a stream of words that Mark needed only half his mind to monitor. After all, they both knew that the only thing that changed in Shepton Mallet was the degree to which the abandoned mills deteriorated every year.

"But times are looking up," Lewis was saying, capping off a monologue on those selfsame mills. "There's a new shoe factory beginning to make its mark. And the crepe manufacturers have been seeing redoubled orders. After Her Majesty purchased the silk for her wedding gown from Shepton mills, we've seen more patronage."

This was what small-town life meant. This last was not news—at least, not in the sense that it was *new*. It was a measure of how slowly time passed in sleepy Shepton Mallet, that the primary topic of conversation was the Queen's marriage, an event that had taken place more than a year in the past.

Mark had been right to come here. Here, they might have *heard* of his book and his knighthood. But in this little town, he could escape the inexplicable swarms that had gathered in London. He would be left in peace.

People might even believe that he was *human*

here—the sort of person who had faults and who committed sins—instead of some sort of saint.

"Why," the rector continued, "I assure you, everyone here feels a debt of gratitude to you on that score."

The first discordant note sounded in Mark's bucolic dream. "Gratitude?" he asked in befuddlement. "To me? Why on earth would anyone be grateful to me?"

"Such humility!" Lewis beamed at him. "Everyone knows it was your favor that brought Her Majesty's eye upon us!" As he spoke, Lewis leaned forward and tapped Mark's lapels lightly.

A deep dread welled up inside of him. This was not a forward, grasping sort of fumble. Instead, it was a reverent little touch—the way one might dip a forefinger into a font of holy water.

"Oh, no," Mark protested. "No, *no*. Really, you mustn't put that complexion on it. I—"

"We here in Shepton Mallet are truly grateful, you know. If the silk manufacturers had failed…" Lewis spread his arms wide, and Mark looked around. The few people dispersed around the square were all staring at him in avid curiosity.

Not again. Please. He'd come here to escape the adulation, not to be feted once more.

"This town owes you much. Everyone's been waiting for me to make your acquaintance, so I might show you around. Let me start with *this* introduction."

Lewis motioned with one hand, and a figure slouching against one side of the Market Cross straightened. The man—no, however tall the figure, it was a boy—came dashing over, nearly tripping over ungainly feet.

Whoever this young man was—and he could not have been a day older than seventeen—he was well-dressed. He was wearing a top hat. He raised his hand to adjust it every few seconds, as if the article of apparel were new to him after years of the quartered caps that boys favored.

"Sir Mark Turner," Lewis was saying, with all the pomp of a high-church official, "may I present to you Mr. James Tolliver."

James Tolliver wore a blue ribbon cockade, artfully formed into the shape of a rose, on the brim of his hat. Mark's hopes, which had so recently soared as high as the church's tower, fell eight stories to dash on the cobblestones underfoot. Please. Not a blue rose cockade. Anything but a blue rose cockade. Maybe the ornament was just an accident. Maybe some peddler had brought through a batch, without explaining their significance. Because the alternative—that he was *not* escaping the hubbub of London, that he had *not* left behind the hangers-on and the constant reports in the gossip columns—was too appalling to contemplate. He'd come to Shepton Mallet to relax into its relative timelessness.

But Tolliver was peering up at him with wide, brilliant eyes. Mark knew that look—that gaze of utter delight. Tolliver looked as if he'd just received a pony for Christmas and couldn't wait for his first ride.

And by the way he was staring, Mark was the pony. Before Mark could say anything, his hand was captured in an impassioned grip.

"Forty-seven, sir!" Tolliver squeaked.

Mark stared at the earnest young man in front of him in confusion. The boy had barked out those words as if they had some special significance. "Forty-seven *what?*"

Forty-seven people who might accost him on the street? Forty-seven more months before society forgot who he was?

The boy's face fell. "Forty-seven *days,*" he said, sheepishly.

Mark shook his head in confusion. "Forty-seven days is a little long for a flood, and a bit short for Michaelmas term."

"It's been forty-seven days of chastity. Sir." He frowned in puzzlement. "Didn't I do it right? Isn't that how members of the MCB greet one another? I'm the one who started the local division, and I want to make sure our details are correct."

So the cockade was real, then. Mark stifled a

groan. It had been foolish to hope that the MCB had restricted itself to London. It was embarrassing enough there, with those cockades and their weekly meetings. Not to mention the secret hand signals—somebody was always trying to teach him the secret hand signals.

Why was it that men had to take every good principle and turn it into some sort of a club? Why could nobody do the right thing on his own? And how had *Mark* gotten himself embroiled as the putative head of this one?

"I'm not a member of the Male Chastity Brigade," Mark said, trying not to make his words sound like a rebuke. "I just wrote the book."

For a moment, Tolliver simply stared at him in disbelief. Then he smiled. "Oh, that's all right," he said. "After all, Jesus wasn't Church of England, either."

Beside him, the rector nodded at this piece of utter insanity. Mark wasn't sure whether he should laugh or weep.

Instead, he gently removed his hand from Tolliver's grip. "One thing to consider," he said. "Comparing me to Christ is…" Ridiculous, for one, but he didn't want to humiliate the poor boy. A logical fallacy, for another. But this young man, however exuberant, meant well. And he was *trying*. It was hard to be angry about a youth throwing his heart and soul into chastity, when so many

others his age were off pursuing prizefights and
fathering bastards instead.

But without any chastisement on his part at all,
the boy turned white. "Blasphemous," he said. "It
was blasphemous. I was just blasphemous in front
of Sir Mark Turner. Oh, God."

Mark decided not to mention he'd blasphemed
again. "People are allowed to make mistakes in
front of me."

Tolliver lifted adoring eyes. "Yes. Of course.
I should have known you'd have the goodness to
forgive me."

"I'm not a saint. I'm not a holy man. I just wrote
a book."

"Your humility, sir—your good nature. Truly,
you are an example to us all," Tolliver insisted.

"I make mistakes, too."

"Really, sir? Might I inquire—how long has it
been for *you?* How many days?"

The question was invasive and impolite, and
Mark raised an eyebrow.

Tolliver cringed back a step in response. Perhaps he'd recognized the impertinence.

"I—I'm sure it's in all the papers," he said, "but
we only get a handful of them, when someone vis-
its London. I...I surely should know. P-please forgive my ignorance."

Perhaps he hadn't. And what did it matter if he
asked Mark? Mark *had* written the book on chas-

tity. Literally. He sighed and performed a rough calculation. "Ten thousand," he replied. "Give or take."

The boy gave an impressed whistle.

Mark was less impressed. If there was a local MCB here, all that remained to cut up his peace was—

"Your worshippers are not restricted to the men, of course," Lewis said. "On Sunday, after service, I hope to introduce you to my daughter, Dinah."

—that. The constant efforts to thrust suitable women in Mark's way. In all truth, Mark wouldn't have minded meeting a woman who *actually* suited him. But beside him, Tolliver frowned, rubbing his chin, and glanced at Mark in consternation, as if the man had set himself up as a sudden rival. If this *Dinah* was someone that interested the youthful Tolliver, it meant that this exchange was following the usual pattern. After all, the only women that others deemed suitable for a gentleman of his supposed righteousness were—

"She's a sweet girl," Lewis was saying, "obedient and chaste and comely. She's biddable—a confident, strong man such as yourself would make her an extraordinary husband. And she's not quite sixteen, so you could form her precisely as you wished."

Of course. Mark shut his eyes in despair. Write a book on chastity, and somehow the whole world got the notion that your preferred bride would be a malleable child.

"I'm twenty-eight," Mark said dryly.

"Not yet twice her age, then!" the rector said, with a smile that contained not a hint of awareness. He leaned forward and whispered confidentially, "I should hate to see her saddled to an old man. Or—" he cast a pointed look at Tolliver "—a young pup, who scarcely knows his own mind. Now. I know you're keeping a bachelor household. I can start drawing up a rotation immediately. If we have you scheduled for tea and supper on a daily basis, why, within six weeks, all of the best families—"

"No." There was nothing for it. Mark was going to have to be rude. "Absolutely not. I came here for peace and solitude—not daily engagements. Certainly not *twice* daily engagements."

The man's face fell. Tolliver flinched, and Mark felt as if he had just kicked a puppy. Why, oh, *why,* could his book not have disappeared into a sea of anonymity, as most books did?

"Weekly," Mark conceded. "No more."

The rector gave a long-suffering sigh. "I suppose. Perhaps if we had larger events. A church picnic? Yes. That should answer. Followed by— oh, dear." Lewis glanced across the square and his voice hardened. "Well. At least this way, we can keep you from the unsavory elements."

Mark followed his gaze. A few rays of sun shone through the clouds, brightening the produce in the market shambles across the square. The patrons at the marketplace had arrayed themselves so that they all had a view of him. But the rector was staring at a woman who had entered the square.

For an instant, all Mark could see was her hair—an ebony spill of ink, braided and pinned up in intricate loops that just kissed her shoulders, covered with the barest excuse for a lace bonnet. He'd always thought of black as a colorless hue, but her hair seemed so black it was every color at once, the rays of the sun spangling it. And there was a great mass of it on her head. Freed from the pins and braids, rid of that flimsy bit of lace, all that dark hair would reach past her thighs. It would be a great warm cloud of silk in his hands.

She moved smoothly, almost gliding over the cobblestones. Her strides suggested long, lean legs beneath her flowing skirts. She stopped before the public house. Even though it was not yet market day, the greengrocer had begun to gather goods for the next morning. She peered at the items and made the act of examining a head of cabbage seem like a verse of poetry.

It was only then that he noticed precisely what the rector was staring at. Her gown was the lightest shade of pink, but she had cinched it at her waist with a cherry-red ribbon. Yet more ribbons were threaded through the bodice of her gown, drawing attention to the curves of her breasts. Not that her bosom needed attention to be drawn to it; her figure was, to put it mildly, stunning. She wasn't impossibly thin and delicate; nor was she extraordinarily buxom. Still, she somehow made every woman around her seem wrong and ill-proportioned by comparison.

For just one second, Mark felt a wistful tug. *Why doesn't anyone ever try and foist women like her off on me instead?*

In London, she would have garnered second and third glances—more out of curiosity and admiration than contempt. Here? No doubt the inhabitants of Shepton Mallet had no idea what to make of a woman like this one—or a gown as daring as the one she wore. But Mark knew. That was the sort of dress that commanded: *look at me.*

Mark had never taken well to commands. He turned away.

"Ah, yes," the rector said. "Mrs. Farleigh." The stuffy tone of his voice suggested that Mrs. Farleigh was an unwelcome inhabitant of the village, but it was belied by the rector's posture. He watched her, his eyes following her across the square with an expression that was closer to avarice than outrage. "Just look at her!"

Mark wasn't one to gawk. In his mind, he built a wall of glass bricks—clear, yet impenetrable. With every inhalation, he reminded himself of who he was. What he believed. Breath by breath, brick by brick, he built a fortress to contain his want before it had a chance to roar to uncomfortable life. He stood behind it, lord of his own desire, until nobody could command anything of him.

Not want. Not desire. And definitely—most definitely— not lust. When he was in firm control, he looked again. Even with that gut-struck feeling of stupidity walled off, she was objectively, undeniably beautiful.

"She arrived almost two weeks ago. She's a widow. Still, she's said little about her people or her past. I suspect it's because she feels it's best left unsaid. One has only to look at her to imagine what she's done."

Rectors, Mark supposed, were as free to imagine lascivious goings-on as anyone else. He didn't think they should *gossip* about them, though. Mrs. Farleigh looked up across the market square, and her gaze fell on him. Her expression didn't change—which was to say, that small mysterious curl of a smile stayed on her lips.

Still, even through his fortress of glass, he felt a tiny jolt of electric resonance, as if lightning had struck nearby. She started in his direction.

Before she could come much closer, the rector snapped into motion. He darted through the stone arches of the Market Cross and took hold of Mrs.

Farleigh's shoulder. Not in a friendly, rectorlike way. Nor even as a rebuke. His gloved hand landed rather too close to her breast for any of that.

Mrs. Farleigh's artful smile suggested that she was worldly. Her revealing gown shouted that she was a temptress. The rector's gossip said she was worse. But when Lewis placed his hands on her, she flinched—no more than a half step backward, a twitch of her skin, but that was enough. For one instant, she had more the look of scalded cat about her than graceful swan, and that half second of response betrayed her air of worldly sensuality. She was not who she appeared at first blush.

Mark was suddenly interested—interested in a way that a low-cut gown and a striking figure could never have accomplished.

From these yards away, he could barely make out the conversation. No doubt neither believed they could be overheard. But they stood just on the other side of the Market Cross, and the acoustics through the stone were unexpectedly good.

"Come, Mrs. Farleigh," the rector was whispering harshly. "As it's not market day, there's no need to display your wares so openly. Nobody *here* is buying *those* sorts of goods."

Mrs. Farleigh had flinched at his touch. But at the intimation that she was selling her body, she did not react in the slightest. "Oh, Reverend," she replied, equally softly. "Whatsoever is sold in the shambles..."

She trailed off, invitingly, and Mark automatically filled in the remainder: *Whatsoever is sold in the shambles, that, eat, asking no question for conscience sake.* The words took him two decades back, to his earliest memories—reciting Bible verses while his mother looked at the wall behind him, her head nodding in time to music that only she seemed to hear. Those words he'd memorized were still burned into him, that sharp juxtaposition of right and horribly, terribly wrong.

Lewis shook his head. "I don't know what you're talking about. We sell corn here. And cattle."

Her smile ticked up another notch, and Mark's respect for her increased. The rector—upstanding, breast-grappling citizen that he was—hadn't noticed that the godless Mrs. Farleigh had just quoted the Bible at him. He probably hadn't even recognized the verse. Mrs. Farleigh's hand drifted to her shoulder, to the point where the rector's hand lay. She picked his gloved fingers up between thumb and forefinger, as if a dead leaf had landed on her, and then let his arm drop to his side.

"I shan't keep you, Rector," she said, her voice gentle. "I'm sure there are a great many things you would like to purchase. Maybe the other wares you examine will actually be for sale."

She turned away, not looking at Mark. The rector stared after her, folding his arms about his chest in dissatisfaction. He watched her go with rather more interest than a rector ought to have had. Finally, he turned to face Mark. "There," he said, in a loud, carrying voice, as he wiped his hands together. "Don't you worry, Sir Mark. We'll make sure that the likes of her never bother you again."

Mark glanced once at Mrs. Farleigh, who was walking back toward the greengrocer. The red of her sash made the stack of radishes look pale by comparison. She made the entire town seem faded and washed out, like a poor watercolor painting of itself.

He was chaste, not a saint. And he was just looking.

But she'd already made a contradiction of herself, one as stark and intriguing as the light color of her dress, juxtaposed against the vibrant slash of color at her waist. She'd called the rector a hypocrite to his face, and the man hadn't even noticed. What would she say if she looked Mark in the eyes?

Would she see a saint? An icon to be worshipped?

Or would she see *him?*

The possibility hung in the air, too powerful to be ignored. No. No use telling himself falsehoods. He wasn't just looking at her. He wanted to know more.

CHAPTER THREE

JESSICA HAD NOT considered what it meant, that Sir Mark was returning to his childhood home for the summer. She'd lived in—or near enough to—London for the past seven years of her life. Her protectors *had* taken her along on their excursions to the country. But improper as her role had been, they would never have introduced her to the neighbors. She'd imagined the country as a smaller, more private version of the city—just with fewer people and no operas. So quickly had she forgotten her childhood.

In a way, she *did* have more privacy. Jessica had found a cottage on the outskirts of town, half a mile past the point where cobblestones gave way to dirt and houses to fields. She sometimes went hours without seeing a soul besides the maid-of-all-work she'd brought with her from London.

But for precisely that same reason, she was unlikely to meet Sir Mark ambling down the country lane that led to her abode.

And that meant there was only one place she

could go, knowing for certain he would attend: church. Early on a summer morning, the stone walls were still cool. But the bodies packed inside made the interior warmer than she'd expected. There was a hierarchy to the rows, no less. The wealthiest families sat up front in reserved pews; the simple folk stood in the back.

The people of Shepton Mallet had not yet worked out where Jessica belonged. She had enough money to let a house and bring a servant with her. But she'd answered no questions about her family or her origins—a sure sign of dubious morality on her part. On top of that, she was beautiful, and beautiful women were not to be trusted.

In London, nobody trusted anyone, and so the mistrust never bothered her. Here, she had taken a place halfway toward the rear of the church.

Sir Mark, of course, sat in the first row, the entire congregation as interested in him as they were in the rector leading service.

Jessica had tried to make his acquaintance before service began, but half the town had the same idea. The other half—having already met him— had been equally determined to keep him from Mrs. Farleigh of the unknown origins. Still, she couldn't regret her dubious reputation. She wanted to seduce him, after all, not inveigle him into offering marriage. She needed to be the kind of woman whom a man like him wouldn't marry. It all made a kind of frustrating sense…but she'd not yet made his acquaintance.

His attention had not strayed from the rector through the entire service. But as Lewis wound into his inevitable conclusion, Sir Mark turned in his seat. It was not idle inattention that turned his head. He looked straight at her. As if he'd known where she sat. As if he had realized that she was watching him.

Their eyes met. She didn't duck her head or avert her gaze—any of the things that a shy, retiring lady might have done. Instead she met his eyes calmly.

His gaze dipped.

For a second, she regretted the unfortunate habit that had led her to wear a respectable gown to service. All these years, and she still reached for a sober, high-necked gown.

His eyes came up, met hers again—and then, very deliberately, he winked at her.

She had only a moment to stare at him before he turned to the front once more.

What had that meant? What had he intended? Her stomach knotted, for all the world as if she were a young girl, wanting to misconstrue every last glance given her by the boy she fancied. But this was no girlish desire that caught her breath. It was her livelihood, her survival, her very future that flashed by her in the wink of his eye. It had to mean something.

Her questions echoed, even after the congregation rose and began to disperse. Sir Mark was surrounded the instant he got to his feet; by the time he'd made his way to the rear of the chapel, he was bethronged.

Jessica waited by the iron fence that surrounded the churchyard. She was not going to him. She would not be one of a score of girls begging for his attention, surrounding him in a positive frenzy of innocence. Still, she almost wished that she could have been one of them—that she could have looked at him and seen bright hope.

Instead, she had nothing but stone-cold calculation. She abhorred trickery. She disliked the idea of deceit. But she was long past the careful weighing of morality. She'd given up that part of her long ago. And if he didn't come to her before her remaining funds ran out, she'd have to resort to a stratagem of some kind.

He caught sight of her and held up one hand. The babble of voices cut off around him, as if it were a conjurer's trick.

"Wait here," he said, and the multitude assembled about him—a motley collection of elderly matrons, young men and hopeful, unmarried ladies—all held their collective breath. He walked toward her across the yard. A few gravestones stood between them; the grass was bright green, the sun too hot. His hair seemed almost too blond, too gold, and it sparkled like a king's treasure hoard.

He stopped a few feet before her. "I did ask for a proper introduction," he said, his voice quiet enough not to be overheard by his waiting audience, "but oddly—nobody was willing to perform it."

"That," Jessica said, "is because I am a very, very wicked woman." She took a step closer and held out her gloved hand to him, steeling herself for his touch. "Mrs. Jessica Farleigh, official town disgrace. At your service."

He didn't bow over her fingers, as any other gentleman would have done. But neither did he falter at this introduction. Instead, he clasped her hand in his and shook it—as if they'd entered into a secret compact together. Even through her glove, she could feel the press of his ring against her flesh. What she needed was so close...

"Sir Mark Turner," he said. "I speak with the tongues of a thousand angels. Butterflies follow me wherever I go. Birds sing when I take a breath."

He relinquished her hand as easily as he'd taken it. She could feel the phantom pressure of his grip against her palm, strong and steady. She stared at him, unsure how to respond to that introduction. If

Sir Mark had actually been mad, surely the matter would have been broached in the London papers.

"That must be rather disconcerting," she finally said. "You appear to have lost your butterflies."

A light danced in his eyes. "I propose we come to an understanding. I won't accept the gossip about you on its face, so long as you don't believe everything that's said about me."

"Sir Mark!" The call came from behind him, and one of his braver admirers ventured forth. No doubt they judged that he'd spent too long in her tarnishing company already. They wouldn't want the town's golden child tainted, after all.

Jessica had only a few moments of this comparative privacy left with him. "You are not what I expected to find, after reading the London papers."

"You've read that? Forget it all. I implore you."

She turned her head slightly and gave him her most captivating smile. As she did, she could see it captivate *him*. He was better at hiding his reaction than most men, but his mouth curled up just a little more. He stood just a little straighter. And his body canted toward hers ever so slightly. He was attracted to her—very much so. He was caught.

And she had only to reel him in. He'd been so easy after all.

But the crowd was bearing down on him. It

wasn't as if she could consummate his downfall in the churchyard anyway.

"You mean," she said, "that you're not a saint? Sir Mark, your public will be shocked."

His eyes met hers once more.

"No," he said quietly. "Don't canonize me. I'm a man, Mrs. Farleigh. Just a man."

He turned from her, just as a lady in purple bombazine reached to tap his elbow. Jessica did not miss the venomous gaze that the elderly woman shot her way. Once again, Sir Mark walked in the throng. The women parted to let him through—and closed about him afterward.

I'm just a man.

If Jessica knew anything, she knew men. She knew what men wanted, and she knew how to give it to them. And if the remnants of her conscience pricked at the thought of what she must do... Well. She wouldn't force him to do anything.

She wouldn't have to.

No; as with all men, she only needed to imply she was available. Sir Mark would be a willing participant in the destruction of his own reputation.

She was only going to need one little stratagem, after all, to hurry him along.

MARK'S FIRST WEEK in Shepton Mallet was taken up in thought.

Ever since he'd been discreetly approached

about filling an upcoming vacancy on the Poor Law Commission, he'd been in turmoil. On the one hand, the Commission, responsible for overseeing the workhouses, was universally hated. He'd been approached simply because they'd hoped his popularity would quell the public outrage about recent mishandlings. Mark suspected that, quite to the contrary, the appointment would merely sink him in the eyes of the public.

After all, the whole present policy of poor relief was an utter mess. Mark might make a real difference in the lives of unfortunates if he threw all his energy into the project—and if he'd been granted popularity by a capricious fate, surely he had the responsibility to use it for good. On the other hand, the entire theory behind the system of workhouses seemed fundamentally flawed to Mark. He wasn't sure if it *could* be fixed.

He'd expressed these rational concerns to the poor undersecretary who'd paid him a private visit. But there was yet another side that he'd not mentioned, and it was one that echoed most strongly here in Shepton Mallet, between the walls of his childhood home. He'd grown up here. His brother had nearly died here. And all because his mother had gone mad.

Dedicating her life to serving the poor had sounded noble in practice. But she'd taken it to the furthest extreme: giving away the family's modest competence, until almost nothing was left. Of his three brothers, Mark was the only one who truly understood why she'd done it. It was no comfort that he so easily made sense of the world as seen through the eyes of a madwoman.

Perhaps that was why he'd retreated here after all. He hated the idea of entering politics. Even if he'd wanted to spend his life serving the poor, he'd not have chosen to do so by regulating the day-to-day administration of workhouses. And yet...

He'd often thought that if he had any work to do on this earth, it was to put his mother's unquiet legacy to rest. She'd insisted on perfection; Mark had written a *practical* guide to chastity, that allowed for the merely human. She'd flown into rages at the slightest provocation; he'd worked hard to bring his own temper, never even, under his control. She'd been every righteous impulse, taken to excess. Mark aimed for moderation.

So he hadn't said no, not yet. Perhaps this was the opportunity he needed to show that he could dedicate his life to the poor while tempering his zeal.

Maybe.

He'd come back here, to his old childhood home, repository of a hundred memories. It had seemed as good a place as any to contemplate the offer. Better; he'd insisted on privacy, and here he'd found it, at least in some small measure.

Today, with rain drumming down on the roof, had been the best day of all.

He'd sent his charwoman home at noon, and the boy who saw to the gardens only came by every other day.

Best of all, with this downpour, the paths were no doubt mud to the ankle. No rational person would come visiting today. Why, Mark might avoid all crowds until the church picnic in two days' time.

He'd have plenty of time to spend in contemplation.

But just as he'd settled down in a chair with one of his mother's old journals, a knock sounded on the door. Mark bit back a groan.

He should have realized. When it came to him, nobody was rational.

For a moment, he stared fixedly at the fire in front of him and considered ignoring the summons. It could be the rector no doubt with his poor bedraggled daughter in tow.

Unbidden, his imagination summoned up another possibility: it might be Mrs. Jessica Farleigh, damp and spangled all over with raindrops. She would be lost, wet and in need of—but no. *That* sort of ridiculous schoolboy fancy made better entertainment in the dead of night, when he could more appropriately deal with the lust it would engender.

It was probably his charwoman, Mrs. Ashton, come to check on him. No doubt she'd taken one look at the rain when it started, donned oilskins and galoshes and trudged the three miles back to his home, just to make sure he was comfortable. She meant well.

They all did.

With a sigh, he rose to get the door. Truly, it was almost certain to be plain, plump Mrs. Ashton, perhaps with a crock of butter and a loaf of freshly baked bread carefully wrapped in oiled paper. No other rational possibility existed. He threw the door open.

And stopped in stupefaction. It was the schoolboy fancy after all. Mrs. Jessica Farleigh stood on his stoop. Whatever gown she'd been wearing had been soaked through by the torrential downpour until it clung to her form in a sodden, limp mass. His hands curled appreciatively, as if to cup the heavy spheres of her breasts and wipe those drops of water away. The dark half circles of her aureoles were visible through translucent muslin; the nub of her nipple itself was occluded—barely—by a corset.

She might as well not have been wearing a gown at all. He could make out individual stitches, pale green vines, on her undergarments. He could see every seam of her stays, molded to her frame. And when his eyes dropped farther—he *was* only human—he caught a glimpse of petticoats plastered to hips that might cradle a man's body.

Schoolboy fancy? No. She was a grown man's desire. Ravishing. Too convenient. And therefore, entirely untrustworthy.

Slowly, deliberately, Mark raised his eyes to her face. *Yes*, he commanded his unruly wants, *to her face, nothing else.*

It didn't help. A drop of water rolled to the tip of her patrician nose, and he had a sudden desire to reach out and wipe it away. Instead, it hung, suspended in midair, in defiance of all the laws of nature.

Well. She wasn't the only one who could defy nature. Glass bricks. He reached for them, building that wall. Behind it, he'd feel no desire. No want. No urge to step forward and lick the beads of rain from her lips.

"Sir Mark." Her voice was clear and gentle, like a caress. "I am so dreadfully ashamed to impose upon you, but as you can no doubt see, circumstances have made it necessary." She held her drenched bonnet in one hand.

He looked into her eyes. They were so dark he could not make out their expression, not in the dim light that filtered through the rain clouds. She spoke that lie without flinching, without even looking away.

"You see," she continued, "I was walking, not paying attention to the time or the weather—"

"Without shawl or cloak or umbrella." His own voice sounded curiously flat to his ears, as stale as water left to sit in a bucket for too long. "Even before the rain began, it was dismally cloudy this morning, Mrs. Farleigh."

"Oh, I should have had the forethought to bring at least a wrap." She let out a too-bright laugh. "But I was thinking of other things."

Her hair was wet. It should have been stringy and unkempt. It should have been flat and colorless, nothing but unrelieved black. Instead, several strands had fallen out of the knot she kept it in. When wet, it curled—just enough to wrap about a man's finger.

It was easy to set aside his arousal, after all. He was actually rather disappointed.

Mrs. Farleigh made herself sound quite stupid—as if she were the sort of forgetful female who regularly traipsed about outdoors in the wet. Some men of Mark's acquaintance might have believed the act. After all, they believed *all* women were stupid.

Not Mark. And most definitely not this woman. If he had to guess, he would have said that she chose every item of apparel with the same care a clockmaker employed when selecting springs.

He let out a sigh. "Mrs. Farleigh, if you were

that idiotic, you would have perished years before now. As you are quite robust, I'm afraid I must call your story what it is—a fabrication."

She blinked up at him, iridescent beads of water clinging to impossibly long lashes. Her brow furrowed in disbelief.

"You see? I am by no means as kind or generous as rumor has it. If I had been, I would never have called you a liar."

Her eyelashes flickered down. She clasped her hands behind her back. "Very well. I admit. I was curious about you. Given my reputation—and yours—I knew we would never have a chance to hold a conversation of any length."

He would have found a way. He'd already been thinking about it—about her clever retorts, about that curious contradiction between her dress and her manner. About her smile, wise and sad and wary all at once. He'd have *insisted* on conversing with her. But this little escapade left him with nothing but the bitter tang of copper in his mouth. No doubt she'd imagined that she had only to present herself in all of her dripping glory, and his intelligence would dry up and dissipate into nothingness.

"If all you wished was conversation," he said dryly, "you could have worn a cloak." He glanced upward. "You didn't even need to wait for rain."

She looked up at him, her dark eyes wide, her

chest expanding on another breath. He hadn't wanted an introduction to a polished seductress. He'd wanted to know about the *other* part of her, the side she didn't present to the world. He wanted to know the woman who whispered clever set-downs to the rector when she thought nobody else listened.

And that, perhaps, was Mark's own personal fancy, exerting a more powerful pull on him than all her wet curves. He'd wanted someone to *see* him. To see past his reputation.

"Mrs. Farleigh, you seem a woman of some experience."

She licked her lips and gave him a brilliant, encouraging smile.

Mark did not feel encouraged. "Do you know what the difference is between a male virgin and the Elgin Marbles?"

That smile faded into confusion. "Oh, I could not say." She peered at him in manufactured befuddlement. "They seem quite similar to me—are they not both very hard?" Her tone seemed innocent; her words were anything but.

He shook his head. "More people come to look at the virgin."

Her eyebrows drew down, and she studied him quizzically. Come, now. If she'd been curious for any sort of knowledge of him, except the Biblical sort, that should have at least garnered a request for explanation. Instead, she licked her lips again.

He tried another joke. "What do you suppose sets a male virgin apart from a pile of rocks?"

"Both seem hard again."

"The rocks," he replied, "are more numerous. And more intelligent."

Laugh at me, he wanted to tell her. *See me—not some obstacle to overcome.*

"Oh, no," she exclaimed. "That can't be, as you're so clever."

Maybe he had imagined that quick wit. He was wont to do so, he knew. He wanted it too badly. He wanted to be seen not as flawless, but as himself, faults and all.

"Very well, Mrs. Farleigh," he said. "You prevail. You went out for a stroll in stormy weather, risking health in defiance of all good sense, just to have a look at me. You did so on a Tuesday afternoon, when the lad who weeds my vegetables is off. And so here we are, completely alone." Mark shook his head. "I cannot in good conscience send you on your way. It's miles back to the village. You are no doubt cold, and I have a fire lit inside. No matter your reasons, you don't deserve to risk your health."

"Thank you, sir. Your hospitality is appreciated."

Not by him, it wasn't. This would pose even

more of a delicate challenge than he'd feared. His was a bachelor household, and she was soaked to the skin. She would need to remove everything and dry her wet things by the fire before he could toss her outdoors again. He could hardly hand her a pair of his trousers while she waited.

He turned and strode down the hallway, thinking. He could hear her follow, her footsteps soft and squelching. A small fire crackled in the parlor where he led her. She turned about, around and around again, taking in the surroundings.

"Thank you," she said simply.

"I'll be back shortly." He watched her face. "With some towels and a dressing gown, so you can dry yourself."

Her face did not change. It was unnatural, that lack of response. It seemed as if she were not entirely present. What exactly did she intend? Once was her landing on his doorstep, wet and bedraggled. Twice was her lying about her intentions. Third time...now, that would be the way to find out what she truly intended.

"Two minutes," he told her. "I'll return in two minutes. And I *am* the only one in the household. It will have to be me who returns. Do we understand each other, Mrs. Farleigh?"

She nodded.

Mark left. He desperately wanted to be wrong about her. It was stupid of him—he knew nothing of her except the gossip in the village and the cut of her gown. But he so wanted to believe there was *more*.

Here was his grown man's fantasy: he wanted to come back and find her fully clothed. He wanted to engage her in conversation without anyone watching with assessing eyes. He wanted, in short, to like her. He'd been inclined to do so from the start. In the market, he'd been led away from her before they'd had a chance to exchange greetings. In the churchyard, they had only talked for a minute.

He'd been curious about her ever since he'd seen that flinch. Like a callow youth, he'd enlarged upon it in his mind. *See? There is more to both of us than anyone else will acknowledge.*

But of course not. He was nothing more than a challenge to be scaled, a man to be brought down.

He took the towels with a shake of his head and returned, steeling himself against what he would see. He'd left the parlor door open. When he entered again, he was prepared.

And it was just as well. She'd shed her gown and petticoats. She was standing, her back to him, her arms wrapped about herself as she struggled with her corset laces. He could see her ankles, delicate and fine, rising to pale calves underneath a thin, wet layer of linen. His eyes traced the curve of her legs up through the damp cloth of her shift.

She turned. "Oh! Sir Mark! How embarrassing!"

"Spare me." His tone was flatter than ever.

She flushed. "But—"

He kept his eyes trained on her face. He felt as if he stood at the top of a cliff overlooking a perilous sea. At any instant, he might be assaulted by vertigo if he dared to look down. "Spare me your excuses. Pay me the compliment of understanding. What was it you imagined I would do at this juncture? Am I supposed to be so overcome with lust that I cannot hold myself back?"

"I— That is—" She took a deep breath and started walking toward him.

"Do you think that an eyeful of breast and buttocks will have me so besotted that I will forget all my principles? I'm a virgin, Mrs. Farleigh. Not an innocent. I've never been an innocent."

Her jaw set, and she stopped in front of him. Close enough that he could have grabbed her. That he might simply push her against the chair behind her and warm the cool expanse of her still-wet skin with his hands.

"At this point," he said scornfully, "I am supposed to be so overwrought with desire that I cannot reason."

He dropped the towels and the dressing gown in a heap on the floor.

"Sir Mark, forgive my forwardness. I just

thought…" She reached out, her fingers stretching for his lapels. Before he could think, he grabbed her hand.

Not lightly. Not kindly. It was a trained grip, one that he and his brother had perfected years ago. No matter how strong a man was, he wouldn't stand up to a boy who bent his thumb backward. He and his brother had practiced the hold for hours, for *days* until the fluid motion came automatically in response to a threat.

When she reached for him, he reacted without thinking, stepping to the side. Her hand crumpled in his, and his fingers pressed against the meat of her palm.

And she flinched. Not because he'd hurt her— he hadn't applied the slightest pressure to the joint of her thumb. But she flinched, just as she had when the rector grabbed her in the market. For no other reason than that he'd touched her.

If he had been the sort to curse, he would have done so now. Because if there was one thing more disappointing than a woman who saw him as a target for seduction, it was this: a woman who tried to seduce him, without even wanting him in the first place. She was standing close to him, and flinch or no, she tilted her head up as if she thought he might kiss her.

"Most men," he said, through gritted teeth,

"would not look a gift horse in the mouth. Not at this juncture."

"And you?"

"If I were of a mind to purchase horseflesh," he told her, "I'd examine every tooth. And if I found one flaw, I would walk away, with no regrets whatsoever."

She brought her free hand up. Even now, with her fingers clenched in his grip, she ran her hand down his jaw. "What a shame. I consider my flaws my primary attraction." She spoke as if she were almost purring. "I'd make a poor broodmare, Sir Mark, but then, I don't think that's what a man like you needs."

She did a good job of pretending to want him. But her tone didn't match the thready beat of her pulse against his fingers. It didn't match the wary tension of her body, strung tight as a harp string and vibrating next to his.

"As it turns out," he said sharply, "I'm not in the market for flesh of any variety."

"No?" Her finger drew a line down his chin. "You're a man. You have desires, like anyone else. As for me…I'm a widow, but I'm not dead. I shouldn't mind a little comfort, and like you, I should very much like it to be discreet, so that no censure falls on me." Her hand traced that line down his neck, his shoulder. "Our interests are much aligned. You might have your spotless reputation, and indulge yourself, as well."

Her fingers, cold and still slightly damp, slid along his wrist. He told himself it didn't matter. She was touching glass, not flesh; granite, not skin. No doubt, tonight he'd relive the sinuous line she'd drawn on his skin. Tonight some lustful part of him would wish he'd pulled her close and taken the comfort she offered.

He made himself stone instead. "You know nothing of my interests. That's not what I want."

"If you don't want me," she asked silkily, "then why are you still holding me?"

"A point of clarification." He pressed his fingers against the joint of her thumb—lightly, not to hurt her, but enough to show her exactly what he could do, should he choose. "I am holding you at bay," he said dryly. "That is far removed from actually holding you. As for the rest, you are the one who is trembling. Not I. Really, Mrs. Farleigh. You must think that because I have never been in anyone else's skin, I cannot be comfortable inside my own."

He relinquished her hand and stepped back through the parlor door. Her hand dropped to her side, and she stared at him, befuddled once more.

"As it turns out," he said, "I don't give a fig for my spotless reputation. What I care about is chastity itself. And, in any event, I doubt I'd ever be tempted to stray by a woman who flinches when I put my hands on her. Dry your clothes." His voice was harsh. "It might take some time. If you become bored in the meantime, there are books to read." He gestured to the wall.

She took one step toward him.

There was only one way to end this argument: Mark closed the parlor door on her. The last thing he saw was the look on her face—not outraged, not desirous, but cold with fear.

CHAPTER FOUR

THE DOOR SLAMMED in front of Jessica's nose. Then, before she could quite understand what was happening, she heard the sound of a key scraping in the lock.

The sound was irrevocable, creaking out her defeat. She was drenched down to her drawers. And she'd failed.

Her hands shook as she undid her corset laces. Not from cold; she'd stopped feeling cold months before. She'd made not one, but two tremendous miscalculations. And she feared that her mistake was irreparable.

Her tiny reserve of capital was in the tens of pounds now. She might make her funds last longer by selling clothing—but, given her trade, that would be akin to eating her seed corn. Besides, a courtesan must never appear desperate for a protector. Men who were attracted to desperate women were worse than the desperation itself.

No doubt Sir Mark thought that she was driven by something like desire—or, perhaps, mere feminine curiosity. He didn't know how truly grave her situation was. How badly she had needed him to succumb. It was that urgency that had made her misjudge the situation.

She'd convinced herself that his seduction would be easy—that he'd fall, if only he believed that nobody would find out. Worse. She'd fooled herself into believing that after what had happened to her, she could stomach another man's touch of ownership on her skin again.

She had been awfully, horribly wrong.

It had taken her months to recover from her illness. Back then, it had only been the physician's commands that had made her take her medicine, choke down a few spoonfuls of gruel. Amalie, her dearest friend, had come over daily and forced her to care for herself. Even now, she still had to remind herself to eat.

That was what had decided Jessica on this particular course of action.

Jessica knew what happened to courtesans who ceased to care for themselves. She had seen it too many times in the years she'd been in London. When a woman stopped caring, she no longer took pains to choose her next protector. One mistake— one man who liked hurting his mistress a little too well, one fellow who managed to hide a bawdy-house disease—that was all it took. Soon, the emptiness in a woman's heart grew to encompass her eyes.

She'd seen women take to gin or opium within months of making that first mistake. From there, it was nothing but a long, slow slide into the grave.

In her first year in this life, when Jessica had been young and naive, she'd told herself it wasn't so bad, being a courtesan.

It hadn't been what she'd dreamed of, but she'd embraced her survival with open arms. And she'd discovered that the scandalous Jess Farleigh enjoyed freedoms that the gently bred Jessica Carlisle dared not contemplate. During the days, she could think about commerce, manage business accounts, talk with her fellow courtesans about the things that happened between men and women. And the nights…she'd wanted to forget what she'd lost, and so she'd thrown herself into the evenings with abandon. At first, it had seemed one endless soiree, where men tripped over themselves to give her what she wanted.

In the years that followed, she'd learned that the glittering finery was a trap, that the soiree was not endless. It eroded you, piece by irrevocable piece. It made a mockery of love, and if you did not look after your heart with a ferocious care, you'd find, bit by bit, that you'd traded it for silk ribbons and baubles on gold chains. It took only one mistake to turn a cosseted courtesan into an empty-eyed whore, willing to do anything to forget what men had made of her. Jessica had watched it happen far too often.

The successful courtesan, Jessica had learned, had much in common with the successful gamester. The trick of winning was knowing when to leave the table. Anyone who stayed past her time lost. She lost everything.

Jessica pulled her shift off her shoulders and hung it to dry before the fire. The carpet was thick beneath her feet—warmer than the stockings she removed and placed on a chair to dry. The fire flickered against her skin. She was sure the flames radiated heat. But she no longer felt it. She no longer felt *anything.*

Sir Mark was supposed to be her final throw of the dice. She'd wagered her reserves on him. And she'd misjudged him—had let her cynicism do all the thinking for her. She had never imagined that his belief was *real,* that he would give up an opportunity to slake his lust. Principles had never mattered, not with the men she'd known.

She'd made a mistake—and one she could ill afford.

It wasn't money she was fighting for—not truly. It was all the things money could buy: the opportunity to escape her past, to have a cottage in a quiet village. To feel the sun against her face as warmth, instead of a cold, pale light. She wasn't going to be one of those women—the dim-eyed cousins of courtesans—giving up her soul to strangers nightly against a cold stone wall, just so she could purchase the gin she needed to forget.

No. After all these years, she was going to do what she did best. She was going to *survive*.

And so it didn't matter that he'd locked her in this room. That his eyes had narrowed in distrust. It didn't matter that she didn't have a whore's chance in heaven of convincing him to smile at her again. She was going to seduce Sir Mark. She was going to get her fifteen hundred pounds. She was going to find a nice cottage in a tiny village, she and Amalie, and together they would finally be able to let go of everything that had come before.

She had to sell her body one last time, but this time, she wasn't trading it for anything less than her heart. Nobody—nothing—not a locked door, nor even the great weight of Sir Mark's morals—would stop her.

She even thought she knew how to do it. She'd mistaken him once. She'd not do it again.

This time, she had to tell him the truth.

THE RAIN HAD STOPPED, and Jessica's clothing had dried by the time he came for her. His knock sounded twice on the door, echoing ominously.

"Come in."

A silence.

"It's safe," she added. And it was safe. For him. She sat, demurely dressed, before the fire. There would be no more mistakes. She couldn't afford a single one.

The key scraped in the lock. He opened the door a few inches. His face was obscured by the shadows in the hall. "The weather should hold," he said to the window near her, "long enough for you to make your way home. I would have offered you tea, but…" He trailed off with a shrug that had more to do with explanation than apology for his lack of hospitality.

She wouldn't have taken tea in any event.

"Let me show you out." He turned his back to her, and she stood. Her muscles twinged, sore, as if she'd run a great distance. Sitting and waiting for him had been arduous enough. His shoulders were rigid as he walked, at odds with the fluidity of his gait. At the front door, he fumbled for the handle.

Jessica stayed a few feet back. "Sir Mark. I owe you the truth."

He'd not looked at her, not since he'd opened the parlor door. But at these words, he paused. His shoulders straightened, and he glanced at her over his shoulder—a brief look, before his gaze flitted back to the door. He pressed the handle down.

"The truth is plain enough." For all the harshness of his words, his tone was gentle. "I was rather too cruel earlier. There's no need to embarrass yourself. Speak no more of it."

He might as well have said, *speak no more to me.* And *that* outcome was unacceptable.

"But I owe you the truth as to *why* I did it."

He didn't turn, but he let go of the door handle.

"I did it," she said, "because I hated you."

That brought him turning slowly around, this time to really look at her. Most men wouldn't have smiled at being told they were hated. And in truth, it wasn't a *happy* smile that took over his face. It was a bemused look, as if he held his breath.

"I hated you," she continued, "because you have done nothing more than abide by rules that every gentlewoman follows every day of her life. Yet for this prosaic feat, you are feted and cosseted as if you were a hero." She felt nothing as she spoke, but still her voice shook. Her hands were trembling, too. "I hate that if a woman missteps once, she is condemned forever, and yet the men who follow you can tie a simple ribbon to their hats after years of debauchery, and pass themselves off as upright pillars of society. And so, yes, Sir Mark. I came here to seduce you. I wanted to prove that you were only too human. Not a saint. Not an example to follow. Not anyone *deserving* of such worship."

Her voice had begun to rise. If she hadn't known better, she'd have thought herself upset, her calm unraveling like the edge of an old scarf.

But she *did* know better. She felt nothing—just the cold sweat of her palms, the tremor of her arms wrapped around herself. Her body, apparently, felt what her heart could not. There was truth in her words—too much of it.

He must have heard it because his eyes widened. The smile slipped from his face. He contemplated her silently for a while. Jessica set her jaw and returned his gaze.

"You are quite right," he eventually said. "I agree with your every sentiment, with my whole heart." And then he did smile at her—not just a bemused little curl of his lips, but a brilliant grin. "Pardon me. I agree with almost every sentiment." He leaned back against the door. "I must make an exception for one tiny particular. You see, I rather like myself."

She'd never met a man before who preferred facts over flattery. He seemed torn from the pages of a child's fable—a dazzling hero, pure and upstanding. Incorruptible. And what role did that give her in this fairy tale?

"You would be a more comfortable man if you were not so good."

"No, Mrs. Farleigh. You mustn't believe that. You were doing so well at avoiding all those pesky illusions. I've told you before, I'm no saint. In fact, I am eaten up by mortal sins. It's refreshing for someone else to notice."

"Sin? You must not mean the typical ones that gentlemen engage in."

"Typical enough." He shrugged. "I harbor a great deal of pride."

"Oh?"

"Oh." He met her eyes. "You see, I'm not some shiny bauble to be strung onto a necklace and displayed for all the world to see. I'm too proud to ever be anyone's conquest."

It was both warning and explanation all at once. She could see that now, in the set in his jaw. Her direct approach to seduction would never have worked even if he'd been more inclined to sin. This was a man who wanted to work for his prize.

"Besides," he added, "I'm much too proud to ever want a woman who did not like me."

"Liking has nothing to do with it. Can you tell me the difference between a mounting block and a male virgin?"

He shook his head.

"The virgin," Jessica said, "is a far easier conquest."

He laughed—simple and uncomplicated. "Yes," he said. "I far prefer this side of you. For what it's worth, Mrs. Farleigh, I don't hate you. I don't even hold you in dislike, however disreputable your intentions may have been this afternoon. I don't imagine your situation is easy." He looked down briefly and then glanced up, his blond radiance almost overwhelming. "I'm willing to forgive a great deal from clever women who see through the veneer of saintliness."

She wasn't certain what he meant by that. But he was smiling at her. He'd not thrown her out and told her never to speak with him again. She had a chance—one last chance at success. It was going to be hard. Practically impossible. And she was going to have to move with painstaking slowness.

"It's becoming harder to hate you, knowing that you're more than a collection of moral aphorisms. But I am rather perverse."

"Be careful." His words were a warning, but his eyes sparkled with mischief. "I'm proud enough that I might decide to convince you to like me after all."

"No, no. We can't have that." She pitched her tone to playfulness. "If I *actually* liked you, I might decide to tempt you again—not to prove a point, but just for the pleasure of having you in my bed."

She hadn't realized she meant it until she said it. She didn't want Sir Mark in her bed in any sexual sense—it had been years since she'd felt true desire.

No. She meant what she'd said in the most wistful sense possible. Despite his protestations, he seemed like a nice man. She'd never had a nice man in her bed.

But standing as close to him as she was, she could hear his indrawn breath. She could see his pupils dilate. He didn't rake his gaze down her body in possessive desire, as the jaded roués of her acquaintance might have done. But he didn't squeeze his eyes shut, like a young boy trying to deny the truth of his vision.

Instead, he raised his head. His gaze caught hers—steady and just a bit mischievous. And she swallowed. Sir Mark wasn't anything like what she had imagined a virgin would be. He was too masculine. Too *certain*. Without breaking her gaze, he opened the door behind him—a signal, perhaps, that they'd passed some threshold and the conversation had come to an end.

"Mrs. Farleigh," he said, "you are interesting. And you paid me the compliment of your honesty." He stepped to the side, and the cool air of early evening touched her skin. The clouds had dissipated enough that the sun, hovering above the horizon, left her blinking.

"And so I shall be honest in return." He gave her a tight little smile. "You can tempt me all you like. But you won't succeed."

She *would*. She had to. But for now, she simply smiled at him. "I do believe you've made that clear." She passed through the door.

He set his hand on her wrist as she went by. His

bare fingers met her glove—not holding her back, but just touching her lightly. She paused.

His fingers brushed up her arm—half an inch across kidskin, no more. An unthinking movement, surely; not a caress. Not from him. For one second she thought he looked hesitant. But then he turned toward her, and the low rays of the sun caught his face, coloring his skin with rust. He leaned in, supremely confident. He was close enough that she could see his eyes—blue, ringed with brown. His scent was fresh male, soap tinged with salt. He was close enough to kiss her.

He didn't.

"True honesty compels me to add one more thing." She could feel the breath from his words, brushing against the bridge of her nose. "If you truly liked me enough to tempt me, I should not mind seeing you try."

And then, as if he had not whispered that wickedness against her skin, he bowed in farewell and closed the door.

CHAPTER FIVE

"You shouldn't have come here yourself, Sir Mark." From behind the bar of the new post office, Mrs. Tatlock, the postman's wife, set her hand on her hip and tapped one foot.

Through the dusty windows behind her, the sun shone brilliantly. The rays caught specks of dust as they rose in the air, turning even the dingy confines of the room around them into radiance. Technically, Mrs. Tatlock was only the letter carrier's wife. She had no duties, collected no pay. But her husband was known to sometimes evade delivering the letters to the houses farthest out, particularly on fine summer days when he preferred to fish. She'd arranged a system where she would hold letters at the post office until her husband decided to deliver them—or the owner decided to pick them up, whichever came first.

Today was a beautiful day, every color chosen from a jeweler's display case. Mr. Tatlock was undoubtedly fishing, and Mark had decided to fetch his own post. He'd had a beautiful, peaceful walk to town.

"Here you are," Mrs. Tatlock was scolding, "the knight of the town, and you're fetching your own post as if you were a servant. It's not fitting!"

Mark swallowed a sigh. "Truly, it's no hardship to walk." And besides, he had a suspicion that his charwoman was sneaking glances at his correspondence. The last time she'd brought him a letter, the envelope had come unsealed. The woman had waved it off, claiming that one could never trust that newfangled paste to stay in place. Mark, however, remained dubious.

"Besides," he continued, "the exercise is good for me. I shouldn't like to become slothful."

Her face softened. "Nobody would ever accuse you of sloth." She closed the drawer before her and handed over two letters. "But we do worry that you're not taking care of yourself. Only the two servants to do for you, and those not even in residence. Sir Mark, that would be a proper arrangement for a gentleman come down on hard times. But you're a knight of the realm. The brother of a duke. It's scandalous, the way you're living. And if those London papers heard of it, Shepton Mallet would never live down the shame. To act as if we are so countrified that we can't do for you…" She shook her head at him mournfully.

And yet they *hadn't* done for him, decades past.

It felt the height of decadence just to live in his mother's house and have new bread. He'd come back here to recall that time, not to bury the memories in luxury.

"Nonsense," Mark said. "The papers will just chalk it up to my eccentricity."

She sniffed. "Eccentric? You? Not likely, that. You're not the one who's decidedly out of place—that is to say, *I* won't speak any ill. Unlike some others." She sniffed, and when Mark didn't ask her to elaborate, she immediately broke her own dictum. "Unlike the *other* newcomer," she said carefully.

Mark set his hand, palm down, on the table before him, keeping the gesture as casual as possible. There was only one other newcomer. He could see her clearly in his mind's eye, drenched from the downpour, her hair sliding out of its pins.

But, no. He wasn't one for gossip. He didn't need to ask. He wouldn't even let himself think of her.

"Ah?" he said.

Ah, he decided, was not asking.

But Mrs. Tatlock understood. "Mrs. Farleigh." Her voice crept low, the syllables rounding out in warm west country tones. "Mrs. Farleigh, she writes letters every week."

Mark felt his chin twitch in the barest of nods.

"Regular, like the crow of a cock, she does. Sends out two or three every time she stops by."

"Ah." The syllable escaped again.

"But does she receive anything in response?"

Mark's hand curled against the wood of the counter. The missives in his pocket felt suddenly heavy. He'd known the letter would be waiting for him, had known that his brother's wife would have penned a thorough response—never mind that she was a busy duchess. Just as surely, he'd expected his other brother's reply—fewer in pages, but no less caring. If the letters *hadn't* come, he would have worried that something had gone amiss.

Mrs. Tatlock smiled grimly. "Well," she said slyly. "She hears from her solicitor."

"Perhaps the letters are written to an invalid," Mark suggested.

"Perhaps. It's the other letters that go unanswered." Mrs. Tatlock shuffled in the mailbags behind her and came up with two envelopes, both stamped with penny reds. The direction was written in a fine, strong hand; no curlicues or spidery lines from Mrs. Farleigh. It was addressed to a Mr. Alton Carlisle in Watford. Mark had heard of the town; he thought it somewhere closer to London, although his memory was vague. The other was addressed to an Amalie Leveque, in London proper.

"She brings these letters by every few days.

And every day, it seems, she asks if she's had any replies." Mrs. Tatlock shook her head. "I do wonder who she's writing to. A Frenchwoman, by the sound of it—and we know precisely what sort of people *they* are. No morals to speak of. And no doubt the other's a lover, and one that's scorned her."

Mark thought of that flinch, of that spark of… of something he'd seen in her eyes two evenings before. He could almost hear her speaking, even now. *I did it because I hated you.*

"No," he said softly, "I don't believe she's pining after a lover."

He'd met women on the hunt for a lover before. She'd made a fair facsimile of one at first—the glances that dared him to draw closer, the state of undress she'd so carefully engineered. But there had been something…something brittle about her come-hither. He couldn't imagine that she was sending letters to a lover in desperation. No matter what she'd tried to do to him, the thought of her sending out letters and receiving no response…it made him want to comfort her.

Mrs. Tatlock snorted. "What, you think she has more than *one* lover, then?"

He drew himself up and looked down his nose at Mrs. Tatlock. "Do you have intimate knowledge of her situation?"

"I— Well—"

"I've heard a great deal of gossip about Mrs. Farleigh since I've arrived, and yet nobody has presented any proof."

She'd presented her own form of proof, true. And if he were the sort of tale bearer who delighted in ruining reputations, he could have destroyed hers by simply recounting the facts of their encounter. He wasn't.

"But, Sir Mark—"

"Don't 'Sir Mark' me. I consider it just as shabby to ruin a woman with talk as with action." Mark leaned on the counter and glared at her.

"Sir Mark—I didn't intend— I truly thought—"

"You thought? You thought I would *want* to see a woman ostracized and left without friends, simply because she had the misfortune to be prettier than usual?" His words slowed. He could almost feel the music of the Somerset accent, forgotten since childhood, pulling at his tongue. "Or did you think I would enjoy making sport of someone who wasn't here to defend herself? Don't ruin a reputation on the basis of simple gossip. Not in my presence."

Mrs. Tatlock took a step back. Her eyes were wide; her hands clutched the gray of her skirt. "Oh, my." She spoke slowly, her voice rising half an octave. "I hadn't thought— I had assumed— No. Perhaps I'd let myself forget entirely. You *are* Elizabeth Turner's son, after all."

Elizabeth Turner's son. Mark shook his head, but he couldn't deny it, not really. He *was* her son—heir to both her best and her worst qualities. Her goodness. Her zeal. Her excess.

His brother, and the rise of dark waters.

He took a step back from Mrs. Tatlock. He took a step back from himself, seeing suddenly his own image superimposed on hers: cruel and unthinking and kind, all at the same time. Even though his hands clenched in denial, he let out a breath.

"Well," he told her, "gossip about *that*, then. At least what you say about me happens to be true."

MRS. TATLOCK, apparently, had not chosen to spread rumors about Mark's defense of Mrs. Farleigh — at least she hadn't by the time the ladies of the church arranged the picnic in his honor. Upon his arrival, he was hailed with good cheer and humor. The commons where they held the event had been emptied of all livestock except a flock of chickens, who squawked in complaint in the corner. But the sheep were not the only undesirables they'd kept hidden; they had succeeded in keeping away the less fortunate members of the community by hosting the event on a Wednesday morning. The common folk were all laboring: in the mills, in the fields, or simply doing the spinning in their own homes. The only laborers present were the servants who danced attendance.

When Mrs. Farleigh arrived, a wave of shock ran through the gathering throng. It started in gasps; it traveled in whispers. By the time she'd come halfway across the field toward them, a horde of concerned women had descended upon her. They buzzed about her, gesticulating and consulting one another in tones.

Even though he could not make out a word they said, he could imagine their scandalized conversation.

"Help," Mark supposed Mrs. Lewis might be saying. "A pretty woman has appeared—and she has lovely breasts."

At least that's what he hoped she was saying. Mark couldn't imagine why else she'd be pointing to Mrs. Farleigh's bosom.

"Oh, no!" Mrs. Finney could have been replying, as she put her hand on Mrs. Farleigh's elbow. "I haven't had chance enough to embarrass my thirteen-year-old daughter by introducing her to Sir Mark. We can't have an actual *woman* close to him—he might want her instead. Come over here, Mrs. Farleigh."

The group moved together, slowly displacing the hens, who squawked in avian protest. One of Mrs. Farleigh's hands had crept to her hip.

Mrs. Lewis gave her a bright, cheery smile, so false that Mark could discount it even from this distance. The women all nodded at her firmly, shook their heads and walked away, leaving her a full twenty yards from the gathering, with no company nearby but the chickens.

Mrs. Farleigh watched them leave. She didn't sigh. She didn't shake her head. She didn't even shrug. She simply reached into her basket and pulled out a blanket. She laid it out, ignoring the poultry who pecked at its edge.

Walking back, Mrs. Lewis, the rector's wife, rubbed her hands together briskly, as if well satisfied.

The conversation Mark had imagined had been for his own amusement. But by the look on their faces—by the stony unconcern on hers—he doubted the conversation had been pleasant for her at all.

The women returned to their places by him, chattering amongst themselves as if nothing had happened.

Really. Had any of them *read* his book, or had they simply placed the volume directly on the altar, as a mute object of veneration?

Perhaps that was why he turned to Mrs. Lewis as she fussed over her daughter's bonnet. Mrs. Lewis was the epitome of a clergyman's wife—staid and proper—and Mark caught the rumble of a lecture about ladies and the sun as she wrestled her daughter's wide bonnet into place.

He was about to upset their shiny, clean social order.

"Mrs. Lewis."

As he spoke, her hand dropped from the ribbons about her daughter's chin. The crowd quieted, hanging on his words. "Why is Mrs. Farleigh seated with the hens?"

Twelve people turned to him as one, their eyes rounded.

Young James Tolliver made a choking sound and gestured urgently.

Mrs. Lewis was not much more cogent. "She— well—have you not heard the talk?"

"I've heard some innuendo," he said carefully. "I've seen a few dresses—but nothing that is outside the typical bounds of fashion." She was dressed beautifully—provocatively, in fact, for the country. But promenading in a London park, she would only be thought a little daring.

Heads turned again to look at Mrs. Farleigh and then turned back to Mark.

"It's…it's… Sir Mark." The rector's wife was flustered. "Truly. Perhaps somewhere in London that sort of *thing* is tolerated. But we're good people here. Upstanding."

"What sort of *thing* are you speaking about?"

Mrs. Lewis flushed. But Miss Lewis spoke out from under the brim of her bonnet. "It's the décol-

letage," she said simply. "If it were *here* instead of
there..." She drew a line on her own breast.

"Dinah!"

"What?" Dinah said. "I saw all the men looking. If you would only let me get rid of this horrid
lace..."

"Don't say such things." Mrs. Lewis glanced
over at Mark and gave him a pained smile. "Dear.
People will think you mean them."

"So it's just the neckline," Mark heard himself
say. "I can fix that." And before anyone could stop
him, he started off down the field. The dim rumble
of conversation slowed behind him. And then, as
it became clear that Sir Mark, the guest of honor,
was approaching Mrs. Jessica Farleigh, the unwanted guest of dishonor, talk ceased altogether.
The chickens scattered before him.

He stopped at the edge of her blanket.

She raised her head slowly. Three afternoons
ago, he'd seen her stripped to chemise and corset.
He wanted her more now.

Maybe it was the sun glinting through her hair,
glancing off the ringlets that framed her face.
Maybe it was the rounding of her eyes, as her gaze
swept slowly up his trousers.

By the time her eyes met his, though, Mark was
sure of one thing. It was not just his sense of fair-
ness that had brought him out to see her. It was
not mere curiosity. It was not even simple lust. He

wasn't sure what to call it. He only knew one thing, by the dazed roil in his stomach.

He was in trouble.

And he was enjoying it.

"Sir Mark," she said. "How kind of you to join me."

She spoke carefully, her words clipped, as if she expected him to cast her out entirely from the dubious heaven of a church picnic.

"This is no social call," he said.

Her chin rose. "And so you've come to finish what they started."

Mark undid one cuff link, and slid it into his waistcoat pocket. "Miss Lewis tells me that all the men are looking at your bosom."

She made no move to cover herself. "Are they?" she asked. "Are they *all*?"

He slipped the other cuff link off. "I wasn't watching all the men. I wouldn't know."

"And you?"

By way of answer, he undid the buttons of his coat, working from top to bottom. Her breath hissed in as he worked. He tugged one sleeve down, and the soft breeze touched the last layer of fabric between his shoulder and the open air. Behind him, he heard the murmur of outraged feminine conversation. He didn't care what they said. He didn't care what *any* of them said. He simply finished removing the jacket, and then, meeting her eyes, he held it out to her.

"Put this on." His voice was betrayingly hoarse. It was not a suggestion.

She stared at the fabric in his hand but made no move to take it. "Why, Sir Mark, that is quite a gallant offer, but I am not chilled in the slightest."

He narrowed his eyes. "And here I thought we had passed the point where you feigned idiocy." He leaned closer. "You know quite well why I wish you to cover yourself."

She shrugged, which did very interesting things to her uncovered bosom. "And here *I* thought you believed your own book. It's chapter thirteen, is it not? Where you say that a man must claim responsibility for his own temptation, and not pin it on the woman who arouses him. It's a gown, Sir Mark. Not even one of my more daring ones. And yet you look at it as if it were a viper, poised to strike at your virtue. Clearly, I must have misunderstood the import of your practical guide."

"Nobody ever understands my book." His tones were clipped. "It's the least practical guide I could ever have written."

"You're not the least bit tempted?" She looked up at him. That sense of dichotomy struck him again—as if she were unsure how she wanted him to answer. As if she wanted him to *want* and yet wanted to push him away all at once.

He *was* tempted. But it was that sense of hesitance more than anything that made him release his coat so that it fell to the blanket beside her. "I don't want you to cover yourself to withdraw *my* temptation." And then—he wasn't precisely sure why—he dropped his voice to a whisper. "More clothing would hardly signify in any event. I could not possibly forget a single curve of your skin, and when I take myself to bed tonight I doubt I will see anything else."

She'd been reaching for his jacket. But she froze at that, her hand held rigidly an inch away. Her eyes widened.

"No," he continued, "the reason I offer is not because I want to avoid my sins, but rather that I must own up to them."

"Sins?" she repeated.

"We've already discussed my sins, Mrs. Farleigh. I am greedy. I am covetous. I am selfish. And one other thing." He leaned in. "I absolutely do not share."

"I— But I haven't— We—" Her eyes fell from his in discomfort.

"Just because I happen to be a virgin does not mean I am content to share my fantasies at night with other men."

She exhaled slowly. "If you were any other man," she said softly, "I would think that you had just threatened to seduce me."

"Worse." He leaned down, close enough to whisper. "I threatened to *like* you. I suspect seduction would be easier for you to understand."

A small smile touched her lips. "Sir Mark, there's no need to threaten me with anything so drastic as *like*. Mere acceptance would be sufficiently shocking."

Mark straightened. "One last thing, Mrs. Farleigh." He took a deep breath and waited for her to raise her eyes to him one last time. When she did, he gave her a wolfish grin. "Red suits you," he said, and then left.

JESSICA PICKED UP the jacket Sir Mark had dropped next to her and shook it out. She watched his retreating back, trying to find firm footing in her mind.

She had thought it would be easy to guide a virgin's first tentative foray into sensuality. But there was nothing tentative about him. He did not deny his lusts, his wants. She didn't know how to seduce such unbending confidence.

Yes, I want you, he'd as good as told her, *but I won't act on that want.*

There was a bigger problem.

He looked at her with an air of such quiet expectation. She remembered what he'd said with a laugh the other day. *I rather like myself.* She could feel that certainty, spreading from him like a contagion. And now he was threatening to like her, too.

Despite her better judgment, she respected him. It was impossible not to. He was so…so forthright, so straightforward. He didn't hide behind rules, didn't accuse others of his own shortcomings. He didn't flinch from his own desires.

He simply…didn't set a foot wrong.

And for the first time, Jessica wished this was real. That she was merely a widow with a slightly tarnished reputation. That she *had* been banished here.

She wished she was free to revel in the heady feel of flirtation without feeling the future press against her in suffocating reminder of the penury that waited.

Sir Mark's long strides had brought him back to the protective crowd of women once again.

Everyone had been watching them. Jessica stood and brushed her skirts into place. Then she shook out the jacket he'd left behind. The fabric was warm with the heat of his body. It smelled of him—clean, fresh male, with a dab of sea spray. Slowly, she donned the garment. It was large on her, and overly warm. Still, it felt like a friendly embrace—comforting and casual, without importuning her for more. She couldn't remember the last time she'd had a simple hug from a man.

He was surrounded by women again—a gaggle of concerned villagers, clucking over him. No doubt making sure that he'd not been tainted by her.

He laughed and then spoke, gesturing with his hands. And then, when he'd tamed their frightened outrage, he turned and glanced at her. A warm breeze swirled up. It lifted the collar of his jacket against her neck.

No. She had no notion how to seduce a man like this. He had no pampered vanity to flatter, no hidden desires to draw out in the open. He wanted her. He thought of her. And he admitted it so openly that she feared it would be impossible to lure him into dishonesty.

Worse; he was luring *her* into the truth. He gave her a private smile, one that made a hollow of her chest.

She had thought that when she felt again for the first time, it would be something gentle, something clean. Some small and silent pleasure, perhaps. But it was not some quiet return to feeling that came to her. It was the sharp, painful tingle of a limb being slapped from sleep.

She wanted to tell him the truth. She wanted to relinquish all hope of seduction, so that she could enjoy the company of a man who didn't lie. She wanted him to like her with the same easy confidence with which he liked himself. The impossibility of it made her ache.

Jessica reached out and plucked a dandelion from the grass. It was a fragile, delicate shell of white spores; when she snapped its stem, a few seeds detached from the round head.

He was still smiling at her, a bright golden grin as blinding as the sun.

She raised the dandelion to her mouth and blew. White seeds scattered on the breeze, whirling in his direction. Maybe it was her imagination. The spores separated too quickly for her to follow their path, and it would have been a strange wind indeed that blew those tiny parachutes across twenty yards of picnic.

Still, after a few seconds he raised his hand, almost in greeting. And then he closed his fingers, as if snatching something invisible from the air.

CHAPTER SIX

"DID YOU NOT SEE me, Sir Mark?" James Tolliver demanded.

Mark pulled his gaze from Mrs. Farleigh's form to contemplate the skinny child by his side.

"Your pardon, Tolliver. Were you trying to catch my attention? My mind is…" He trailed off, thinking of the red silk of Mrs. Farleigh's skirts, spread on the blanket she'd set out. The carmine of her gown had been in perfect contrast to the pale perfection of her skin. But it wasn't the cold marble of her complexion that drew him. It was the hint of fire that he'd sensed beneath. As if she were unstable, dangerous and all too enticing. The buzz of insects swirled around him, loud in his ears. "My mind is elsewhere." Mark turned his head to focus on the young man. "My thoughts have all gone awandering."

"I didn't mean just now. I meant before you left to speak with Mrs. Farleigh. I made the signal." Tolliver held up his hand, his thumb curled to meet his two middle fingers. He twisted it at an angle.

"A signal?"

"*The* signal," Tolliver corrected.

Mark stared at the boy's hand in puzzlement. With his little finger peeled back that way, his hand looked like a small dog, ear cocked, looking on quizzically.

Tolliver tapped the blue rose on his hat, glanced at the women around them with a glare that bespoke a world of suspicion and dropped his voice. "*You* know. *The* signal."

"I'm not familiar with that." Mark *didn't* lower his voice.

Tolliver blushed and looked about furtively. "Shh! Do you want them to *hear?*"

"I hadn't realized we were in enemy territory. Who is this *them* that we fear?"

Tolliver made *the* signal once again and pointed to his hand. "Didn't I do it right? It's supposed to be the signal for 'Watch out—Dangerous Woman Ahead.'"

Mark counted slowly. One. Two. Three…

"Tolliver," he finally said, "where did you learn that signal?"

"It was in the introductory pamphlet. *A Youth's Guide to the MCB,* by Jedidiah Pruwett, which I—"

"There's a pamphlet?"

"Yes, advertised in the paper! Send one shilling to…" Tolliver trailed off, glancing at Mark. Maybe it was the curled fists, or the clenched teeth, that gave away Mark's anger.

"That…that wasn't *your* pamphlet?"

"No."

When Mark had sold the rights to his book to a publisher, he'd not given a thought to any potential profit. Philosophical volumes—even ones written for the common man—rarely sold well. And besides, he didn't need the money. His publisher had paid twenty pounds for exclusive and unlimited rights to the work; Mark had been convinced they'd only given so much because his brother was a duke. Said brother had tried to convince him to hold out for royalties, but Mark only cared to see the volume in print. He'd donated his twenty pounds to charity and thought nothing more of it.

He'd not minded when he heard that the book was in its third printing—or even its twelfth. But then had come the Illustrated Edition. Followed shortly by the Royal Edition—printed particularly for Queen Victoria, bound in leather dyed to match her favorite color. The Floral Edition. The Edition with Local Commentary—that one had included little woodcuts of Parford Manor, Mark's room at Oxford and his brother's home in London. Not to mention the infamous Pocket Edition.

He suspected his publisher had a Woodlands Edition ready for production, complete with illustrations of adorable talking deer. Somehow, they would find a way to make the creatures look like him.

No. It wasn't the *money* Mark regretted relinquishing. It was the *control*. And even without a Woodlands Edition, he'd lost it completely. Between the newspapers that tracked his every move and Jedidiah Pruwett, who'd founded the Male Chastity Brigade, he'd had no peace at all.

"Don't tell me where you sent your money." Mark drummed his fingers against the seam of his trousers. "I'd really rather not know."

Tolliver shook his head in confusion. "In any event, that's where I learned that signal. And I used it today because she's a danger, she is."

"*That's* what the MCB is teaching? To avoid dangers like that?"

Tolliver swallowed, looking around. Mark's outburst had drawn the attention of everyone around him. Miss Lewis, the rector's daughter, had frozen midconversation with her mother and a few others. They turned to Mark as one.

He hated being the center of attention. *Especially* here in Shepton Mallet, with the green, familiar silhouette of the hills framing the gathering. It reminded him of his childhood, of those months when everybody would pay attention to his mother, watching her as if she were some crazed beast about to spring. As if they might goad her into doing so.

Nobody was thinking of that now—nobody but Mark. His own personal preferences counted not one whit when it came to a matter of right and wrong. He took a deep breath. Unlike his mother, he didn't need to gibber. He didn't need to scream. He didn't need to threaten. People *liked* him, and that gave him a responsibility.

"I assure you," Mark said, more quietly, "I have never endorsed such unkind behavior."

"But, Sir Mark! She's wearing scarlet. She made you give up your coat. You can't really believe she's an innocent. She…she could be a fallen woman!"

"There is no such thing as a fallen woman—you just need to look for the man who pushed her." He shouldn't say that, not here. So many people might recognize its source. But no one cringed from his mother's aphorism. Instead, the rector's wife gave a thoughtful shake of her head, looking back to Mrs. Farleigh.

"Tolliver," Mark said, "I adhere to the law of chastity because I don't believe in pushing women. That's what it means to be a man. I don't hurt others simply to make myself feel superior. Gossip can ruin a woman as surely as unchaste behavior. True men don't indulge in either. We don't need to."

Tolliver raised stricken eyes to Mark. "I—I didn't think of that."

Most people didn't.

Mrs. Farleigh had donned his coat. Even that unrelieved, ill-fitting navy could not dim her beauty.

"When someone falls," Mark said, "you don't throw her back down in the dirt. You offer her a hand up. It's the Christian thing to do." But the thought of taking her hand didn't make him feel Christian at all. His mind kept slipping back to that evening. Not to her form, dripping wet, but to the wild light that had come into her eyes the moment when she'd told him she hated him. The memory still sent a queer little thrill through him. He didn't understand it at all.

To his credit, Tolliver didn't flinch. "What... what do I do?" he asked.

Miss Lewis stood and said, "We go and escort her over here." She cast her mother a defiant glance. Mark held his breath as the two started across the field. But nobody stopped them.

JESSICA WASN'T SURE what Sir Mark intended when he came up to her an hour later. The picnic was breaking up. Blankets were being folded, and the remains of the repast tucked away for future consumption.

He'd not talked to her in all that intervening time, but she was sure he'd said *something* about her. The rector's daughter had come up to her and had admired her gown and hair. The girl had even walked with her, introducing her to women who'd not so much as turned in her direction a week ago at service. She'd promenaded beside Miss Lewis in a growing muddle of confusion, and the passage of time had only served to strengthen it.

Sir Mark stood before her now, and she wasn't sure if she should be grateful to him. She had been practically an outcast before this afternoon. He'd diverted the flow of gossip, as if he were Hercules and shifting a river on its course was no hardship.

It wasn't merely that the people had heeded his sterling reputation. Another man might have been diffident and uncomfortable, standing before everyone in his shirtsleeves. Sir Mark, though, acted as if his dishabille were normal. He managed to look fully attired—so much so that she would have felt awkward and ungainly had she pointed out that he lacked a coat.

He didn't say anything. He simply watched her from a few feet distant. She snapped the blanket she had brought in the air. He snagged one corner as it floated past him and helped her fold it once, then twice, before he passed his gathered ends to her.

He did it so carefully that their hands did not touch. Still he didn't speak.

Jessica broke the silence. "Thank you for your assistance. You must be…here for your garment."

One of her hands had already gone to the cuff when he shook his head.

"You're wrong about that. I'm here to walk you home," Sir Mark said. "You live up the road beyond the old sawmill, do you not?"

Jessica placed the blanket in her basket. "What do you mean, *walk me home?*"

"Walk." He held up two fingers and mimed. "Most people learn how to do it at a young age. I've observed that you're reasonably proficient in the activity."

"That's not what I meant," Jessica sputtered.

"Then perhaps you are unsure as to the meaning of the word *home?* Although—fair warning—I do mean to take you a roundabout way, if you can bear my company for a full half-hour. I thought we'd go along the Doulting Water, and then up the hedgerow."

"But—"

"Ah, it's the middle word you're objecting to, then."

"Middle word?"

His eyes met hers, intensely blue. She swallowed hard, her stomach clenching. "You." He said the word as if no other person existed, as if the dissipating crowd stood at a distance of many miles.

She couldn't say anything. She carefully set her basket on her arm and looked away. She glanced about helplessly, but for once, nobody was hurrying over to separate them, to save Sir Mark from conversing with a woman like her. What had he *said* to them? And why was he doing this to her?

She straightened, not wanting him to see her confusion. "Surely you plan on defining that term as well?"

"Even if I had the temerity to explain you to yourself, I lack the ability. I don't know you well enough. That is, after all, the purpose of the endeavor in the first place." He held out his arm for her. As if she could take it. As if they were just two friends walking together.

Sir Mark did not make any sense at all.

"But—but— This can hardly be—"

"Proper?" He shrugged. "I have been assured it is. Country rules, after all—I have it on the best of authority that a demure little walk is perfectly acceptable, so long as we stick to the lanes and the hedgerows." He reached out and took her hand, just long enough to guide it to his elbow in unthinking assurance. Even through her gloves, she felt the warmth of his arm through the linen of his shirt. And it was *just* his shirt that lay between his flesh and her hand. He wasn't wearing his coat— she was. But he took no notice of it, while she was painfully aware of the lack.

"The best of authority! I should like to see that etiquette book."

"I didn't consult a book." He gave an unconcerned wave to the rector's wife as he walked her out toward the gate, as if the woman's suspiciously narrowed gaze were nothing to worry about. "I wrote to the Duchess of Parford and asked."

She bit her lip, her hands clenching. It took her a moment to identify the emotion that fluttered in her stomach: dazed bewilderment. "The Duchess of Parford. You wrote to the Duchess of Parford about me?"

"Twice now."

Jessica fell silent, unsure how to respond. He spoke in such an easy way—as if he dashed off letters to duchesses on a regular basis. Well. His brother was a duke, after all. He probably *did*. She supposed it shouldn't come as such a surprise. She'd simply forgotten how high his family was. No, not forgotten; he'd made her overlook it, through some trick of his easy manners.

Perhaps that was why she let him guide her down the cobblestoned street in comparative silence. It wasn't until they reached the shade of the trees that lined the water that Jessica spoke again.

"What did you say to the duchess?"

"She *is* my sister, you know—married to my brother. And not nearly so intimidating as her title makes her sound. I wanted to stave off any talk in town, so I thought that getting her imprimatur would be useful. After I'd sent the first letter, Margaret naturally bombarded me with questions."

"Questions?" The river was running through high, grass-covered banks. A wood bridge crossed over one arm of the water, rushing into a millrace, but the main body burbled by noisily to her right.

"She wanted to know how long I've known you. Are you pretty? Clever?" He cast her a sly glance. "I told her, not long enough, and to the last two— very."

If she'd been fifteen, she'd have blushed. As it was, Jessica felt a warmth collect on her skin, in her lungs. "If I didn't know better, I should think you were flirting with me."

He gave her an unreadable look. "Well. If you say I'm not, you must be correct. Still, I don't endorse your conclusion."

This left her equally confused. "But you're— you're "

"A virgin?" There was a note of amusement in his voice. "True. But just because I don't believe in poaching out of season doesn't mean I can't hunt."

Her mouth dried.

"And here I'd thought we had left those polite protestations behind us," he said. "I like you, Mrs. Farleigh. It's that simple."

"I—I—"

"And you hate me." He smiled at her, as if he'd seen through her contrivance. "You see, it's perfectly safe for the both of us. You know I shall never impose upon you. And until you've decided not to hate me, I need not worry that you'll enlarge on our acquaintance. We neither of us have expectations."

"Safe. *You* think *I'm* safe." She glanced at him. He seemed perfectly sane——no hint whatsoever of madness showed, except his appalling words. "Must I remind you that I tried to seduce you?"

"True." He shrugged. "But I don't put much store by that, as you weren't very good at it."

Jessica gasped, pulling her hand from his arm. "Why, you——you——"

"You didn't really mean it," he said, with a wave of his hand that wasn't much of an apology.

Jessica turned on him. "I'll have you know I meant every word of it! If you'd been any other man, I'd have succeeded. And you'd have——"

"You'd have lost your nerve." But he was watching her now, the solemn expression on his face belied only by a tiny quirk of his lips.

"And I don't know what you mean when you say I wasn't any good at it. I was *excellent*." She turned to him. "I *am* excellent. Why, I could still have you, *right now*, you arrogant cad. And I would, except——"

"Except for the little fact that you hate me." His eyes twinkled at her.

"Yes." She folded her hands. "Except for that."

They walked on in silence. Any other man, at being told that he could be seduced were it not for the fact that the woman in question hated him, would have been livid. Sir Mark, however, whistled tunelessly as they walked and leaned to pick up a stone. He skipped it across the water, as soon as they passed a calm section.

"I'm learning a great deal about you," he finally remarked. "For one, you're a competitive little creature. I'll wager you were one of those children who would do anything, if dared to do it."

"I am docile as a *lamb*."

"A great big bull, you mean, tossing its horns."

"If this is your idea of *hunting*," she threw back, "you aren't very good at it."

But the insult did not seem to bother him. He merely smiled. "You needn't think you can put me off that way," he said calmly. "It's what I like best about you—your willingness to insult me to my face. I like a great deal about you, which I must say gives you a deuced unfair advantage, since you despise me so."

"Oh?"

"You see, you remind me of my brother."

She paused, her eyebrows raised. "I remind you of your *brother*? Sir Mark, scores of men have flirted with me. I do not hesitate to tell you that you are absolutely the *worst*. You must work on your compliments. No woman wants to be told she brings a man to mind—even if the man happens to be a duke."

"Not my brother, the duke. My middle brother. You see, if you want to know what Smite means, you have to watch what he does, not what he says. His speech is entirely at odds with his actions."

"Now you're calling me a liar." She shook her head. "You're hopeless. Truly hopeless."

"You see," he barreled on, ignoring her protestations, "you keep telling me that you could seduce me."

"I could bring you to your knees."

He stopped dead in the road. Slowly, he turned to her. "That," he said quietly, "should have been obvious by now."

The lane they had turned down was empty. A hedge of blackberries in full white flower hid the house that stood nearby. Suddenly, the dusty track seemed very small—too small for the both of them. He took one step toward her, his eyes pinning her in place. Her lungs filled with some hot, molten liquid. She willed her feet to stay rooted in place, her backbone to remain straight and tall. She looked into his eyes, unflinching.

Slowly, he raised his hand. He was going to touch her. Her skin tingled with anticipation. And despite that, under it all, there was still that cold prickle, that silent protest. *No. No.* There was nobody about—it was just her and him, and if she was to have any hope of success, she had to yield to him, to let him touch her, anywhere he wanted without protest… She imagined herself an automaton, constructed of some ungiving metal. Something that would freeze in place when his hand landed on her. Something that had no feelings, no heart.

No misgivings.

He raised one eyebrow. "Mrs. Farleigh," he said gently, "you are steeling yourself not to flinch."

"No. No, I am not. I don't know what you mean."

"You know precisely what I mean. You are frozen in place, as if you were some statue made of ice."

"I am not."

He reached for her and placed his hand near her cheek. She caught her breath, not wanting it to hiss in.

"Yes, you are." His fingertips grazed her skin.

That light brush was too much. Even tentative as it was, she stepped back, her heart pounding. She could taste the dark despair in her mouth, the certainty of failure. She waited until her voice ceased to tremble. "Nonsense. I—I—"

He didn't move. "I can't make you out," he admitted. "You can't bear to be touched. And yet…"

"I have no idea what you mean."

"No?" He pulled his hand away, and she took

in a gasp of air. He cocked his head and peered at her. His eyes were so intense, so inescapable.

She felt as she had in his parlor, two days prior: stripped bare before him and nothing to show for it. Nothing to offer him but a taste of the truth. Her eyes fluttered shut. "Men touch their horses to calm them," she said distantly. "They caress their falcons to remind them that they are bound. Touch smacks of ownership, and I am weary of being a possession."

"Has no one ever touched you for comfort? For friendship? No brothers or sisters?"

She didn't dare open her eyes. It had been seven years since she'd seen her sisters. Ellen would be almost grown now. She had Amalie, her dearest friend, but she was back in London.

Amalie had held her close, afterward. And so, no. It wasn't the *comfort* she minded. It was the sense of proprietary ownership.

"And is that why you would touch me?" she asked. "For *friendship?* Or *comfort?* I had not thought you were the type to employ euphemisms."

He straightened. "I'm not."

"Everyone else thinks that because you're a virgin, you're safe. But I know how you look at me. I know what you see. You're a man like every other man, and you want what every other man wants. Truly, Sir Mark. Why *else* would you be standing with a woman of no particular reputation on a deserted road?"

Surely it was an illusion, that she could feel the heat of his breath against her cheek. He wasn't close enough.

"Mrs. Farleigh." His words were choked. "You have no idea how long I have waited for someone to recognize that. I'm not an innocent. I've *never* been innocent. And yet I'm treated as if I were some sort of divine being, untouched by lust."

She swallowed.

"It cheapens what I've accomplished," Mark said, "to imagine me a saint. To believe I am untempted, that I pass through this life without feeling lust or want or desire. I said it in the first chapter of my book, and yet nobody seems to believe me. Chastity is *hard*."

"I hadn't thought—"

"I want. I lust. I desire." He scrubbed his hand through sandy blond hair at that, shaking his head. "No. You're right. You don't deserve euphemisms. I want *you*. I lust after *you*. I desire *you*."

She might have been the only woman in the world, pinned by his gaze.

"But what I don't do is act."

Her gut twisted.

"If you want to know what I am doing with you on this deserted road…I would trade every one of my hangers-on for one true friend. For someone who would look in my eyes and tell me that I am a man like any other man. I don't dare possess you, Mrs. Farleigh. I fear that I'd break something irreplaceable."

She swallowed. "Sir Mark."

He reached out one hand again, almost to her face, before he stopped himself. "I *do* want, but you're safe with me."

Safe. The earth seemed to spin about her with alarming speed. For years, every conversation she had with a man had been colored by calculation. Would she put him off if she spoke her mind? What did he want her to say? When a man took a mistress, he purchased not just the rights to her body, but the content of her thoughts.

Sir Mark wanted her as she was, not as he wished her to be. The thought made her head hurt.

Safe? He was the last thing from safe.

He tipped his hat at her, with that dreadful smile on his face—as if he knew that he'd rattled her to her core, and he was pleased. He was halfway down the lane before her mind cleared.

"Sir Mark!"

He stopped, turned.

"You've forgotten your coat." She started to ease her arms out of the sleeves.

But he simply shrugged. "No, I haven't. I left

it with you on purpose. That way, I'll have an excuse to accompany you home from service."

Her mouth dried.

He winked at her. "Until then."

CHAPTER SEVEN

WHEN THE KNOCK SOUNDED at Jessica's door the next day, her heart leaped. The neighbors did not call on her, she expected no deliveries, and the letter carrier always managed to avoid her house.

But while the name her maid whispered to her seemed familiar, she didn't quite recognize it. Confused, she followed the woman to the front room. A small, weedy man stood before her. His hair was a brownish-red, mostly taking the form of a florid mustache. His coat was wrinkled, his cravat poorly tied. When he saw her, his eyes narrowed. And then he frowned at her, letting his fob watch fall back into his pocket as if she were late for an appointment.

He patted a pocket, as if in reminder, and then drew himself up.

"Can I help you?" Jessica asked.

"I should think not." The fellow spoke in belligerent tones. "Can *you* help *me*? Hmph."

His mouth was set in a stubborn line, and his shoulders hunched, a pose that would have been menacing if he'd not been half a head shorter than she.

Jessica was quite used to being insulted but not in her own home.

"Pardon me." She crossed to the front door and opened it pointedly. "Have we been introduced?"

The man folded his arms. "You know damned well we haven't." He spoke in an accusatory tone. "Just as you know damned well what I'd told you— I'm Mr. Nigel Parret, *the* Parret, of *London's Social Mirror.*"

Oh. The name suddenly fell into place. Parret was the man who had published all those articles on Sir Mark—in fact, he'd made them the cornerstone of the little paper he owned. She'd studied his accounts faithfully.

When she'd first heard of Weston's offer, it had been from a woman who'd tried and failed to seduce Sir Mark. She had thought to have her money anyway, by manufacturing a story. But it wasn't the first time a woman had claimed to have seduced the man. It was Parret who had investigated the claims, Parret who had denounced the few stories that had first come out, by proving that Sir Mark could not have been where the women claimed. It was Parret who had told her friend, and through him, George Weston, that he'd never believe a story of seduction unless the woman in question took Sir Mark's ring—a thick gold ring with a dark stone. It was supposed to be an heirloom from his father, and he was never seen without it.

So why on earth was Parret *here?*

"Here you are," Parret was saying, "tramping all over the turf that I have so faithfully developed, without so much as a by-your-leave. From what I'm hearing in the village, you somehow managed to get an exclusive interview with him."

"What are you speaking about?"

"Oh, don't play so *innocent,*" he sneered. "I'm all too familiar with your type—inviting confidences, taking in good men who otherwise would not stray."

The comments cut rather too close to the bone. "That's quite enough. Good day, sir." Jessica took the man's elbow and guided him the three steps out the door. But before she could slam it on his nose, Parret insinuated his foot in the doorway.

"And you think you can get rid of me so easily! After stealing from me. Yes, *stealing!*" He nodded emphatically as Jessica stared at him in astonishment. "That's what I call it! Theft! Taking the very bread from my daughter's table!"

"Sir, you seem to have forgotten yourself. I must insist—"

Mr. Parret had gradually turned red all over his bald head, as if he were a sunburnt little egg.

"Insist! You have no right to *insist* upon anything. Now, who are you working for?"

His hands were on his hips, his chest thrust forward. Jessica felt her cheeks chill. He *knew.* Somehow, he knew what she was trying to forget. She'd come here for money; she planned to betray Sir Mark to his enemies, to ruin his reputation. This man knew.

"Ha!" His face lit, and he jabbed a finger at her. "I knew it. Your silence reveals everything. Is it Miller, of *Today's Society?* Or Widford, at *The Daily Talk?*"

Jessica shook her head, confused all over again.

"You can't hide it now," Parret gloated. "I know what you are. You," he said, in stentorian tones, "are a *reporteress.*" His hands landed on his hips in righteous indignation. His chin jerked, once, in satisfaction. And his nose twitched, as if being a female reporter were somehow an occupation that made one smell more vile than a chimney sweep on the day before his yearly bath.

"I see you don't deny it," he continued on. "We must stand together and resist all such incursion! We must come together in brotherhood and toss out those like you—women who take a man's job, who rob a man of the ability to feed his family."

"Who is 'we'?" Jessica peered at the empty green hedge behind him. "You appear to be alone."

"I speak for all working men! Sir Mark is my

territory. *My* story. I developed him. I created his reputation. I made him the darling of all London. And now you seek to profit from my hard work. I heard all about what happened in the church-yard the other day—he greeted you privately, away from all the others. He's agreed to allow you an interview, hasn't he?"

"You're laboring under a misapprehension," Jessica said. "I'm not working for anyone—"

"A mercenary?" The word came out as an indignant howl. "Thinking to auction off your story to the highest bidder! Such crass concerns with filthy lucre show your true colors."

Jessica was still shaking her head and contemplating kicking his foot out of the door when he leaned in, crafty once more.

"Sell it to me," he suggested. "We can split the proceeds evenly, yes? For an exclusive interview with Sir Mark on the most mundane of subjects, I could promise you at least five pounds. Think of that staggering sum."

"Are you trying to drum me out of business, or prop me up?" Jessica asked in bewilderment. "If you're going to browbeat me, the least you can do is be consistent."

At that, Parret's shoulders sank, and he let out a mighty exhale. "Whichever happens to be most lucrative," he admitted, his righteous indignation evaporating. "Business has been *bad,* with Sir

Mark away from London. Revenues have fallen. Mrs. Farleigh, you see before you a desperate man. I have a daughter, not yet five years of age. She is an *angel*—and I've put everything I have into educating her as a proper lady. I have the highest of hopes that she might marry high indeed."

"You think she can catch Sir Mark?"

Parret paled and shook his head. "Oh, no. No. Never. But…a wealthy tradesman, yes? A captain in the navy. Maybe a man of the cloth, you see?" He made a fist and ground it against his palm. "Every ha'pence to my name, I have dedicated to her. Surely you would not steal from so worthy a cause as a young girl's dowry?"

"Mr. Parret," she said gently, "I don't believe a word that you've said. What in heaven's name am I supposed to think, when you accuse me of theft, offer me a business partnership and then try to enlist me in a charitable cause? The only thing I am certain of is that you care about money, and you somehow think that I am either going to deprive you of it, or hand it to you in quantity. Both beliefs, I assure you, are idiotic. I am not a reporteress. I have no intention of hurting your…your trade."

Parret gave his head a short little nod. "I see." He looked at her. "Well. Perhaps it is so. And yet why else try to inveigle him into your confidence?"

He seemed genuinely puzzled on that point.

Hadn't he managed to come by his daughter in the usual fashion?

"Surely a gossip columnist can manufacture an explanation of why a woman would want to talk with a man."

"But everyone knows Sir Mark is immune to all feminine blandishments," he mused. "I've watched him for months and months. Look—I don't suppose you'd care to report for me?"

She choked.

"It would be worth a great deal to you," he said slyly. "What is he reading? Is he working on his next volume?" Parret smiled at her, which made him look weaselly rather than friendly. "I would be willing to reward you."

"You're mad," she informed him.

He didn't deny it. "My card." He held it out to her. When she made no move to take it, he shrugged and set it on her threshold. He walked off whistling. Jessica watched him leave through the side window, his footsteps punctuated by the thud of her heart.

Her hands were clammy. She waited until he slipped through the hedgerow and was gone.

She didn't know what to think.

She didn't know what to say.

She almost wanted to laugh. He'd thought she was a *reporteress*, come here to tell Sir Mark lies, to ferret a story out of him? No—she practiced a different species of dishonesty.

Not so different, she remembered. She was here to seduce him, to *ruin* him—and if she wanted to have any chance of collecting at the end, she was going to need this man to believe her story. She had more in common with mad Mr. Parret than she did with Sir Mark, and it wouldn't do to forget it.

Grimly, she opened her door and knelt down. His card weighed nothing in her hand. So why did it seem so heavy?

Because, her conscience answered grimly, she still intended to seduce Sir Mark. Even now, even knowing he was unwilling. Her self-respect had tarnished over time, but she had never stooped so low before as to harm a good man.

And Sir Mark…Sir Mark *liked* her. He liked her when she forgot herself, especially when she did not try to restrain her speech.

Nothing was fair in love or war, but Jessica conjured up the memory of his smile.

"I'll make you a promise." She might have been speaking to him. She might have been speaking to herself. "I'll seduce you," she said. "I *have* to. But no strategems. No tricks. No, Sir Mark—I'll seduce you as myself."

MARK HAD FOOLISHLY imagined it would be *easy* to extricate himself from the crowd after church service on the next Sunday. He'd been mistaken. After the last song had been sung, and the rector had stepped away, he felt as if he were wading in a sea of people just to get to the yard outside the building. Once there, all possibility of escape disappeared. He was mobbed—and aside from a few straggling gravestones that offered scant cover, there was nowhere to hide.

"Sir Mark, we were hoping to convince you to come over for dinner at some point this week," said the woman before him—a Mrs. Cadfall.

At his sleeve, a man spoke. "Sir Mark, we would be most grateful if you could give us some advice as to the cattle—"

A hand landed on his collar, another on the cuff of his coat. It was London all over again—the crowds, the din, the *attention*. All that was needed was a pair of reporters and a paper at breakfast that listed precisely what he'd done the night before. Mark was caught up in a cacophony of voices, all demanding his attention.

"Sir Mark," chimed in a voice from behind him.

"Sir Mark, the MCB wanted—" That was James Tolliver, but what the MCB wanted was swallowed up in further clamor.

"Sir Mark!"

"Sir Mark?"

"Sir Mark, I—"

"Silence!" Mark finally shouted. "Please, all of you. Can you not speak to me one by one?"

Of course, they all apologized. All at the same time. Mark pointed at people then, going through their concerns as carefully as he could. He was mindful of Mrs. Farleigh at the edge of the crowd. He'd promised to see her home. It was the only thing that helped him keep down his temper.

No, Mrs. Cadfall, he would be unable to come to dinner. Also, he knew nothing about cattle—any other person would be a better choice than he was. Truly.

"As for you, Tolliver, what is it you wanted?"

Tolliver winced, and Mark realized he'd let himself become a little short with those around him. He took a deep breath and reminded himself that there were worse things than being well-liked.

"The MCB thought we might sponsor...a debate, or some such." Tolliver looked down, scuffed his shoes against a paving stone. "We thought it might encourage chastity."

"A debate?" Mark asked. "For the MCB?" He didn't particularly like the idea of the MCB. He disliked the secret hand signals, the cockades. He especially didn't like the handbooks that the founder was selling for tuppence. The whole thing smacked of exploitation, and Jedidiah Pruwett had attached Mark's name to it. "You want me to join a debate?"

His displeasure must have come across in his tone, because Tolliver wilted further. Mark wanted to kick himself. It wasn't this youth he objected to, it was—

"You're right," Tolliver said, dispirited. "I hadn't given the matter any thought. Who, after all could possibly take the other side from you? It's not as if you could *debate* chastity, after all."

This, said glumly, cast a pallor on the waiting crowd.

"Come now," Mark said. "It's not so bad as that. There are plenty of—" He shut his mouth again, before he came up with a justification for the de- bate *and* the MCB.

"Plenty of *what?*"

"Plenty of arguments one could make at a de- bate," said a voice to his right. Mark felt a tingle travel down his spine. He turned slowly to see Mrs. Farleigh at the edge of the crowd. Nobody moved to let her through.

Tolliver frowned. "Such as?"

She shrugged, nonchalantly. "Well. I shouldn't know them. But a hypothetical debate might say something about an organization that privileges the wearing of ribbons and armbands over any actions that had meaning."

Mark couldn't argue with that. "Go on."

She met his eyes. "And I suppose someone—not *me,* of course—might even take to task a moral system that rigidly emphasizes adherence to a few select principles, without any attempt at considering the relative value of those principles in individual circumstances."

Tolliver frowned. "What sort of *individual circumstances* could you mean? If it's right, it's right. If it's wrong, it's wrong." He shrugged. "What's to argue?"

"Oh, certainly. *I* could not make such an argument. But a skilled debater might ask what one would do if one were forced to choose between saving an innocent child's life or engaging in unchaste behavior."

Tolliver's frown deepened, and he rubbed his chin.

"This is, after all, the choice that some unfortunate women are put to—sell their bodies, or see their children starve."

Tolliver's eyes grew round, and his mouth screwed up. Had nobody ever posed him a basic moral dilemma before?

"I— That is—" He glanced over at Sir Mark in supplication. "I'm sure that's wrong, because…because…"

Mark took pity on him. "Yes," he said briskly. "It's the old 'tupping for kittens' argument. I hear that one a lot."

She choked. "Tupping for *which?*"

"Kittens. It usually goes like this—suppose that

a madman has sixteen precious, innocent kittens in a sack. He threatens to throw them all in the river to drown unless I engage in intercourse with some woman, who is agreeable. What do I do?"

Mrs. Farleigh stared at him. "What *do* you do?"

"Assuming those are my two choices—tup, or the kittens shuffle off this mortal coil—well, it's simple. My moral code is not so rigid that I would let innocents suffer."

"But—"

"I would also tell lies, strike another man in the stomach and blow my nose in the Queen's presence. All for the benefit of kittens."

"Lucky kittens," Mrs. Farleigh managed. She was doing a poor job of suppressing a smile. Around her, the crowd shifted in confusion. Mark wanted to see her laugh.

"I admit there are some times when chastity is not the right answer. You see? You have me there. In most circumstances, though, there are no kittens. No madmen. There's just a choice to make, and a simple one at that. One mustn't justify day-to-day morality with extraordinary circumstances. Otherwise, we would all feel free to rape and murder at the drop of a cat."

Stunned silence reigned. But he'd won. The corners of Mrs. Farleigh's mouth curved up. "You've convinced me," she said. "No debate is possible."

She was mocking him with that. It had been a

long time since someone had questioned him. It had been a *very* long time since he'd had this much fun.

"In any event," she added, "if one wants to save kittens, I suppose it's more effective to beat the madman into smithereens."

"Still, if I'm ever faced with the prospect," he said casually, "I'll think of you."

Her eyes widened in shock. In fact, everyone's eyes widened in shock.

Had he really just said…? Oh, yes. Yes, he had. In front of *everyone.* He could feel his cheeks heating.

Mrs. Farleigh was the first to recover. "Don't," she replied solemnly. "Impending kitten death would ruin the atmosphere. Besides, you've convinced me. Your moral code seems not just flexible—in fact, it might be a bit floppy."

If it had been silent before, it was like death now. *Actually,* some wicked part of him whispered in response, *I have no problem being rigid, too, if that's what the situation demands.*

Thank God that this little public slip had happened in Shepton Mallet rather than London. People here would talk—but gossip would alter their words entirely. And while the gist of the conversation might be repeated in shocked tones from here to Croscombe, at least it wouldn't be trumpeted in every paper by breakfast tomorrow.

As if conjured entirely from his imagination, a thin weedy voice spoke. "I say, Sir Mark. Could you repeat that?"

No. No. It *couldn't* be.

The owner was hidden by the crowd. But Mark knew the speaker all too well. He could see the fraying edge of a top hat at the very edge of the group, obscured by heads and shoulders.

Nigel Parret. What was he doing in Shepton Mallet?

No point even asking the question. Parret pushed through the crowd, closer to Mark. He held a tiny notebook in one hand and a pencil in the other. He looked up at Mark. No man with a mustache like that should *ever* try to look innocent, Mark decided. It could never work. Besides, Mark knew the man all too well. Nigel Parret was not just a reporter. He was the worst kind of gossip.

"My dear Sir Mark!" Parret shouldered in front of Mrs. Farleigh, casting her a glittering look that Mark could not quite decipher. "It has been so long. So, so long since we last spoke!"

It had been weeks, glorious weeks, since Mark had last brushed the man off.

"Perhaps you could tell me your feelings on seeing me after such a lengthy vacation?"

"Certainly," Mark said. "Two words."

The reporter's pencil poised over paper. Ten

thousand people really *would* read those words, if Parret had his way.

"Push. Off."

Parret looked up. "Sir Mark. That's not a very kind thing to say. And we are such friends, are we not?"

Mark simply stared at him.

"Now," Parret said, "what were we saying then?"

He looked up through the crowd and caught Mrs. Farleigh's eyes. Mark could feel his minor flirtations, all the nascent *like* he felt for her drying up. Nigel Parret could ruin Mrs. Farleigh faster than Mark could decide what he wanted with her.

He'd imagined seeing her home from church. He'd imagined conversations. Walks outside. Oh, very well—he'd imagined more, but what he'd truly yearned for was not the touch of her hand, but to break through the brittleness of her facade. He'd wanted to slowly come to know her—all without the entirety of London watching in vicarious interest.

"We weren't saying anything," Mark said coldly. He tipped his hat to the crowd, avoided Mrs. Farleigh's eyes and gave the man a jerk of his head.

Not now. Maybe not ever.

He watched her go out of the corner of his eye, letting the village conversation swell up around him.

No. *No.* He wasn't going to let this one slip away. Not without a fight.

CHAPTER EIGHT

JESSICA HAD NOT YET finished her breakfast the next morning when her maid interrupted her.

"*He's* here to see you," she whispered.

It took Jessica a few moments to realize who the woman meant. Sir Mark had *not* walked her home after service, as he'd promised. After their too-public exchange—and after Mr. Parret had appeared—he'd seemed to abruptly lose interest in her.

Her heart thudded painfully in anticipation. What was he doing here, and so early in the morning? Her hair still hung loose around her shoulders, just brushed after being taken from its braids. She didn't take the time to put it up, instead ducking out to the front room of her cottage.

Sir Mark stood there, contemplating the items she had on her shelf: two porcelain figures that she'd obtained over the past seven years, and one broken shell—a present her youngest sister had given her nine years ago, and her only memento of home.

"Sir Mark?"

He turned to her. For a moment, he simply froze in place, his mouth open. Then he shook his head.

"Oh, that is utterly unfair. I came to make my apologies, and make amends. But that—*that* is utterly beyond the pall. I don't think I can ever forgive you."

"What? What did I do?"

He rubbed his forehead. "Never mind. I came to ask you whether you had any interest in taking a walk with me this morning."

"Sir Mark, I feel that I must remind you of the last few words we have exchanged. Twenty-four hours ago, you announced to an entire crowd that you wanted to have intercourse with me. This morning, you tell me that I am appalling. Now, I'm supposed to step out with you?"

He looked up into the corner of the room and then shrugged. "That's pretty much the lay of the land, yes."

"Do you know what people are going to *think* if they see us together after what you said on Sunday?"

"I'm not planning to see people. We'll see cows." He sighed. "Besides, one advantage of having a sterling reputation is that no one thinks the worst of you. Even when you're thinking the worst of yourself." His gaze slipped again, down to her waist, below, and then slid up to her face. "I must ask one question. Have you ever cut your hair?"

Suddenly, the disjointed nature of his conversation began to make sense. "No."

"Hmm," was all he said.

"I need to go put my hair up. Get half boots and a spencer."

"Yes," he said absently.

"I'll just slip out the back, while you're waiting, and fetch a pig to serve as chaperone, too."

"Mmm-hmm."

"She breathes fire," Jessica clarified. "The pig, not me."

He looked up, shaking his head. "My apologies. What were you saying?"

"If I had challenged you to a debate and taken my hair down, would you have been able to string together one coherent sentence?"

His eyes rose to meet hers ruefully. "What do you think?"

She clucked sympathetically. "Never mind."

But in her upstairs room, with her maid pinning her hair into a ruthless bun, she could make no sense of it. Sir Mark liked her. This didn't surprise her; men usually liked looking at her. She was accustomed to that much.

But he was not like other men. He wasn't indifferent, not in the least. But for all that he claimed to be attracted to her, he'd rejected her advances.

What kind of man did that? If he didn't plan to take her to bed, what did he want from her? And if he *did* want to take her to bed, but refused for chastity's sake…why was he throwing himself in temptation's way?

She had uncovered no answers by the time she descended the stairs one last time. He didn't offer her any. Instead, he guided her up the lane, away from the water. From her cottage steps, if she listened carefully, she could make out the distant clack of wool-mill machinery. The rumble was soon swallowed up by the sound of the country. It was never silent; the rustle of wind through leaves was punctuated by the call of birds and the hum of insects.

Up a hill, over a stile, across a pasture, thick with purple-flowered thistles that crunched under her half boots. He followed a trail that did not seem to be outlined by any path. They went down one hill, crossed a narrow brook by means of a wide wood plank and then marched up the incline on the other side.

"I hope you know where you're going," she told him after jumping down from the fourth stile.

"We're going to Friar's Oven. We're almost there."

"I'm not sure if that name is supposed to sound ominous or delicious," Jessica said.

They were walking through a cow pasture. It

sloped gently downward, toward a short rise. Over the top, she could see a long blue horizon.

"Neither," he said. "These cows have the best view in all Somerset."

They reached the upward slope again in a matter of minutes. There were a few large rocks strewn about, rose-gold in the morning sun; then a few more. Just as the grass gave way to stone, the rock turned to cliff, falling away at their feet. An immense valley lay before them, and Jessica caught her breath. Somewhere in the distance, she caught a glimmer of blue river.

Morning mist still clung to the valley floor; she could see only a hint of emerald. And in the middle of the mist, a terraced, conical hill rose. Through the fog, she could make out a stone tower on top of that hill.

"That," Sir Mark said from behind her, "is Glastonbury Tor."

She didn't know what it *meant*. A wild wind blew off the valley, fluttering her skirts behind her, whipping a tendril of her hair free.

"What do you think?" he asked.

"What is it for? Defense? Worship?"

Sir Mark came to stand beside her. "They say King Arthur is buried at Glastonbury."

She turned to him. "Is he really?"

"Oh, yes. Queen Guinevere died in Amesbury. On nights when there's a new moon, they say the road between Shepton Mallet and Glastonbury is lit by the torches of her bier." He pointed into the mist, as if sketching out a ghostly path.

"It is *not*."

"My brother and I snuck out here one night when we were young to watch for it. But we fell asleep." He gave her a wicked smile. "That must have been the moment when she passed by."

Jessica had lived the past years in London. It had never really struck her before how new the city truly was. After all, it had been burnt to the ground not two centuries past. The buildings out there were terribly modern—new stone, recent construction. But out here, there was something positively ancient in the air. Stones had been set here a millennium before in inexplicable patterns. Battlegrounds had lain fallow and had been turned to the fields beneath her feet centuries before the foundation of her house in London had been laid. It was not quite magical, but perhaps it was a touch mythic.

"They also say," Sir Mark mused on, "that if you can see Glastonbury Tor, it's going to rain."

Today, the honey-warm stone of the tower was outlined in marvelous precision. She didn't want to *think* of rain, not on a day as marvelous as this one. "What a shame," she breathed. "And if you *can't* see it?"

"Then," he said thoughtfully, "it's already raining."

She burst out laughing. "You," she said, "are very bad."

"I'll own as much." He stared at the tor a while longer and then shook his head. "Guinevere," he said pensively, "should have held out for Lancelot."

"Pardon me?"

"She married too soon, you see. It wasn't Arthur she wanted—she just didn't know it yet. He seemed like an acceptable fellow—King of all Britain, big army, bigger sword—and so she said to herself, 'Well, I suppose a king will do.' She should have waited for Lancelot."

"But then who would Arthur have had?"

She waited for some acerbic remark from him—something like, *a wife who was not an adulteress.*

But he scratched his chin pensively, looking off into the mist-filled valley before them. "The Lady of the Lake," he finally said. "That's who I would have picked, had I been him."

"The Lady of the Lake? She's not even human."

"Mrs. Farleigh, imagine that you are a man, and a king, and you must choose a wife. On the one hand, you can have a beautiful woman—a very nice one, too—who will respect and fear the power that you wield. One the other, there's a woman who is a bit frightening, but she has already given you an ancient sword and a scabbard. She's made you stronger, more powerful. Deep down, you respect the power she wields, and fear it exceeds your own. Whom do you choose?"

"Any man would choose the first—the beautiful woman who fears you. What man wants a woman who overpowers him?"

"A man who is sufficiently strong in his own right need not be jealous of power in others." He glanced at her. "I know ugly men who insist on ugly wives, believing that they will not stray." He shrugged. "For myself, I've always wanted a beautiful woman."

She let out a little laugh. "Because you are so beautiful yourself?"

"Because I intend to win her affections to me, mind and soul." And then, as if in an afterthought, he added: "And body. I definitely look forward to winning her body."

"Is that why you haven't married, then?" she asked. "Because no woman is good enough for the great Sir Mark? You have confessed to the sin of pride. Is this just more of it?"

"Not quite."

"Not quite." She smiled at him and walked a few paces away before turning, her skirts whirling around her ankles. "I don't understand you. You want. You desire. You lust. You also believe in chastity. But this is no impossible dilemma, Sir

Mark. Find an acceptable girl, marry her and assuage your lusts to your heart's content."

"Oh, I've thought it over, often enough." He shrugged again and looked away. "In excruciating detail, sometimes. A quick marriage would serve, I suppose, for a few months. Maybe a few years. But marriage is for a lifetime, and male chastity means there must be fidelity afterward, as well."

"For a man of your temperament, faithfulness should not prove a problem."

He shrugged. "No? Imagine that I chose a girl who was simply acceptable—someone who would simply *do.* And then imagine that two years later, I met someone who was everything I wanted— clever, kind and beautiful. The sort of woman who has the integrity to make a better man of me. The kind of woman who might laugh at my pride while still loving me."

He turned and looked at her.

"Imagine," he said, "I met her, and I was tied to someone who would just *do.* I want a wife I can love, Mrs. Farleigh. One who I *want* to be faithful to because there is simply nobody else for me, not because it is the right thing to do. I don't want to resent my fidelity. Or my wife. And so...I wait."

"What are you trying to *do* to me?" she asked, stepping back from the intensity of his gaze.

Her foot slipped on a rock—enough to unbalance her, just a little. He reached for her. She *knew* it didn't mean anything, knew that he meant only to steady her arm—and yet still she flinched from his outstretched hand. It threw her entirely off balance. She went sprawling, her palms smacking painfully into rock.

"Did you hurt yourself?"

She examined her gloves—easier than looking up. Tiny bits of gravel had ripped through the fabric, abrading the flesh beneath. Her ankle stung, but only a little. "Just my pride."

He started to extend a hand toward her to help her up and then grimaced and pulled it back. Instead he crouched down beside her, so that his head was level with hers.

"Look here," he said quietly, "I'm not trying to do anything to you. I wish you'd understand that."

"But—"

"But nothing. I don't want to take you. I don't want to possess you. Right now, I just want to see whether you've injured yourself."

Jessica swallowed hard and stared at the ground. Then, tentatively, she held out her hands, wrist up. He made no move to take them. Foolish of her to be thankful for that. But his finger traced the frayed edge of her glove, brushed at little bits of gravel that had embedded itself in her skin.

"I'm not even bleeding," she said.

"No."

She looked up. Their eyes met. She didn't know

what to think of him, didn't know what to think of herself.

"I'm hunting for sport, not meat," he said. "Because I *like* you. Because in London, my every last step is dogged by gossipers and hangers-on. If I talk to a woman once, it's in the papers the next day. If I talk to her twice, people start making bets. I hardly dare talk to anyone a third time." He let out a sigh and sat back on a rock. "I intend to wait until I find the right woman. But I miss female companionship—and no, that's not a euphemism for anything except...this. I *like* women. I like you."

"There are a great many other women besides me."

"I had noticed. That is the worst of London. I don't dare let myself admire anyone. Not even a little. It's an impossible dilemma. How can I know if a lady is the right one, without paying her some attention? But the instant I show even the slightest interest, the public assumes that marriage is a foregone conclusion. If I were later to decide she wasn't right, I would embarrass her. Publicly. All it would take was three dances, spread over two weeks, and speculation would run wild. I can't decide to marry on the basis of three dances."

His fingers hovered over her wrist. She could feel her pulse beating against them.

"There's a reporter in town now."

"I'll get rid of him." He looked off into the distance.

She nodded mutely.

"You understand, then, what I'm telling you? I just want more than three dances. And you're perfect." His hand skimmed down her palm, down the joints of her fingers, to her fingertips. "I can't possibly lead you astray, because you hate me already." He was smiling as he said that.

Jessica swallowed. Just the touch of his fingertips—nothing more.

She might have responded with artifice. She was *supposed* to, if she meant to seduce him. But she could hardly seduce him, when even a touch made her flinch. Besides, she'd spent months in a dark haze. This feeling, this tentative flutter in her belly—this was *hers.* This was sunlight on her face. It was the warmth she'd dreamed of. It was a curl of honest attraction, the first she'd experienced in years. And so slowly, deliberately, she crooked her fingertips under his, so that the curve of his hand caught against hers.

She let her weary fear flow through her, found that cold, hard center of protest. She'd been letting Weston own her, though she'd tossed him out long before. She'd been flinching from every good thing, from even this simple touch. But she could at least possess this again—this electric feel of honest attraction.

His breath caught as their hands clasped.

"I don't hate you," she whispered.

"Oh." His voice dropped. His thumb encircled her wrist. "Oh, dear." And then he pulled her to him, gently.

She had a second to look up into his eyes, to breathe in the taste of him. "Sir Mark?" she asked, her voice suddenly quavering.

His lips touched hers.

It wasn't a fierce kiss. It wasn't an extravagant kiss. It was just his breath, feathering against the skin of her face, his lips, soft and gentle against hers. But there was not the slightest sense of hesitance to it, either.

She'd been kissed more times than she could count. She thought she'd known how to translate the language of lips. After all, kissing was a communication that spoke of only a few possibilities. A kiss was an offer or an acceptance; it was an invitation to commerce, or, on rare occasion, the conclusion of a bargain. Kisses were money. They were a mark of possession.

Or, at least, they were supposed to be.

But this wasn't a claim, his kiss. His fingers curled around hers; his lips brushed hers. He wasn't taking ownership of her. She didn't know what to make of it. She didn't know what to make of *him*. Most important, she didn't know what to make of *herself,* of that impossible tangle of fear and want and attraction that she harbored inside.

He lifted his head. His eyes met hers.

He didn't apologize. He didn't make promises.

Another man might have made a joke, to pretend that it hadn't meant a thing. Sir Mark blew out his breath and uncurled his hand from hers. "I *did* tell you I liked you."

His words lingered in the air between them, charging it subtly with every breath she inhaled.

So that was what this was, this kiss. Not commerce. Not ownership. Affection, untinged by anything else. She'd never been kissed out of affection before. Her hand rose, as if of its own accord, to touch her lips. To ascertain that her skin belonged to her, that it didn't bear the imprint of him. That feeling lingered inside her, unfamiliar and yet so welcome all at once.

She *liked* him.

Not a good idea. Not a good idea at all. She wasn't sure what to do with that feeling—whether she should stomp it out or encourage it to grow. She'd spent all that time wondering what he wanted of her and none thinking about what she wanted of herself.

She turned to look back at Glastonbury Tor. The wind and sun were making short work of the mist. The tor itself shone distinctly; only the valley floor was a smudged green. It was going to rain. That's what they said.

She hadn't needed a folktale to know that. It always rained.

"And what do you do, Sir Mark, if you meet your Guinevere, and she is already claimed by another?"

He said nothing for so long that she turned back to see if he'd heard. His eyes met hers. She remembered them as blue, but they were changeable in the light. Right now, they seemed stony-gray.

"I'm not worried about that," he said quietly. "I'm not worried about that at all."

WHEN THE CLOCK struck eleven later that evening, Jessica was alone in her bed, clad in nothing but a linen shift.

It had been a long time since she'd felt desire. The feeling didn't bother her; she'd come to accept it as a practicality, a tool for survival as much as any other trick in her arsenal. But there was nothing like performing for pay to render the pleasurable prosaic.

Over the past seven years, her desires, her wants, had been submerged in the service of the men who'd paid for her. It had been years since she'd owned her own sexual response.

It wasn't an intelligent thing, what she did now. It was one thing to tempt him. It was another, entirely, to tempt herself, to fool her heart and her desires into focusing not on his seduction, but on *him*. Still, she couldn't help but revisit that kiss. That moment of startled intensity, when he'd looked into her eyes and said, "Oh, dear." She relived the touch of his mouth against hers and didn't stop there. Not with a simple kiss.

She wanted another and another. She wanted his hands on her, not just chastely touching her fingertips.

She wanted to banish the cold fear she'd felt and replace it with the true warmth of his want.

Her imagination sketched in the naked form of his body, stealing the imagery from the remembered curve of his biceps under her hand. He would be lean, but muscular, the lines of his body firm and strong. Jessica felt a slow shiver run through her at the thought, and her eyes fluttered shut. She'd worn his coat; she knew there wasn't the slightest padding to it. The breadth of his shoulders owed nothing to clever tailoring.

At the thought of his coat, the memory of the scent of his clothing wrapped around her once more, a hot blanket enveloping her in the midst of the cool evening. Mark's scent was clean male, with a hint of salt and starch. No extraneous perfumes; no pomade, no cologne attempting to mask more intrusive fragrances. His skin would smell like that all over—subtle, strong and attractive—

an aroma she couldn't pin down, somewhere between clean sunshine and the clear, cold water of
a mountain spring.

In her imagination, she didn't touch him. She
didn't need to. In her imagination, there was no
reason to put his pleasure above hers, to set aside
her own desires to make sure that he was fulfilled.
He thought of *her*. He touched her. He took care
of her.

It was just her imagination, but, oh, she wanted
him. And it had been so long since she wanted
anything, let alone a man.

She let herself want him in the safety of her
own bed. She could want him without thought or
analysis, without calculating the effect of every
touch. She could want him purely for herself.

She gasped, and the night air was cool against
her lips. Fantasy-Mark had no hands, and so her
own had to do. She touched herself, taking back
territory that she had ceded to others over the last
long years: her breasts, her thighs.

She imagined his hand at her nipple instead of
her own. His mouth. His fingers, spreading her
legs, his palm brushing her thighs before he found
the nub between them.

It didn't belong to anyone, that spiraling twinge
of pleasure she felt. Not to anyone except herself.
It was *her* want, her *desire*. Nobody else mattered.
No one else needed to be satisfied. She had no

need to falsify a response, to try and inflame another person.

It shook her, that final moment. Ecstasy raced through her. It was stronger and more powerful than just physical release, and she almost wept from the joy of it.

Hers. *Hers.*

She belonged to herself again, body and soul, pleasure and heartbreak. She was every inch *hers* again, her body reclaimed from those long years of bitter ownership.

She was hers.

She drew a tremulous breath, shaking, her eyes opening to see only darkness before her.

She thought of Mark. "Oh." She exhaled slowly. "Dear."

CHAPTER NINE

THE FIGURE THAT STOOD on Mark's doorstep the next evening was not nearly so attractive as the one that had greeted him days ago in the rain.

It was coming up on suppertime, but in the height of summer, the sun was still warm. The man before him wore a jacket of serviceable wool, creased by wear and dirtied around the cuffs. His skin had the look of a man constantly in the sun— spotted with liver and wrinkled. He held a shape-less slouch hat of dark fabric in his hands, turning it nervously as he avoided Mark's eyes.

"How can I help you?" Mark asked.

His visitor smelled of sweat—not the sour sweat one might scent on a London vagrant, but the stronger, cleaner smell that belonged to a man who labored all day, every day.

Large hands wrung the hat. "I…I wanted to… You see, sir, my wife and I—we're not the sort to take charity. I'd offer you my thanks, but…"

Something about the man's tone, the way he avoided Mark's eyes, suggested that he wasn't talking about the pale gratitude that the wealthy townspeople offered because Mark had written a book. Had he seen this man before? He searched the man's wrinkles for some memory of the person he might have been, but even if age hadn't stolen any similarity, all his childhood memories had blurred into indistinctness.

"You've nothing to thank me for," Mark said. "I assure you, it's all been forgotten."

The man shook his head. "I? Forget what your lady mother did for me? I'd be ashamed. I can remember it like yesterday. With my Judy alone with the children…" He shook his head. "Please, Sir Mark. If you won't let me repay you, I'll feel the shame of it the rest of my life."

Shame. It was Mark's foremost emotion when he thought of his mother—that headlong rush into madness, the laughing looks the villagers had exchanged at every one of her tirades.

He stepped to the side and gestured. "Please. Come in."

"I couldn't. Didn't mean to enter your home—"

"But I'm inviting you. I should be honored if you'd accept my hospitality."

In many ways, despite the heights he'd ascended to, Mark felt more comfortable around this laborer than he did around the rector. The man followed him down the hall. From the corner of his eye, Mark detected a slight limp in his step—not so much to incapacitate him, nor even to render him lame. Just an old wound.

The man thought nothing of Mark putting on a kettle for their tea on his own. He didn't protest the simple bread and jam that Mark laid out or ask why Mark had no servants. For all the wealth his elder brother had won, Mark's first memories were of sweeping the floor while his elder sister finished the washing-up. In his brother's house, he was constantly fighting his urge to do things for himself—to fetch his own paper, to shrug on a coat, instead of standing still while a valet eased it over his arms.

"I tend Bowser's sheep, now," the man said. "My wife—she's Mrs. Judith Taunton."

"Taunton," Mark said slowly. "I remember her." The memory was dim—a single room in the village. She'd been a young woman, with two small children. His mother had visited her; Mark had come along. He'd always come along. "That was years ago. Decades."

"Aye," Mr. Taunton replied, then met Mark's eyes. "That would have been before I returned from transportation. I don't know what Judy would have done without your mother."

"Ah."

"Yes," Taunton said stiffly, "I was one of those young firebrands." He stretched out his arms. "I helped burn the mill down, when they brought in the spinning jenny and sacked half the workers." He glanced at Mark and colored—as if perhaps remembering that the mill he'd destroyed had belonged to Mark's father. "The magistrates sent me away for my sins. It was your mother who made sure my boys had enough to eat. Your mother paid my passage back when my time was done. She found me work, posted a bond as surety for my good behavior, when nobody would hire a criminal."

"Maybe this is true," Mark said quietly, "but I'm guessing it was my father who sacked you. The scales are balanced between us." His mother would have agreed. She'd been mad, but there had been a frightening lucidity to everything she had done. She'd sold everything the family owned and had given it all to the poor. But she'd never seen it as charity. She'd always imagined she was giving it *back*.

Mr. Taunton looked up at him. "I'll beg your pardon, sir, but I don't feel so balanced. I am very much in your family's debt." He rubbed his head. "Didn't come here to argue with you, in any event. You see, I have this dog. A bitch—the finest sheep dog in all of Somerset, she is. She's a breed from Scotland." The man's eyes shone with a sudden light. "She came into heat a few months back. All the men hereabouts are mad for a chance at one of Daisy's pups. There's five of them, seven weeks old now. Four are spoken for. I've held the last one back, because…" The man spread his blunt fingers. The fingernails were lined by dark grease. "Sir Mark, are you by any chance in want of a pup? I'd be honored to know that Daisy's whelp went to one of Elizabeth Turner's sons."

Mark swallowed a lump in his throat. The wealthier members of the community—the mill owners, the landowners—had offered him a few scant meals around their table. Even that hospitality had not been freely given. They'd wanted to trade gossip and to boast that they'd had him as a guest.

But Mark knew what a good sheepdog meant to these men. Not just income, but companionship, friendship, the difference between a hardscrabble life and comfort. It was as if the man had offered him his firstborn child.

"Mr. Taunton, I came to Shepton Mallet to think…to think on an opportunity that presented itself to me. You see, I've been asked to join the Commission on the Poor Laws."

Taunton, for all the dirt he carried, nodded sagely. "That's…an honor," he said, his mouth twitching.

Mark rubbed his forehead. "You mean it's a nuisance. I'm not a proponent of the Poor Laws, and the Commission has bungled the administration worse than Parliament. I've no wish to spend my time attending to details like the allotment of gruel at workhouses around the country."

Taunton drummed his fingers against his knee. "If it's a mess, mayhap you could clean it up. Happen they could use a good man."

"I know. It's the only reason I haven't turned the offer down flat."

And people—*important* people—would listen to him if he said the system was falling to pieces. He could make a difference. He'd been granted a measure of popularity by fate; he had an obligation to use it to do good. He just wished it didn't sound like such an ever-loving chore.

"But, you see, if I accept the position, I'll be traveling constantly. I'd have nowhere to keep a dog. Surely, Daisy's pup deserves better."

Mark looked across into a face that was slowly shuttering.

"Of course," Taunton muttered. "You'll be going into the finest drawing rooms. No room *there* for a filthy mutt." His shoulders squared. "Well, perhaps I might be of service some other way." He looked around the room.

Maybe *Mark* didn't think of his mother's actions as pure charity. But this man—this proud man—undoubtedly did. Mark could as soon have cut the man's hand off as refuse the offer.

"But my brother," he heard himself saying. "My elder brother—he'd not lock the animal up in a tiny

London parlor. And I know he'd enjoy having an animal around. I was thinking just the other day that I ought to get him one."

The man looked up, the light returning to his eyes.

"In fact," Mark promised, "I'm *sure* he'd want it. And the dog would be happier with him."

Taunton broke into a broad grin. "It needs a few days yet with its dam. But you're right. I suppose there'd be more room to romp at Parford Manor."

"Actually," Mark started to say, and then realized that he didn't need to clarify *which* brother he'd intended the gift for. "Actually, I won't be visiting him immediately in any event, so a delay is just as well. Thank you. You've no idea what this will mean to my brother."

Taunton gave him a jerk of a nod. "Truthfully, Sir Mark—this scarcely means anything. All these years, I've carried the shame of knowing I should have done more. About...about your sister. And you and your brothers. I saw what was happening, when I first came back, but didn't dare to speak up."

Mark sat still, not wanting to move. Not wanting to acknowledge by so much as a breath that those words reached any part of him.

Taunton continued, "Only one person in all of Shepton Mallet would have stopped that kind of wrong when it happened. And she was Elizabeth Turner."

One nod, that was all Mark could manage.

"I always thought that what happened to you and your brothers after she passed on—that was her way of looking out for you, once she found her way round to herself again."

"Yes." Mark felt as if he were standing at a great distance from the conversation. "Yes. I suppose it was." The silence grew after that, and the man took his leave.

After he'd gone, Mark wrapped his arms around himself. Sometimes he thought he was the only one of his mother's sons who could see her clearly. She'd always been stern and earnest; devout, too. Even before she went mad, she'd had no balance, too much excess. She'd afflicted all her children with Bible verses for names, after all.

She'd seen a great deal of suffering and had thought it her duty to alleviate it. She'd also seen a great deal of sin and had railed against that, too. Mark didn't remember his father at all, but he remembered his mother. All too well.

She'd let Hope, his elder sister, perish by neglect. She'd beaten Ash. She'd locked Smite in the cellar for…for longer than Mark could truly remember.

But Mark… Mark she'd spared. She'd not felt it necessary to cleanse the devil from his soul.

She'd told him once she didn't need to, because he alone was *her* son, not his father's. That she'd seen herself in Mark, that she'd identified in him the same unwieldy imbalance that had torn her to pieces, he kept first and foremost in his mind. Perhaps that was why he'd become who he was. He'd had to prove to himself that his mother's finest qualities—her compassion, her charity, her goodness—could be married to peace and tranquility. He wanted to prove that he could be *good* without going *mad*.

The thought of dedicating his life to the Poor Laws made him feel frenetic and unbalanced. It would be *good*. It would be *righteous*. But he didn't want to do it.

He'd come to Shepton Mallet to find himself. Instead, he'd met Mrs. Farleigh. Mark smiled faintly and thought of her fingers, warm and curling about his. The soft pressure of her lips—he'd have wondered what he'd been thinking when he kissed her, except it was perfectly clear he'd not thought at all.

And now, he didn't want to do good. He wanted to do it again.

London, the Commission and every gossip rag in the country could wait another week.

LONDON, IT TURNED OUT, had other thoughts.

Three days later, Mark ventured into town. He

was on his way to the square to deliver another handful of letters when a familiar voice stopped him.

"Sir Mark!"

Parret was the last man Mark wanted to see at the moment. Still, the tiny man hurried over, his boots clattering over cobblestones. He held his hat to his head with one hand as he ran, lending an odd, undulating appearance to his stride. "Sir Mark. I was hoping—it's just you and me, out here in the country." Parret stopped a few feet before him next to the gray stone of the Market Cross, doubling over. His words spilled out between gasps of air.

"Indeed," Mark said ironically, indicating the people around them.

But Parret appeared gratified. He removed his top hat, revealing a pate covered by a few sparse, carefully combed strings of hair, and wiped beads of sweat off with a yellowing handkerchief of doubtful cleanliness. "Perhaps you might consider an exclusive interview?"

Nigel Parret was nothing if not persistent. Mark would have admired him—or, at a minimum, felt sorry for him—except that the man published the most intrusive articles. On one particular occasion, he'd actually picked through Mark's household trash and had published a piece in which he had explained, on rather dubious grounds, that Sir Mark preferred leg of lamb to beef.

It happened to have been true…at least, it had been true until Mark was served lamb at every dinner he'd gone to for a fortnight.

And that hadn't been the worst of Parret's sins. Three months ago, Mark had danced one dance with Lady Eugenia Fitzhaven. She had seemed a sweet girl—emphasis on *girl*—and he was friends with her father. It had also happened to be the supper dance, and so he'd taken her in to the meal. A hundred men in London had done the same for a hundred ladies throughout town that evening, and nobody had spoken of those conversations again. But Mark was not a hundred men. He was Sir Mark.

Of course, he'd observed the brightness of her eyes, the color of her cheeks. He couldn't help but notice that she was utterly tongue-tied in his presence. He couldn't prevent impressionable young girls from imagining themselves in love with him. All he could do was recognize when the infatuation started and do his best not to offer them encouragement. Girlish appreciation had a way of working itself to nothing if he offered a polite distance. It didn't take long for most ladies to shift their attentions to a source who would appreciate it.

But Nigel Parret had found Lady Eugenia before

her affections had a chance to alter. He'd spoken to her, and she had told him every detail of her unrequited fancies. She'd outlined her childish plan to win Mark's affections—mainly this had involved looking radiant in his presence. She'd enumerated the children she planned to have with him once they were married. Mark *still* winced, thinking of it.

Parret had published her juvenile dreams on the front page of his paper. Mark's reputation hadn't suffered—the article had made it painfully clear that Mark had done nothing whatsoever to encourage the girl—but children of that age hardly needed encouragement to dream. There was no way to stop them from wishing for the impossible.

No way, that was, except to expose their aspiration to the ridicule of all London society.

Lady Eugenia had become a laughingstock; Nigel Parret had collected a small fortune selling papers. And Mark had stopped talking to young, impressionable ladies.

Parret stared up at Mark now with a certain speculative hunger. Mark could almost see the next article brewing in those calculating depths. Maybe, this time, he'd analyze Mark's woodpile. What his column would make of Mrs. Farleigh, Mark didn't want to know.

"One little interview," Parret said, in what Mark

supposed was intended to be a cajoling tone. "Just a few questions."

"Not a chance. You are the last person on earth to whom I would grant an exclusive interview."

Parret nodded as if Mark had not just insulted him, pulled out his notebook and started scribbling.

Mark glanced down uneasily. Parret wrote in a large, round hand—visible even upside down at two paces.

Your correspondent met with Sir Mark in his birthplace of Shepton Mallet. The man wrote with astonishing speed. *Upon seeing his dear friend—for so, my readers, I dare to believe Sir Mark thinks of me—Sir Mark greeted me with effusive superlatives.*

"I did not!"

"Last person on earth," Mr. Parret contradicted aloud. "Very superlative indeed."

He continued writing. *He displays his usual good humor and humble nature, disclaiming the compliments I bestowed upon him.*

Enough of that game. Anything Mark said would be twisted to feed Parret's rapacity for gossip. Mark folded his arms and tried to figure out some way to ask Parret to take himself to the devil—in a way that couldn't be twisted about. Parret looked up at him, his head tilted, as if waiting for Mark's next comment.

Mark pressed his lips together and tapped his fingers against his elbow.

My kindness in visiting him, however, mostly shocked him speechless. Still he agreed to conduct an exclusive interview with me—one which I now convey to you.

"I agreed to no such thing," Mark said through gritted teeth.

Parret's head bobbed as he wrote. "Here I am, speaking with you, no other reporters present. This implies a certain degree of exclusivity."

Mark shook his head, turned and walked away. Naturally, Parret followed. "Communication," he said, "is an amazing thing. I can read responses in the turn of your head. The set of your chin. So long as I don't put quotation marks about your words, and I speak no ill of you, you can't possibly stop me."

Mark didn't respond and lengthened his stride.

Parret trotted beside him, his breathing labored. "I *am* the only reporter here," he continued. "No matter what any other enterprising souls may say. And you know, it is *I* who have investigated some of the cruder reports about you and discredited them as jealous whispers. If it were not for my tireless reporting, that *incident* last year with Lady Grantham might have taken hold."

"There was no incident with Lady Grantham," Mark said. "Everybody knows that. Nobody believes the lies that some people try to spread about me."

"True," Parret said. "But, I flatter myself, I have done quite a bit on that count myself. If you knew the number of stories I had heard about you, the number of allegations made without support." He shook his head. "And that little bit of wordplay I heard the other day...that was not an allegation made without support, was it?"

Mark stopped dead and turned to Parret. "Are you trying to *blackmail* me into giving in to your demands?"

"No, no!" He paused and rubbed his mustache. "Well, only if it would serve."

Mark rolled his eyes. "You may put quotation marks about this, if you choose, and place it in your paper—I would rather sell my soul to the devil than have you make another shilling off my reputation."

"The devil can have your soul. I just wish to maximize my income."

Mark turned away once more, walking as swiftly as he dared. He could see the churchyard now, and a knot of townspeople collected in front. Maybe if he waved them over, he could...

He could what?

Have them toss Parret out on his ear? Lock him up on trumped-up charges? Either option seemed a fine idea. Almost as good as getting his hands on the man, lifting him bodily by the collar...

Mark shook his head to clear it of the violence of those thoughts. He wasn't about to lose his temper, his *balance*. Not to a little puddle of ethics like this man.

"And if you *won't* speak to me," Parret said, "someone else will. I'd love to write about the woman you spoke with—Mrs. Farleigh, was it? It could be like Lady Eugenia all over again."

A swell of ugly emotion bore down on Mark. It slammed across him, knocking him practically breathless. He felt like a chip of wood, riding raging floodwaters. And before he could think better of it, he turned, abruptly, and tripped Nigel Parret. As the tiny man went sprawling, Mark grabbed his arm and wrenched it around. His other hand twisted in the collar of the man's greatcoat. He picked the man up bodily.

"Sir Mark!" Parret squeaked, his feet kicking out in midair.

Mark had a mental image of himself slamming the man repeatedly against the stone wall of the tavern. The thought was almost too satisfying— Parret's nose bleeding, his hands scraped.

Mark took two steps toward the nearest house. *Stop. Stop.*

But he didn't *want* to. He fumbled for calm. It

felt like floundering. His knuckles scraped against the greasy fabric of the man's collar.

Mark turned to the side and lifted the man skyward. Parret gave a little shriek, one that was all too pleasing to some corner of Mark's vengeful soul. His feet kicked out. And then Mark let go.

The resulting splash sent a shower of droplets into the air, misting Mark's face.

In the murky water of the horse trough, Parret sputtered and wiped his face. A horse, tied to a ring nearby, let out a great sighing bluster, as if to say, *Oh, please. Not in my water.*

"You're wrong," Mark said. "I *can* stop you."

But there was no sense of righteous victory in these words. Instead, he felt a sick, hollow regret. He'd lost his temper. *Again.*

That vision—of his slamming Parret's limp body against the stone wall of the public house—lingered still, an uninvited, unsavory guest. Mark could almost feel the reverberations in his arms, as if the ghost of his awful want had taken up residence.

Parret stared up at him, speechless for once.

It wasn't the first time Mark had crossed the line between that red, hazy want and violence. It wasn't the first time he'd regretted it, either.

Mark sighed and shook his head. "Understand, Parret. You are not going to have an exclusive interview with me. Not in reality, nor will you print one in the public imaginings you call articles."

"But—"

"No."

"But—"

"Certainly not." Mark set his hands on his hips.

"But—"

"And not that."

"Sir Mark," Parret pleaded. "I have a daughter. I—I have cultivated your reputation, as carefully as any steward. Have I ever printed anything maligning you? I've made my reputation—my career—on telling the truth about you. Should we not work together on this?"

The crowd of women was beginning to drift from the churchyard. No doubt they were intent on finding out why Sir Mark had just dumped a man in the horse trough.

"I know what it is," Parret said, a sudden note of jealousy infecting his voice. "You *have* had a better offer from someone else, no matter what... what I said. That *other* reporter has offered you a cut. What was it? Ten percent? Fifteen percent?" He dropped his voice. "I can better it. I will. I promise."

"I'm not interested in your promises." Mark could not make himself focus on any of the people who were coming this way. None of them, that was, except one. Jessica. Mrs. Farleigh was there.

She was not a calming influence; she never had been. But his attention focused on her.

"You think you're more powerful than me," Parret spat. "That your run of popularity is your *own* doing. I made you, Sir Mark. I could break you, if I chose. You owe me your success."

Mark shook his head and turned away "I don't owe you a thing," he said. "And I'm only going to warn you once. Get out of here. Leave town."

Parret scrambled out of the slick trough, doing his best to invest the clumsy exit with a sullen dignity. "Someday," he said formally, "you will regret this."

"Interview me in London," Mark said with a wave of his hand, "and I'll tell you precisely how much I regret it."

JESSICA HAD WANTED to see Sir Mark again but not now. Not like this. Not with the letter from her solicitor folded in her skirt pocket, with its precise measurement of her freedom—or lack thereof.

Over the past few weeks in this small town, she'd found some sense of peace. She had begun to reclaim herself. But the first paper from her solicitor laid out her debts—too many—and her assets—too few. Rent on a flat in London, the amounts she'd spent here... In three weeks' time, when the quarterly bills came due, she'd find herself at the end of her savings.

The other paper, enclosed by her solicitor, had come from Weston.

Sir Mark's decision is expected in the next few weeks, the man had written. *Seduction is of no use to me if it comes too late. Finish it now.*

Weston had not said "or else." He'd not needed to. Without his promised money, she would have no way to survive except to find another protector.

And even that would only stave off the darkness for a little while. Once that man left her, she'd need another, and another, and another. Each time, she'd lose a little corner of herself.

She *had* to do this. She hated to do this, to Sir Mark least of all. She *liked* him. But he looked up, away from—was that Mr. Parret he'd tossed in the water trough? Yes. *Good.* He saw her. His gaze fixed on her, and he strode forward until he stood before her.

"Sir Mark," said a woman next to her. "Did my son James invite you to our shooting competition next week? I know that—"

Mark didn't even look at Mrs. Tolliver. "He did," he replied shortly.

"And will you be there?"

"As I told your son, I'll be there so long as Mrs. Farleigh is invited, as well."

Jessica's breath sucked in.

"She…she was invited." Mrs. Tolliver didn't

look in Jessica's direction. "And...and she's very welcome indeed. But can we be of help?"

Whatever emotion had prompted Sir Mark to dunk a man in water, it had left him angry. "In fact," Sir Mark continued, "I had promised to see Mrs. Farleigh home earlier and never did make good on that promise."

She didn't want to like him more, didn't want to bring him that much closer to his downfall. She didn't want to think of George Weston, waiting for the lascivious details he expected her to divulge. "I don't need—"

He glanced at her. "I know you don't need the accompaniment. But I do."

He was going to create a scandal, speaking to her like that. Scandal was precisely what she was supposed to want him to cause. The women watched him turn and leave, and Jessica gave them one last unapologetic shrug before hurrying after his retreating form.

"What are you doing?" she demanded. "Do you have any idea how...how much those women are going to talk?"

"Let them." His shoulders were taut. "What are they going to do? Talk to Parret?"

Sir Mark made no attempt to moderate his steps to match hers, and Jessica found herself half running to keep up with his long stride. In the hot sun, she was overheated within several streets. Still, he kept the pace through the heart of town, past the point where the paving stones gave way to dust. Sir Mark stared fixedly at the horizon as he walked. It wasn't until five minutes had passed that he addressed her again.

"I was rather too unfair. I'm not much company right now." Droplets from the horse trough had splashed him all over; the darker spots that the water had left across his coat had almost faded.

Jessica didn't say anything.

"In truth," he said, "I'm in a bit of a temper."

"I could never have guessed."

He did look at her then—a slow, sidelong glance. His eyes fairly snapped with intensity. And her insides sparked with the fierceness of his gaze.

"You're formidable when you're angry," she said. He jerked his head toward the front once more, and she breathed again.

Formidable didn't quite cover it. She couldn't imagine crossing him in this mood. She wouldn't have known how to seduce him from it. There was something about the way he walked, the way he held himself—he seemed larger and more lethal than he usually did. As if his anger had stripped away some civilizing influence and left this version of him: less voluble and more vicious.

She should have been wary.

"I don't trust myself when I'm angry," he said, as if hearing her thoughts.

"Well," Jessica said slowly, "*I* do. So that's all right then."

"Hardly reassuring. You've no familiarity with my temper." Little clouds of dust rose up from the ground with his every footfall. He walked so quickly, he could have kept time with the beat of her own heart.

"I try not to lose my temper," he said gravely, "because it is so very, very bad when I do. Even today, I nearly slammed that unfortunate scribbler into a wall. I only recalled myself at the last moment."

"Consider me shocked."

"I *like* balance," he said. "I like quiet. I like calm."

"You must hate me, then."

"Hardly." Sir Mark snorted. "When I was younger, I...I picked a fight with a distant cousin, Edmund Dalrymple. He'd been making some remarks about me, about my mother. I broke his arm in two places. The incident precipitated a rift between our two families. It took years to heal, simply because I couldn't keep hold of my temper."

"I'm stunned," Jessica returned. "Boys, fighting? How outrageous. How abnormal."

"Actually," he said, "it was. Now my brother's married to his sister—and doesn't that make for the cheeriest of gatherings? Edmund and I still have not had a cordial conversation. By now, I suppose it will never happen." Mark trailed off. "It's more complicated than that. My elder brother, Smite, was once friends with Edmund's elder brother, Richard. But after we fought, they argued. Now Richard won't come to Parford Manor if Smite is there, and the same holds true in reverse. So, yes. I don't trust my temper. When I truly lose it…"

"Smite," Jessica said. "Your brother's name is *Smite?*"

He let out a great sigh. "You see what happens when I'm in a temper? I can't keep my mouth shut. He'll hate that I mentioned that. These days, I'm Sir Mark, and Ash, of course, is Parford. Smite goes by Turner—just Turner. He hates his name, for reasons I am sure you can imagine."

"Your eldest brother is named *Ash?* That's an… odd name. How did your brothers come to be named *Ash* and *Smite,* and you were lucky enough to be called *Mark?*"

The ruddy flush of his complexion had faded. Now he blushed—ever so faintly, back to his quiet, slighter self. "Listen here, Mrs. Farleigh. This conversation is going rather far afield. And I've just talked to a newspaper reporter, who reminds me that every one of these details would be worth a fortune to the right man."

"And yet I am the soul of discretion."

He cast her an unreadable look. "My brothers

and I all have Bible verses for names. Mark, Ash—those are just shorter versions of our real names."

"What is your name, then?"

"Soul of discretion or no, I'm not stupid enough to tell you that." He looked up at her again. "It's not the sort of thing one discloses to a woman when one is trying to impress her."

"Well." She sighed. "I suppose you were lucky that your verse was chosen in the Gospel of Mark, instead of, for instance, the Book of Zachariah. You don't much look like a Zachariah. Or a Habakkuk."

He smiled, which had been her purpose in the first place. "Your father must have been quite devout," Jessica continued. Even her own father, a straitlaced vicar, would never have considered such a path. And then she looked up into his face, remembering something he'd said earlier...

"My mother," Mark said softly. "My mother actually had the naming of us. My father wasn't around when any of us were born. And yes, she was very religious. She..." Mark trailed off. "She didn't have much to believe in. What she did have, she believed with her whole heart."

Jessica chewed this over slowly. "You said you wanted peace and balance, Sir Mark. Might that be why?"

Sir Mark looked at her for a good long while. His lips pressed together. His eyes met hers, and she suddenly was struck by the realization that while she knew his tailor and his record in school, she knew very little about him. For a man who had his every move trumpeted in the papers, there was a great deal more to him than anyone had ever reported. She'd not known that "Mark" was not his given name.

He smiled so often, spoke so easily. She'd thought him straightforward. Now, a shiver went through her—not fear, but an almost resonant sense of recognition. This was a man with secrets.

She knew what those felt like.

"There are some things," he said, "that I don't want in any of the papers. Ever. I've had my life picked over often enough. Some risks I just can't take. It's not that I don't trust you."

He *shouldn't* trust her. She was planning to seduce him and to proclaim that fact publicly. She held her breath, feeling appalled with herself.

"Some things," he said slowly, "I should like to keep private."

When she'd volunteered herself for Weston's plan, she'd thought she was just going to ruin his reputation. He'd had his name picked over in the papers so often, she'd imagined it would be just another story to him. That was before she'd known him. Sir Mark was going to utterly hate her if she succeeded. She was going to hate *herself*.

"Then don't tell me," she said, with more airy

unconcern than she would have believed possible. "We're at my house anyway, and I see Marie in the window. So we'd not have any privacy to speak of."

He gave her one sharp nod.

"I'll see you…next week, is it, then? At Tolliver's shooting competition."

He let out a breath. "Hope that Mr. Parret is gone by the time someone hands me a rifle." She *thought* he was joking. As she turned to go into her house, he caught her hand in his. "Mrs. Farleigh. Thank you."

His fingers twined with hers briefly. And then she pulled her hand away, thinking of all the things he wanted to keep private. "Don't," she said quietly. "Don't thank me."

CHAPTER TEN

THE SUN HAD BARELY burnt away the morning mist when Mark arrived at the green beyond the river, where the shooting competition would start. James Tolliver—whose father was hosting the activity—greeted him enthusiastically as he walked up.

"Sir Mark!" He sounded genuinely excited, as happy as a puppy whose master had returned home. "You came! I set up targets two and four—when you see them, tell me if I've done a good job."

"I'll be sure to do that."

"And I was the one to come up with the rules for the competition. It's two rounds—shooting to be done in pairs. The first round will determine relative ranking, and then, everyone will be paired off based on ability."

Mark wasn't quite sure how that would work, but he'd little experience with such competitions. All he hoped to do was pull the trigger when they said shoot.

"That seems like a sound structure. You must have put quite a bit of thought into it."

"Well." Tolliver preened a bit. "Will you partner me, first round?"

Unbidden, Mark glanced across the lawn toward the knot of other contestants. He caught a glimpse of Mrs. Farleigh— a flash of a long gown of buttercup yellow with smart white cuffs.

"And you needn't worry about *her,*" Tolliver continued innocently. "Dinah—Miss Lewis, I mean—has agreed to partner her. I *did* take what you said to heart."

"Huh." Perhaps the boy might actually have done so.

"And besides," the young man continued, "Dinah *wanted* to talk with her. She wanted to know how she did her hair. Can you believe it?"

Mark took in Mrs. Farleigh again. Today her bonnet matched her gown—gold silk with white ribbons. Underneath it, her hair coiled in braids that glistened and intertwined, as impossible to unravel as a blacksmith's puzzle. "I don't blame Miss Lewis," Mark said absently.

"Um." Tolliver cleared his throat, and his tone turned sly. "Maybe we should go talk to them. See if Miss Lewis needs anything."

Oh, the unsubtlety of a randy teenager. Mark glanced at Tolliver, and that false nonchalance evaporated in pink cheeks.

"That is to say—truly—I can resist—not that I am at all tempted! An upstanding member of the MCB—"

"What has the MCB to do with talking to a lady?" Mark asked. "You're allowed to flirt. When have I ever said otherwise?"

"But the membership card!"

"*Membership card?*"

Tolliver fumbled in his waistcoat pocket and pulled out a rectangle not much larger than a calling card. The edges were fraying and soft, as if it had been carried around for a great while.

"There. Item number three. 'I solemnly agree that I will not engage in flirtatious or other lascivious conduct, as such leads to Peril.'"

"Give that here."

Tolliver handed it over. Mark fished in his own pockets and found a stub of pencil. With a flourish, he drew a line through number three and then added in tiny letters: *Flirtation privileges restored, 21-6-1841. M947T.*

"There," he said handing the card back. "Just in time, too. The ladies are coming over."

Tolliver stared at the card. "How is it that the MCB is…is so not in accord with your own beliefs?"

Because I was avoiding the entire organization. You were all embarrassing. But…he was beginning to understand that he'd let this happen through his inattention.

"Tolliver," Mark said, "it's because I made a mistake. A very bad one, and one that you've helped me realize."

"You? A mistake?"

"I should have spoken with the MCB before this moment. Perhaps. . ." He sighed, looked at the confused look clouding the boy's eyes. "Perhaps you'll let me start here."

"You want to give a speech to the MCB? Oh, brilliant! What of Tuesday next?"

Mrs. Farleigh and Miss Lewis were approaching. They'd been given rifles. Miss Lewis held hers delicately, between thumb and forefinger, as if she planned to drop it at any moment.

"Best get it out of the way. Tuesday it is. Now go say hello to your sweetheart."

Tolliver blushed furiously. "She's not my—oh. You're having me on."

And then the women joined them, and Tolliver began talking—explaining the system of the competition once again, this time in an even more disjointed fashion. After he'd managed to confuse everyone, he complicated matters by asking Miss Lewis about, of all things, her father's intended sermon.

Flirtation privileges, Mark decided, were not

about to lead Tolliver into Peril. They were more likely to take him toward Embarrassment.

Mrs. Farleigh glanced at the two and then over at Mark. They shared a half smile, poorly suppressed.

Mark reached forward and took the card from Tolliver's hand. "I'm revoking these," he said to Tolliver, "until such time as you learn to use them properly."

"What?" asked Miss Lewis.

"Nothing," Tolliver said urgently, waving at Mark. "It's nothing."

But Mrs. Farleigh glanced at the card over his shoulder and burst into laughter.

It wasn't fair. He'd never seen her laugh before. When she did, her whole face lit. She held nothing back. Mark felt utterly, stupidly bereft of intelligence. He'd have babbled about sermons to her in that moment, if he could have thought of a word to say.

"Ignore him, Mr. Tolliver," Mrs. Farleigh plucked the card from Mark's hand and slid it into Tolliver's pocket. "You're doing quite well, considering. And you—" she pointed at Mark, and he felt his breath come to a rumbling halt inside his lungs "—I've a question to put to you."

She turned and walked away. When they were a few steps distant, she shook her head. "Poor boy. He can't impress both you and Miss Lewis at the same time. You are his hero, you know. Show some compassion."

"You're quite right. I shouldn't have teased."

"No." She sighed, and then looked up at him. "You signed your initials to that card, didn't you?"

"Yes?"

"Mark 9:47? Isn't that rather a gruesome name to attach to a young child?"

Mark felt his smile fade. "My brothers are named Ash and Smite. My mother wasn't concerned with choosing happy names for her children." He paused. "You know what verse that is offhand? You keep trying to tell me that you're wicked."

"I am."

"You're the worst fallen woman I've ever met."

"My father was a vicar," she returned with asperity. "I can't help it if some of my early childhood lingered, despite my best intentions. And really—you were named after the verse that suggests that in order to enter the Kingdom of Heaven, you have to—"

"I know. You don't need to tell me," he said with a growl. "Really. Next time, I'm just signing Sir Mark, do you hear? Forget it."

There was a long, awkward pause. From this distance, Mark could hear Tolliver burbling on to Miss Lewis. By the way she was looking up at him, *Tolliver* was doing better than Mark was.

He could even hear the rector, twenty yards away, talking about the same catechism that Miss Lewis had recounted to Tolliver.

A new subject of conversation was definitely warranted.

"Are you a good shot?" It was a fumble, but as soon as he said it, he knew it would distract her. There was something about the way she held her rifle. She didn't seem to be conscious that she was holding it at all, and yet it seemed as if she might close the breach and raise the weapon to her shoulder at any moment. That bespoke a facility with firearms, one that had been trained so consistently that it was now beyond thought.

But Mrs. Farleigh simply shrugged, still looking at him. "I've not spent much time shooting rook rifles," she said absently. "You?"

Ah. So these were rook rifles. They all looked basically the same to Mark—long barrels, wood stock.

"Indifferent," Mark confessed. "When I was young, we had no shooting range. And over the last years, I've spent most of my time with my eldest brother in London, which means I've had little chance to shoot in the country. I hope only to avoid coming in dead last."

She let out a little gasp. "Wha-at?" She drew the word out, making a mockery of her surprise. "The indomitable Sir Mark has an imperfection?

Oh, dear. And here I left my hartshorn and vinegar at home."

It had been a long while since anyone aside from his brothers had teased him. It felt good now—better than he dared admit—to look into her dark eyes, glowing with humor.

He schooled his own expression to sobriety. "Well, it's only the one flaw," he said. "And if I speak very loudly, surely nobody will notice." His eyes darted across the lawn to the rector, who stood across the lawn, still pontificating.

Mrs. Farleigh coughed on a sputter of laughter. Yes, it had been a *very* long time since anyone had dared to tease him—let alone understood when he teased back. His thoughts from the past days—his lingering anger, his unresolved thoughts about the commission   seemed to weigh less. "You, on the other hand," he said, "are an excellent shot."

"You can't know that." But her cheeks took on a faint flush that had nothing to do with the sun overhead.

"What think you of the course?" He gestured toward the first target—a simple shot across twenty yards of green.

Beyond it, the track cut through low oaks. Barely visible through the foliage, the second target peeked out. The stations increased in difficulty. The fifth target, invisible now, was hidden like a partridge in the bracken along the Doulting Water.

Jessica narrowed her eyes briefly—perhaps sizing up the course—before turning to him. There was a stubborn set to her chin. "Interesting," was all she said.

"Can you win this thing, do you think?"

She had not yet admitted to any aptitude for shooting, but the fierce intake of breath beside him was all the answer he needed.

"Ah," he said aloud, drawling the syllable out. "The imperfect Mrs. Farleigh has a talent."

She didn't breathe, simply looked at the first target in front of them. She seemed taut and wary, like a deer deciding whether to stay and snatch a few more mouthfuls of grass, or bound away into the underbrush. Her lips curved, not in pleasure, but in want instead. He had no idea what he would do if she ever looked at *him* like that.

But he was saved from finding out when the rector recalled himself from his lecture. He motioned to the elder Mr. Tolliver, and the man called out for everyone to take their places. Reluctantly, Mark touched his hat and made to leave.

But she held up one finger.

"I *could* win this thing," she said. Her voice had a hint of a rasp to it. "But I shall do you one better."

He couldn't imagine what might be better than winning, but he had no opportunity to question her. Instead he let Tolliver guide him away. The young fellow was a better shot than Mark. Hardly surprising, but Tolliver flushed every time he out-shot his...his hero. Mark waved away the apologies, annoyed.

In the first round, he scarcely had a chance to speak with Mrs. Farleigh. She walked arm in arm with Dinah Lewis. The two of them strolled after everyone else, whispering to one another. If she'd been shooting brilliantly, he ought to have heard the congratulations.

And so Mark didn't realize what she'd done until the first round was finished, and the evidence of his prowess—or lack thereof—was placed before him. Between pairs, servants had covered the targets with fresh sheets of paper, the more accurately to score and to resolve disputes. On the first target, Mark's shot had gone wide, to the upper left, where it had lodged in the second ring from the center. She'd hit the target in the upper right, also in the second ring. Had he placed a looking glass down the meridian of the paper, her shot would have been the reflection of his. Target after target, she'd mirrored his shots. Precisely.

Nobody else seemed to notice this. And why would they? Nobody shot to *miss*.

Her performance meant that they were paired together for the second round—and due to their equally poor scores, they were the last pair to go through the course.

While they were waiting for the crowd to clear around the first target, he found her once more.

"Where did you learn to shoot like that?" She was standing to the side of the lawn, watching the men take aim. Despite the exertions of the past hour, her dark hair had not slipped from the complicated knots and braids she'd made of it.

"Why, Sir Mark. My aim is indifferent—as I am sure you noticed." She fluttered her eyelashes at him—a self-satisfied little feminine gesture. Even knowing that she teased him, he could not help but feel a swell of desire. He wanted that flutter to be real. He wanted to have at least that much power over her—to know that he could fluster her, even a little bit.

"Your aim was unerring," he said. "It was your target that was indifferent. Now, are you going to answer my question, or is this an attempt to maintain an air of mystery?"

She let out a sigh. "I've spent a good amount of time in hunting boxes around men. When they go off on their own to shoot, one has to find some way to amuse one's self."

"Your husband took you hunting?"

She shrugged once again. "It amused him to have female companionship. And I discovered that I had a...a natural affinity for shooting. Once I discovered that, I *had* to learn greater proficiency, for the sake of self-preservation."

"Self-preservation? Truly?" He raised an eyebrow at her. "What, was your life threatened by pigeons?"

She didn't smile. "No man enjoys being outshot by a woman. I had to learn to shoot exactly where I wanted, every time. Because. Well." Her lips pinched together, and still she didn't look at him. It was the first time she'd mentioned her late husband. If he'd thought of the matter, he would have guessed that she had disliked the fellow.

And perhaps this started to explain why.

Mrs. Farleigh was beautiful. No, not just beautiful—there were many beautiful women. She drew every eye, male and female, in a way that beauty itself could not have done. It was not just women who felt jealousy. She could so easily have outshone a husband. No doubt she had done so. A bridegroom might have imagined her as some kind of a keepsake to be placed on a shelf, a possession he could point to. But someone who wanted to bolster his image with an expensive wife would not have been pleased to be outdone.

"So you learned to lose," Mark said flatly.

And she flinched when men laid hands on her. Of course she did. The most important man in her life had made her small.

"I *chose* to lose." That hint of wariness had crept back into her face. "Perhaps you cannot understand what it is like, to be dependent on—on someone

else. If I had not lost, there would have been endless rounds of sulking, culminating in…"

But she sighed and shook her head, before
she could explain what the result of her competence would have been. And now he felt a flush
himself—anger, perhaps, that she thought he might
want such a thing from her. Fury, that she supposed he needed to win by artifice. Or maybe it
was just desire, plain and simple.

The pair shooting in front of them—the hapless
Tolliver and Miss Lewis—finished their round and
marched on to the next target, and he and Mrs.
Farleigh were left alone on the green. She started
for the line where they were to shoot from.

"Mrs. Farleigh," Mark called. She stopped and
gave him her shoulder, not quite meeting his eyes.
Still wary, and that made him angrier yet. "I want
you to trounce me."

Her head snapped up. "Pardon?"

"It is down to you and me. We are battling it out,
to see who will be the king of the indifferent shots
in this competition. Only one of us can prevail. I
shall be shooting to win." He really was angry,
he realized—furious to imagine her spending her
autumns deliberately hiding what she could do,
hiding the extent of her ability from the man who
should most have treasured it. It was as if she'd
left a vast swath of her ability unclaimed, hidden

behind a swirl of feminine smiles. He didn't like the idea. He didn't like it at all.

He raised his firearm and sighted at the target. He hated shooting. There were always too many things to remember—to compensate for the slight breeze, the distance, the kick of the weapon in his hand. Still, he juggled all those considerations in his mind and then fired; even twenty yards away, he could barely spot the single hole burnt in the paper. It was level with the bull's eye, in that first ring. It was the best shot he'd made all day.

"Of course you'll outdo me," he told her.

She didn't respond. Instead, she lifted her arm, steadily. Without seeming to make any calculations or even to take aim at all, she fired.

They strode forward as one, to mark their positions on the target. Mark had been inches from the bull's eye. Mrs. Farleigh, however, struck it. Her bullet was not quite dead center; instead, the dark circle of her shot was at the very edge. If Mark had been angry before, he was furious now.

"Do you think you need to hold back because you'll anger me?" His throat felt tight. "Do you think me so small and pitiful a creature that the sign of the slightest competence on your part will send me into a spiral of depression? You have it quite wrong. I know you can do better. I expect it of you."

Her eyes widened.

"I meant it. I don't just want you to win. I don't want you to put on a showing barely more respectable than mine, to leave the outcome in doubt, and assuage my pride. My pride doesn't need your cosseting. I want you to win."

"I *am* winning."

His memory matched up the precision of her shooting earlier in the day, and he gave her one scorching glance. "You can do better."

Her lips thinned, and she turned from him, her shoulders rigid, and marched to the next target. He followed after her. She didn't say a word in response, just lifted her chin, loaded her rifle and then fired in one smooth motion. He couldn't see where her shot landed, but it must have been dead in the center, because she gave him a smoky, self-satisfied glance.

Mark fumbled with his weapon and then raised it. He wasn't sure what precisely he was supposed to call this emotion that raged in him. He wasn't calm; he could scarcely string one logical thought after another. He wasn't sure how much higher to aim, how to judge the distance. Was the target on lower ground? He thought it might be. He felt like a pot of water, on the verge of a boil. He shook his head and squeezed the trigger.

The bullet barely winged the edge of the target.

Beside him, Mrs. Farleigh said nothing. Instead, they walked forward together, to examine her shot.

She'd placed hers dead in the center. Mark groped for words. Congratulations, under the circumstances, would have been a little too condescending. But to leave the accomplishment unacknowledged? That he couldn't do.

She took the decision from him. She turned to him and raised one quizzical eyebrow. "You," she said without a trace of emotion in her voice, "can do better."

And on that pronouncement, she marched away from him, leaving him on the verge of spouting blasphemy.

He stalked after her, only to catch her up at the third target. This one had been set thirty yards away on the top of a hill; the elevation difference was supposed to add difficulty. This time, when he took the position, she came to stand next to him.

"You're thinking too much," she told him. "I'm sure that if you had pencil and paper you could calculate the precise angle at which you should shoot. But your body is smarter than your mind. It knows what needs to be done. Trust it."

Heat broke around him once more. His body knew *exactly* what it wanted to be doing right now, and it had nothing to do with shooting bullets at targets. He wanted to tear her rifle from her hands and let it fall to the ground. He wanted to wrap his arms around her. He wanted to crush her frame against his. This welter of heat had nothing to do with anger. This wasn't fury. It was passion.

Stupidly, he groped for some semblance of peace. Calm. But his body was having none of that. He was painfully, horribly excited. He turned away from her and fought for nothingness. He hadn't tried to solve mathematical problems since his days in Oxford, but it seemed like a good idea now. If Newtonian physics couldn't break through this arousal, he wasn't sure what could. If a bullet fired from the muzzle at a velocity of one hundred feet per second, at an angle of fifteen degrees, traveling over thirty yards and a substantial incline... then Mrs. Farleigh was still going to be standing next to him, gorgeous and capable and telling him that he could do better.

He fired.

She shook her head. "Too much thinking."

Too much thinking of the wrong sort. Now that the image of holding her was lodged in his head, he could not banish it. He did not trust himself to speak, not even to say a word when she once again hit the center of the target. He flubbed the fourth station entirely, missing the target altogether.

She simply shook her head once more. "You can do better."

That wave of heat—sheer arousal—crested and crashed around him. It was white-hot desire. He couldn't have explained what was happening or why. But her breaths lifted her chest more rapidly. She looked at him—taunting, yes, but playful. And…and… Oh, dear. He was undone. Because her pupils were wide, her tongue touching her lips. If he reached for her, she wouldn't flinch.

"I did tell you I was an indifferent shot," he growled.

"A fine excuse." She turned and disappeared into the track through the woods. The last target was down by the water, half obscured by branches and a fallen tree that had been overgrown by ivy. He wasn't sure he could hit this target when he was calm. Now, it seemed altogether out of the question.

"You need to let instinct take you forward."

"Ridiculous."

"Truth."

His hands clenched as he loaded his weapon. "Even if it were true, I've had no opportunity to practice, to hone that instinct—"

"More excuses. I won't hear them, Sir Mark. I make you a wager. Defeat me on this last target, and I'll let you kiss me."

He should have stopped to think. But on those words—*kiss me*—logical discourse dropped from Mark's mind, disappearing as the blood rushed from his head. He couldn't think, couldn't imagine anything except the soft touch of her lips on his, the palms of his hands about her, her body strained flush against him. He wanted to pick her up and hold her against a tree. He wanted to taste her.

And so it was not thought that made him turn from her, made him approach the flag that marked thirty paces from the target. He did not think as he raised the rifle to his shoulder, did not contemplate as he focused on the bull's-eye. He just squeezed the trigger. Black powder and sulfur surrounded him in an acrid haze. His arm ached from the force of the recoil.

The cloud cleared, and they strode forward.

Somehow, he'd hit the bull's-eye—barely nicking the dark edge of it, true, but the best shot he'd made all afternoon. Perhaps it was coincidence.

Perhaps it wasn't. He swallowed and looked at her. He could almost taste success, sweet and smelling of black-powder smoke.

She didn't say anything. Instead, she turned and paced back to the flag. He followed. It was only now, watching the curve of her backside, the languid sway of her stride, that sanity began to trickle back.

She could beat his shot easily; he'd seen her do it three times in a row.

But did she want to?

Did he want her to? No. And yes. He didn't want it to happen like this. He didn't want to kiss her because he'd lost his temper. He certainly didn't want her to grant him a kiss because she ceded him the win out of pity. He didn't want her to make herself small for him.

She waited until he stood behind her before raising her rifle, and then she fired in one fluid movement. She didn't look at him as she walked forward. She must already know the outcome.

He didn't want her to shoot to miss—not for any reason, not at all.

She stopped at the target. There, embedded clearly in the center, was her shot.

She'd beaten him.

He felt a wave of relief, coupled with a tight sense of loss. Yes, he'd wanted her to win. But still…

"You know," he said, his voice hoarse, "this was a poorly formed wager. We never did decide what *you* got if you won."

Her eyes lifted to his lips. Her tongue darted out to touch the corner of her mouth.

Suddenly, wildly, he wanted her to lay claim to the same reward. He shouldn't want it. He shouldn't even think it. If he'd had a membership card in the MCB, he'd have taken it out now, because Peril was reaching for him. But her breath cycled in time with his. Her hand fluttered at her side, reaching for him and then falling away, as if she, too, did not know.

She shook her head, as if shaking off a tight

little spell, and drew in a shuddering breath. And then she gave him a smile—not a cruel one, but understanding, as if she knew that her goading earlier had aroused him to the point of pain. As if she'd traveled that road alongside him.

"What do I get?" she asked. Her voice echoed in the clearing. "That's obvious. I get to know you wanted to kiss me."

The white-hot emotion returned, and this time, he couldn't control it.

"Bollocks on that," he said scornfully. And before she could move away, before she could take back those words, he'd stepped into her arms. His hands caught her waist. She tipped her head up to his. And then roughly—stupidly—his lips found hers.

CHAPTER ELEVEN

JESSICA HADN'T REALIZED quite what she was doing.

At first, the only thought in her mind had been to do to Sir Mark what he was doing to her—insisting that he could do better. But up until the moment when he'd faced her, his mouth set, she'd not understood. Not truly.

She'd incited men to passion before. But she'd not been considering any sort of strategy. She'd not thought of seducing him, not since the moment when he'd told her that he wanted her to trounce him. She had thought in that moment only of herself—her own wants, her own desires, so long ignored.

As he lowered his lips to hers, what she felt was not victory or even a sense of success. It was a purely feminine response, a delight that had nothing to do with her campaign of seduction, and everything to do with the fact that it was Sir Mark kissing her.

For all that his hands held her tightly, his lips landed gently on hers. His skin was slightly rough with unseen stubble. And without thought, she opened for him, unfurling as gently as a flower reaching for the sun. He was pure heat against her skin, and she drank him in. Her hands clutched his chest.

All thought washed from her mind. Targets disappeared. The other contestants who had gone before, who were now undoubtedly waiting back at the Tollivers' estate for the final tally…they vanished. There was nothing in this world but Mark and the taste of liquid sunshine, her own desire filling her to the brim and overflowing.

His body was flush against hers. He made no attempt to hide his erection, poking into her. Still, it was just a kiss—just his lips on hers, his mouth, growing ever confident, his tongue, tangling with hers.

It was just a kiss. It only felt as if it were more.

He raised his head, took his hands from her waist. All Jessica's breathless desire was met by the crisp air rising off the nearby water. The chill slapped against her face.

She took a step back, raising her hand to her mouth as reason returned. Another man might have looked embarrassed or guilty. Another man would have blamed her for that kiss and called her a temptress. Or worse.

Sir Mark wasn't looking at her with anything

that resembled shame or anger. Instead, his face echoed her feeling of lightning-struck wonder.

"Well." He rubbed one hand against the seam of his trousers and looked away, as if searching for the right words. "At this moment, I believe a proper gentleman would apologize for taking liberties."

"If you do," Jessica said, "I will find a stick and beat you over the head with it."

He regarded her closely. "Tolliver would see you brought up on assault charges if you did," he said. His tone was grave, but his eyes flashed at her with a sly, private humor. "And I don't suppose you would take well to picking oakum at Cornhill. I've heard it's quite damp and unhealthy there. So it's just as well that, in defiance of all propriety, I don't feel the least bit sorry."

"No?" Her breath caught.

"No." He reached forward and lightly touched her cheek. She could feel the warmth of his hand even through his glove. She wanted to press her own arms around him, to hold him closer.

Instead, he released a sigh and pulled his hand away. "No," he repeated. "And I should. Under ordinary circumstances, I should be delighted to accompany you home. Too delighted, in fact. I hope you'll understand when I say that tonight, I must leave you to make your own way back."

Jessica looked up at him. And in that instant, she

remembered what she was supposed to be doing. She'd vowed to seduce him. She *needed* to do it, needed the money quite desperately. He'd made her forget all that. She'd forgotten everything— everything except the feel of his mouth on hers.

"Surely a saint like Sir Mark can stand up to a little temptation," she said.

But he didn't smile at the jest. Instead he shook his head. And this time, he truly was grave. "Not tonight, Mrs. Farleigh. Not tonight I can't." And before she could answer, he turned and walked away from her.

She watched him go, her stomach twisting. It wasn't supposed to happen like this. She wasn't supposed to want him, too. She was supposed to seduce him—but it felt dreadfully as if he were the one seducing her.

You can do better.

All she had to do was take her own advice and stop *thinking* about seduction. She liked him. She liked his style, to the point and honest and unstudied. She liked that she could make him lose his head. She liked that he made her forget, if only for a few minutes, everything but the primal attraction between them.

But most of all, she *loved* that he'd wanted her to win.

Men had complimented her beauty, and she'd stayed detached. They'd written poems about the timbre of her voice, and she'd been unmoved. But just the thought of Mark, saying in a voice roughened by desire that she could do better…that had brought her to the edge.

It was the first time in years that she'd liked it when a man kissed her. And therein lay the danger.

Maybe she could seduce him simply by not thinking too hard, by letting herself slide into an infatuation that came all too naturally to her. But could she then turn around and heartlessly betray him to Weston?

She'd done a great many stomach-churning things in the name of survival. She could do this, too. It wasn't as if she had so much choice. All she had to do was let herself feel the heady thrill of attraction. She could tumble headlong into… into *like* with him, letting that nascent admiration grow. And then, when she respected him— when she appreciated him—when she longed for his touch and couldn't bear to see him hurt, why, then all she had to do was betray him.

She wanted to vomit.

Instead, she sighed, took a deep breath to settle her stomach and collected her rifle.

THERE WAS ANOTHER letter from her solicitor when she stopped by the post office on the way home from the competition. The envelope was thicker than usual; it must have contained several pages. She ripped it open as soon as she was in private.

The first sheet was little more than an introduction—a few more bills left off the last note sent and a final tally of her accounts. The amount—something under nine pounds—was not something she cared to contemplate.

That sense of nausea had not dissipated, and the truth of her finances did nothing to ease her worries.

There was another letter from Weston enclosed—a terse note, really, demanding that she give him news. She passed over that one quickly and turned to the final sheet.

It was filled with her solicitor's writing. She frowned and began reading as she walked.

I regret to inform you...

Her steps slowed in the path, then came to a standstill.

She read on. Her hands didn't dare to tremble. Her feet didn't dare to misstep. She could not look away from the page—the words it contained seemed impossible.

She'd had one good thing in her life, and while she'd been here in Shepton Mallet, flirting with Sir Mark, it had been ripped away. And Jessica hadn't even had the chance to say farewell.

She should have been crying, but her eyes

stayed dry. There was nothing tears could do to change the situation in any event.

Amalie had taught Jessica all the rules of being a courtesan. Stupidly, they came to mind now.

Never trust a man who gives you diamonds; whatever he needs to apologize for isn't worth the jewelry.

Every new man is a risk; better the man of moderate means, who stays for two years, than the wealthy protector who abandons you after a month.

And most importantly of all: *Every courtesan needs a friend. We would never survive without each other.*

For the past seven years, Amalie had been that friend. Amalie had taken the place of Jessica's sisters. She'd been the constant warmth in Jessica's life.

But Amalie wasn't here, and none of her advice could see Jessica through this blow.

Don't think. Act. That wasn't Amalie's advice; it was what Jessica had told Sir Mark earlier today. And like that, she was turning in the path, fighting the burn in her lungs for breath. It might feel like a mistake tomorrow, but tonight, she needed a friend.

IT HAD BEEN a mistake.

That was all Mark could think as he made his

way home from the competition, his long strides sending up clouds of dust around him. He forced himself to keep to a walk, even though he wanted to run, to put as much distance as he could between himself and what had just happened.

Rationally, logically, he knew that it was the sort of slip that anyone might make. Mrs. Farleigh was a widow, not some virginal miss. It had been nothing but a kiss—a heady kiss, to be sure, but he'd not shoved her against a tree as he'd wanted. He'd not flung her to the ground and lifted her skirts. He hadn't even let his hands stray past her waist, and he'd wanted to drink her in.

It was just a kiss. A flirtation gone too far. If he'd been any other man, he'd have enjoyed the feel of her lips on his and then thought nothing more of the matter.

But Mark knew himself better. For him, it had been a catastrophe.

He'd lost his head before, and he hated the feeling. He knew what it was like to act without thinking, to have no control over what came next. It felt like close kin to madness, plain and simple. And he had seen what madness could do.

His mother, in her madness, had beaten his brothers. She'd done good works, yes, but she'd also nearly killed his brother.

He didn't fear that he would become mad. He'd never detected the slightest propensity toward unreason in himself. Still, he hated the feeling of rage overtaking him, hated the feeling of want overpowering his intellect. It reminded him that no matter what he did, a piece of his mother had lodged inside him. He'd inherited a fragment of her temperament alongside her hair and her eyes.

As he'd grown older, he'd watched his mother ossify into a shell of a woman, nothing to her but rage and anger. He'd eaten porridge throughout his childhood, too; today, he could no longer stomach oats. He'd developed a distaste for excess emotion to go along with his dislike for gruel.

Mark had thought about his ideal wife before. He'd not yet found her, not in the myriad subdued and pliable debutantes that had been pushed his way. Mark's ideal wife was intelligent. She would be a perfect companion: clever enough that he would never tire of her company, outspoken enough that she did not simply bow to his whims. She would challenge and confront him when necessary.

But there was another, more important component to this wistful dream. He wanted a woman who would calm him. She needed to be level-headed enough that he might trust her with the truth about himself. She would bring him to balance. She would be a source of peace and quiet.

Yes. Of course, he also hoped that his wife would satisfy his physical desires, too. Still, every

time he'd imagined marital intercourse—far too
often for his peace of mind—he'd imagined it as
a rational endeavor. Heated, of course, and pleasurable, naturally. He had no problem with pleasure regulated by reason. But sexual congress was
supposed to leave his head clearer at the end.

When he'd met Mrs. Farleigh, he had wanted
time to consider her. She'd seemed…possible.

She was beautiful. She was intelligent. And
most important of all, she challenged him. She
hadn't believed all the folderol about his perfection. She was the first woman in a very long while
who had seen through the claptrap of his inexplicable success to discover that underneath, he was
still just a man like any other man. He needed
someone who could turn to him and say, "Sir
Mark, you are failing, and you must get yourself
under control."

Mrs. Farleigh might have done. He'd begun to
hope that she was the woman he'd been waiting
for, no matter what the townspeople said.

But now it was quite clear that he would have
to discard that hope. There was one way in which
Mrs. Farleigh was completely wrong for him. She
didn't calm him. No; she enflamed him. When he
let his eyes flicker shut, he could see the fall of her
eyelashes, the look she'd given him over her shoulder. He could see the pink of her lips, her mouth

opening to his. He could still taste her sweetness on his lips.

She made him smolder. She took his logical thoughts, and instead of arranging them in calm and clean order, she shook them until he could not tell up from down, right from wrong—could only think in terms of *her* and *not her*.

No. Despite her intelligence, despite the connection he felt to her, there was no question about the matter. She was wrong for him. Utterly, completely, and in all other ways wrong.

His reason knew it. But the rest of him was discontent with that decision.

Mark turned off the dusty track onto a lane. It headed straight down the hill, through a path lined by birch trees. The way was shaded; it wended down until it ran parallel to the briskly moving water of a mill-leat. Cool air rose around him, the temperature welcome against his skin. The walk, if nothing else, helped to bleed the edge from his sexual frustration. Deliberately, he kept walking past his mother's house. He needed to regain his equanimity, to find the smooth imperturbable silk that normally surrounded him. Nothing like physical exertion to work his wants out of his system.

Glass bricks. He imagined them, cool against his skin. Distancing. Anything seen through glass must be far away, unable to touch him. If he laid them just right, he would be able to block off this smoldering powder keg of desire. He would be in control once again. He'd no longer sense the echoes of his mother but would again be a man whose emotions were all that was proper and gentlemanly.

He concentrated only on the distorting wave of the glass. It would mute out color, heat, shape— everything, really, except that which was sober and seemly. In his mental exercise, he built those glass walls high, higher, stretching until his mental tower of bricks rivaled that of Babel. It didn't help that at every step along the way, he was confronted by reminders. The shadow of oak on water recalled the dark gleam of her hair. An errant beam of light, cutting through the gloom, brought to mind the sun-warm lips he'd touched. He waited until his breathing evened out. Until his wants fitted inside his skin once again.

It was only then that he let himself observe his surroundings. He'd traveled miles upstream from his mother's house. In the distance, he could see the blackened bricks of a factory—one that no doubt had been burned back in the troubled times. Times his own family had precipitated. If he'd needed another reason to avoid the dangers that awaited him if he gave in to his animal needs, those dark stones stood as a whispering reminder. This wasn't about him or his selfish, burning want for a woman.

Mark wasn't his father. He wasn't his mother. But…he might duplicate their mistakes, if he let himself slip.

Even with an hour between him and that kiss, even with his every thought bent toward expunging the sense of heat, he could still feel the pressure of her lips against his. No. There was nothing for it. He was going to have to stop indulging himself. He was going to have to stop pretending that his want for her was anything other than animal desire.

He was going to have to stop seeing her.

So why did that decision feel so *wrong?*

That twinge of regret he felt, that soul-deep gasp that filled him…

That was only further proof that she was the last woman on earth he needed to be thinking about.

With that decision firmly in hand, he turned and headed for home. The walk back took longer, now that he was no longer trying to outrace his own desires. If anything, he was almost reluctant to turn to his house again. It was cold and empty, filled with the ghosts of his childhood: precisely not the calm comfort he needed to keep his life in regular order.

When he was a child, there had been scant opportunity for quiet and comfort. But still, there had been times when his mind cleared, when the everyday bustle had been taken away. In times like this, with his fears cascading about him with no escape, he found an almost meditative calm in reciting words he'd long memorized.

Lo, thou requirest truth in the inward parts: and shall make me to understand wisdom secretly.

The words were familiar, restful. A muttered incantation, offered to his own fitful spirit.

Thou shalt make me hear of joy and gladness. Renew a right spirit within me.

That was what he wanted more than anything— to be refreshed, to not fear his own thoughts. But peace didn't come. Nothing eased the turmoil he felt. No quiet. No calm. His thoughts made a whirl-pool around him.

He made his way along the embankment of the mill-leat, the water running fiercely beside him, until he saw the familiar shape of home. It was just as he remembered it: gray and chilly in the late afternoon, fading into the brackish fenlike un-derbrush around it. Tonight, it would be dank and lonely. Mark sighed, wishing for the first time that one of his brothers had come with him.

When he was within a few yards of the en-trance, movement off to the side distracted him.

He turned.

There was a moment of staggering stillness, as if the maelstrom of his discontent had simply fro-zen in place. As if every argument he'd conducted with himself had fallen in on itself. As if she had come here in answer to his desperation.

She brought him no calm. No quiet. If he hated excess, he should despise the sight of her.

He didn't.

Jessica, his body whispered.

"Mrs. Farleigh," he said instead.

"Sir Mark." She was wearing a heavy cloak, covering her from neck to ankle. Her head was bowed, not in reverence, but as if she were carrying a heavy burden. She looked up, and her eyes sought his.

At the look in them—that haunted, sad look— he wanted to go to her and put his arms about her. He wanted to turn and barricade himself behind the heavy wooden planks of his door. He wanted her never to feel sorrow again. He wanted to make it all better. He wasn't sure if she was the answer to his desperate prayer, or temptation sent from the other side.

"I know how improper this must seem," she said. "Particularly after what transpired earlier today. I know what you must think. But I did not come here to enlarge on our prior...discussion. Truly. I came because there is no one else I can turn to."

She took another step toward him, and he could make out the tight lines around her eyes, the tremble of her hands. There was nothing fabricated about her distress.

"Mrs. Farleigh," he repeated. He should send her away. He'd just decided that he could have nothing more to do with her. He should tell her to unburden her problems on the rector and be shut of the situation.

Right. And the man would no doubt paw at her breast and then blame her for tempting him.

No. Mark was many things, but he was not the sort of man who would walk away from a woman in trouble. Especially not *this* woman. This maddening, tempting, arousing woman.

He hadn't responded, and she clasped her hands in front of her—not in entreaty, but in an unconscious movement. "We can speak out here, if it makes you more easy. I brought my cloak and an umbrella, just in case. But I want—no, I *need*—to talk with someone."

And that's when Mark knew that he was in even more trouble than he'd believed. Because all it took was that one plea, and the objections he'd had against her, so carefully considered, disappeared in smoke. And all he could think of was her.

CHAPTER TWELVE

JESSICA GASPED in relief when Sir Mark silently opened the door and ushered her inside. He took her cloak and hung it on a hook. But he didn't say anything as he conducted her down the long hall she'd walked once before. Once they'd reached the parlor, he silently gestured her to a seat in front of the fireplace. It was beginning to cool down; inside, it was actually cold. He set logs in the cavern of a fireplace with easy assurance before reaching for a small bellows and encouraging the embers to spark to life.

He did all of this without touching her, without a brush of his fingers against her neck. She was glad of it.

Flames licked up, devouring wood. He pulled the grate in front of the fire once more and turned to her. His gaze touched her eyes, dropped to her hands, pale and clasped together.

"You're chilled," he said. He spoke so matter-of-factly, she would never have known they'd kissed earlier. She might have thought there was nothing between them but bare facts. "Would you like some tea?"

"No." Her fingers spasmed, and she burrowed them into her skirt. "No. I don't like tea."

He must have heard something in her voice, because he cocked his head and looked at her. But he didn't press her any further. "Coffee?" he asked. "Warmed milk?"

"I don't suppose you have any port." The words escaped her.

But he didn't look offended at the notion that a woman might do something so unladylike as take strong spirits. Instead, his eyes crinkled in amusement, and he turned and left. Rustling sounds, and then a long creak, floated into the room. He came back a few minutes later, with a pair of tumblers and a dusty bottle.

"No port," he told her. "But—" he hefted the green glass "—I do have a bottle of the local apple brandy. Have you ever tried any?"

She shook her head.

He wrested the cork from the bottle and then poured a splash of the caramel-colored liquid into a glass. "It's a local tradition." He handed this over—their fingers did not touch—and then he poured himself a more generous measure.

She just needed to steady her nerves. A sip, that's all. She was beginning to feel foolish for having come here.

He set the decanter on the side table and sat on the divan. She might have said that he sat next to her, but it was a long divan, and he'd settled on the opposite edge from her. If she stretched out her arm full-length, and he held out his hand, their fingertips might scarcely touch. Still, a little frisson went through her. They were sitting...*almost* next to each other. The cushions against her back moved when he leaned back. Her hand stroked the silk of the seat.

"To your health." He raised his glass and drank.

Jessica sniffed the liquid tentatively. Above the sweetness of apple, she scented something strong and raw. It tickled the back of her throat. "Sir Mark," she said tentatively, "are you trying to inebriate me?"

"I didn't even give you an inch." He raised one eyebrow. "Can't you hold your liquor?"

She pressed her lips together and focused on the challenge. "I could drink you under the table," she informed him flatly. But her heart wasn't in it. She raised the glass and took a gulp.

She'd expected something smooth like cider. But what hit her was alcohol, raw and unfinished, burning her tongue, stealing the breath from her lungs. She coughed, barely swallowing the slug she'd taken into her mouth. This wasn't the smooth taste of well-aged spirits sipped by gentlemen in London clubs. This was the sort of hash brewed

by backwoods laborers, reserved for raucous gatherings. And then the effect of those spirits struck
her, like a kick applied to the seat of the pants. It
felt like a fire, igniting in her belly and pushing
aside her worries.

She cleared her throat and stared at the seem-
ingly inoffensive liquid. "You could have warned
me. This is a death trap."

"That, too, is a local tradition." A small smile
touched his lips, but faded as he looked at her.
"And, truthfully, you looked as if you needed a
bit of something to pick you up. I figured that
would do the trick." He took another sip from his
glass. His gaze shifted from the apple brandy to
her hands, wrapped around the tumbler. And then,
he followed her arms, up, up until his eyes met
hers. "Also, I believe I am trying to drown out my
better self."

Fire? The brandy had nothing on the heat in his
gaze. She might have found her forgetfulness in
the look in his eyes alone. The dark need. The desire. It was all there, too much to grasp with both
hands.

Jessica took another gulp of brandy. Easier to
swallow fire than to meet his eyes. If she'd *had* a
better self, it was Amalie. "Lucky you," she said
bitterly. "I haven't got one of those."

He picked up the decanter and poured himself
another inch.

"It's not goodness that leads men and women to sin, Sir Mark," she said. "It's the dark, ugly portions that drive men and women together. Our better selves have no need to be held."

She'd not realized what she wanted until she said the words aloud. But perhaps that was why she'd come—not for unapologetic lust, not for mere physical intimacy, but for something that ran deeper than the blaze of want.

She'd come for *comfort*.

He took another swig and then met her eyes. "Need more brandy?" he asked conversationally.

Jessica rubbed her neck tentatively. "It appears that the lining of my throat has not yet been entirely stripped away." She held out her glass. "Why not?"

He lifted the decanter. But instead of taking the tumbler from her hand, he slid across the divan toward her. His eyes held hers. His hand wrapped around hers. If the brandy had seemed hot as tongues of flame, Sir Mark was the heart of the fire. His fingers engulfed hers, steadying the glass as he poured.

She pulled the cup to her mouth. He didn't let his hand fall away, letting her draw him toward her until his hip rested against hers. She couldn't breathe. She didn't dare drink. He was alive and warm, and when he touched her, he drove shadows from the dark corners of her vision.

"What are you doing?"

"I'm contemplating." His voice was dark. "Thinking about right and wrong."

His hand slid down her forearm to cup her elbow. Her whole body leaned toward his. His other hand took her cup, set it on the floor next to the decanter. And then her fingers were wrapping around his arm, little shivers traveling through her.

"I see you've decided against right." Her voice shook.

"Not precisely." He leaned toward her, his face fitting into the space between her chin and her neck. She could feel his breath against her neck, his arm curling around her waist.

How did he know that this was what she needed? That more conversation would have left her falling to pieces?

How did he know to trace her chin with his thumb, to cradle her head in his hands? How did he know that she needed to rest her forehead against his? Because any other man in his position would have thought nothing of her comfort. He'd have wanted to claim her, not hold her.

"You're shaking," he said.

"I've had some bad news."

He didn't demand that she divulge it. He didn't demand anything of her, and that made her feel wrong and dirty—because she came to him for comfort, and he gave it without asking questions.

It recalled her nausea of that afternoon once again. Her hands shook anew.

If she seduced the one good man she'd met, she'd surely earn her place in hell. But if there was a hell, she'd already earned her place in it. That's what it meant to be a fallen woman. She'd already lost all hope of heaven.

All hope except the scent of Sir Mark, his arm wrapped around her now. If there was any such thing as salvation, surely it felt like the gentle kiss he laid on her throat. The feel of his nose, brushing against the line of her jaw. The light calluses on his hands, sliding across her shoulder.

It didn't feel like damnation when her fingers found his chin, when she lifted his head so that his eyes met hers. His mouth touched hers, sweet and gentle; her hands dropped to curl about his elbows, as if she could cradle the comfort he offered her. His kiss seemed some blasphemous prayer whispered against her skin. His lips caught at hers. His arms encircled her, as if she were some fragile, precious thing.

And, oh, it felt *good*. He held her without restraining her—as if his every caress was a supplication. As if every touch of his lips was a question, one she could answer as she willed, and not a demand.

There was only one answer. *Yes. Yes* with her

tongue; *yes* with the heat of her breath; *yes* with her hands digging into his shoulders.

And then his fingers were brushing up her ribs, setting her afire. His mouth slid down to her chin, her neck, leaving a cascade of warmth in his wake. His palm cupped her breast, his fingers exploring it. His touch was neither tentative nor practiced—just slow, excruciatingly slow, as if he were unearthing some kind of archaeological treasure, and he feared it would break.

"Jessica," he murmured against her skin.

He'd found the nub of her nipple. She gasped as he circled it with his thumb. The pleasure was like drink—intoxicating, stealing away memories she wished forgotten.

Her hands slipped down his chest to the wool of his waistcoat. Copper buttons twisted in her grip until she revealed the starched linen of his shirt, warmed to his touch. She tugged, and the tails came loose. She reached beneath the fabric.

His skin was hot. His breath hissed in as her palms skimmed up the wall of his abdomen. His muscle tensed into hard curves under her touch, corded and inflexible. Any other man would have flipped her onto her back by now. His lips found the side of her neck. He kissed her slowly.

"You know," he whispered to her, "this afternoon, I had vowed never to talk with you again."

"Why ever did you change your mind?"

He shrugged. "You were waiting on my doorstep. And I believe my first coherent thought upon seeing you was—so much for that promise, then. The resolution would not have lasted past seeing you. You may be utterly wrong for me, but I don't believe I can give you up."

"That's precisely how I feel. You're the worst man on *earth* for you to be."

"Am I so bad, then?"

"So good." She swallowed. "Sir Mark—the village gossips were too kind. I have been intimate with men who are not my husband." She stopped, forced herself to go on. "More than one."

"Have you, then?" He didn't move from her.

"My morals are not what they should be. Surely you must know that by now."

"If you were truly bereft of morals, surely you would feel no compunction about lying to me. Is there anything else truly dire I need to know about you?"

"Oh, Sir Mark. I don't even know where to begin with my direness. At this point, I've made so many mistakes I'm riddled with impossibility." She shrugged. "And it's not just my...my lack of chastity."

"I suppose I should care about that."

"You don't?"

The fire cast his face into unforgiving shadow— an agony of expression that she could not dissipate.

"Oh, no." His voice rumbled. "All I can think—the only thought that enters my mind—is…" His body canted toward her, and she could not help but sway toward him. Until her bodice brushed his chest, until her fingers slid from his shoulder to his wrist, and the air in her lungs turned to fire.

"All you can think," she breathed.

"All I can think," he whispered, "is that you would *want* to be faithful to me."

His hand slipped under the neckline of her gown and drew it down to expose her shoulder. A swelling ache went through her. It should not have made her gasp aloud, that innocent touch—nothing but his fingers against her collarbone, his skin against hers. But it was *his* fingertips that dragged across her shoulder, *his* caress that sent sparks shooting down her arm. And the intent in his eyes—serious and deliberate—transformed that touch beyond all possible innocence.

"If you were any other man," she said, "I should think you were trying to have your way with me."

"If I were any other man," he said, "you wouldn't let me do it. But I'm me. And my way doesn't involve any *having*. I am making you a promise, not a proposition."

Men always made promises at times like this, and Jessica had long learned to discount them. But Mark didn't spell out the content of his promise. His lips brushed hers once more—gentle, not demanding. He didn't fit into her understanding of the world.

"You told me once that I was safe with you." Jessica ran her hand up the linen of his sleeve, leaning into him as she did. His body was hard planes of muscle, strong and imperturbable. "One of the most damning things about celibacy is this—this inability to touch another person. Not to engage in intercourse. Just to touch."

He did not say anything, but his eyes fluttered shut.

"Back when I was home with my sisters, I took touch for granted. That every night, there would be someone who would do up my hair in braids, that I might receive an embrace at bedtime, that I might jostle my sister in the morning with my elbow, to have her hurry while she washed."

She could *not* forget, it seemed, why she'd come. It returned to her, no matter how she tried to drive it away. Because now his hand had drifted to her hair in a sweet caress. He'd given her the comfort she'd needed.

"After I left home," she said, "I found a friend. Her name was Amalie. She wasn't...she wasn't what she should be, either. She gave me advice— hard advice that I needed to hear. She saved my life. For seven years, she was my reason to live— my one true friend, who I could count on through the most impossible hardship."

And now her eyes were beginning to sting. The tears that had evaded her earlier built.

"I received word today that there was an accident in London." Jessica took a deep breath. "And so now I am truly alone. No touch is innocent anymore. Even before this, there were days I was so hungry for simple warmth that I would have given up anything—*anything*—to have it."

He leaned into her. Her lips tingled in anticipation, but he didn't kiss her. Instead, his arms came around her, pulling her close. His hand stroked down her spine, slowly, as if he were counting each vertebra and storing the memory in some cool cellar. She could feel his breath on her neck. Her eyes shivered shut, and she held on to him.

Just an innocent embrace. And yet…not. He inhaled raggedly.

"No," he said softly. "No, you're not."

"I'm *starving* for affection."

"That's not what I meant. You're not alone."

And maybe that was the substance of his unspoken promise. The muscles that held her so tightly were rigid with restrained want. His fingers bit into her spine, as if anchoring himself to reality. Just one caress from her, one little kiss, and she might unleash all his dammed-up desire. She could win. And if she did, even this embrace would be tarnished in her memory, all the warmth stolen away into sick certainty.

No. She *was* alone, and she couldn't let herself forget it. It was idiotic to nourish this sense of being wanted, to soak in his touch. To treasure, one last time, something sweet and unsullied. It was a foolish indulgence not to press her advantage now, not to slide her fingers under his waistband and inflame him further. Because if there was one rule that Amalie had burned into her memory, it was this: *Survive. Survive at all costs.*

Now, she had to live for them both.

He held on to her until his breath evened out, until the urgent tension faded from her grip.

She was weak. She was indulgent. Because she couldn't make herself ruin him today.

She reached her hand up to touch his face and whispered to him. "Now…" she said quietly. "Now, I think it's time I go home."

And this time, she let him go.

THE RED LIGHT of the setting sun invaded Mark's bedchamber. The rays bombarded him when he tried to look out his window. He could see only a trace of a silhouette—the echo of a hill, limned in crimson, impossible to focus on through the harsh sunset.

When he turned away, an imprint of the sun remained, etched indelibly over his vision.

Jessica was rather like that. When she was about, he burned. He couldn't even see straight anymore. And when she was not... He had only to shut his eyes, and he could see her smile at him across a field of dandelions.

Lust wasn't a stranger. It wasn't even an enemy. Lust had always seemed something of an itinerant peddler to Mark: always showing up when least expected, clamoring on his doorstep. Either you stopped up your ears and hoped that it would give up and go away, or you were driven past all hope of ignoring it. At that point, you made a token purchase—something you didn't need and shouldn't want.

After what had happened earlier that night, his lust wasn't going away. It had lodged underneath his skin, taking up its complaints in the form of a persistent throb.

A breath of night wind curled through his window. Even that hint of coolness could not calm the storm of his thoughts. God, he wanted her. There was only one way to calm the clamor of his body.

What he was about to do was classified as a sin. He unwound his cravat from his neck, setting his mouth in a grim line. But it was a case of kittens: better the little sin of relieving this tension, than risk losing his mind entirely the next time he was in her presence. And there *would* be a next time. And a next. And a time after that.

The sun blinded him as he worked. But his vision was ruined in any event. Even without the sun, he wouldn't have been able to see himself pull the tails of his shirt out. He wouldn't have been able to make out the buttons on the fall of his trousers.

No. In his mind, no matter what he willed, he saw her: the pins slipping from her hair. Her curls, drifting past pale shoulders. And in his mind, it wasn't the dark red dress that she wore. It was the black shift he'd glimpsed underneath, clinging to her every curve.

When he let his trousers fall to the ground, he was thinking about taking off her chemise. Of raising it, to show ankles he'd seen—and then more that he hadn't. Calves. Thighs. If lust had clamored in him before, it rose up in him now—powerful and impossible to displace. His skin seemed on fire.

He was still standing. He shrugged out of his shirt; in his mind, he was not the only naked one. He caught hold of the carved wood post of his bed with one hand. With the other...

It should have been a clinical act, what followed. It *was* a sin, after all—a lesser one than actually taking a woman to his bed, but a sin nonetheless. But it didn't feel like a sin when his erection filled his palm. It didn't feel like a sin when his grip tightened around his member. And when he thought of her lips against his, remembered the taste of her mouth, sweet against his tongue—she felt *right*, no matter what his reason said.

It was not his own practiced touch that he felt, but the cool brush of her fingers. His imagination conjured up her body, sliding against his. Her hair, draping like cool silk over his chest. He strained forward, as if he might find her mouth.

His hand worked, quick jerks that sent little shocks of pleasure through him. As he moved, as he grew harder, as his lust grew more insistent, Mark opened his eyes and stared out the window into the dying sun. But even that fierce, red after-image couldn't steal the vision he had of her.

He was tight all over—his muscles contracted—thought washed away in a rush toward pleasure. His eyes shut at last, and he was bombarded by sensation, a barrage of images. Her hands. Her lips. The curve of her waist. And then, at the very end: Jessica, fully clothed, standing on the edge of the harsh rocks of the Friar's Oven. Her skirts belled out around her in the wind, and she looked out over a sea of mist.

His release pounded through him, sweeping him away. It was welcome, so welcome. All that pent-up lust burnt like so much tinder in a wildfire. It savaged him, choking him, ripping his breath away.

Passion ebbed, and he was left with the furious pound of his pulse, the only echo of what had come before.

Mark opened his eyes. The light in the room

was fast fading to navy-darkness. He breathed out; one final jolt of pleasure shook him, before his body subsided.

It was done. He'd banished his want.

Mark gingerly unwrapped his fingers from the wood post and walked to the basin on the other side of the room. The water was cold against his skin, the towel rough as he cleaned himself. He washed his hands, his skin. He could see the night sky outside his window. A lingering line of light painted the edge of the hills in claret.

With his want satiated, his thoughts should have been clear and rational. Instead, he felt even more muddled than before. He was alone with himself in the dark.

And he was in trouble.

With the sun of his want set, he'd expected relief from the blinding light of lust. He'd hoped for an utter absence of desire. Instead, he'd discovered stars—a thousand pinpricks dancing around him; an entire constellation of yearning, sketched into his skin.

He got into bed by rote. Once there, he longed for her touch as he drifted off to sleep. For her body, to pull parallel against his, that he might explore her skin with his fingers, his mouth. Not for lust. Not for sin. For…comfort. He'd uncovered a cavernous desire that was impossible to satisfy with fingers and palm.

Mark opened his eyes and blew out his breath. With every exhale, he banished her image. He called to mind dark, cold things: caves under water, winter storms blocking all hint of the sun. He concentrated on the reckless cry of a cricket somewhere in the night. Nothing danced in front of his vision but darkness now—black of night, shadow playing on shadow.

Even with his mind cleared, he could feel the subterranean tug of his desire.

Mrs. Farleigh—*Jessica*—wasn't comfortable. She wasn't demure. She wasn't even respectable.

She was none of those things. And yet… Mark inhaled deeply and faced a truth that he had been trying to avoid for far too long.

He was done resisting her.

CHAPTER THIRTEEN

"I DON'T SUPPOSE there's anything here for me again today?" Jessica asked.

The post office was dark—dim enough, she hoped, to hide the familiar flush of humiliation that touched her cheeks. She hated asking after the post. It always made her feel like a beggar, ringing her bell on the street corner while passersby slunk to one side, avoiding her eyes.

The letter she'd received a handful of days past had taken away everything she'd hoped for. It was foolish to think that she'd receive any communication today. Still, hope, obstinate as that creature was, whispered that maybe she would receive something to make up for recent pain. She was owed something good in the post. It had been years since her family had sent her away. Why should today not be the day on which the embargo was lifted?

Because, Jessica thought grimly, *I've already had a letter from my solicitor this week.*

But the proprietress crinkled her forehead instead. "Happens there is."

Jessica hadn't realized she was holding her breath until she sucked air in, light-headed all at once. She squeezed her hands together, hard, and tried not to lunge at the woman and demand her letter. Possibilities flashed in front of her—her father had written; her mother, maybe Charlotte—

"That is, assuming you are who is meant by Jess Farleigh."

Jess. Her family had never called her *Jess*. Her excitement turned to heavy lead.

"I suppose I am."

Only one person called her Jess. If he was writing her directly, instead of sending his missive roundabout through her solicitor, he must be feeling anxious. Only a few days had elapsed since she'd last heard from him.

She didn't want another letter reminding her of what awaited her in London. Still, the woman handed the envelope over, and Jessica took it gingerly between thumb and forefinger. Weston's hands had covered this paper. His thumbs had rested where hers were now. It made her skin crawl, just to think of his touch on her gloves, even in such an indirect manner.

She wandered out into the square. She shouldn't have told herself that fable about her family. Hope was a fickle friend. Gorging on it was like eating too much pudding. All that sweetness would feel wonderful for a few minutes, but once the first heady rush of energy faded, it left you tired and worn through.

After seven years, she needed to accept that she no longer existed. Her sisters had almost certainly forgotten her. Her father had banished her entirely. She was a fading memory to them. It wasn't a crushing blow not to receive a letter from them.

It was only today that it felt like one.

She ripped open George Weston's envelope and pulled out a half sheet of paper.

Jess, it read. *Hurry it up. Lefevre is announcing his retirement at the end of next week. I want that sanctimonious ass discredited immediately. A seduction's no good to me if I lose the role as Commissioner before you deliver.*

She checked the date on his letter and calculated. Adding in time needed for her to return to London, time to secure publication, that left her with... Three days. She only had three more days to spend in his company before she had to ruin him.

"Well, then."

The voice sounded behind her, and she whirled around, crumpling the paper in her fist.

"Sir Mark," she gasped. She could hear the thrum of her heart, beating hard in her ears.

"Mark," he said.

"Your pardon?"

He was serious, unsmiling. "It's just Mark," he said quietly. "To you."

The sun suddenly seemed overbright. There was nobody else on the paving stones, but the taproom window looked out on the square. Anyone might see them here.

I want that sanctimonious ass discredited immediately.

"How are you today?" he asked.

She *could* destroy him. She had to do it. And he'd just asked her to address him by the naked intimacy of his Christian name and then inquired as to her well-being.

She wanted to scream at him, to shove him in the chest and tell him he was an idiot. She could destroy him. What else was she to do?

"Jessica?" His voice was soft and low. They stood in public, in full view of anyone who could see. "I may call you Jessica, may I not?"

"Don't." The word squeaked out.

"Don't what? Admit to feeling a sense of familiarity? You know I can't deny it. Or do you mean I shouldn't want more? I've tried. I can't help it."

"Sir Mark, perhaps I did not make myself clear last night. I've been intimate with men who were not my husband. Don't trust me."

Just as he had last night, he didn't flinch at her

words. "Yes," he allowed, "but still, you have this odd sort of integrity to you."

He might as well have punched her in the stomach. Weston's letter, crumpled in her hand, burned. She needed to hurt him. How was she to do that, when he made her want to weep?

"That's lust talking, not discernment." Her words were sharp. "You're supposed to have written a *practical* guide to chastity. Be practical now. My integrity is not odd—it is nonexistent. You can't like me."

"Would it be better if I pawed over your body, rather than feel an ounce of honest affection?"

"Yes," she spat out. "*Yes.* It would be a great deal easier."

"Come, Jessica. One mistake doesn't damn you to unhappiness forever." His eyes softened. "And I know that you must be upset about your friend."

One mistake. *One* mistake. Oh, that she could count her mistakes. Instead, they filled her to the brim with choking bitterness.

"Don't make a romance of me, Sir Mark."

"No?" He shook his head, mystified. "What do you want, then?"

She stared at his lapels, as if all the answers she sought might be contained in the brown wool. He waited.

Finally, she lifted her chin and looked him in the eye. "I want to feel alive again." She kept her voice calm as the sea between tides—but, oh, the undercurrent pulling at her. "I want never to have to tell a lie again." She stopped at that and shook her head. "Sir Mark. *Mark.* Please don't make me have to do this."

She *had* made mistakes, yes. But he was right. Even while she'd lived in the utmost sin, she'd tried to hold on to the last vestiges of her integrity. She'd sold some of her morals to survive. This was the first time she'd sacrifice her honesty. If Mark succumbed, she'd lose everything.

He couldn't understand what she was begging him to do, and she had just enough sense of self-preservation not to tell him. Still, she wanted him to hate her, to resist the threat she posed.

"You know," he said softly, "it's not a romance I want to make of you."

"What *do* you want?"

His gaze slipped down her form. She could feel where he'd touched her last night. More, she could feel where he hadn't—the untouched skin of her belly, the nakedness of her inner thighs. But he didn't move. "For now?" His tone was nonchalant, so at odds with the heat of his gaze. "For now, I'll be satisfied if you call me Mark. And I wanted to ask if you'd…if you'd heard about the address I agreed to give tonight. I'm talking to the MCB."

"About chastity."

He nodded. "These days, I think I should deserve a medal for my restraint." He shook his head. "Come. Let me see you home afterward. I thought…I thought you might want the company."

She'd warned him. She'd told him to take himself away. If he insisted on throwing himself, mothlike, into her flame, who was she to tell him no? It must have been her fate to ruin him, her destiny to lead him astray as surely as Guinevere had ever seduced Sir Lancelot.

"Yes," Jessica said softly. "I'll be there." The words sounded like blasphemy on her lips.

THAT EVENING, Mark noted, the church was filled well before the appointed time. There was nothing quite like the hum of whispers before one addressed a crowd. Before he started to speak, he could imagine anything happening. Riots could break out. Or, more likely, he might put everyone to sleep.

The rector had ceded the church this evening for the use of the MCB, the town hall being insufficient for the size of the crowd. The pews had filled up. It seemed as if everyone in the parish—in fact, everyone in every neighboring parish—had found their way here to attend the lecture that Tolliver had arranged, even on so short a notice.

Jessica sat near the front. They were beginning to accept her now. He liked that. No longer ostracized, she was seated next to Mrs. Metcalf.

But Mark still could not help but noticing that the nearest man to her was three feet away. The nearest man, that was, excepting Mr. Lewis, who sat next to her. Jessica looked straight ahead, her face blank, as the rector spoke to her. He couldn't hear a word, but he seemed to be lecturing her. Jessica was accepted but not trusted. It made him ache inside. He wanted her to have more than that.

The very front rows were taken up by young, male faces—eager, eyes shining, intent on hearing Mark's words. They sported the blue armbands that designated them members of the MCB. The armbands, he'd once been told, were for indoor use, when hats—and their cockades—were not allowed. James Tolliver stood to Mark's immediate right, and as the crowd finally found their places, he motioned for silence. It took very little time.

"Our guest tonight needs no introduction," Tolliver began. "We are all familiar with the great, the magnificent, the inestimable Sir Mark."

Mark wanted to bury his head in his hands. Magnificent? Inestimable? He'd have preferred less effusive praise—"decent" was all he strove for, and considering how close matters had come with Jessica over the past week, he didn't even merit that any longer. The thought should have made him feel guilty.

"Sir Mark, as you all know, is the author of that famous tome, *A Gentleman's Practical Guide to*

Chastity. We here in Shepton Mallet are familiar with every sentence in that holy book."

Holy? Mark imagined hitting Tolliver with the oversize prayer book that lay open on the podium before him.

"We have memorized its every commandment," Tolliver intoned. "We have committed its advice to memory."

They had made membership cards distorting said advice. It was a book, a human-written one, not deified advice engraved on stone tablets.

Tolliver continued, solemnly. "We have adopted its creed as our own—as members of the Malc Chastity Brigade—and, having solemnly sworn ourselves to righteousness, we have learned to cast out temptation. Wherever we may find it."

Mark thought of Jessica, and the way they'd cast her out at first. His fists curled.

"Tonight," Tolliver said, "Sir Mark will address us, and tell us how best to keep to chastity. I, for one, plan to listen."

Applause rang out, accompanied by cheers. Mark's thoughts churned.

He couldn't count the people who had turned out to see him. Several hundred, at least. If it was the entire parish, it might have been *thousands.* Mark had delivered lectures before. He never enjoyed the prospect. The only thing worse than being forced to make idle conversation with one person was to have to address hundreds. The crowd's expectant stares stabbed into him like a hundred tiny knives.

They always expected him to be some kind of extraordinary orator. In truth, he usually managed to be an indifferent one. He'd prepared his usual remarks for tonight, a summary of a few important points he'd made in his book, followed by a plea to remember that he was just a regular man and not some kind of a saint.

The first few times he'd mouthed the latter sentiments, he had waited for the disappointed buzz. Perhaps he'd secretly hoped that someone would stand up and say, "He's right! Did you hear what he just said? Sir Mark is a horrible fraud—why on earth have we been listening to him?"

There would be riots. The papers would turn on him as quickly as they'd taken his side, and in a few months, everyone would have forgotten him and turned their inexplicable zeal toward some more worthy object.

But the more he protested his ordinary nature, the greater the adulation. They acted as if he spoke out of some misguided, foolish humility, instead of simply giving him credit for speaking the truth. He could have announced that he had formed a financial partnership with Lucifer himself, and they would have crowded about him afterward, praising him for his business acumen. They'd have patted him on the shoulder and, when told that he had an interest in their souls, would have swooned because the great Sir Mark had taken notice.

His gaze drifted to Jessica again. He could do no wrong. Up until he'd interceded on her behalf, they'd thought she could do no right. They both commanded attention—one for praise, the other for censure. And yet Mark was certain that *he* had been the one who had cupped his hand around her breast when last he saw her. *He* had been the one to take her mouth in a kiss. And he was the one standing before a crowd now to talk about chastity when his thoughts over the past week had been increasingly obscene.

It seemed an unbridgeable gap between them, that disparity. And then he saw the rector beside her. She was wearing an evening gown, perfectly respectable for a lecture given at night. Respectable...but creamy curves peeped from behind the lacy décolletage. The rector turned his head so he could look down her bodice ever so discreetly. And like that, Mark's carefully planned, dull speech disappeared from his mind.

"Good evening." His voice carried. The murmurs ceased instantly, and the crowd leaned forward. "Normally," he heard himself say, "I would tell you all that I am just a man—not anyone special, not anyone to listen to. Normally, I'd admit to my fair share of hypocrisy. And have no doubt about it. I am a hypocrite. But for now, I'd like to set that aside. There are worse hypocrites in the room.

"For instance," Mark said, sweeping his gaze over the blue-arm-banded boys who sat in self-satisfied honor in the front of the room, "the members of the MCB are the biggest lot of liars I have ever met."

There was a pained silence at that—as if several hundred people had suddenly forgotten how to breathe.

Mark glared at Tolliver beside him. "You claim that you've committed my book to memory, but as far as I can tell, you haven't bothered to read a single word. At least, I must presume you haven't, because the MCB has failed to understand the central message. Let me start by revealing your secrets."

He made the hand signal Tolliver had showed him at the picnic earlier. "That is not a signal that appears in *A Gentleman's Guide*. Not anywhere. And yet I was told that it is a warning. A signal that men might use, to let each other know that a woman is dangerous."

Tolliver's nose crinkled, and he frowned at Mark.

"The import of the whispered accusations, those sly hand signals, is that a man who has been unchaste is a man in need of saving, and he can redeem himself by a renewed adherence to principle.

A woman, however, who makes a mistake—well, she is unclean, and must be forever cast from good society."

A few fans rose at this and worked the air furiously.

"I don't blame any of you," Mark said. "It's not as if you could learn proper conduct from a rector who sees nothing wrong with manhandling a woman, simply because he thinks that nobody will notice."

Across the distance, Jessica lifted her eyes to his. She smiled faintly, but her eyes were still sad. The rector started, his chin lifting suddenly, as he pulled his eyes from her bosom. *Good.*

"And so," Mark continued, "I will explain this to you, since you seem to never have heard the concept. There is no such thing as a dangerous woman. If a woman makes you want to lose your head and forget what is right, it is *you* who are dangerous—to yourself, and even more possibly, to the woman in question. I simply do not believe that any of you who claim to hold me in adulation could have read my book, if you do not understand that basic principle."

He was caught on the tide of his fury now. For once, he felt no need to restrain his temper.

"There are no unchaste women, or profligate men." He set his hands on the podium. "There are no saints. None of you men want to hear me say that. After all, if it's not a woman who's led you astray, you've gone down the wrong path all on your own. If I am just an ordinary man, it means that chastity is attainable for everyone. It means that you are all responsible for your own mistakes, that you must own up to the wrong you have done without laying the blame on anyone else's doorstep. It means you can never hold a woman scapegoat for your shortcomings again, not even if she is pretty and lively and intelligent."

Jessica had not taken her eyes from him. They were wide and luminous—and still sad.

"When you make the secret hand signal that suggests that a woman is dangerous, you do not prove yourself strong. You prove yourself weak. What kind of man hides his weaknesses behind a woman? What kind of man places the blame on someone else, rather than admit that he is fallible? And so, yes, I don't think much of the lot of you right now. I think you're a pack of cowards and cheats."

Jessica's mouth was ajar. Had nobody ever taken her side, then? Who had ever stood as her advocate? Who had defended her? An emotion besides rage presented itself—something cold and prickly, rising up from the depths of him.

"There is one other basic concept that I think you have failed to comprehend," Mark said. "If you think that women are your nemesis in some struggle for your soul…well. You've bungled everything. Completely."

Mark met her gaze and delivered the next words for her and her alone.

"Women are the point of chastity, not the enemy of it. You should hold to chastity not because you fear what your cohort will say, but because when you indulge your own lusts, the woman you indulge them with is hurt. She is the one who will weather the censure of society. She is the one on whom the burden and expense of an unanticipated pregnancy will fall. She is the one who will be cast out. Men? Men will survive the temporary opprobrium of society. Only an unfeeling cad ignores the plight created by his passing desire. Only a juvenile lets the weight of his actions fall on someone else, and then blames her for his own weakness."

The crowd had disappeared from his vision. He could see no one but Jessica, could think of no one but her. She watched him like a stone statue, her cheeks marble.

"I know what integrity looks like," Mark said. "A person with integrity takes responsibility for his own failings. And I respect and admire *that* more than any number of false protestations of honor."

If he'd not known better, he'd have thought her on the verge of tears. He looked away. Proud as she was, he didn't think she'd want him to see it.

"And so when you say a woman has caused your downfall?" Mark swept his gaze back to the members of the MCB. "You're acting like a pack of irresponsible infants."

Tolliver actually cringed under Mark's glare. And for the first time since Mark, swept up in his rage, had begun to speak, cold reality asserted itself. He'd truly let his anger get the better of him. He'd called them all cowards and babies, as if he were the worst sort of hellfire pulpit-thumping preacher.

But thinking of Jessica, sitting isolated and scarcely tolerated, infuriated him. He couldn't even feel a mild regret.

What was left?

"There," he said, brushing his hands together as if he were Pontius Pilate disclaiming all responsibility. "I'm done with you."

He began to walk away. For his first three steps, there was silence. Then the crowd surged to its feet, applauding, shrieking wildly.

He couldn't believe it. "Are you mad?" he protested aloud. "I just called you all fainthearted infants!"

But they didn't hear him, not over the whistled accolades. It hadn't done any good—they still sprang from their places as he tried to escape, slapping his back, *thanking* him—-even though he'd done his best to make them hate him.

"Brilliant speech, Sir Mark!" Tolliver was saying.

"Such heartfelt conviction!"

"I feel inspired," someone was saying by his elbow. "Truly inspired to live a righteous life."

"Everyone loved it." That was Tolliver again. "Except, um, Mr. Lewis. I think he's looking a bit angry. And Mrs. Farleigh—she's leaving already."

Mark turned toward the exit. In this crowd, he could scarcely see more than elbows and hats, wide sleeves and cloaks being claimed in the entrance. But he didn't need to see more than her elbow— more than the tip of her finger—to recognize her.

She was leaving. After all that, she was *leaving* without saying a single word to him.

"Tolliver," Mark said, "do me a favor, there's a good lad. Tackle anyone who tries to stop me."

"What, sir?"

But there was no time to explain. Mark shoved through the crowd after her. Not a chance he'd let her go, not now.

CHAPTER FOURTEEN

"JESSICA!"

She didn't want to turn, especially not at the sound of his voice. She didn't want to look at him, didn't want to have to sort through the confused welter of emotions that coursed through her.

But his footfalls pounded on the dirt road behind her. He must have run clear from the center of town.

"Jessica," he repeated as he came up to her.

"Sir Mark. I told you not to make a romance of me. You…you are the dearest *idiot*."

He didn't flinch. "Is that what you think I'm doing, then? Seeing some idealized version of you? Didn't you hear a word I just said? It's not about *you*."

"No? Then you must have been making a champion of yourself."

"Jessica."

"I'd quite forgot," she said, "you *are* a knight, are you not? I suppose it shouldn't surprise me that you occasionally play the part."

He shook his head and rubbed at one eye. "Are you yelling at me because I *like* you?"

"Yes!"

"Well, get used to it," he shot back. "Because I can't get you out of my mind. I think of you all the time. And you can't shout loud enough to make me stop."

"Would you care to place a wager?"

"Just go ahead and try," he said coldly, rummaging in his pockets. "Here." He pulled out his fob watch, flicked the gold face open. "It's three past eight. Now go on. Scream as loudly as you like. Don't mind me. I'll just stand here and keep time until you're bored."

He didn't need to tell her about the ticking of time. She had two days to seduce him, and she couldn't bear to do it any longer. He stared back, tapping his foot. And it was only then that the utter, impossible ridiculousness of it swept over her and she began to laugh. He was by her side in a trice, his arms around her. Her shoulders shook. She wasn't sure if she was laughing or crying until his hand ran down her head.

"There now," he said. "Has it really been so long since someone took your side?"

"It's been ages. Too long for me to remember." It had long ago ceased to be a matter of *if* she would have to rely on herself—just how much it would sting when her legs were kicked out from under her.

After they left the buildings behind them, she took a deep breath.

"Sir Mark. What you said at the meeting to-night—it struck me." That didn't describe what she'd felt. He'd looked like an avenging archangel, ready to rain fire and brimstone down on the men around him.

"You don't say." His tone was dry.

"Why have you chosen to champion male chastity? Why not focus on—oh, the Corn Laws or suffrage or education? There are myriad social causes you could champion. Most of them are easier than the one you've chosen."

"Well." He slanted her a look. "When men are unchaste, women bear the burden. You see—"

She moved in front of him swiftly, and he stopped. She raised one hand to his mouth, touching his lips. Cutting off those words, before he could speak them. His breath wafted through the knit of her gloves.

"No," she said. "I don't want to hear the theory. I've read your book. But when you spoke today… A man doesn't get so angry about something unless it's personal. I am not asking why *someone* should be chaste. I am asking why *you* in particular have dedicated so much of your life to the pursuit."

He stared at her. No warm breath touched her fingers.

Slowly, she pulled her hand away, wondering if he was about to denounce her.

Instead, he shook his head. "You know, nobody has ever asked me that question before. Not even my brothers."

"I have always been particularly impertinent."

Mark met her eyes again. There was nothing importunate about his gaze—no ogling, no sense that he was measuring her for his bed. Still, she saw in him a fierce, possessive hunger. "Impertinence suits you," he finally said and held out his arm for her. She took it once more, and they began walking again.

He said nothing more for a few minutes, but by the tense jump of the muscles in his arm, she could tell that he'd not forgotten her query.

"It was my mother," he finally told her.

"I've heard of your mother. People talk of her sometimes."

His tone grew warier. "What have you heard?"

"She was a generous, godly woman." Jessica didn't want to say much more. Men reacted strangely when you criticized their mothers—even if they'd just done it themselves.

"Ha. Surely the gossips have told you more than that."

"She was a mill owner's wife. I heard that when

your father passed away, she grieved. And that in her grief, she became a little…strange."

"She went mad."

Jessica nodded in acquiescence. "It must have been difficult, to have a mother so overtaken with sadness—"

"She didn't go mad with grief," Mark interrupted. "She hated my father. She was always quite religious—extraordinarily so. He, in turn, scarcely cared to attend service. That alone wouldn't have done the trick. But he was not faithful to her. She got the notion in her head that he'd forced the women who'd worked in his mill years before to whore for him in exchange for a position. And that when they complained, he brought in laborsaving machinery, so he could sack the ones who caused the unrest."

"Oh."

"She wasn't entirely wrong about that," he added. "A handful, certainly. All of them? No. But she had this notion that our entire family wealth was built on his debauchery. She began to see sin everywhere. She began to hate money, to hate everything that reminded her of him. If she saw a woman on the streets, she instantly believed her to be a victim of my father's profligacy. She began to sell…at first, just *things*. Then she started to give away the respectable competence my father had left. When my sister fell ill, she refused to pay a physician, saying it was God's will whether she lived or died."

The sun was setting. It hung, red and warm at the edge of the field. It painted his cheeks in orange, his hair in rust.

"She died. I scarcely remember that. I was still young at the time. But I think my mother took her death as a sign of God's judgment. After that, she became very strange indeed. Soon, very little remained of the legacy my father had left. Very little except my brothers. Have I mentioned that my brothers look a great deal like my father? That didn't help. I take after her more. So she beat them, and took *me* along with her on her errands of mercy. I met the poor, the weak, the afflicted."

"She was mad."

"I know," he said quietly. "But...underneath that insanity, there was a core of truth to everything she said. I've seen the ones who are destroyed in the wake of profligacy. The man takes his pleasure, and women and children suffer. My mother most of all. I don't know what she would have been like if he'd been faithful. She never would have been comfortable, I don't think, but at least she might not have tried—"

He caught himself and stared off into the distance, his shoulders pinched together. He looked miserable, so lost in memory.

"Ah," she said softly. "Is that all, then?" She'd

meant to interrupt his grim reverie, to put a soft smile on his face. Instead he looked at her, his eyes haunted.

"No," he said softly. "It is not." He turned from her and began to walk down the path again.

She followed.

"She nearly killed my brother, Smite. It was a…a matter of punishment and neglect. Not intentional, I don't think. But she'd gone so far beyond rationality. She put him in the cellar and hid the key from me. Ash had been in India at that time, and we'd gotten word that he'd be coming home soon. When I managed to get Smite out, we walked the thirty miles to Bristol to wait for him."

He wasn't looking at her, but when she put her hand on his arm, his fingers closed around hers.

"We waited three months. We ran out of the shillings we'd taken within the first month. We spent the next two months on the streets. I don't know if you can understand what it means to be starving—not merely hungry, nor even famished, but slowly *starving*. You stop caring about anything except food—not laws, not manners, not right nor wrong. The world disappears, until there is nothing but you and the constant struggle to put something—*anything*—in your belly."

She'd never got to that point. She'd never come near. All she could do was listen in horror.

Mark didn't look at her. "At least," he said, "that

was how it felt to me. My brother, now…Smite would have fed his last scrap to a hungry cat. He had no sense of self-preservation, not even when matters were at their worst. We hid in an alley one evening. I woke in the middle of the night, to see a woman walking through the gloom. She didn't see me. There was a pile of refuse in the back of the alley—moldering bits of food that even I would not have tried to eat, discarded fabric that had worn so thin it was little more than a collection of threads—that sort of stuff. She set a bundle on the heap, and then, without looking back, walked away."

Jessica felt a pit in her stomach. She could feel her hands start to shake. She knew what was coming. In the wretched sisterhood of whores and courtesans, there were some things that never changed.

"I went," he said. "I looked. Of course I looked. But the bundle was an infant—tiny and red. It could not have been more than a few hours old."

He paused. The sun had disappeared beneath the horizon; only a ring of red painted the hills.

"Even starved, homeless and desperate, I knew what the right thing to do was. As little as my brother and I had, we had more than this wretch. We could have done *something*. And knowing Smite, he would have done it." His hand balled into a fist. "I knew the right thing to do. And I also knew that if I picked that child up, my brother would not let it starve—even if it meant that we would. And so I walked away. And I didn't tell him."

He stared off into the twilight.

"You cannot blame yourself for that. How old were you?"

"Old enough to know right from wrong."

"Fourteen? Fifteen?"

"Ten."

She balled her hand and brought it to her mouth. Ten years old and starving on the streets.

"Ash arrived that afternoon. I insisted that we go back, but the infant was gone by then."

"You were ten. You had nothing. And in any event, that baby needed a wet nurse, not your left-over scraps."

He said nothing in response.

"While we're at it, the reason it was gone was probably that someone else found it and brought it to the parish."

"But *I* didn't. Every time I have been tempted to sin since—and I have been tempted a thousand times since—I have remembered that discarded, unwanted bundle of humanity. I think of the woman who left her newborn child in an alley. But mostly, I think about how alone she was. I think about the man who was not there in that alley at all. I am not going to be him."

Her hand was on his elbow. She let it slide down

his forearm until his hand engulfed hers, warm and alive.

"I see," she said. He'd earned his knighthood years ago.

His grip tightened around hers. "That's what I mean when I say I'm not a saint."

"You're a good deal better, Sir Mark."

He reached with his free hand and caught her other elbow. Their fingers twisted together. In the fast-fading light, his expression was shadowed. "No."

"Yes."

"I meant—no. After what I've told you, I had better be just Mark to you. Only Mark."

"You will never be *only* Mark to me," she said fiercely. "Not in a thousand years. You're—you're—"

"What, just because I know a little thing like chastity would make the world a better place? I've said nothing that every woman does not already know. Tell me, Mrs. Farleigh—if your Mr. Farleigh had kept to the laws of chastity, what would your life be like now?"

There was no Mr. Farleigh. There never had been. But there had been a man, once…

She shut her eyes. "He seduced me," she finally said. "At that age, I didn't think. Or if I did, I believed I was indomitable. When you're young, nothing can ever go wrong. Bad things happen to other people—people far less clever, and far uglier—than I was. The rules of propriety existed for stupid, unlucky girls."

She swallowed. "I thought nothing would ever happen to me. Until it did. He kissed me, and I didn't think about chastity or right or wrong. I didn't think about the consequences, or what effect my choice would have on my parents or my sisters. Before I knew it, I was compromised so thoroughly that my family wouldn't have me in the house. It *did* happen to me, and I *was* the stupid girl."

His hand twisted in hers, slipping, caressing her palm through her glove, her wrist. Then his fingers found the edge of her glove. Slowly, he stripped it off, baring her hand to the cool night air. To his touch. Skin slid against skin.

"I've been miserable ever since," she finished.

"How old were you?"

"Fourteen."

He didn't say anything to that, just drew her closer, pulling her hand, leading her as if in a dance until she stood inches from him.

His other hand moved to her chin and tipped it up.

"Jessica," he said gravely, "I will be your champion, if you let me. If I have to take on the role of knight, I want to be yours. Let me be your protector."

The words sent a flurry of confusion through her. "You're offering to be my *protector?* You'll get no honor from association with me."

In response, he kissed her. Not a short, chaste kiss. Not even a long, lingering kiss, sweet and yet still chaste. No. It was heat. It was fire. It was everything he'd been holding back. His body pressed against hers, hard, leaving no secrets. His mouth took hers without question.

She dissolved in his touch, disappeared as his hands cupped her face, pulling her closer still. Not chastity, this, but an invitation. A prelude to sin and scandal. It made no sense, not with what he'd just told her.

"Hang honor," he whispered, pulling away to breathe kisses against her neck. "Hang my reputation. I don't care what the world thinks of me."

He pressed against her once more. His words were as drugging as his kiss, threatening to overwhelm her.

She set her hands on his chest and pushed away. "You can't mean it. You've lost your head over a kiss. You can't mean that you'd give up fame, your prestige, your rank in society—"

"It will hardly be so dire. But yes, Jessica. If that's what it means to have you." He sighed, blew out his breath. "I'm getting rather ahead of myself." His voice was rough. "I...I'd like a chance to do this properly. Might I call on you tomorrow evening?" His voice dropped. "Alone."

Tomorrow evening. She'd have precisely one day to ruin him, then. How…how convenient.

Yes, Sir Mark. I'll ruin you.

Yes, Sir Mark. I'll meet you alone and take you to bed.

Yes, Sir Mark. I'll steal your honor and your good name, and trade it for thirty pieces of silver.

"Don't freeze up on me. I've been thinking of nothing other than you for days. Nights, too."

Oh, yes. She'd won. But this wasn't the victory she'd hoped for when she first came up with this plan. She needed it to be strictly lust that drove him to her bed, not this quiet consideration. She wanted her own emotion to be calm and disengaged. She wanted his surrender to be nothing but the cold, clinical slide of male into female.

There was nothing clinical about the touch of his hand on her face. It wasn't lust that had her sipping the air he breathed. And it wasn't just her body he wanted.

You are not alone. Let me be your protector.

Victory was bitter. It *hurt*.

She looked up into his eyes. *There's an odd sort of integrity to you.*

He was wrong. He was *so* wrong. Still, what was she to do? If she walked away from him now, she'd have nothing. If she did this to him…

But what choice did she have? Nothing awaited her in London but more debts, more dishonor. She couldn't do this to him, but she couldn't go back to London, couldn't resume her old life. She just couldn't.

No, Jessica. If you can survive Amalie's death, you can survive this, too.

"Jessica?" His hand touched her cheek. "I want this. I want *you.*"

It would utterly damn her to destroy the trust of the only good man she'd ever met. But then, she was already damned. If she was going to be hanged for a lamb, she might as well be hanged for the entire flock.

"Yes, Mark," she said softly. "You may call on me. Shall we say seven in the evening? I'll make sure we're alone."

He nodded briefly and then leaned in and touched her lips once more with his. The contact was quick, warm—and yet it felt like a death knell, sealing her fate.

She was going to ruin him. She only prayed that she didn't destroy herself in the process.

JESSICA HAD HOPED Mark would change his mind. Instead, he brought her flowers. He'd even picked them himself—a riotous mess of cow parsley and lilies. She could almost hear her heart crack when he handed the bouquet over.

While she found a container to put them in, he removed his hat and gloves. He held them in his hands, turning them about uneasily before setting them in a heap on a side table. It was the first time he'd seemed visibly uncomfortable.

"You're nervous," she remarked. "Don't be."

He smiled faintly. "I'm still unsure of my reception."

She raised one eyebrow. "Truly, Mark?"

His smile flickered, fading into resolve. His chin rose. And he took a step toward her. But he didn't take her in his arms. He didn't press his body full-length against hers. He didn't even press a kiss on her. Instead, he took her hands in his. His fingers were warm and smooth.

And then, to her horror, he sank to one knee in front of her. He fumbled with the ring on his finger and slipped it into her waiting hand. "Jessica," he said, his voice low, "will you do me the very great honor of granting me your hand in marriage?"

Her whole body went cold.

She hadn't ruined him. She'd thought herself prepared for the evening, but she hadn't expected this. Even if she'd never fallen—even if she'd been Jessica Carlisle, the virtuous vicar's daughter, Mark would have been miles above her station. He was a duke's *brother*. Queen Victoria had knighted him. She was nobody.

She didn't know what to do.

Say yes.

She wouldn't have to ruin him. He could obtain a special license in a few days with his brother's help. They could be married before the truth of her background was discovered. She would never have to sell herself again. She could have her freedom and Mark, too.

But there was a difference between ruining his reputation and ruining his life. The gossip she would stir up by seducing him would blacken his name for months, but it would pass. Entrapping him into marriage? She'd be robbing him of all chance of future happiness under a cloud of lies. And that would be a lie she couldn't escape, if she were bound to him—not with any amount of money.

She couldn't do that to him. She couldn't do that to herself.

"Jessica, darling," Mark said, still on one knee, "you have to say yes before I can kiss you again."

She hadn't let herself think the words before. Love had seemed as futile an emotion as hope. What had been the point? But she knew it now. She loved him—loved that he would care so little for the difference in their stations, loved that she hadn't been able to seduce him from his principles after all.

But love was not gentle. Love was not kind. And love was furiously, powerfully jealous. She couldn't have him, and in just a few minutes, he wouldn't want her. Every good thing that touched her life had always been ripped away. And Mark had been more wonderful than...than everything she'd had since Amalie.

She pulled her hand from his. "Sir Mark—"

"Mark." His eyes clouded slightly.

"Sir Mark," she continued, "I didn't think you were coming here to offer *marriage*."

He frowned in puzzlement. "What else would I offer?"

She met his eyes. "You told me yesterday you wanted to be my protector. You said you wanted me."

"I did. I *do*." He pushed up off the floor, awkwardly coming to his feet. "Whatever is the matter?"

"*Protection* isn't synonymous with marriage. It's what a man offers his mistress."

He simply shook his head, still baffled. "Having never offered for a mistress, and having had no occasion to do so, I'm unfamiliar with the precise vocabulary. But, Jessica, I've been talking to you of marriage since the first day we walked to the Friar's Oven."

He had.

She'd noticed, too. Perhaps she shouldn't have been taken by surprise. But somewhere in her mind, after every one of his sentences, she'd appended a but. He told her he was making a promise, and her imagination whispered *but not that sort of promise.* He'd said she wasn't alone, and she'd heard an unspoken *for now.*

He'd flat out said he wanted to know her beyond the space of three dances, so he could determine if she was the sort of woman he would marry. But the notion that he would actually decide to marry her had never entered her mind. She wasn't the kind of woman men married. She knew that. Apparently, he didn't.

If she could go back to the beginning, start over by telling him the truth... No. There was no way to roll her past into a neat, honest ball. Her lies trailed behind her, hard and unflattering.

"I had no first marriage," she said, turning from him. She walked away, so he couldn't see the betraying liquid collect in the corner of her eyes.

"What was that?" She could hear him following after her, drawing close.

"You heard me correctly," she said to the whitewash on the wall. "I have never been married. Just ruined. Again and again and again. I've been lying to you from the start."

"Perhaps—that is—surely you had a good reason." A note of uncertainty crept into his voice. "A very good reason." He took a step toward her.

Stay away.

"I'm not a lady, down on her luck. I'm a courtesan. A whore. George Weston offered a bounty to any woman who seduced you, and I put myself forward for the task. I planned to announce the particulars to the *ton,* and to destroy your reputation." She swallowed her tears. Love was *angry,* furious that he could make her feel such dreadful *hope* again and rip it from her in the same breath. She turned to face him, her hands in fists. "I thought you'd come today to hand me my victory."

He had gone pale. Worse than pale; his eyes glittered, freezing, losing all the kindness she'd grown accustomed to seeing. "George Weston?" he repeated. "You kissed me because *George Weston* paid you to do it? What the devil does Weston have to do with any of this?"

"What does it matter? If you'd come here to take me to bed," she told him, "I would have betrayed you. I would have let you tumble me any way you wanted, every way you wanted, as much as you wanted. And then I would have written an account and sent it in to the papers."

"Ah." His voice was arctic. "I see. But—but didn't you— Surely you—" He swallowed. "No. I can't believe that you've been telling me lies this whole time."

It had been hard to tell him the truth. It was harder still to force her lips into the semblance of a smile, to let her eyes reflect nothing but smug satisfaction. She turned back to him. "Yes," she said, "I was very believable, wasn't I? I can't believe you ate up every word."

And, oh, how she wanted him to protest again.

Foolish, foolish hope. He looked at her with the tiniest curl to his lip, as if she were a snake polluting his garden and he was about to cast her out. "And here I thought that you'd overcome your initial distaste of me. Apparently I was wrong. You must have been laughing at me dreadfully, then, behind my back—mocking my lovesick ways—"

"Lovesick?" Her temper flared. "You don't know what love means. If you think you have been sick with love, you must never have had the influenza. You've held yourself back at every turn. Every time I provoked a passionate response from you, you drew away. And why did you do it, Sir Mark? Because you're not that kind of man. Because you wouldn't stoop to letting yourself *want*. Do not pretend that I have done anything other than hurt your pride, substantial as that is."

He stared at her grimly, his hand contracting at his side. "I would have forgiven almost anything—"

"Yes," she said. "And how lovely that would have been for me, ten years down the road. To know that my husband had condescended to *forgive* me. To know that he always thought himself above me, that my sins were always a blot on my record, one that I could never make up. That every day he woke up knowing that he was my superior. I wager it made you feel quite proud of yourself, knowing that you were good enough to stoop to my level."

His jaw set. But he didn't deny what she'd said.

"You know," she said, "I had some moral qualms about my role in this piece. It didn't seem right to me to use you so. But truly, Sir Mark, you could stand to be knocked into the dust once or twice. Then you might think twice about how magnanimous you are in *forgiving* me my sins."

"You have no idea." His voice was low. "You have no bloody idea where I've been. And you have no idea what I want—*wanted* of you."

Jessica raised her chin in the air. "I know enough to know that whatever it is you wanted, deep inside your skin, you'd never have let it out. Just as I know that as much as you'd like to smack me at this moment, you never will. No, Sir Mark. I do believe that whatever you might be feeling right now, you'll bottle it up with the rest of your sentiment. You've kept yourself in too much of a cage to let a whore like me truly overset you."

He took one step toward her. "By God. If you knew—"

She waved one hand in the air. "But I won't know, will I? You'll forget this all soon enough."

He stepped toward her, his eyes darkening from

furious to murderous. "Don't. Tell. Me." His hands landed on her shoulders. "Don't tell me what I'll forget." His grip tightened. Had he been any other man, she would have been frightened. But this was Mark; even now, his body gave the lie to the harshness of his tone. Her breath cycled in tune with the heave of his chest. His grip was firm, not hard.

"You," he said, "have absolutely no idea." And then his lips were on hers, pressing into her. Not just a kiss; nor even an embrace. His body pressed into hers. His skin was heated with passion; the hard ridge of his member pressed into her belly.

Love was angry. Love was hurt. And love would take anything it could get, even if it was his hands pushing her against the wall, his tongue slipping between her lips in furious anger. His hips grinding against hers. There was no love in his touch, none of the cherished sense of wonder she'd sensed in his kiss before. Just lust.

His head dipped. His teeth nipped down her neck. Jessica threw her head back and let him touch her.

I love you. Her hands found his elbows, cupped them.

He pulled away. "Print that in the paper," he said scornfully. "I'm sure Nigel Parret would love to see it. Print that you brought me to the last edge of desire, to the point where I could scarcely pull away from you."

"Sir Mark—"

"Print that I told you secrets I'd never dared to tell another soul." He raised his hand to her face, moving slowly, as if to touch her in farewell. "Print that you brought me to my knees, and that when you had me there, you laughed."

She didn't much feel like laughing. Jessica felt beyond tears—as if she'd killed something sweet and innocent. And she had—as she'd known she must. Everything good always failed. She'd known from the start that this—his regard, his goodwill— would not last past her unmasking.

"I—I had so little choice, Mark." Her hands fluttered. "I had to get away. I needed the money. It was this, or—"

He shook his head. "Or what? Participate in the ruin of a man who was *not* a willing dupe?"

She bowed her head. Her hands trembled, and she pressed them into her skirts. "You'll never have to see me again. I'll be gone by tomorrow." Although heaven knew where she would go now. Or what she would do.

"Don't bother." His voice was tight. "I'm leaving in the morning. I don't want to see you again, not ever." He stepped back from her.

She reached for him. But this time he flinched from her. Her hand dangled uselessly in midair, and she let out a covert breath. "Mark. Be well."

He gave her a jerk of a nod. And as if he hadn't

bid her farewell for life, he turned and grabbed his hat and gloves from the table. Without one backward glance, he stumbled through her doorway, and then he was gone, swallowed up by the coming evening.

He'd escaped her, and if it left her in an impossible situation…well, better her than him.

It was only when he was gone past all point of calling him back that she realized she was still holding his ring.

CHAPTER FIFTEEN

THE RAIN RAN DOWN Mark's face in slick tracks. He clutched his cloak to him, readjusted the lumpy satchel that lay warm against his side and knocked on the door.

The streets of Bristol had fallen into darkness; an oil lamp on the corner had not yet been lit by the lamplighter and only a sliver of the moon peeked out from behind a breath of ragged cloud. The satchel shifted against his ribs and then subsided before the door opened.

"Mark."

Of course Smite answered his own door. His older brother stood in the entry, barring his path. He stared for a few seconds before he turned. "Come in. Come in." He cast another glance at Mark's wet form. "I wasn't expecting you in this weather. Come to think of it, I wasn't expecting you at all."

Twenty-four hours ago, Mark had been so full of hope for his future. Now, he'd landed on his brother's doorstep. He hadn't been able to think of anywhere else to go. On the ride here—half on horseback, half by steam train—Mark had imagined himself telling the entire story to his brother a thousand times. Sometimes he'd raged; mostly, he'd been confused. But he couldn't imagine saying a word now. It was too humiliating, for one.

Mark handed off his wet things and then set the leather satchel he'd brought from Shepton Mallet on the wooden floor.

"Can I put that away for you?"

The bag wasn't twitching, which was a good sign.

"Never mind," his brother said. "You look like you need a drink. Never tell me she said no."

Why, oh, why had Mark committed his foolish, burbling hopes to a letter? And why had he sent it before he'd had a reply from her?

"Can we…can we *not* talk about that?"

It must have been obvious from his face that something was wrong, because instead of teasing him, his brother shrugged his shoulders. "Suit yourself."

Anyone else would have heard that airy dismissal as unkind or uncaring. But Mark had come here because he knew his brother would understand without Mark's having to say a single word on the subject. That was the way it was between them.

He had been to Smite's home before. Any other

man in his brother's financial position would have set himself up in high style—a home crowded with servants eager to do his bidding. Smite, of course, eschewed all of that. He'd been branded by their mother in a way that Mark scarcely comprehended and could never explain to anyone else. Smite was too proud to admit to the difficulties under which he labored. Not even to servants.

They didn't ask each other for anything. Perhaps that was why Mark felt comfortable giving his brother everything.

"Your satchel. It's moving," Smite said.

"Oh, good. That means your gift is awake."

"A gift?" His brother stepped back, suddenly wary.

Mark felt a rush of affection. Only Smite would quail at the thought of a gift. "Yes, a gift," he said. "A good one." He knelt beside the satchel and unbuckled the heavy, oiled leather. He'd shielded it with his cloak through the worst of the rainstorm, and the satchel was dry inside. Still, a rough wetness swiped his fingers as he reached in.

"Here." He pulled out the bundle—it was wriggling, and that made it feel twice as heavy—and held it out.

Smite simply stared at him. "Dear God," he said finally. "What is that thing?"

"Somewhere in the furthest reaches of your voluminous memory, you will recall seeing similar creatures."

"Yes," Smite said, gingerly extending a finger. "Perhaps. Somewhat similar creatures. But in all my prior experience, I have generally encountered puppies that have…eyes. Not great mounds of fur, topped by a big black nose." He parted the gray fur on its head, almost tentatively. "Good Lord. There are eyes in there after all."

Mark thrust the bundle out; Smite took it, his face a pattern of bemusement. "What sort is it?"

It was all long fur, gray everywhere except the white of its feet and chest. "It's the progeny of the most capable sheepdog in all of Somerset. But don't think you need to rush out and purchase a flock. The owner tested it for herding instinct. Apparently, it failed utterly, thinking it much more interesting to turn up grass."

"Hmm." Smite set the animal down, where it stood on clumsy legs. "And I suppose you thought I needed a puppy to dribble on the floor? You imagined I wanted a beast that would demand to be taken on great circuits of the surrounding areas? You wanted to make me a slave to sticks thrown and sticks fetched? Have you any notion how much *work* a dog is?" His words were harsh, but his tone was light, and he gently caressed the little dog, who immediately sank its teeth into his cuff. Smite tried to pull his hand back, but the dog dug its claws in and growled in mock play. "Don't tell me. This is all part of a clever plan to see my shoes chewed to bits."

"Not in the least," Mark informed him. "I didn't think you needed a dog. I thought the dog needed you."

Smite looked up, his expression momentarily stricken. He looked down at the dog. "Thank you," he said quietly. It was the only acknowledgment Mark was likely to get from him.

Gently, his brother disentangled the dog's teeth from his coat. "Cease that behavior, Ghost," he admonished. "Here—you may chew on this instead."

Mark clouted him on the shoulder. "That's my satchel, you buffoon."

Smite didn't answer, and when the pup grabbed one end of the strap and pulled clumsily, a smile lit his face. "Good dog."

It was almost an hour later—after the dog had been taken outside twice, and then fed remnants of chicken, had a ball of rags constructed and rolled on the floor, and a box found for it and lined with blankets—before Smite looked over at Mark. "In the normal course of things," he said, "I would send you out to a hotel, where you might be comfortable. I assume that's not a good idea tonight."

Mark had almost forgotten it. But with those words, the past few weeks crashed in on him. He'd been certain that Jessica was the one, right up until he'd had the numbing realization that she most decidedly wasn't. It hurt all over again.

"Probably not," Mark said, aiming for nonchalance. "It's nothing. Don't worry about it."

"Hmm." Smite tucked the edge of a rag into the ball. "You told me she was gorgeous and intelligent. I presume she's virtuous, too. If she has any brains at all, I can't imagine what the problem could be. Don't tell me her parents don't approve. Just get Ash to charm some sense into them."

"Not you, too." Mark put his head in his hands. "Why does everyone think that my dearest wish is to have some innocent little wisp of a virgin?"

"I can't imagine," Smite said dryly. "It couldn't be because you wrote a book about chastity."

Sarcasm. It flowed between them as naturally as breathing. He needed that, now—something familiar to grab on to, something besides anger and some deep, dark, cavernous want.

"It turns out George Weston hired her to seduce me. She's actually a courtesan. Can we talk of something else?"

"You asked a courtesan to marry you?"

"Just be quiet about it already."

Smite was silent for a while longer. "Do you care for her?" he finally asked.

"I asked her to marry me. What do you suppose?"

"That answer goes to whether you cared for her

in the past. I did not ask you that question. I asked you whether you care for her *now*. In the present."

"I don't know. How could I? I was utterly misled. How could I have been so *wrong* about her?"

His brother leaned forward and set his hand on Mark's shoulder.

"That's simple," Smite said. His voice was low and soothing, the gentle brush of his fingers comforting.

Smite was not one to indulge in physical affection. He froze when Mark embraced him, shied away from all contact beyond a handshake. Mark could hardly blame him, under the circumstances. And so if Smite thought it necessary to touch him in comfort, he must be in a bad way indeed.

He'd always wanted to protect *Smite* from this. For all that his brother was the elder, they'd been forged in the same place—Smite the anvil, Mark the hammer. They'd come to blows often enough when they were younger. But when it had come down to it, they'd faced the fire together.

Perhaps his brother was right, and it was a simple case. Just clouded judgment.

But, oh, how his judgment had clouded. He'd wanted her, yes—but he'd wanted other women before. He knew what mere physical want felt like. With Jessica… He'd wanted *her*. He'd wanted to win her regard. And he'd thought that she'd seen him, really seen him, both bad and good. This was so much more than a simple rejection. He'd wanted to know her, not just her body, but her entire self.

She'd not wanted to know him at all.

"I wish it were simple."

"It *is* simple," his brother corrected. "I know precisely why you were wrong about her."

"You do?"

"Yes." Smite patted his shoulder. "It's because you're an idiot."

That won a weak chuckle, but at least it was real. So. There was hope after Jessica. It only *felt* as if he was being torn to pieces. He would survive.

"Probably," he admitted. "But you know—it runs in the family."

THE CARD THAT Jessica had saved directed her to the middle floor of a Cheapside flat. A young maid-of-all-work let her in and deposited her in a faded parlor. The white of the walls had gone to yellow, and the brown of the upholstery had bleached to sand. Even the wood of the furniture seemed muted. Jessica sat on a chair, as directed; it squeaked ominously, even under so slight a weight as hers.

Jessica was *tired*. After Mark had left, she and her maid had spent the night packing frantically so that Jessica and her trunks could be loaded onto a dogcart in time to reach the railway station at

Bath. The train had been delayed, though, and she'd stayed on the smoky platform two hours.

Her last few coins had paid passage for herself and Marie. When they'd arrived in London, she'd scrawled a note to her solicitor, advising him to give the girl enough to survive on and a reference. Jessica, after all, would soon have no need for a maid.

Her muscles ached from the train ride. She'd not thought it would be so strenuous to simply *sit* in one place—but the car had rocked back and forth in an ungentle, insistent rhythm, and the strangeness of the noise had kept her from nodding off. It had given her time to think. By the time she'd reached London, she had known how to proceed.

She was going to do what she always did. She was going to survive.

The curtains in Mr. Parret's room were thrown back to show a dark London street. Maybe it was not the room that was muted. Maybe it was her.

"Oh, my."

Jessica turned at the words. A young girl stood behind her, one hand on the door frame.

"Are you a lady?" the child asked.

The girl was undoubtedly Parret's offspring. On her, those weedy features had muted into delicate femininity. Nigel Parret hadn't been lying about having a beautiful daughter.

"No," Jessica said, "I'm not a lady."

The girl's eyes widened, and she took a step forward. "But you cannot be a *gentleman!*" she exclaimed. "And you don't look like a maid."

The girl was maybe four years of age— a bit younger than Jessica's sister, Ellen, had been when Jessica left home. Clearly not of an age to learn the various sordid distinctions among women.

"Belinda!" Mr. Parret's voice interrupted from the hall. "Sweetheart, where is your governess? How many times must I tell you, you're not to disturb my guests?"

"Miss Horace fell asleep."

Parret turned the corner and lifted his daughter into his arms. "Very well, then. I'll just—"

He stopped, looking at Jessica. "Ah," he said, the good cheer vanishing from his voice. "You. *You're* the one who had me sent out of Shepton Mallet. You've cost me a pretty penny, you know. *Reporteress.*"

Perhaps that was what she'd become, over the course of one train ride. A reporteress. Jessica simply inclined her head to him.

"I *knew* it." Parret's arms clasped his daughter, and he half turned from Jessica, as if to shield young Belinda from the horror of a woman with a vocation. "Have you come to gloat, then? You had the exclusive interview. These last days, since Sir Mark tossed me out on my ear, I've had precious little to write about. I suppose you're very happy indeed."

"No, I'm not happy," Jessica said. "But it happens that I came to sell you a story. I've written it partway already."

"Oh, and now you'll come crawling to me." He snorted. "And why should I do business with you?"

"Because otherwise I shall go to your competitors. They haven't your reputation for the truth, but in a pinch—"

"Go! Why should I care?"

In response, Jessica reached up and undid the simple chain at her neck. The unwieldy pendant that hung on its end emerged from between her breasts. She set it atop the papers she'd brought.

Mr. Parret stared at the item she'd placed in front of him.

It was, of course, Mark's ring. The onyx in its center winked up at her.

Slowly, Mr. Parret set his daughter on the floor. "Belinda," he said quietly, "go find your governess."

"But I want to hear about the lady."

"Go. Now."

He waited until she'd disappeared. Then he walked forward, slowly, and picked up the ring. He dangled it from its chain, turning it from side to side. "Well," he said softly. "One of the complexions that could be put on the matter I observed in

Shepton Mallet was…precisely this. I didn't want to think it. After all, I don't want to ruin Sir Mark's reputation."

No. Jessica had thought long and hard about her options. There were only so many ways she could find money, and she wasn't going to—she *couldn't*—sell herself again. But even if she wasn't selling her body, she could still sell her integrity.

You have an odd sort of integrity to you, he'd told her once. Maybe…maybe after this was all said and done, she could have her security and her integrity, all at the same time.

"I think," Parret said, settling into a chair, "that you need to tell me your tale."

Jessica took a deep breath. "It began," she said, "when I met Sir Mark in Shepton Mallet. I had come there, you see, with the express purpose of seducing him…" The story she conveyed was *mostly* truthful. It required only a few alterations to change the entire tenor of it. She spoke, and Parret listened, nodding intently. When she was done, he picked up the pages she'd scrawled that morning and read through them.

"You write well," he said in surprised tones, as he turned over the first page.

"For a courtesan, you mean?"

"For a woman." He spoke absently, his fingers drumming against the table. He turned another page. "For that matter," he said, "you write well for a man."

Jessica searched for an appropriate response. Her mind covered everything from sarcasm to outrage. Finally, she settled on the simplest reaction. "Thank you," she said graciously.

When Parret reached the end, he looked up. His mouth was set in a grim line beneath the ragged line of his mustache. "I don't think this will work," he told her.

"Then I'll have to take it to your competitors." She tried not to hide her disappointment. She'd hoped that Parret would be able to give her enough to survive—enough that she wouldn't have to think of money for a good long while yet.

Parret scowled. "Oh, not the piece," he explained. "I meant that we can't call you a courtesan. It's too risqué. Why don't we call you a 'fallen woman' instead, and leave the precise circumstances of the fall a mystery? That way, the public will be free to imagine anything they wish."

Jessica took a staggering breath of relief.

"Of course," Parret continued, "I can offer you my normal rates—a shilling per column inch. It's a fair offer—what I would give a man under the circumstances."

Jessica almost smiled. "My dear sir," she said, "you must be *joking*. No man could possibly have told this story. We are talking about the most incendiary article that London has seen in years. You can't fob me off with a few shillings. This isn't piecework. I want fifty percent of the proceeds."

His eyes narrowed. "All the expense of production is mine, and all the risk. Two pounds, no more."

"Forty-five percent. I can take my account to anyone else. I'll have a share of the proceeds, or you'll have nothing."

He slapped his hand on top of the papers, as if to ward off that threat. "Twenty-five."

"Thirty, and I get five pounds upfront." Enough to clear the debts in her name. Enough to survive for months. Enough for the future to become suddenly possible, and not some grim, looming fate. Even the city street outside the window seemed to lighten.

Mr. Parret cocked his head to the side. "Very well. I accept." He reached out one hand.

Jessica took it carefully. "You bargain well," she told him. "For a man."

He pursed his lips ruefully and shook her hand. And apparently, that was all it took to turn a courtesan into a *former* courtesan. She'd just earned enough to survive for a good long while. Before this ran out, she would find a way to earn more. She wouldn't need to sell her body ever again.

"Sir Mark will be furious." It was the worst part of this deal, knowing how much he hated private inquiry—and knowing that she would be thrusting him into the public eye with a vengeance.

But Parret didn't even shrug as he smoothed out the papers. "He usually is. I never let it bother me."

Maybe one day she'd be able to view Mark's response with such equanimity. That day was a long way off.

"I want to publish this one section each day, for five days—that will *really* get everyone interested, and we can charge double for the last printing. As for a title, I thought to call it 'The Seduction of Sir Mark.' That has a nice ring to it, doesn't it?"

"But what is he going to do, when he sees that?"

"Hopefully," Parret said, "he'll get very angry. It will confirm everyone's suspicions, and make us a great deal of money."

CHAPTER SIXTEEN

TWO DAYS AFTER Mark arrived in Bristol, his brother suggested a walking trip.

"My duties are reduced during the summers," Smite said. "And Ghost could use some country air." He'd said this with a gesture at the puppy, who gamboled about their feet.

Mark had translated this as: *Stop moping about.*

They'd sent a letter to Ash, informing him that they'd be gone a few days —eldest brothers *did* tend to worry, even over grown men— and Mark spent the remainder of that day losing himself in procuring supplies and planning the trip. He'd pored over maps and railway timetables, finally deciding to take the train to Reading, and from there, a meandering journey through country roads until they reached Basingstoke. It would be four or five days through tracks and lanes. Mark made note of a few smaller hostelries along the road where they might stay.

"None of the big ones now," Smite had said lazily. "I don't know how they'll take to a dog."

They'd have taken an entire menagerie from a duke's brothers. But then, Mark didn't need Smite to explain his peculiarities.

It was good to have something else to think of. It was better still when they disembarked from the passenger car in Reading to a bright, sunny day. It was a day so glorious that Mark could almost forget that everything else in his life was far from perfect.

The locomotive pulled away from the station in a cloud of smoke, leaving Mark and his brother pushed about on all sides by the crowd leaving the platform.

Smite met Mark's eyes and jerked his head toward the road. In this dry weather, the track was dusty with all the passing traffic. His brother would naturally prefer to choke on road-dust than spend time in a crowd. Mark shouldered his burden, happy to bear a little discomfort. It would get his mind off the interminable spiraling back, the uncomfortable thoughts of her...

No need to speak, thankfully. They made their way out and started through the clouds of hanging dust, holding their breaths. The fields weren't far beyond; once there, they might not need to speak to anyone until they reached their destination for the evening.

The whole notion sounded lovely.

"Oy!" A voice sounded behind them, recognizable and yet impossible at the same time.

Smite paused, turning on the shoulder of the road. A man—tall, burly—was striding toward them. He moved quickly, without once seeming to hurry. He had a satchel thrown over his shoulder; he barely glanced down the road for traffic before darting across.

"I had thought," the man said without any additional greeting, "the two of you would be civilized enough to stop in the public house before sallying forth."

"That's where you went wrong," Smite said. "We didn't intend to do anything so dramatic as *sally*. We had just planned to start."

Mark stared at the newcomer in dumb confusion. "Ash," he finally said stupidly. "What are you doing here?"

"Got Smite's message about the trip late last night," his eldest brother replied. "I can't have the two of you haring off on your own, can I?"

"We don't hare, either. We walk. With dignity."

Beside them, Ghost gave the lie to that by jumping up on Ash, his paws leaving two dusty footprints on his trousers.

Ash was protective, sometimes to an overbearing degree. Mark should have realized how suspicious it was that he'd not responded to their letter with a lecture on walking safely. In his normal course of events, he would have offered them an armed guard…or…or whatever other ridiculous thing he might have dreamed up.

He must have spent the entirety of the morning riding here. All that, just to meet them for an hour?

His eldest brother showed no sign of fatigue, however. Instead, he simply shifted the satchel he carried.

"Well." Smite spoke first. "I suppose we could set aside our *haring* and *sallying* long enough for a brief repast."

"Not at all. There's no need to make the slightest alteration in your plans on my account." Ash grinned. "I can keep up with the lot of you."

Smite glanced at Mark, his eyes widening. That slight entreaty was as good as a plea on bended knee for him.

"Keep up?"

"I'm coming with you," Ash said. His jaw set as he spoke, and he looked away from them. "Unless—"

"Can you neglect your business affairs so long?" Mark asked.

"Can you neglect your wife so long?" Smite asked, perhaps a little more slyly.

Ash let out a sigh. "Margaret suggested, in very strong terms, that I should come along."

Mark exchanged another glance with Smite.

Ash and Margaret had been happily married for five years; Mark couldn't imagine Margaret sending him away.

He was trying to work out a way to politely ask what might have happened, when Smite broke in, no politeness at all. "Good Lord, Ash, what did you do?"

"Nothing!" Ash said. "Or—at least—nothing I shouldn't be doing."

The track across the field, this close to town, was wide enough that they could all three walk abreast, and so they started down the path.

"Nothing?"

"If you must know," Ash said in patronizing tones, "she is increasing."

"Oh, congratulations!" Mark clapped his brother on the back.

Smite shook his hand, and Ash's smile broadened, as if he'd done something very clever.

"But now I'm doubly astonished," Mark continued. "I wouldn't have thought you could be pried from her side under those circumstances, not with a full harness of oxen."

His eldest brother stiffened. "She says," Ash muttered, "that I *hover*."

Mark stifled a laugh, just as Smite hid his face.

"I don't hover," Ash said. "Do I hover?"

"Surely not!" Mark said, overly polite.

Smite grinned. "Never."

"I couldn't imagine such a thing."

"Never in a million years."

"Hovering," Mark said, "puts me in mind of a butterfly—a light creature, flitting about from flower to flower, delicate as you please, vanishing at the first sudden movement."

"And that," Smite said, completing Mark's thought, "seems rather too circumspect for you. My guess is that you were circling overhead, like some kind of obscene vulture."

"Waiting to pounce on any weakness."

Ash put on hands on a hip. "You unholy pack of ruffians," he said in amusement. "I do not—"

"Only to give aid, of course," Mark said. "You are perhaps the most benevolent vulture I have ever met."

Smite sniggered. "Albeit not the most polite."

"You two are the most captious lot of ingrates ever to walk the face of Britain." Even though Ash's words were harsh, his tone was playful. And for the first time since Jessica had rejected his proposal, Mark realized that *he* was smiling. The future no longer seemed quite so bleak and barren. His brothers were together; and whatever waited could not be so impossible. "In all seriousness." Ash took a deep breath. "Will I be in the way?"

It wasn't Mark's place to answer that question. He looked to Smite, who looked away.

He'd told Jessica that it was hard for Smite to

make friends. That wasn't even the half of it. Smite didn't keep overnight servants. He wouldn't stay at a hotel where they might be bothered in the evening. He wouldn't even stay in Ash's townhouse in London; he had a flat he kept there for precisely that purpose. There were maybe three people in the world who understood *why*. Ash wasn't one of them.

Smite's lips thinned. He took a deep breath. "Don't worry, Ash," he said. "We're an unholy pack of ruffians here. You should fit right in."

A walking trip. Nothing to do but move and talk with his brothers. He'd not have to see a thing that reminded him of Jessica for close to a week. Mark smiled. Why, by the time he got back to London, he would have forgotten Jessica entirely.

THE HEADLINE on the London paper read: *Sir Mark: Seduced?!*

Jessica could read the words from across the square. The post-boy was already mobbed by a crowd, eager to fork over their coins for this news—and this was only the first issue to be printed. In a week or two, she would be able to collect the remainder of her earnings from Nigel Parret, and she could leave London. What she would do thereafter, she didn't yet know.

But she had one last piece of business to conduct. She ducked into the taproom where she'd seen Sir Mark for the first time. She had put off this interview as long as she could. She needed to tell George Weston what she should have told him months ago. She needed to tell him to go to the devil.

He was waiting for her at a table in the back. He wasn't unpleasant to look at—brown hair, brown eyes and an indistinct nose. Still, as she smoothed her skirts away and sat down before him, her teeth gritted. Every inch of her skin remembered what he'd done, recalled it in a visceral way that she could not forget. She felt faintly nauseous. The very air around him felt like a punch to the stomach.

Not that he had ever hit her. If anyone had asked, she wouldn't have said that he was a *bad* man. He went to church service regularly. Back when he'd been her protector, he'd even been... well, she couldn't call him *kind*. But he'd never beaten her. Up until the end, she would have said that he seemed like a decent fellow.

But he'd set a bounty on Mark's head in an attempt to ruin the man's reputation. And there was the matter of what he'd done to her. He wasn't *bad*. Still, she could never forgive him, and now that she knew what a good man was, she could recall precisely how awful he'd made her feel. She'd been steeling herself to endure his presence ever since she'd made the appointment.

He smiled as she sat. "Congratulations, Jess. I knew you could do it—you just needed a little prodding on my part."

Jess again. Mark had called her *Jessica*. As if she were a full person, not a truncated portion of one. "That's a bit premature, don't you think? I've not yet given you my report."

"I can guess." His smile stretched out, lazy, sure of itself. "Today, the first installment of a fallen woman's account appeared in the *London Social Mirror*. It's titled, 'The Seduction of Sir Mark.' The afternoon edition of every paper has picked up the refrain. I'm not an idiot, Jess. Well done. Everyone is already talking. And serializing the story? That was brilliant. Nobody will ever forget this. When Lefevre retires, I'll take his place."

Jessica thought of Mark's ring. It hung on a chain from her neck. What would he do, if she showed it to him? "I admit, I don't understand the ambition. You never struck me as one who cared about the poor."

He shrugged. "What, and pass up the chance to determine which of my acquaintances can harness the product of the workhouses? The Commission decides who gets the contracts for the food, the blankets. They decide what the workhouse pro-duces, and who benefits from it. A man who has that kind of power can get a great many favors.

And it will undoubtedly serve as a stepping-stone to other, greater, callings."

Jessica felt her lip curl a little.

"The opportunity would have been wasted on Sir Mark," Weston said. "He has no head for politics or organization—just philosophy and ethics. You've not just done me a favor—you've done a favor to all of England."

Jessica shook her head. "You are still making a great many assumptions. I came here because—"

He smiled at her indulgently. "I know why you came. You always did want to make sure the details were squared away. Here." He pulled a piece of paper from his jacket pocket and slid it across the table. "You've earned it."

She waited until he pulled his hand away before she looked at the paper. It was a bank draft. She hadn't come here to take his money. She'd come here to denounce him.

But that was before she'd seen that he'd made the cheque out in the amount of three hundred pounds. She tasted bitter charcoal. She lifted her eyes to him. "How odd. We agreed on fifteen hundred."

He gave her a negligent smile. "Come, Jess. You know I'm not overly wealthy. Besides, I've a reputation to maintain—I can't be throwing all my free capital into whores, no matter what sort of benefits they offer me."

Jessica tapped her fingers against the paper. "I don't see how the state of your funds is any concern of mine. I certainly don't care about your reputation. We had a deal, you and I. It was spelled out. Quite clearly."

"What are you going to do?" he asked. "Take me to court? You know that our little bargain is quite unenforceable." He leaned across the table, his hand reaching to brush against the side of her cheek. "If you want to earn the rest, you know how you can get it."

She slapped his hand away. "Why would you suppose that you could motivate me to enter into one contract with you by reneging on another?"

He didn't say anything, simply shaking his head.

It wasn't as if it was the first time he'd done this to her. She'd had a contract with him before—she'd insisted on it. And when it had come down to it, he'd broken that one, too—splintered it clean in half, nearly killing her in the process. He wasn't a *bad* man. He was just…an unthinking pinchpenny. He'd put his pocketbook before his obligations once before. She shouldn't have been surprised that he'd done so again.

"I wouldn't touch you for twice that amount." She glanced down at the bank draft. "For *any* sum."

"Come now, I wasn't that bad. I would think that

after being pawed over by a virgin, you'd welcome a man of some experience."

She stood. "Sir Mark made me feel more when he touched my hand than you ever managed."

His jaw worked, and he reached for the cheque. Without thinking, Jessica slammed her hand over it and glared at him. She hadn't earned it—he only *thought* she had. In truth, she had no right to the funds. But then…

The memory of those months after he'd so casually broken their last contract came to mind. The illness. The *darkness*. The feeling that she would never hope for the future again. He could never repay her for those months. He could never banish the sadness she would carry, not with every penny in his accounts. He *owed* her.

She couldn't collect. But she had already humiliated him; he just didn't know it yet. When he read the final chapter in the serial she'd written, he would understand precisely what she'd done.

By the time that happened, she'd have taken his funds. He didn't know where she was staying, and in a few weeks, she would leave London for good. It wasn't justice—she could never get justice for what he'd done to her. But it was indubitably *right*.

"Jess," he said. "Do be reasonable."

She folded up the draft and slipped it into her pocket. "My name isn't *Jess*."

"No? Then what should I call you?"

"Weston," she said simply, "you're not going to see me. If you look for me, I'll leave."

"And what if I insist?"

She lowered her voice. "I'll shoot you. Stay away from me."

"Jess!" he called after her.

But she wasn't turning back, not for him. Not ever. She held her head high and marched onward.

AFTER MARK'S WALKING trip, London was…gray.

Even though they'd not talked about Jessica, Smite must have sensed Mark was still unhappy, because he'd accompanied Mark and Ash to London without a word of explanation. He'd even agreed to attend a soiree. He'd probably done so to make sure Mark had no time to think on that first evening back.

It was the first time that all three of the Turners had ever appeared at a soiree together. They'd arrived in town only just in time to wash and dress for the event that evening. They entered the room, Mark's brothers flanking him on either side.

Heads turned as they were announced. Mark shouldn't have been surprised. Ash was a duke; Mark still seemed possessed of an inexplicable popularity. And Smite was wealthy, good-looking…and never around, which made everyone wonder about him.

Mark had been away from London—away from

polite society in its entirety—long enough that he'd forgotten what it was like to attend one of these events. Everyone was looking at him. This was *normal,* he reminded himself. Everyone was *always* looking at him; it was only his imagination that found a trace of pity in their gazes. They didn't know what had happened while he was gone. None of them did.

This was just the usual adoration that he collected, simply because he was a knight, because he was popular and because he was wealthy. It chafed more than usual tonight.

But when he looked to either side of him he realized that he *was* wealthy. Just not in the way that these people thought. There had been lean years before Ash had made his fortune; Mark could still bring to mind the feeling of hunger, not so much a memory as an occasional itch that sometimes tickled the back of his mind from time to time. And yet…if there was luxury in this world, it wasn't velvet waistcoats or top hats. It wasn't a perfectly sprung carriage or marchpane delicacies served on silver platters.

It was this—this certainty that without his even asking, his brothers would stand at his side. Even Smite. Even in this crowd. All his life, his brothers had protected him. He'd been born rich.

Perhaps that was why he found the strength to paste a false smile on his face, to clasp hands with a friend he'd not seen in months. Perhaps that was why he could dismiss the sidelong glances, the murmurs behind shielded hands. Perhaps that was why he could converse easily and pretend that nothing had happened in his absence. He knew that his brothers were there for him, a foundation that would never crumble no matter what he faced.

It was even easy to ask a young lady to dance, although he somehow missed her name when they'd been introduced. He could pretend perfectly; all he had to do was act by rote, like a clockwork knight wound up for a performance.

But he had only to think of what he was not pretending about, and the memory returned, shocking and vivid. The women at the ball were faded portraits of femininity compared to Jessica. She was warmer, more vibrant. And though the woman he was waltzing with—a debutante who watched him with a puzzled look on her face—was quite pretty, he could hardly attend to her conversation.

It still hurt to think of Jessica. But that pain was beginning to fade to the dull ache of a wound that was healing.

"Do you still think of her, then?" the young lady asked.

Mark frowned at her. Had he spoken those last words aloud? He hadn't. He was sure he hadn't. He shook his head uncertainly.

The young lady was looking at him. She didn't

have the usual look of adoration that a debutante in her position might have exhibited. "Did you love her?" she asked breathlessly. "It is the question everyone wants answered, after all."

He barely managed not to trip over his own feet. "What are you talking about?"

"The woman in the papers," she said, "of course. What else should I be talking about? Nobody has been talking about anything else for *days*. And now that the last of the serial has run—"

"The serial? What serial do you mean?"

"You haven't seen it?" Her eyes widened. "And here all my friends had deputized me to get the particulars from you. You *must* have seen it."

"I've been out of town for weeks." He felt faintly sick. Why hadn't anyone told Ash?

But, no—they'd arrived hours after his men of business would have departed. Mark could see precisely what had happened. No doubt they'd deputized Jeffreys, Ash's right-hand man, to deliver the bad news. No doubt Jeffreys had left Ash a report, and the remainder of the servants, delighted to know they would not need to bring it up, had kept quiet.

Or not so quiet. Was *that* what his valet had meant when he said Mark had been busy in the country?

"My brothers and I—we've been out of town

these last few days. We've been utterly unreachable."

They'd purposefully traveled through isolated villages, on roads with little traffic. Mark hadn't wanted to meet one of his hangers-on. They'd shared the road with cattle drivers and peddlers— people who didn't care about polite society and did not read the gossip papers. On the train into London, people *had* stared at him and whispered. He'd not thought anything of it, though. People always stared. These stares had seemed more pointed than before, but then, he felt all the more vulnerable.

"What was her name?" he heard himself ask. He already knew. *Jessica.*

"Nobody knows," she replied. "But surely *you* can tell *me.*"

Mark could remember his last words to her with almost cold clarity. *Print that you brought me to my knees.* Fine words, then. Now…

Did all of London know of his courtship, his disappointment? Had everyone truly been looking at him with pity? How was he ever supposed to forget her under those circumstances?

"Who printed it? What was it called?"

"It's—it was called—" She gulped and then glanced across the room. Mark couldn't see what she was looking at—probably her friends, waving her on, urging her to find out more of the sordid tale. What on earth had Jessica said? His dancing companion had a faint blush across her cheeks, and she whispered all in one breath, "It was called 'The Seduction of Sir Mark.'"

"Seduced, was I?" That much, at least, was true—in mind and soul, if he'd managed to barely restrain himself from the final physical act.

"Oh, no, sir!" she said innocently. "That is to say—it was the most romantical tale. I wept *buckets* at the last installment. Can you tell me, is there any truth to it? We all want to know," she explained earnestly, gesturing toward the side of the room. Indeed, there were five ladies sitting there, watching them intently—they raised fans to cover their faces as he turned in their direction.

"I can't know if it's true. I haven't read it. What is it that I have purportedly done?"

"Why… You encountered a woman, not knowing that she'd been hired by your dastardly enemies to ruin your name. And you—you treated her kindly, in the most Christian manner, and made her decide to change her ways."

Mark looked at her. "That's the entirety of it? I treated her *kindly?*"

She nodded.

No mention of kisses? No mention of that moment when she'd curled her fingers around his? *Kindly* did not begin to cover the truth. He could almost feel the humiliation creep over him. Still, she might have mentioned his own feelings. He'd told her about his *mother*. He'd told her about Smite—or at least, some portion of that. Had he mentioned *Ash's* secret? That would be more devastating.

No. No. He didn't think he had. That much, at least, was safe. Still.

No wonder everyone was casting such pitying looks at him. They all knew that he'd been stupid enough to fall in love with a liar.

"Sir Mark," his companion said earnestly, "I think I speak for every lady here when I tell you that I could have fallen in love with you myself, except I so want you to love her."

From across the room, he caught Ash's eye. His brother's expression was grim, and he jerked his head. *Get over here quickly.*

The waltz was winding to a close.

"Do you love her, Sir Mark?"

He'd thought his emotion had begun to burn down, to sputter and fade. But this news had fanned it to life, had made his every wound feel raw once more.

"Love her?" Mark said, his voice low. "When I find her, I'm going to *kill* her."

CHAPTER SEVENTEEN

THEY GATHERED in Ash's study, the three brothers.

A report was there, on Ash's desk. "'Urgent,'" Mark read aloud. "'Read immediately upon arrival.'" *Immediately* was underlined three times. There was a scrawl on the bottom, too, a note to Ash from Jeffreys, telling him that *this* time, as he'd been eccentric enough to have disappeared entirely, he'd have to settle for a written report.

Ash looked over at Mark. "I—I didn't see it." He glanced over at his other brother. "Truly. I had no idea. I don't know why—"

Mark reached over and pushed his brother's shoulder. "I know precisely what you mean, Ash. Nobody could hold it against you."

Mark shuffled through the first pages of summary to find the newspaper clippings that had been so carefully collated. The paper seemed too flimsy to contain anything of so much weight. For the first time in days, his brothers' presence annoyed him. He'd managed to barely talk about the matter at all. To have someone else talk to his brothers about it…it seemed even more horrible than having all of London know.

Read it when I'm done, he wanted to say. But then he looked up into Ash's eyes. Ash was looking at that report with something like regret in his eyes. Mark's brothers had stood by him all these past days. They didn't deserve to be pushed away now.

"There's just the one copy," he said instead. "I suppose…I suppose it'll go fastest if I read it aloud, yes?"

"If…if you could." Ash didn't meet his eyes.

Mark sank into a seat on a settee. His brothers settled to either side of him as he flipped through the sheaf of papers. Jeffreys had included not only the original serializations, but the commentaries thereon. Mark didn't care what anyone else said. He just wanted to know about…well, about Jessica.

There. This flimsy newsprint was the start of it.

"'When I first met Sir Mark,'" Mark read, "'he said he spoke with the tongues of angels.'" Mark had forgotten that. He didn't glance to either side. He didn't want to know what his brothers thought of that introduction.

"'But it took me a week to understand that he spoke not as a saint, nor as an ascetic, but as a man. He was just a very, very good one.'"

If he'd had any doubts that Jessica had written this account, they vanished with those words. He could almost hear her speak them. What he hadn't imagined was the swell of emotion he felt in response. Not anger. Not betrayal. Just a sensation of recognition—as if he'd jumped into deep, cold water. It felt as if she were telling him something he didn't want to hear but had known all along.

He read on. "'I must admit that at first, I wanted to hurt him...'"

It was disconcerting to see himself through someone else's eyes. For the past days, he had thought she'd been laughing at him. She'd watched him fall in love with an illusion. He had supposed that she had somehow intuited what he most wanted in a woman and had presented it to him. He'd felt trapped and angry, furious that even knowing all that, he still desperately longed for her.

But as he read, her version of the story corresponded with the woman he'd believed she was. Even though she did not voice them, he could hear her doubts. Even though she did not speak of it, he could sense her falling under his spell as surely as he'd fallen under hers. He felt as if he was rediscovering her in those pages. She was still the woman he'd come to know. There was that familiar prickly integrity.

All the hurt he'd nursed this past week...it

was beginning to feel a little childishly resentful. Because if she had told the truth, she'd been seduced. She'd been thrown out of her home. She'd lost her dearest friend, had no family to speak of. He glanced at his brothers to either side of him.

In truth, she'd had no wealth at all. Not of any kind.

He read on and on, unable to stop. He didn't stop hurting; the pain just began to alter. She left off all accounts of their physical intimacy—the touches, the kisses, everything except the moments when he'd looked in her eyes and found himself unable to look away—but still he could sense their echo. She kept his secrets through every installment. The narrative went through to his ill-fated proposal.

And then Mark scanned the last words she'd written and set the page down before he read them aloud. He felt as if he'd had the breath knocked out of him.

He couldn't say those words. Next to him, Smite leaned against him, offering unspoken comfort. Ash's hand touched his shoulder.

If *she* could write these words, all alone, he could surely speak them aloud to the people who loved him best. Mark picked up the account again. "'I left. What else could I do? I hated him for the same reason I loved him: because I could not break him, and because no matter how hard I tried, a woman like me could never have a man like him.'"

I hated him. I loved him. His heart raced. He could almost reach out and touch the loneliness in her words.

I loved him. After the spare, quiet words of her narration, those three words echoed. It might have been a lie. It might have been a dramatization.

It felt like the truth.

He'd held to the notion that she'd lied to him because he'd not wanted to contemplate an alternate possibility. He had imagined her laughing at him. He'd imagined her meeting with George Weston and mocking his tentative adoration. He'd believed all that, because the alternative was that he'd promised her she wasn't alone, and he'd lied.

I loved him. He felt drunk and uncertain, as if he'd been assailed by a vertigo of the soul.

I loved him. But she'd lied to him. He grasped for the fading shreds of his righteous indignation, but it fled. She'd *hurt* him. Wasn't that worth something?

I loved him, but a woman like me could never have a man like him.

He'd been blind. And stupid. And wrong. So focused on his own hurt that he'd not stopped to question. She'd practically begged him not to like her. She'd told him she was ruined and outcast. How was she surviving? If she'd stooped to seducing him, how badly had she needed the money? And what was she doing now?

Mark was wealthy beyond imagining. He'd had letters and love and companionship all his life.

But where was she? Whom was she with?

How was he to find her?

He stared into the darkness, questions dancing about him. He stared until the night seemed to take on colors of its own before his unblinking eyes. He stayed there for minutes longer, listening to his brothers' silence, until finally Ash punched him lightly on the shoulder and then, as if deciding against it, converted the motion into a gentle pat. The fire snapped behind them.

"How much of that was a factual account?" Ash asked eventually.

Mark shook his head. "She omitted the portions that don't reflect well on me. I told her about Mother—if she'd wanted to embarrass us, she could easily have done so."

"Hmm." That was Smite.

"Do you want me to have the paper print a retraction?" Ash asked. "I could…buy the building in which it resides. Make life difficult for the owner."

"It's all true. She actually painted me in a…a fairly flattering light. She didn't even mention the times I kissed her."

Mark felt his brothers turn next to him, as if exchanging careful glances.

"*You* kissed *her*?" Ash asked.

"Times?" Smite echoed. "Plural?"

"There's no need to sound so surprised. I'm chaste, not dead. Although it was close on more than one occasion. *Really* close." He hunched into the cushion and shut his eyes.

"Oh, well done," Smite said. "Well *done*."

"It wasn't done at all," Mark mumbled. "Well or poorly."

"Honestly," Ash said, "what is it you want, Mark? Do you want this stopped? I'll stop it. Do you want her found and silenced? I'll pay her whatever you want. You have only to ask and it is yours."

What did he want? He felt as if he were on the edge of a precipice, posed to fall. He reached for the shreds of his balance, sought out calmness, peace, quiet…

But no. She thought that a woman like her could never have a man like him. He'd excoriated the MCB as a bunch of hypocrites. *Women are the point of chastity, not the enemy of it,* he'd said.

Fine words. But what was the point of holding one's own balance on the cliffside only to see the woman you cared for topple over the side?

"Yes," Mark said. "Ash, I *do* want your help. Let me explain what I need…"

THE RAIN SLASHED against Jessica's cloak as she fumbled in her pocket for the key to her London flat. The few rooms she had were in Whitechapel, and the streets were dingy. She'd taken them late in the spring as a temporary place to store her things while she went to Shepton Mallet, and so that she would have someplace to retreat to once she'd finished with Sir Mark. The rooms didn't feel like home, but until Parret delivered the final payment, she needed somewhere to stay.

The dark clouds had come on quickly that night. She ducked her head in front of the door, her fingers chilled and clumsy. Iron rattled in the keyhole. It had been a few days since the last serial had been published. It should have made her feel queasy, knowing her words were out there for anyone to see. She'd heard that Mark was in town—that he'd arrived last night.

She didn't want to think of him. Of what she'd done to him. She had done what she always did: she had survived, and never mind the cost. The key finally turned in the lock, and she wiped the water that trickled down the side of her face. In the doorway, she turned to wring the wet wool of her cloak into the street.

A single street lamp burned on the corner, scarcely cutting through the dark night storm. The gaslight didn't seem to illuminate. It cast only shadows—long, dark slashes of cold dreariness.

One of those shadows moved. A form, hidden at first by an alley, started forward across the street.

Jessica's heart quickened as the form—the *man*—moved closer, stride by stride. She took one step into her flat, her hands going to the handle of the door.

"Jessica," he said.

It was *him*. A welter of confused emotions assailed her—panic, relief, hope, fear. By contrast, Mark's voice was flat, devoid of all feeling.

She drew back farther. "Sir Mark. What are you doing here?"

He took another step forward. She could make out his face now. His coat was sodden; underneath his hat, his pale hair was plastered to his head in strings. Rivulets of water ran down his face and dripped from the tip of his chin. His eyes burned into hers. "What do you suppose I'm doing here?"

She winced at that tone. "You must be angry."

"Furious."

"What are you *doing,* venturing out in the rain without a greatcoat? Or an umbrella? Or even a…a…"

He took another step toward her. He was close enough to touch her now; she looked up into the shadow of his face and swallowed the remainder of her sentence.

"It wasn't raining when I left," he said simply. He set his hand on the door, as if to forestall any chance of her escape.

Her heart beat faster. "It's been raining since three."

"I've been waiting since noon." His words were calm, and that frightened her more than any amount of shouting. "Besides, this way I know you can't throw me out. Turnabout is fair play."

The intensity of his eyes called to mind that long-ago day when she'd arrived on his doorstep, wet to her underthings. She'd tried to seduce him. She'd told him she hated him. Jessica shivered and pulled her cloak around her.

"I know you are unhappy with me," she said. "I know how much you hate attention. I knew you would despise me when I placed such intimate details of our conversation before all of London." Her words left puffs of white in the rain. "I haven't any defense."

He reached out and touched her chin. "Really? Not one defense?"

She stepped away, turning her back to her open doorway. "I just did what I have always done. I did my best to survive. I won't apologize for that, but I can't ask you to forgive me, either."

He took another step forward, and she instinctively retreated. The entry was small and cramped; her hands found the wall too soon. He stepped forward again, until he'd backed her against her wall. Slowly, deliberately, he set his hands on either side of her head. She was trapped. Closed in. There was no way to escape.

"Mark," she begged. "I know you must resent me, but—"

"Resent you?" he asked. "Why, in the name of everything that I hold holy, do you think that I am angry at *you?*"

Her fear turned to crystal inside her. She shook her head, not knowing how to answer. Not knowing how to respond when he leaned in even closer.

He touched her cheek. His fingers were wet and cold but solid and real. He touched her gently, as if he expected her to disappear if he pushed too hard. "When you told me Weston had hired you, all I could think was that you'd been laughing at me the whole time. That you'd pretended everything. That you'd never cared. But it wasn't a lie, was it?"

Her heart thumped. He couldn't be excusing her. He couldn't possibly think to forgive her. "I told you I was married."

"But you were fourteen." He brushed water from her forehead and then swept a thumb down her nose. "You were fourteen when you were seduced, and your father threw you out of the house."

She couldn't speak. She was choked by an emotion that she couldn't name, something bigger than mere relief and more powerful than even hope.

"Since then, you've made your way on your own."

She nodded.

He turned from her and shut the door. When it closed behind them, the scant light from the outside was cut off. She was left in darkness with a man she couldn't see.

"It was true, what you said." His voice floated out of that nothingness, close and yet so far away. "You hated me at first."

"Yes. But it didn't last long. It couldn't."

He let out a sigh at that, soft and warm. "That's what I hoped, Jessica." He paused, took a deep breath. "I must humbly beg your forgiveness."

"*My* forgiveness?" Her breath seemed to belong to someone else; she had to fight for every lungful of air.

"I told you I would be your champion. I haven't done very well by you."

It would be foolish to cry at those words. In the dark, she could pretend it was just rainwater. She reached out, clumsily groping for his hand. He gripped her tight.

"You don't need my forgiveness."

"No?" His hand curled about hers. "Tell me, then, why I have been reliving that awful moment when I left you, again and again. Tell me why it hurts me here—" he pulled her hand against the wet wool that covered his chest and spread her fingers "—when I remember that I walked from you. Explain how I am to ever deserve your trust, if I can't have your forgiveness first."

"You don't need my forgiveness. You've had it since the day you gave me your coat. I think I was already half in love with you then."

His hand crept to the small of her back as she spoke, drawing her close. When she was silent, she could feel the steady beat of her pulse in her throat. That pounding could not fill the impossible silence. It sounded like the opening strains of a symphony, quiet and subdued, with the entire orchestra poised to join in. Her hand curled in his coat in prelude. She could feel his entire body shift, leaning in toward her.

And then he kissed her. That first taste of him overwhelmed her senses with a pleasure so sharp it could have cut. His clothing was wet against her; his lips cold at first. They warmed. She tasted the rain on him, and then the heat of his mouth. He jolted her to life with that kiss. There was no hiding from her wants, no pretending that she could simply *survive* any longer.

No. He'd become necessary to her, and this was more frightening than anything she'd experienced before. At any second, he could break her. He could break her more easily with kindness than a thousand cruel words. She almost cried out at the tenderness in his touch. Every brush of his lips felt like falling.

Maybe she was just waiting to hit the ground.

His hands slid to her hair, finding pins in the dark. He pulled them out one by one, until her hair tumbled down her back, a heavy mass, half wet, half dry. He caught it in his hands as it fell. Then he pulled from her and let out a little breath.

"Oh, Jessica." He leaned his forehead against hers. "You should have told everyone what a hypocrite I was. I lectured you with a straight face about how profligacy hurt women, and then refused to see how it had hurt *you*. Don't tell me I don't need your forgiveness."

That almost did break her. He was vulnerable, too. They were both groping about in the dark, afraid to find one another.

Jessica found the clasp of her cloak in the dark and released it. The sodden weight slid from her shoulders. "Mark," she said, "I would never wish you harm." Her voice shook. "Whatever you need from me, I'll give it. Gladly."

"I need this." His arms came around her. Water from his coat soaked through her dress. She couldn't make herself care about it, not now, not with his mouth seeking out hers once more, not with his lips covering hers, his body hard against hers. He was so firm, and yet she had only to set her hand on his chest and he pulled back. No; he wasn't going to hurt her. Not today. Not now.

But what of tomorrow?

Jessica shook her head, clearing it of those worries, and gave herself up to his kiss. There was nothing but the give and take of lips and tongue and teeth, nothing but the ebb and flow of breath cycling into kiss cycling back into breath again. She pulled back briefly, fumbled in the dark until she guided him to the sofa in the front room. They sank onto it, and he kissed her again, leaning over her. The cold and wet of his clothing gave way to a warm, damp humidity.

His hands cupped her cheeks. He held her as if she were precious. Tonight, maybe, she *would* be precious to him. This minute and for every minute it lasted.

The buttons of his coat were hard lumps pressing against her; she undid them, at first absently, and then in earnest. He paused only to strip the garment off. And then he found her lips in the dark once more. Not just lips; their bodies met, her hips nestling against his, her chest brushing his. It felt so right to cradle him, so right to feel that pleasure flooding her. He felt so good, she was sure this couldn't last.

When he pulled away, she wasn't surprised; she'd been expecting it for minutes. But instead of calling a halt, he knelt before her. His hands

tangled in her skirt, lifting it, pushing her petticoats up to gather at her hips. Cool air touched her
thighs. Her whole body tingled in anticipation.

And then his hands, hot now, slid up her knees.

"Jessica." His thumbs slid farther up, finding the
wetness of her sex. He made a strangled sound.

But it was nothing to the shock that filled her.
His caress, tentative at first, slid against her most
intimate parts. His fingers were hesitant in their
discovery, then became more sure.

"Is that right?" he asked, his thumb sweeping
over the nub of her pleasure. It felt so *good*.

"Yes."

"This?"

Her hand joined his. "Right *there*. Like that.
Oh, yes. Like that."

Again he tempted her, tormented her, his hands
uncovering all her secrets.

"I want—" she began, but stopped, letting out
a small cry, as he caressed her once more.

"Tell me what you want." His voice was strong,
urgent.

"No—oh, Mark—we can't. We have to stop. I
don't know what you're thinking."

He paused. And then he pulled his hands away,
letting her skirts fall. She ached all over. Her body
screamed at her for completion. Still, she scrambled to her feet.

"There's a basin over there, if you want it." She

pointed, realized he couldn't see her, and stumbled over to a side table near the entrance. Her hands shook as she found a lucifer by shape, shook when it failed to light once, twice—on her third try, a sharp sulfurous smell filled the room. She cupped the precious flame and lit a candle. The light danced, too bright, and too late she realized her mistake. If he could see her eyes, he would see…everything.

Behind her, Mark had found the basin. He washed his hands methodically before turning back to her.

"Let me explain something to you," he said. His trousers were tented out in front of him; she tried not to focus on that telltale bulge. "You warned me once not to make a romance of you." He advanced on her again. But when he got to her, he didn't try to kiss her. He turned her around, so her back was to him, and folded his arms around her. "You have only one chance to escape."

His hands slid to her waist, curled in the sash of her dress.

"I plan to thwart you," he said against her neck. "I am going to make you understand that you deserve to have romance. And you, my dearest, will not be able to stop me."

He pulled the ends of her sash, letting it float to the ground.

"Mark?"

He undid the top button at the nape of her neck. "I never should have listened to you about that anyway."

His lips touched her ear—the lobe of it, just a brush, the heat of his breath in sharp contrast to the chill of his hands. Her nipples tightened, pointing; a well of warmth rose up inside her. And then he was not just kissing her ear but catching it lightly between his teeth, his mouth tracing the edge. His tongue—oh, heavens, his *tongue,* flicking out. She felt it in her hands, her breasts, that rising sense of pleasure.

"What are you doing?"

He didn't answer, just finished unbuttoning her dress, his fingers moving slowly. "Thank you for lighting the candle," he said quietly, as he slid the sleeves down her shoulders. He pressed his lips to her neck. "I wouldn't have been able to do *this* without light."

His hands slid to her corset laces. He leisurely untied the knot, unlaced the ribbons and pulled the garment away. She wanted to grab for it, to pull it back. It wasn't just her body he wanted; it was intimacy, and that was more than she'd given in years. She couldn't help but feel that at any moment, he would come to his senses and leave her where she stood, trembling and hurt and wanting.

"Is there a trick to the petticoats?" He found the first button that held the top layer in place.

"Mark, what are you doing?"

"You know what I'm doing." He peeled away one layer of muslin and started in on the next. "I'm undressing you." The second petticoat joined the first on the floor. "I feel like I'm taking apart a watch," he said. "It's easy enough to disconnect the parts, but I'm fairly certain I couldn't reconstruct the whole without expert help."

"Truly, Mark, you have to stop." She was beginning to shake.

Her last petticoat slid to the floor, and she stood in her shift.

"Is that what you want?"

She turned in his arms. His eyes slid down her form—uncluttered now by skirts and excess fabric.

All her scampering vulnerabilities froze in the heat of his gaze. She felt like a rabbit staring up at a hawk. But this hawk didn't pounce. Instead, he simply leaned in and kissed her. It was a sweet kiss—just his lips against hers, his hand on her shoulder. Her body melted against his. She carried her fear inside that rising tide of pleasure, like shattered glass waiting to slice her.

As he kissed her, his hands moved. He traced her form as if he wanted to commit it to memory. The hairs on her arm stood up, brought to attention by that gentle touch.

"If we go much further, I'm going to lose my head," she confessed.

He pushed back and looked her in the eyes. "Lose it," he advised, and then he leaned down and fastened his lips to her breast. Heat washed over her. Her protests, weak and halfhearted as they'd been, disappeared, swallowed in the swelling need of her body.

"You like that." His voice was hoarse. "I've thought about doing that for ages. I couldn't get it out of my mind."

Jessica nodded, not trusting her voice. And then he leaned down and did it again—his tongue swirling around her nipple, gentle and yet firm. His breath was growing ragged—she could feel it washing against her skin. The sensation rippled out from that point, powerful and intensely pleasurable. She could feel her own want grow.

Any other man, having paid this bare attention to her pleasure, would have been eager to sate his own desire. But Mark touched her as if every stroke of his tongue was new, as if she were a sweet to savor, a prize to treasure, as if her enjoyment were vital for more than just easing his way inside. Her skin burned to feel his body pressed full-length against her.

"Hurry," she said.

He raised his head and gave her a knowing, wicked smile—one that made her feel as if he were drawing on a wealth of experience. "I've waited twenty-eight years for this. I don't suppose another few hours will change anything."

It was unlikely that he would have come here. It was improbable that he would think well of her after everything he'd learned. But her mouth dried at that bald statement. There was no mistaking his intent. He wanted her, and that was impossible.

His hand drifted down her ribs, slowly, as if he were counting them out. He found the edge of her shift and pulled it up, the fabric sliding over her sensitive flesh.

"A few *hours?*" Jessica said, hearing her voice rise. "You *are* optimistic."

His lip quirked up at that. But he kissed his way down her body, to her navel.

"It is the most astonishing thing," he whispered against her skin. "To touch you, to feel you tremble. To know that I'm the cause of it." His thumbs made circles against her hips. And then he reached out tentatively and touched her thighs. Slid his hands up, parting her knees, his fingers brushing against the slick folds of her sex once more. "It is so much better than I'd imagined."

She reached out and ran her own hands through his hair. "Just wait until I start to touch you."

"Oh. That's nice," he breathed. And then he met her eyes. "Here?" he asked. She felt his thumb brush her between her legs. "Or here?"

"There."

More sure now, the pressure he exerted; more certain, the light in his eyes as he looked at her. "And what about here?"

Sparks cascaded through her. "Yes—that."

This time, he did not just part her sex. His finger slid inside her, and she shivered, her inner muscles tightening around him.

"And this?"

"Too much—oh, Mark, and not enough."

He pushed back, stood up. He undid his waistcoat quickly, unwound his cravat from his neck. He didn't rush, not even when he pulled the lawn of his shirt over his head. His chest was pale and smooth, furred over with light golden hairs that caught the candlelight.

Jessica reached up and caught his upper arms, glorying in the curve of that muscle, so strong, and yet trembling under her touch. She ran her hands along his chest, found the smooth circle of his nipple. His breathing caught, and he canted over her.

"Jessica. Please. Darling. Do that again."

She did.

Men sometimes talked as if curves were something that only a woman possessed. But his body was a construction of subtler curves: the gentle swell of his forearm, racing down to the blunt tips of his fingers. The ripple of his abdomen. That arc where torso met pelvis. His body seemed the pinnacle of masculine artistry.

He reached for the fall of his trousers. Her breath scalded her lungs. She reached out and set her hand over his. "What are you *doing?*"

His hand found hers, clasped it. "Do you know *why* I professed to believe in chastity? Because I don't believe in doing harm, least of all to someone I care for."

He relinquished her fingers and proceeded to undo his trousers.

"But it's the woman that matters," he said, his voice low. "Not my pride. Not my reputation. Not even my principles. I should have put you first." He pushed the fabric to his hips, and then farther down. "I wanted peace and balance. But I should have put you first. First. Last. And, Jessica— always."

This had to be a dream. A fantasy. He couldn't mean those words, not to her. He couldn't be standing naked before her. But his hand, when it found hers, was warm and real. Her feet touched the floor as he led her back to the sofa. And she would never have imagined him sitting unclothed before her, could never have believed that he would pull her to straddle him. He was warm beneath her; his mouth found hers.

He didn't just give her a kiss, he pulled her body to his, his hands entangling with hers, her tongue darting out to taste him. His hips pressed up against hers.

And his member… He was thick and strong and hard. He twitched when she touched him. And that finally grounded her. This wasn't just a passionate kiss. It was something more. He thrust up against her, instinct instructing him where experience could not.

This was *impossible.*

She reached down to touch his erection. It was heavy in her hand, the head wet already. He hissed, his hands clutching her arms, as she stroked down his length.

She slid up onto her knees. One of his hands clasped her waist. He was the one to adjust his member into place, the one to set his hands on her hips. He was the one to apply just the slightest pressure. This wasn't possible.

It was possible.

And then, it simply was.

His hands clenched around her arms. His breath came in explosive little gasps. His body entered hers—not in possession, but in desire. She could feel herself stretching around him. He was thick, hot.

"Jessica," he said. Her hips sank to meet his; her body sparked above his. She could feel the tension in his arms, the tremble of his muscles as he held himself back.

It had never been like this before. His eyes met hers. He watched her intently, his gaze slitting as she rose up on him. His hands slid up her ribs to her breasts, touching her. Overriding her every thought. She wasn't sure when she began to move, wasn't sure when her need began to consume her, spiraling out from their joined bodies. Her hands clenched. Her toes curled. Every commingled movement sent an agony of pleasure through her, until she threw back her head and let out a little cry as ecstasy overtook her.

He grabbed her hips as she came, thrust hard into her. She could feel slick sweat on his shoulders, his entire body tensing beneath hers. He made a short, strangled sound in the back of his throat. His hips pounded into hers. He was hot, so hot, and yes, he was coming, too. He came to her without any lies between them.

He was still breathing heavily when his body stilled. His arms came around her, hard. His lips found hers in a long, drawn out kiss—the passion not the slightest dimmed by the act they'd just performed.

And Jessica still didn't understand. She didn't understand what had happened. Oh, she knew the mechanics of it. And she understood ecstasy. But this…this had been a new kind of pleasure. Something Jessica had never experienced before, something strange and inexplicable. She didn't quite understand what it meant at first. Her fingers intertwined with his, her body wrapped around his. His forehead pressed against hers, and their mingled breaths waxed and waned in an intimate rhythm.

It took her a few moments to hit upon the difference. Normally, a man took, and she gave. He *owned* her, for those minutes. The pleasure was *his*. And if his desire provoked her physical response—well, that, too, belonged to him.

But this…this pleasure hadn't been his. It hadn't been *hers,* either.

No. It had been something that seemed both foreign and intimate all at the same time.

It had been theirs.

CHAPTER EIGHTEEN

MARK TOOK HER to bed afterward.

There was nothing that quite compared to the glory of her bare skin.

In the tepid light of the candle, his fingers had to fill in what his eyes could not. The smooth curve of her shoulder. The silk of her hair, softer than he'd imagined.

He didn't understand how men could flit from woman to woman. He had thought he was infatuated back in Shepton Mallet. That had been nothing compared to this—to the feel of her spine against his hands, each vertebra dear to him. Then there was the taste of her neck, subtly different than that of her collarbone. The flickering illumination showed bits of her in turn: pale skin and dark hair and pink lips, all enticing.

He wasn't sure how long he spent afterward just touching her. Trying to memorize the feel of her. Long enough that the candle in the other room eventually guttered out. Long enough that wonder turned into lust once more, that he positioned himself over her, sliding into a heaven that he'd tried to imagine before and had utterly failed.

Her body. Her hands, grasping his. Every thrust he took, every gasp he wrung from her, was a precious gift. Her desire magnified his want. Instinct merged with intuition. He waited for the change of her breath, for the moan she tried to hold back. He waited until her body clenched around his, and he lost all sense of anything but her, her, her.

When sanity returned, he found himself collapsed atop her, chest to chest, her hands clasped around his lower back.

"Try as I might," she said, "I can't make you out."

He caught her lips in his. "What's to make out? I'm not so complicated." He disengaged himself from her as best he could without relinquishing her. Now that he'd had her once—well, twice—he didn't plan on letting go again.

She said nothing in response, simply waited.

"I suppose there are two things you really should know," Mark said. "About the past. And about the future."

At the word *future,* her breath sucked in. He could almost feel the tension steal into her limbs. But all she said was, "Hmm?"

"The near past," he said. "You must know that I would never have risked making love with you, if there were any chance that you would be unprotected afterward. There are always risks, and even if I intend to make it right…well, I could have been struck by lightning. I wouldn't risk the possibility that you might not have the funds to care for a child." He could still remember that infant in Bristol and the woman who had walked away. He *needed* to know it wouldn't be her. That it wouldn't be his son there, one day.

"I—I had wondered about that." Her hand found his face.

"Which is why this morning, I went to my solicitors and signed five thousand pounds over to you."

She sat up abruptly, pulling the covers with her. "You did *what?*"

"I gave you five thousand pounds." His words were calm, but his pulse beat wildly.

She curled in on herself. "I don't need it. I don't want it. I refuse."

"Too bad. It's already been done—the money's signed into a trust. I couldn't take it back, even if I wanted it." He reached a tentative hand to touch her back.

She inched away. "I hope you don't think you're paying me for services rendered."

"That would be ridiculous. You hadn't rendered anything at that point, and by the time I touched you, you were already a wealthy woman."

She huffed. "Your pardon. I…I don't quite comprehend what you've done."

He let the silence flow between them, unsure how to respond to that.

"I had some money," she said stiffly. "I wouldn't have needed it."

He shrugged. "Now you have more."

She let out a puff of laughter. "Oh, honestly. I can't understand this. I just can't understand what is happening. Yesterday, I was alone. And now…" She shook her head. "Things like this do not happen to women like me."

And there were those words again. "Women like you?" he asked, forcing his voice to calm. "What kind of woman do you suppose you are?"

"Mark, I'm a woman who has been unchaste outside of marriage."

"Jessica," he parroted, "in case you failed to notice—I am a man who has been unchaste outside of marriage."

She fell silent.

"Why do you think I came to you like this?" he continued. "I told you once—you are the point of chastity, not its enemy. What was the use holding on to principles that only served to make you feel as if you were beneath me? When I marry you, I want you to know you're my equal."

"Marry you? You can't really want to marry

me. You shouldn't feel obligated, just because we were intimate."

"I gave up twenty-eight years of chastity. It wasn't on a whim. I'm not asking for your hand out of a fleeting sense of obligation or regret. I want you in my life. I want you to meet my brothers. I want you to bear my children."

She took a shuddering breath. "You can't convince me that you've dreamed of marrying a courtesan. And—oh, I'm trying to imagine it, but I just can't."

"Hmm." He reached out a hand to her, found her fingers. "True. I never dreamed of this. But now that I've found you, anything else seems a nightmare. Dreams change with circumstances. Often for the better."

"Not in my experience." Her voice was still and flat, but she let her fingers twine with his. "Two months ago, my dearest dream was to never sell my body again. A far cry from my childhood fantasies."

"Am I so far from your childhood dreams, then?"

She shook her head. "I always believed I would be married. I was pretty. Everyone told me so. So I thought that one day, my perfect husband would find me. He'd ask me to marry him. We'd call the banns in my father's church, and three weeks later, I would walk down the aisle."

Her nails bit into his hand.

"That's right." Mark kept his tone carefully neutral. "Your father is a vicar."

"He was very formal, you see. Very proper. He…he never knew quite what to do with us. I don't believe he'd expected to have beautiful daughters. My mother is pretty. But…the three of us, we were something else. We turned heads, and it confounded him." She shook her head in wry bemusement. "I was a confounding child, even before I ruined myself."

"Was he angry, when it happened?"

"Angry? No. He was very frightened. He was not wealthy. A poor vicar with three beautiful daughters must be very careful. Gossip will magnify the slightest mistake. If my reputation had the tiniest blemish, it would have reflected on my sisters and damaged their prospects. Perhaps it might have ruined them altogether."

"Was there a great deal of gossip?"

"No." She shook her head. Her hair covered his hands momentarily, before she flicked it away again. "Just sympathy."

His eyebrows flickered downward in confusion.

"Nobody ever found out. My father threw me out of the house. Then he put it about that I had become ill, that I went to stay with relatives in Bath for my health. After a month, they told everyone I had died."

His breath sucked in. "Oh, Jessica."

He'd thought the other night that he was rich because he had his brothers. He felt it doubly now. He set his hands on the curve of her shoulders.

"Don't. Don't feel sorry for me. It doesn't sting any longer."

He didn't believe that, not one bit.

"And he was right," Jessica said. "He was right when he told me I should not take risks with my reputation. He was right when he told me I should not go driving with an older man. And he was right to throw me out of the house and disown me entirely. I was born Jessica Carlisle. Since then, I've called myself Jessica Farleigh. I relinquished all rights to my family name when I lost my family."

The silence ate into him, caustic as acid.

"Your father. The man who first ruined you." He tallied marks on her shoulder as he spoke. "And when you finally told me, I walked away from you. Jessica, has anyone ever stood by you?"

"My sisters." A tiny whisper. "Charlotte and Ellen." Jessica smiled. "We used to talk. If they'd been asked, I don't want to think what they would have sacrificed for me—but I know they would—" She cut the sentence short. "Maybe it does still hurt a little."

She drew in careful breaths, as if measuring them precisely would stave off tears.

"I send my father letters," she continued. "So

they'll know I'm alive and well. But I've not heard one word from my family in seven years. Every year, I check the church records, just so I know where they are."

Seven years. Mark tried to imagine what that would feel like, tried to envision himself cut off from his brothers for even so many weeks. He couldn't comprehend it. Even when he and Smite had spent those months on the streets of Bristol, his brother had protected him. He couldn't imagine a world in which his siblings didn't exist. He had never been alone.

"Oh, Jessica."

She smacked him on the shoulder—not hard, but enough to get his attention. "Look at me, Mark. Look at *me*, and stop feeling sorry for me. I'm not fourteen any longer. I lived. I survived. I did what had to be done. And it could have been worse."

"How?"

"He might not have taken me to London," Jessica said simply. "And I might have ended up in the hands of a procuress, or in a brothel. I…I may have been fourteen when I left home, but I met Amalie the first week I arrived. She had had the same protector for five years. She taught me how to get by. How to avoid the worst mistakes. Don't you feel sorry for me, Mark. I *survived*."

"Stop simply *surviving*. Marry me. Forget all of that—"

She leaned back into him. Her fingers found his lips, cutting off his words. "Don't. Don't. The most important thing that Amalie taught me is when it was safe to stay, and when you have to walk away."

"You're going to walk away from me?" Mark felt something dangerous building in his chest. "Not a chance."

"No. You don't know the worst of it." Her voice was small. "There is something else. Something you don't know."

"Something worse than being cast out at fourteen?"

She didn't answer right away. He reached out to her and pulled her to him. He could feel the subtle tremble of her hands. But she didn't push him away. And when he held her, stroked her hair, she leaned against him. That was an illusion, though; he could feel her tension.

"It happened when I discovered I was pregnant."

He started in surprise, and she stopped speaking. Her breath grew shorter. His had, too.

"I had taken precautions, of course, but no precaution is ever entirely effective. By the time I realized what was happening and told my...protector, I was months along."

Mark's throat closed, swallowing all the words he could imagine. He breathed, forcing them out anyway. "Did he cast you off?"

"No." Jessica swallowed the lump in her throat.

"He was actually quite kind. Or so I thought. He told me he would take care of the matter, that I should have nothing to worry about. I thought—I thought he meant…"

She didn't say anything for a while. She had, perhaps, thought he meant to care for her. To keep her, in a more permanent capacity—to make some provision for her.

"The next time he saw me, he offered me a cup of a special blend of tea. He told me it had been mixed particularly for him, and he wanted me to try some. It was supposed to be a flavored tea, he said. An experiment, released only to a few."

He couldn't speak at all, could only hold her.

"It wasn't just tea leaves in there. It was pennyroyal and lady's lace and I don't know what else from the apothecary, all brewed to bitterness, and then mixed with milk and sweetened. I didn't know what was in the pot. He said he liked it. And so I drank it all. Just to be polite. You always have to be polite."

Mark's mind had descended into utterly horrified confusion.

"I didn't know," she said again. And this time, he could hear the edge of tears in her voice. "I didn't know what he'd mixed in."

"What—what had he—" But he already knew.

"The mix promoted female bleeding," she said. "When taken in sufficient quantities…"

He could feel the wet of her tears against his shoulder. In fact, he could feel his own eyes prickle. His hands stung. He held her as tightly as he could, not daring to let her go.

"He told me later that he didn't know how strong a dose I'd need. To be certain, he tripled the apothecary's suggestion. That evening, I began to bleed, and it didn't stop. It just came and came. I nearly died. And when the physician arrived and examined me, and was made to understand precisely how I'd been dosed…" She trailed off. "The physician…he's one that a great many courtesans have used. He's not the sort to make cruel remarks, or make us feel uncomfortable."

He stroked her forehead, the side of her face, not sure what else to say.

"It was so idiotic of me." Her voice caught. "When I discovered I was pregnant, I was scared. I was worried. I didn't know what to do. But there was also part of me that was secretly pleased because I wasn't going to be alone any longer."

He didn't know what to say to this.

"He took that from me. Without asking. He made me weak and powerless—made me into so much nothing, that I could not even decide my own future." She was shaking now, her hands trembling in his. "Every time I think of it, I remember that. I survived everything else. But that…that nearly killed me."

"Jessica. Don't cry. Please don't cry. You *did* survive, and thank God for that."

"I knew I had to get out. Had to stop being a courtesan. That's why I had to seduce you—I needed the money so I wouldn't have to go back. I couldn't go back. Not to that."

"Hush," he said. "Don't worry about that now. I understand."

"There's more. The physician told me there was a good chance I'm barren because of that. You want a family. I'm not sure I can give you one."

Mark thought of a dark alley and a deserted street, many years ago. "If it comes down to it, there are children enough in need of parents. As for family…I *have* a family. I want to share mine with you."

"But what would happen to them if you wed me?" Her fingers bit into his arms. "The man… the man who did this to me was George Weston."

Of all the surprises Mark could have had at the moment, this was the least welcome. His mind washed blank. "George Weston," he repeated. "George *Weston*. George Weston?"

"If we were to marry, I could not avoid him. He's a part of your social set." Her hands clenched into his arm. "He hates you—he'd tell everyone who I was. You can claim that I'm your equal in sin all you like, but you know society will not agree."

"Hang society," Mark said thickly. "I don't care."

"But I do. If I were in society, I couldn't escape him. I couldn't escape myself. And most of all, Mark...I can't bear to remember."

Alongside his horror, another emotion was growing. It was white-hot in its fury. It would consume him, if he let it. It was offensive that Weston had ever offered a reward for Mark's seduction. But it was downright repulsive what he'd done to Jessica. He remembered Jessica flinching when he'd reached for her. Weston had committed an assault without fists, as determined an act of violence as rape. He had nearly *killed* her.

"To hell with Weston," Mark heard himself say fiercely. "To hell with all of that. We'll figure it out."

"There isn't any we."

Maybe there hadn't been, for her. But this wasn't the time to dispute what she'd said with words. No; he had better arguments. Now was the time for him to hold her, to whisper soft reassurance in her ear. Now was the time to nuzzle her neck and tell her that everything would be all right.

"I will not leave you. Not for my reputation, not for my wealth, not for my hope of heaven. We'll work it out in the morning. I refuse to give you up just because one man happens to be an unmitigated ass."

"And if I ask you to leave?"

His lip curled. He shook his head. "Bollocks on that," he said.

And then, despite everything she'd said, despite everything she'd told him, he felt her smile against his shoulder.

Balance. Calm. That's what he gave her now, what she needed from him. But deep inside himself, something dangerous whispered.

Calm now; retribution tomorrow.

CHAPTER NINETEEN

TOMORROW CAME ALL too swiftly, and with it, Mark's plan for revenge. It didn't take long to find his quarry. Weston was too much of a creature of habit to escape.

The sun was high overhead, and Weston was scurrying across the lawn of Hyde Park when Mark found him. Ironic, that he was headed to meet with men whom he hoped would put him forward for the position on the Commission on the Poor Laws. The upcoming vacancy had been announced today; the nomination to fill it would soon be made.

"Weston," Mark called across the expanse of the park.

Weston paused and turned, a puzzled expression on his face. That expression faded to annoyance as he found Mark striding toward him. His jaw stiffened; the corners of his mouth ticked down.

"Sir Mark." He made the words sound like an insult.

After Mark had listened to Jessica's tale last

night, anything out of Weston's mouth would have seemed an insult. Mark walked forward. "I heard you had some interest in the Commission."

Weston scowled and folded his arms. Around them, people were promenading. Mark knew his appearance would draw attention. He'd hoped for it, in fact. He felt almost calm, floating in a sea of inaction.

That was going to change.

"And what does it matter to you?" Weston growled.

Mark smiled. "I'm going to make sure you don't get it," he said.

"You sanctimonious prig. I should like to see you stop me."

"Pardon me." Mark needed to stay calm. "You don't think there will be any…any interest in the fact that you hired a woman to seduce me? Now, that would be an amusing addition to the serial that concluded in the papers a few days ago. I wonder what that should do to your reputation?"

"I—" Weston looked about and lowered his voice. "You can't prove that." He swallowed. "I don't know what you're talking about," he added, belatedly.

"Oh, I could prove it," Mark said. But he wouldn't. He wasn't about to thrust Jessica into the center of attention over this. The last thing she needed was to be permanently linked with this man in the public's eye.

"How much power do you think you'd have," Mark said, "if people knew the true you? A man so cowardly he resorts to hiring women to do his dirty business, and so untrustworthy he cheats them in the end."

Weston took a step forward, his fists balling. "I am not a coward. You don't want to start a fight with me, Sir Mark. I warn you."

"No." Mark smiled placidly. He didn't want to *start* the fight. "I'd imagine you're afraid. It's not so easy to be powerful, when you have to face down someone your own size." His calm was a scant layer of civility over an anger that had taken control of his entire being. He could almost see the moment when Weston's temper snapped, could see his hand curl into a fist, draw back from him. Everything seemed to happen so slowly. Mark could have moved, could have stepped out of the way of the punch that Weston threw, so languidly did it seem to drift toward him.

But if he had dodged, all of Hyde Park would not have seen Weston hit him unprovoked. Mark barely felt it land, in the haze of his fury. His head snapped back; the force of the blow knocked him to the ground. He saw the limbs of a tree wave overhead, green leaves obscuring blue sky. All around him, gasps rose, and people turned, rushing over to them.

Mark jumped lightly to his feet.

"I box regularly," Weston said, raising his fists. "I shoot, too. There's more where that came from. I *told* you not to start a fight with me."

"I don't box at all." Mark stood in stillness, a calm contrast to Weston's bouncing on his toes. "I wasn't going to start a fight with you. But I was rather hoping I could finish one."

Mark had never seen the need for boxing—especially not with the newly adopted rules that brought civility to the fighting. But then, he'd lived on the Bristol streets as a child. He'd learned to fight in a harsher environment than the London Prize Ring.

And so when Weston threw a second punch, Mark swiveled to the side. He caught the man's fist in his hand as it passed, jerked Weston to the side and let the man's own momentum send him crashing to the ground.

Weston gasped like a fish as the wind was knocked out of him. Mark set one hand idly against the trunk of the tree and waited.

"You tripped me," Weston said in confusion. "But don't think you can beat me for sheer power."

Mark didn't have to wait long for Weston to stand. The puzzled ridge of his eyebrows faded to anger as Mark smiled at him. With an outraged cry, he ran forward once more. Mark had no intention of grappling with the man. He side-stepped again and grabbed his arm. Weston *did* have sheer power. He was fast, and his arms were locked in position with all his strength. So when Mark swung him in a circle, he had no way to stop before he crashed into the tree behind them. He hit it face-first, barely able to raise his hands to protect his nose.

Shouts rose up behind them.

Mark wasn't even breathing hard.

Weston turned, unsteady on his feet. He lifted one hand to his mouth and spat out a tooth. For a second, he simply stared at it in disbelief. Then he raised his head.

"You goddamned dirty bastard," he breathed, starting forward once more. He was more wary this time, keeping his distance. Still, the next time he darted forward, Mark stepped behind him and slammed his elbow against the back of the man's neck. As Weston fell, Mark caught his arm and yanked at an awkward angle. He could almost feel the pop as the man's shoulder jerked out of its socket.

To his credit, Weston didn't scream, even though his face scrunched up. "Pax," he whispered. "Pax. Truly. I had no idea." He backed away, leaning against the tree.

Mark strode forward.

"Truly, Sir Mark." Weston spoke so quietly, Mark could barely hear him. "I give up. I surrender."

Mark could dimly recall the last time he'd lost his temper this badly. At the time, he'd been at Eton and surrounded by bullies. He'd beaten the lot of them, and when they'd begged for mercy, he'd still not stopped. For years, he'd felt guilty every time he thought of his actions. He'd feared his anger, his passion, as proof that he, too, could fall prey to his mother's excesses.

But now, seeing Weston cower before him, he realized one last thing. After he'd beaten those boys, they'd never set on anyone else again. He'd been ashamed for no reason. There *was* a place for righteous anger. And sometimes the only way to balance the worst kinds of wrongs was to meet them head-on. He didn't stuff the tide of his anger behind a glass wall. Instead, he stalked forward.

"You misunderstand," he said, his voice low. "I know what you did to Jessica Farleigh."

"What I did? Hired her to seduce you. That bitch—she took my money, and—"

Mark grabbed the man by his hair and twisted. Weston hissed in pain. "I'm talking about the tea," Mark said.

"Ouch!" Weston tried to pull away and winced instead. "Good Christ almighty, is she still going on about that? I saved her the pain of having to make the decision herself."

"You stole the decision from her. You nearly killed her."

"It was an accident."

Mark let his anger take hold of him. He gripped Weston's hair, then slammed the back of the man's head against the tree trunk.

"Ow!" Weston groaned. "You can be commissioner. Just…just don't hurt me anymore."

There was a time for mercy. This wasn't it.

"You're pathetic," Mark informed the man and slammed his head against the tree one last time. Weston's knees crumpled underneath him. Around them, the crowd gasped. Mark let go of his hair, and Weston fell the rest of the way to the ground. For a long moment, Mark stared at the still body at his feet. He couldn't hear anything except the rushing in his ears, could barely feel the cool breeze of afternoon insinuating itself around them. Finally, he knelt and found the man's pulse. It was strong and steady.

He wasn't going mad. He'd not lost control of his temper. He'd used it, and he was glad.

"Someone fetch a physician," he said over his shoulder. "He'll do very well, but he's going to have a monstrous headache when he awakes."

He pushed to his feet and walked away. Behind him, he heard the murmurs of the crowd.

"That was Sir Mark," someone was saying.

"Weston must have truly deserved it," another responded, "for Sir Mark to hit him that way. He's a gentle, kind-spoken soul, Sir Mark is."

"What did he do, then?"

"Something awful," a third person responded. "Besides, I saw him. He attacked Sir Mark for no reason—he can't be a steady character, can he?"

So easily was a reputation ruined. There was a peculiar sense of justice in that. Mark shook out his hand, which was just now beginning to sting, and headed for his next destination.

"GUESS WHAT I have?"

Mark stood in Jessica's doorway that evening. He'd donned a wide, worn hat—one that shielded his face from view. Still, this close, even in the gathering shadows, she could see the bruise forming on his cheekbone.

She stepped aside, and he came in, shutting the door behind him.

"You forget," she said grimly. "It's already in the paper." She held up the offending item, letting the headline show.

Sir Mark: Fights Weston, Obtains Special License.

"Be thankful," Jessica said. "Parret made no untoward speculation about the object of your license, and he could have."

Mark took off his hat and gave Jessica an unapologetic grin. "Well. So much for the surprise, then."

"Don't you think it's a little premature to be purchasing a special license?"

"I'm never premature," he told her. "I'm always precisely on time." He pulled his greatcoat from his shoulders and set it on a hook.

She'd once dreamed of a little country cottage, of a life spent in solitude with only Amalie to keep her company. Perhaps…perhaps she'd been afraid to wish for anything else. Hope was painful, after all. But now, she couldn't beat it back, couldn't shove it away. She could almost make herself believe in a future that contained Mark. And not only Mark—a family.

Because when she'd seen the headline across the square, her thoughts had flown for the first time to her sisters. Surely, married to Sir Mark, she might see them again? Perhaps, with the news of her death, they'd have to meet in secret. But she wouldn't have to be dead to them entirely, would she?

She squelched those thoughts viciously. Best not to want; that way, she'd feel no disappointment. Hope hurt.

So, she imagined, did that dark bruise on his face.

"Come here," she said severely, taking his hand

and leading him to a chair that she'd set near a basin. He sat, looking at her in bemusement. Jessica concentrated on the task before her. She steeped a cloth in the cool water of the basin and then laid it on his face.

"Ah," he said. "That feels good."

She'd scented the water with herbs. They released their sweet aroma into the air. It made the atmosphere take on the aspect of a dream as if this were some wooded glen, taken from her imagination and not a room in dirty London. Her hands moved to his shoulders, and she rubbed them.

"Did Weston scream?" she asked. "Did he grovel?"

"Indeed."

"How gratifying."

He snorted under the damp cloth. "It was, actually. I wish you could have been there."

"Oh, the account in the paper was lovely." She sighed again. "I wish…I wish…"

"What do you want?"

Her hands were cool and moist from the compress. His fingers reached up and intertwined themselves with hers, warm and dry.

"It's lovely what you did, Mark." She shook her head. "I…I never thought he'd pay for what he'd done."

But. She left the word unspoken. But it didn't make it any better. Mark couldn't make the man give back what he'd stolen—not with any number of beatings. She still felt sick when she thought of Weston, like some creature cowering in the underbrush. It hadn't made her feel any better. It had just made Weston feel worse.

A cause for celebration, to be sure. Still…

"Dearest," Mark said, taking the cloth from his eye. "You *will* marry me, won't you?"

She could choke on the hope he made her feel. Her hands shook. "I— Even if Weston stays silent and hidden, someone might recognize me. And the paper—it says you're likely to be appointed Commissioner of the Poor Laws, with Weston in disgrace. You'll constantly find yourself in the public's eye. Perhaps even more than you are now, hard as that is to believe. *Someone* will speak out about me. We would be disgraced."

"You haven't met my elder brother." Mark smiled. "The Duke of Parford. He'll make sure nothing goes wrong."

"Even a duke can't stop gossip."

"Stop worrying." He said the words lightly, but she could see the tic in his cheek, the tension in his hand as it balled lightly into a fist.

"And you're going to be Commissioner now. You didn't even *want* to be Commissioner."

"Well." He didn't deny this. "But I did want you."

Jessica had suffered the waning of a man's interest often enough to know the course of *want*. At first, a man was willing to give up almost anything. But soon enough, want settled into familiarity. Soon, those little deprivations would start to sting and then fester.

She could barely accept Mark's regard. She couldn't manage his resentment.

She held out her hand to him. There was no hope to be had, not in this. There was only tonight.

"Will you come to my bed?" she asked. It wasn't an answer to his question. It was, instead, a different sort of offer. He looked at her hand. Slowly, he raised his own to touch her fingertips. His fingers curled about hers again, so warm, so confident.

"Yes," Mark said, his voice low and throaty. "Yes, I will."

CHAPTER TWENTY

WHEN JESSICA AWOKE, Mark was asleep beside her. In the pale light of morning, he looked innocent. Young. She was almost afraid to touch him, lest she break the spell that had brought a man like this to her.

It felt like Christmas morning as a child—that sense of unreal anticipation, that feeling that something good might be waiting for her, if only she hurried to meet the day. But it was only in bed that they could be together like this. For all his fine words last night, he had to know that she didn't fit in his life. *He* didn't fit in *hers*. He was a knight, Her Majesty's own moralist. He was London's proper darling. He was Sir Mark Turner—and she was still the woman who had seduced him.

Everything innocent about her was dead—almost literally. She could shut her eyes and remember the obituary her father had placed in the paper. She wasn't Guinevere to his Lancelot. She was a courtesan. No knight, however skilled he was in the art of war, could take on the field of windmills that had taken her prisoner.

Still, she placed her hand against his chin. His skin was warm and rough with stubble. Whatever had happened that fate had brought her this man? How was she to send him away? And had he really given her five thousand pounds? What an idiotic, absurdly…romantic…gesture.

On that thought, his eyes fluttered open. He blinked twice and looked at her.

"There's nothing to eat," she told him gravely.

"Just as well." He sat up, rubbing his eyes. She waited for him to come to his senses. Surely *now,* he must have reconsidered.

"Good morning," he said, and he leaned over and touched his lips to hers.

For one lovely second, she could believe the promise in his kiss: that this would not fade, that she would wake up to him for a thousand mornings to come. Ten thousand mornings.

She pulled back abruptly. It had seemed *safe* to love him, when she'd believed him far beyond her touch. But she didn't know what she believed any longer. She only knew that everything she held dear eventually crumbled to dust.

"I wish we'd put some thought into your clothing last night," she mumbled. "It's been lying on the floor all evening, and it's probably wrinkled."

"I hung it in front of the fire," he offered. "After you'd gone to sleep."

She cast him a baleful look. Really. He was *too* good, sometimes.

"I'm sure there'll be some wrinkles," he continued, "but nothing too unseemly. Can you tie my cravat?"

"Tight around your neck," she muttered.

He shrugged away her foul mood. "Oh, stop worrying. Come. Break your fast with me."

"I told you—"

"Not here."

"You want to have breakfast with me, out *there?* You are mad."

His eyes glittered at that last word, and she almost called it back.

But he spoke in precise tones. "I want to have an entire life with you, out there. Do keep that in mind."

She couldn't even imagine breakfast. She tried to envision Sir Mark entering a public house and asking for kippers and tea. Here in London, he would be besieged within minutes. One look at his wrinkled shirt and his disreputable companion, and his good name would cease to be so good. And once he'd tasted the censure of society, he'd not be so sanguine about linking himself to her.

"In any event," he said, "I don't intend to go *out* precisely. I had in mind somewhere private."

"But the servants—"

"Will say my intended is beautiful and gracious." He glanced up at her. "You do recall how to be gracious, do you not?"

Jessica winced and set her hands over her face. She was being uncivil and for no other reason than that Sir Mark had not yet given her up. He was anticipating marriage; she, despair.

"You're quite right," she finally said. "I'll feel more myself once I've had something to eat." After all, it wasn't fair to punish him for sins he had yet to commit. "Help me dress," she added, "and I'll help you."

It took Jessica too long to get ready—in part because Mark's help was of dubious value. She had no sooner pulled on her shift than his hands fell on her hips, smoothing the fabric into place. And instead of pulling her corset tighter when she asked, he put his own arms about her, holding her tight. Kissing the back of her neck. His hands roamed the front of her body. She twisted in his grasp—she'd intended to tell him to get on with it, then—but even her foul mood couldn't last when he held her face and kissed her as if she were some precious thing.

It felt fragile, that kiss. As if this, too, would break. As if the future could rise up and choke the life from even this mutual desire. But he pressed her against the wall, and there was nothing delicate about his want. She couldn't envision the future, but she comprehended this *now*—the hard ridge of his lust against her belly, the demands of his mouth, her own lust rising, hard and fast. She brought one leg up to draw him in. "Hold me," she explained, guiding his hands to her hips. It took a few moments for him to get the idea—a few seconds until he slid inside her once more.

Each thrust speared through her uncertainty, each kiss grounded her. His hands held her up. When she came, it shattered her anxiety, splintering dark fears away.

His orgasm followed, fierce and relentless. Jessica shut her eyes and held on to his arms, letting the fury of his pleasure sweep everything else away. When he was done, he pressed another kiss against her skin.

He was the first man who had ever cared to kiss her *afterward.* Maybe this would work. She opened her eyes to see him watching her.

"Mark," she whispered.

"Yes?"

"Good morning." And she smiled at him then.

This time, they really did manage to dress. Jessica found a threadbare cloak for Mark—one that would keep off the drizzle and simultaneously shield him from public view. And it turned out that nobody looked twice at him under his immense hat. Mark spoke to the driver outside Jessica's hearing; the carriage jerked to life shortly after he entered. For the first ten minutes, Jessica made no sound. Their hands tangled together in slow, steady exploration.

Finally, she spoke up. "Where are we going? I should have thought we could find a private hotel not half a mile away."

Mark ran his thumb over her fingers. "It will take longer. We're not going to a hotel."

"Perhaps you should have let me arrange it," she continued. "After all, I have considerably more experience in anonymity than you."

His fingers covered her lips. "I never said I was looking for a place where I would be anonymous. I said I was looking for one that was *private*."

"There is a difference?"

The carriage jolted over a rut in the road.

"Yes. It has never been my plan to hide you away," he told her. "You aren't some hideous, shameful secret of mine."

A curl of unease crept into her. Jessica shook her head. "What on earth do you have planned? Where are we going?"

There was a window in the door, but the glass did not appear to have been cleaned anytime in the past eight months. It was so smudged over that she could only make out vague impressions of shadows passing her by.

"We're going to Mayfair."

"Mayfair?"

Mark shot her a strangely reluctant look before he confessed. "My brother's house."

Jessica stood, cracking her head on the top of the carriage and biting her tongue in the process. The physical pain stung, but it only increased the abject horror that filled her. "Your brother!" Her wounded tongue didn't seem to be working quite right. "You cannot be theriouth."

"But I am." He pulled her down to sit beside him once more. And then he ran his hand over her head, finding the sore spot where she'd whacked herself. He rubbed it gently, soothing away the hurt.

"Stop it." Jessica pulled from his arms. "You're mussing my hair. I didn't dress to visit a duke." Her panic was beginning to rise. "He's going to toss me out the instant he claps eyes on me. What are you thinking, bringing a courtesan to see the Duke of Parford?"

Mark simply shook his head. "You misunderstand. I'm not bringing a courtesan to visit a duke. I'm bringing my future wife to see my brother. It just so happens that he is also a duke. But Ash is… Ash is… Look, he just doesn't care about that sort of thing. He's not the kind of person who will toss someone out simply because she doesn't fit some preconceived notion of his. Trust me, Ash will be *delighted* to be able to do something for me."

"Mark." All her fears came rushing back. "Mark, I am a *courtesan.* I don't fit in your world. Your reputation—your good name—is at stake."

"So far as I can tell, I would greatly benefit if my reputation were to suffer. No reporters following me about. Nobody writing about my household refuse." He sighed and leaned back. "It sounds idyllic. We could live in the country. Would you mind that?"

That notion she'd once had, of a cottage in the country, came back to her. But this time, she wasn't alone. Mark was with her. And that made her country cottage not a place to hide away and lick her wounds, but a place to start afresh, the situation for a new life where she was liked and respected, where she had Sir Mark, where she found herself Lady Turner and not some woman who would be snubbed by the meanest letter carrier. It was so powerful a thought that she was staggered.

"Do you love me?" he asked casually. "You said you did."

She gaped at him, unsure how to answer.

"Thought so." He grinned at her. "I can understand that you may feel some trepidation now. But wait until you meet my brothers. They'll adore you."

"Awk," Jessica managed.

"Don't worry."

She shook her head. "Those are the two most

ineffectual words ever put together by man—don't worry. I can't stop worrying just because someone assures me it's unnecessary."

He blew out his breath. "Then do worry, if you prefer."

His assurance did nothing to calm the fluttering confusion she felt. It peaked, sharply, as the crunch of wheels on gravel sounded, and the carriage jerked to a halt. A few moments later, a liveried footman opened the grimy door. Mark handed her down, onto a pristine half ring of white rocks outside a Portland stone building. He took her arm and then swept her through the front door as it opened.

"Sir Mark," the butler greeted him. He did not seem to think anything was amiss with Mark's wrinkled attire. Still, Jessica could almost envision the headline that afternoon. *Sir Mark: Turning to Dissipation at Last?*

"Is Ash still at breakfast? Is Smite here?"

"No, sir, and yes, sir. Mr. Smite Turner is at breakfast." The butler paused, contemplating his words. "Mr. Smite Turner informed me that you've spent the last two nights with him, and that I'm to expect you to be out of sorts."

That latter, Jessica decoded, was a hint that his brothers were already spinning stories to save his reputation.

"Ah," Mark said. "I see. Is Ash in his office?"

"Yes, sir."

"Busy, is he? Could you have him duck into the blue parlor when he's got a chance?"

"Yes, sir."

"This is…" Mark paused and cast a look askance at her.

How *awkward*. He probably didn't even recall her true name. "This," he said again, "is my fiancée. Do tell Ash."

There was a slight pause, as the butler turned to look at her. He waited, no doubt expecting a name. When none was forthcoming, he nodded. "I'll do that."

"Oh," Mark added, "please send a tray up, as well." He conducted Jessica into a room on her right.

She'd known his family was wealthy—he had, after all, thrown five thousand pounds her way without thinking. But she hadn't quite understood the extent of it until this moment. She felt as if she might have been in a royal palace. Blue velvet cushions lay on delicate rosewood chairs. A tapestry covered one wall; a globe sat on a table, the countries fashioned of amber and turquoise and lapis lazuli.

Jessica didn't even have a name worth giving. She set her finger on Africa and gave the globe a spin. Mark came to stand by her as it whirled.

"I didn't introduce you properly," he said in a low voice.

"I noticed." Continents passed under her gaze.

"Until I speak with Ash, and we determine how to proceed, I thought it best to wait." He reached out and stopped the earth as it turned on its axis. "Once we tell the servants who you are, there's no going back."

"Of course." It all made perfect sense. Still, it heightened the feeling that she might not truly be present. This was a room for other people— wealthy, respectable people. Even the candle sconces were decorated with crystals that sent rainbows shimmering about the room.

In the hall, footfalls sounded, heavy and fast.

"*That* didn't take long." Mark turned.

The door burst open. "Mark," the man in the doorway said, "what in God's holy name can you have been thinking?" The man crossed the room in three strides and engulfed Mark in what looked like a ferocious hug. "You idiot," the man was saying. "You mope for a week, and then you disappear for forty-eight hours without leaving word at all. I've heard nothing of you but what Margaret was able to glean from the papers. Have you any idea how worried I was?"

"Stop fussing, Ash. I am an adult. I *told* you where I was going." Mark pulled away, and Jessica got her first good look at the newcomer. The two men looked…nothing alike. The Duke of Parford was broader than Mark and taller—a physique that seemed suited more to a laborer than to a peer and a businessman. His hair was coffee-dark; his skin tanned.

"Fuss, fuss," Parford muttered, and he reached out and ruffled Mark's hair.

Oh, to be part of a family again. It almost hurt to watch. It hurt more when Parford looked over and his eyes fell on her. She could see the wariness creep into his expression, the tight lines collecting on his cheeks. Not much reaction from him, but she felt as if he'd slammed a door in her face.

"We do have a great deal to talk about," the duke said.

Mark was turning to her. "Ash, this is Jessica Farleigh. She is—"

The duke looked her over, and then slowly, he crossed to her and put out his hand. Jessica blinked at him and then took it.

"So. I suppose we'll have to figure out how to keep you from hanging in the court of public opinion."

"I…I suppose we will," she said.

He nodded politely to her. But as he did, he spoke under his breath. "Hurt my brother," he told her, "and I will hang you up myself."

For some reason, the threat made her feel more at ease than mere friendliness.

The duke pulled away and gestured. "Come, Mark, speak with me in my office."

"Don't try and exclude Jessica. This is about her, too, and—"

"Leave off, Mark." Ash rolled his eyes. "Margaret arrived here yesterday—didn't you hear me say so? She wants to talk to your Jessica. It's some sort of woman conversation. We're supposed to take ourselves off and leave them alone."

"Oh, well, then." Mark brightened. "You'll like Margaret. And she'll love you—I'm her favorite brother."

In Jessica's estimation, duchesses didn't take kindly to women who preyed on their virtuous younger brothers. Especially not when the brother in question was her favorite. "Hmm," she said. "How comforting."

Mark was already half out the door.

The room seemed darker after he left, and smaller. She'd come to know Mark when he lived in an isolated house, all by himself, with a few servants to come in and look in on him from time to time—as if he were mere gentry, surviving on a few hundred pounds a year. Even then, the gap between their stations had seemed enormous.

But this... The candelabra on the wall were edged with faceted crystal. The dark, polished wood of the wainscoting met gold and cream and red paper. And when she craned her neck, she saw a ceiling of clever plasterwork, gilt-and-blue edging cunning landscapes. She felt as if she'd walked into a royal hall while wearing a sack. She reached out one finger—not because she wanted to stroke the impossibly delicate vase before her, but just to make sure that it was *solid*. It couldn't be real. None of this could.

A tap-tap sounded behind her. Jessica whirled around, knotting her hands together behind her back. She felt as if she were a thief, caught in the act of slipping valuables into her skirt pockets.

But this wasn't the Duchess of Parford standing in the doorway—not unless the duke was even more broad-minded than Mark had represented.

"Mrs. Farleigh." The man who stood before her was thinner than Mark, and taller. He was dressed in dark blue. His hair was ebony, his eyes blue. She could see traces of Mark in his face—and none of Mark's innocence in his eyes.

"You must be Mr. Sm—Mr. Turner, I mean."

"I see my brother has disclosed my appalling name." He didn't smile at her, and she swallowed. They stared at each other a long time, like strange cats, not sure what to make of one another. If she looked away, she feared he might be upon her in a second, rending her fur.

"I don't bite," he finally offered, and he came into the room.

"No? You *are* the magistrate, are you not?"

He sat next to her. "Guilty conscience? Never fear. My jurisdiction doesn't extend to London."

She swallowed and looked away.

"That," he said, "was supposed to be a joke. I'm starting this off completely wrong." He scrubbed his hand through his hair. "Welcome to the family."

That had to be some kind of trap. "You can't want a connection with one such as I."

He shrugged. "Has Mark told you about me at all? I live alone in Bristol, and I infuriate the local gentry by letting various ragtag scoundrels go from time to time, simply because I believe they're innocent of the crime with which they've been charged."

"Oh."

"They've taken to calling me Lord Justice," he said. "Which normally I would object to, but it's a damned sight better than Smite."

"So you and Mark have both captured the *ton's* imagination."

"Ah. It's the common people who call me Lord Justice."

He still wasn't smiling, but Jessica caught something suspiciously like a twinkle in his eye.

"What do the gentry call you, then?"

"Your Worship," he said, drawing himself up. Then he winked at her. "To my face. Behind my back, now…"

She laughed, then, and finally he did smile at her.

"That *is* all that matters," he declared solemnly. "Let them say what they wish behind your back. You need only be strong enough that they don't say it to your face."

Jessica swallowed. "Well. Then. Lord Justice, what should I do?"

"You had better marry my brother."

She stared at him. "You can't hope that. The scandal—"

"Will be tremendous." He shrugged. "But not impossible. I would list my brother's many sterling qualities, but if you are not yet aware of them, you don't deserve him. You appear to be intelligent, but so far you've exhibited the decision-making capabilities of a lizard."

"A lizard!"

"Don't misunderstand me. Lizards aren't stupid. But they also drop their tails and flee at the first sign of danger."

"That's amusing," she tossed back. "Mark told me once that I reminded him of *you*."

"Really?" He glanced at her, then twisted up his mouth. "I'm not sure this reflects well on either of us."

"You are not the cruel, sober magistrate I was led to imagine," Jessica said, shaking her finger at him. "I have been deceived."

"I'll only say this once." His voice was very quiet. "You will not understand, because Mark does not see it. We want very desperately to like you, and for you to like us. If I had an appalling wife, it would make little difference to..." He spread the fingers of his hand, indicating the household. "But Mark. It would be too impossible, you see, if Mark's wife disliked me. He keeps everyone together."

He met her eyes and looked away. She didn't know what to say to that, and yet she could see it so easily, just as she could see Mark smiling at her and telling her he liked himself. Of course he did; everyone liked him.

"Besides," Smite said, his voice shifting slightly, "I am the trustee of the funds that Mark has given you. I can hardly be your trustee if you don't trust me. This is all a piece of my plan to put you at ease."

"About that," Jessica began. But she heard something behind her. She turned her head and then jumped to her feet with a noise that sounded suspiciously mouselike.

"I didn't mean to frighten you." The woman who stood in the doorway wore a dark green silk day dress covered by a net of black lace. Her hair was pulled into gentle curls, and she observed Jessica with wide, mobile eyes.

"Margaret," Smite said. "Mrs. Farleigh. I'll be off, and let you two converse."

"I—" Jessica bit her tongue. What was she to say after all? *Please, scary magistrate, I'm frightened of another woman.*

"You can stay," the duchess said as she walked in.

Smite shook his head. "No, dear," he said firmly. "I'm quite certain I don't dare." On those words, he disappeared.

"Sit back down," the woman said, patting the cushion next to her.

Jessica sat uncomfortably, as far away as she could.

"You should call me Margaret."

"Your Grace." Mark's sister by marriage didn't say anything about her use of the title, but her eyes narrowed slightly.

"You must be Jessica. Mark's written to me about you. As soon as I heard what had happened in town, I came down. I've never seen him in such a tangle, do you know?"

"I'm so sorry—"

The Duchess of Parford dismissed this with a wave of her hand. "My husband would advise you never to apologize in polite society. They'll take it as permission to savage you."

They sat in silence, Jessica gripping her knees.

A servant came in with a tray and the duchess turned to it.

"Do you take cream? Sugar?" The duchess was a perfect lady—born to the position and then married as highly as possible. Jessica wasn't sure why the woman was treating her so politely. "No. Thank you. I…I don't take tea."

"Coffee? Chocolate? I can ring for something, if you'd like."

Apple brandy would likely be out of the question. Jessica shook her head. The duchess poured herself a cup. "Of course I have an ulterior motive in coming here. I want to meet the woman who has turned Mark upside down."

"Did he tell you I was a courtesan?"

"Well, no." She set her cup down. "Not directly. But Ash did. Really, if I'm to introduce you to everyone, we're going to need a better story. Which is why I am here. Mark is too much of a gentleman to ask, and Ash would never think to do so. But…how likely is it that you'll be recognized?"

"I…I wasn't a particularly famous courtesan."

The duchess made an annoyed sound. "Pardon my directness on what must be a delicate and uncomfortable matter. Nothing else will serve. If you've lain with half the men in London, please tell me now, so we can pack you off to the country before the truth inevitably comes out."

"Oh." Jessica shut her eyes. "Not half." Her voice was quiet. "Not a quarter. Not any sizable fraction. My friend Amalie and I, we had a rule. You see, every man is a risk, so…"

She opened one eye and bit off the rest of the sentence, before she offered the Duchess of Parford an explanation of how to pick a protector.

"But it doesn't matter. It takes only one," Jessica said, her throat closing. "And…and more men knew of me than knew me, so to speak."

The duchess nodded sagely. "So it shall be a small family wedding, then, and a formal wedding trip abroad. Then you can retire to the country to start a family. Is Jessica Farleigh your true name, or was it one you adopted for the profession?"

"I'm Jessica Carlisle."

"Good. We'd best use that, then. That way, the announcement won't cause a stir in and of itself." The duchess picked up her cup again and took a tentative sip.

Jessica shrank back in her seat. "I… If I marry Mark, Your Grace, I promise not to intrude too much. You'll not need to see me—"

The woman set her cup down. "Not *see* you? My dear, Parford Manor is in the country. I'm afraid I've given you the wrong idea." She took Jessica's hand. "You must excuse my forwardness. I have been thinking of you as a potential sister ever since

Mark wrote and asked whether it would be proper to take a walk alone with you outside. I never had any sisters, and none of my brothers have shown the slightest inclination to provide me with one up until this moment."

Jessica gathered her arms around herself, her heart filling with emotion. A *sister*. She'd never thought she'd have another, besides Amalie.

"You cannot want Mark to permanently ally himself with someone of my reputation."

"No," the duchess said easily. "I can't. But you have to understand who Mark is in this family. He taught me how to defend myself against a man. He's…he's just a good person. His brothers would do anything for him. And that means—until the moment you hurt him—we will do anything for you."

It had been so long since anyone had done anything for her.

"That's what families do, after all," the duchess was saying.

For the first time, Jessica began to believe. Maybe she *could* win out. Maybe she could marry Mark, could leave behind the nightmare of the past. Hope…for such a fragile, futile thing, it was incredibly robust.

"I…" Jessica trailed off and glanced to her side.

"Do you think I might have that cup of tea, after all?"

"But of course," the duchess said. "We've your entire wedding trousseau to plan. It's thirsty work."

CHAPTER TWENTY-ONE

MARK LEFT JESSICA with Margaret. She looked at him in faint entreaty when he disappeared, but there was one last duty he needed to see to. He had a responsibility that he'd put off for far too long, and it was recalled to him with every blue-cockaded hat he saw on the street. He'd been avoiding the thought of the MCB and his supporters, but Shepton Mallet had shown him the error in that.

At this point, with Weston discredited, he was as good as on the Commission, however painful the thought was. And if he was to take on that charge, he couldn't sidestep this responsibility, either.

Which is how he found himself in Daniels, a club for young gentlemen. The organization was so exclusive that no sign indicated its provenance on the door. Any man who didn't know where he was wasn't fit for membership.

Mark was *not* a member, but still he walked in. The footman who stood in the entry was wearing a blue armband. His eyes widened when he saw

Mark. He didn't glance at the membership list, didn't come forward bearing obsequious regrets. When Mark told him what he wanted, he nodded gravely.

He took Mark's hat and cloak and handed them off to another fellow; through the door in the cloakroom, Mark caught a glimpse of hats festooned in blue cockades. Truly, he was entering the den of the lion.

In the club itself, young men were gathered around tables, talking quietly. Fully half of them sported the MCB's blue armbands. There were no wagers here, no raucous laughter, as in some of the less sober establishments. Daniels, after all, was considered a proving ground for the future leaders of the country—men who were expected to take seats in Parliament one day, or inherit dukedoms.

The footman escorted Mark to a small back room, where a man sat alone. Mark had heard the fellow's name often enough, but this was the first time he'd seen him in person. The other man was almost Mark's age, he supposed. Strange that their paths had never crossed at Eton or Oxford. Mark wondered where he'd gone instead. How odd.

Jedidiah Pruwett had close-cropped dark hair and a scarce inch of sparse beard. His eyes were obscured by spectacles. The only color of his dark, sober attire was the blue of his armband—and that was starched and unwrinkled. He didn't look up as Mark slipped silently through the doorway, so engrossed was he in his reading.

Mark pulled up a chair and sat. Pruwett was reading the Bible; as he read, he fingered the frame of his glasses. He seemed utterly oblivious to Mark.

Mark waited. Pruwett turned a page, glanced up—and dropped his book on the table, overturning a glass of some clear liquid.

"Sir!" Pruwett shot to his feet, nearly knocking over his chair as he did so. He made an attempt to both reach for his chair and grab his book before the water soaked it through. Instead, he managed to trip over his trousers and land on the floor.

Mark picked up the Bible, stood and offered his hand to the man. Pruwett let out a sigh and took it.

"How embarrassing," he said, as Mark hauled him to his feet. "I'd never wanted to meet you like this, sir. I promise—I'm usually a good bit more agile. It was just, just the surprise of seeing you." Pruwett hadn't let go of Mark's hand. Instead, he pumped it up and down. "You must know what an inspiration you have been to me. You have meant the world to me. Truly, before I read your book I was…" The man colored faintly. "I was lost. I started the MCB to help others find the way, as you have helped me."

Mark took his hand away and felt an awkward twinge. "Well. Thank you."

Pruwett rummaged in his pockets for a handkerchief and threw it over the spill. "Is there any other way I can be of service to you?"

Mark had come here to ask the man to be of... well, of *less* service. But Pruwett was studiously avoiding his gaze. He stood and walked to the door, signaling for a servant. Silence stretched while a footman mopped up the mess.

"Are you thinking of taking a more active role in the MCB?" Pruwett asked. He bit his lip. "We should love to have you."

He didn't look as if he would love to have Mark. He looked nervous.

"I have a great respect for you," Pruwett added, and at least that seemed sincere.

"I'm flattered. I never expected anyone to take my work to heart, let alone a cadre of thousands of men. I'm grateful—and this is rather awkward—but the MCB is not precisely my sort of organization."

Pruwett seemed to relax at that. "Well, I'm delighted that this is just a social call, then. I'll promise not to overset any more liquids, if you'll stay and have a drink with me."

Mark sighed. "No. This is rather difficult to say. I know you mean well. But when I said the MCB is not my sort of organization, I meant...I dislike what you have done."

The color ran from Pruwett's face. Mark felt as

if he were kicking a puppy, but there was no easy way to deliver the news that he carried.

"The teachings of the MCB imply that women are the enemy, that men must avoid them. That sort of attitude gives rise to the precise stigma that all good men should avoid."

"With all due respect, sir, that's not the intent. It's about developing a sense of camaraderie, about finding things to bind good men together."

"Yes, but you do it by resorting to blatant insult and exclusion." Mark frowned. "I don't understand why you can't just…just remain chaste without a club."

"There must be something for men to do together. Elsewise, it's back to the brothels in groups for fun."

"And it's *fun* to tell everyone else how many days it has been since you've been unchaste?" Mark shook his head.

"Not *fun*—necessary to establish appropriate standards of accountability." Pruwett adjusted his spectacles. "Without that, we'd have nothing but hypocrisy. The meetings, the hand signals— they're all necessary, sir, to bring men together, to make them *want* to choose chastity over…over ruination."

"Huh," Mark said. There was something distractingly *odd* about the man's eyes.

"Look around you." Pruwett was warming to

his subject matter. "All these men here—they have something to do. But think of the third sons, boys who are given too much money and too much license. They're wasted, utterly, given no calling, no place in life. They drift aimlessly. They'll never sit in Parliament, never serve on a committee. They've nothing to show for themselves but their family name and a few idle pleasures. I wanted to give those men something to do." He swallowed. "I wanted to give myself something to do."

"Are you saying you started the MCB because you were *bored?*"

Pruwett's eye's widened behind his spectacles. And, with that, Mark realized precisely what had bothered him about the man's eyes. Usually, glasses made a man's eyes look owlish, distorted by the magnification. But Pruwett's eyes were exactly the normal size.

Mark reached out and plucked the man's spectacles from his face, lifted the lens to his eyes.

"Sir…"

"These are plain glass." Mark looked over at Pruwett. Without his spectacles, his nose looked larger. Mark imagined him without that beard… "Davies?" Mark asked in disbelief. "Peter Davies?"

Pruwett—or was it Davies?—crumpled into his chair, as if all the starch had deserted him. Mark *had* known the man at Oxford. Davies had been a...well, he'd been something of a rake. He'd poked fun at Mark often enough.

"Is this some kind of an elaborate jest?" Mark asked.

Pruwett-Davies reached out and snatched his spectacles back. He fitted them on his nose primly. "Jest?" He sounded affronted. "I've spent the last year of my life building the MCB from the ground up, without any help from you, I might add."

"I know what you were like."

"I know what I was like, too." He hid his face in his hands. "I'll thank you not to remind me. I was an irresponsible ass." He let out a great sigh, and his shoulders slumped.

Mark felt a short-lived twinge of sympathy.

"I meant it," Pruwett-Davies mumbled into his hands. "When I said you saved me. I'll admit that I bought your book because I intended to laugh at it. But after the first chapter, I wasn't laughing. You made me feel so ashamed—so ashamed to call myself a man, when I was basically worthless. I had nothing to do but spend my allowance. For months after I read it, I tried to devote myself to good works, just as you suggested. But nobody who did good wanted anything to do with me. It turns out I had made too many jokes." Pruwett uncovered his face and straightened his shoulders. "So I took my mother's maiden name and combined it with a Christian name from the Bible. I put a notice in the paper, too—the new name *is* legal, not merely a ruse. Peter Davies had nothing to do but to make a mockery of his life. But Jedidiah Pruwett—now *he* had a purpose. You gave me that purpose, but I'm not going to let you take it away. If this is a joke, I won't be the butt of it."

"I don't want to make you one," Mark responded. "But I don't wish you to take out your... your excess zeal on anyone else."

Pruwett readjusted his glasses carefully. "Perhaps the MCB has become too...too excessive. But what *else* am I to do with my time?"

Mark sat and laid a hand on the man's shoulder. He'd not wanted to find himself in sympathy with the man. The MCB had made Mark's life miserable. Peter Davies had been an annoyance. Yet he could not help but feel pity for the fellow.

"You know," Mark said, "you did some very good work. How many members does the MCB have?"

"Several thousand."

"And you...you wrote the bylaws, and arranged the meetings. You handled the details of printing the cards and the pamphlets, and arranging for all the different organizations. That's quite a bit of responsibility."

Pruwett nodded, hardly mollified. "I also organized the small group sessions, the entire system of reporting, really. Those help keep a man on track.

I'd like to think that I've made a difference. I only wanted to have a chance, sir, and since nobody was giving me one, I had to make my own."

Mark cocked his head and looked at the man, as an idea—a glorious idea, a wicked idea—insinuated itself into his head.

"Pruwett," Mark said, "do you have a particular passion for chastity, or do you just want to spend your time doing something *good?*"

"I—sir—that is…" Pruwett put his hands in his lap. "Sir, I *tried* to get involved with something else. Anything else. Truly, I did. But nobody had any need of me."

Mark smiled wolfishly. "Oh, Mr. Pruwett," he said. "Believe you me—*I* have need of you. *England* has need of you. There is someone I should very much like you to meet, and he has a calling for you."

BY THE TIME Jessica had gone back to her flat for the evening, Margaret had assured her that they'd announce the betrothal and perform the wedding ceremony in the next few days. Her head was spinning.

She'd never imagined that there could be so many good people in the world. She'd never believed they might be willing to help her. Even fate, cruel as it was, could not possibly take all of this bounty from her. She sat in her chair and let herself believe in not just warmth, but kindness, happiness…love.

A knock sounded at the door.

She ran to it eagerly. But when she opened it, it was not Mark come to see her that evening. It was Nigel Parret. Her first thought was that he'd come to congratulate her—and, of course, to inveigle an invitation to her wedding, so he could beat out his competitors. But no—even though every paper, Parret's included, had discussed the special license Mark had obtained, her name had not yet been announced. And all similarly happy thoughts vanished as soon as she set eyes on his grim expression.

He handed her a letter. "This came to me. The writer thought that, as I'd published your story, I would know your direction."

The envelope had been opened. She glanced at him suspiciously, and he shrugged. "Can you blame me?" he asked.

Her name was scrawled on the front. No, not her name—*Jess Farleigh.*

That name seemed like a dark, cold shadow. She scanned the text.

Jess—

No doubt you're feeling quite proud of yourself right now. You defrauded me. If that license he obtained means what I think it means, you still managed to seduce Turner. You seem to think you can marry him and simply take your place in society at his side.

But I know who you are and what you've done. If you marry Sir Mark, I'll make both your lives a misery. I hear the Duchess of Parford is increasing, too. I wonder how she'll like you when she realizes her child will be shunned for your sake?

You're never going to marry him. But if you'll denounce him—if you'll write an account saying that he accosted me in the park because he was fighting over a whore—I'll at least agree not to prosecute you for fraudulently taking my money. I'll meet you tomorrow morning at five sharp in Harford Square. Bring Sir Mark's ring. I'll need it.

By the time Jessica reached the end of the first page, her hands were trembling. By the time she finished the letter, she was plunged into cold again.

"It's rough," Parret was saying. "But—at least I won't be the one printing the story. You can trust in that."

"That's kind of you." Her words emerged as a dull whisper.

"Humph." Parret shifted uneasily. "The duke would likely sue me for defamation of character. There's no profit in that."

Jessica smiled wanly. "You do a lovely imitation of a greedy man, Parret. But could you…could you please leave me?"

He set one hand briefly on her shoulder, in scant comfort. And then he left.

The door shut behind him, and Jessica collapsed against it.

Nothing had changed; she'd only been reminded how little had altered.

There was something about *surviving*. She felt a constant fear, a pressing worry. Her muscles never truly relaxed. Her belly always felt a little sour. These things had been her stalwart companions for seven years.

She had hoped—just today, she had led herself to believe—that she'd left all that behind. But no. She could still taste fear.

Mark was good, better than anything she'd imagined. So good that he scared her. How could she have forgotten? *Good* never lasted in her life. Instead, she brought its opposite with her. He wasn't going to save her; she was going to destroy him.

By the time Mark came to her door, she had worked herself into a near panic. She would have fled, if only she knew how to flee her own desires.

He smiled, and she felt warmth. He took her hands, and she felt safe. And it was all an illusion—an illusion that she'd allowed herself to believe, because she was so desperate for comfort from any quarter.

He smiled at her. "I have good news," he said

cheerily. "I've found a new Commissioner of the Poor Laws. Neither Weston nor I are suitable for the position. But it turns out, there is a fellow who has a passion for good works and a good amount of administrative experience. He even has some measure of popularity. I needed only to broach the idea and perform the introduction. After we marry in three days, I'll have no reason whatsoever to stay in London."

"Marry," she said wildly. "Three days?"

"How many times must I say it? There's no need to worry. Nobody is going to hurt you."

No. *She* was going to hurt *him*. She was going to hurt his family. She was going to be the wedge that Weston used to break apart their lovely little group.

"And besides," he said, "I love you. You cannot doubt that."

No. She couldn't. She knew it was true, and that's what scared her the most—the sheer rightness, the wonder of it all. How had London's most desirable bachelor fallen in love with *her*? How much would it hurt when he *stopped* loving her, when he began to resent what she'd cost his family?

"Mark," she said faintly, "You can't change fundamentals. I'm—"

"You are the woman who can outshoot me. Who will argue me to a standstill—and don't think I don't love that about you. I love you, Jessica. And I believe you care for me. What else matters?"

"You're a duke's brother. A knight. And I'm a whore."

He grabbed her wrist. "Don't call yourself that. I wouldn't let anyone else talk about you that way— why should I let you?"

"Very well. Call me a fallen women, then."

"Do you think that matters to me? My mother used to say that there was no such thing as a fallen woman. You just had to look for the man who pushed her down."

The look in his eyes made her want to scream. But this, at least, was something she could dispute. Something she could argue. She needed something to fight, because she couldn't push away the darkness that filled her.

Jessica took a deep breath and came to a realization. She couldn't win against Weston, but she could thwart him. If Mark walked away from her, if she simply left... Weston could threaten him with nothing but innuendo, and *that* society might simply chalk up to jealousy. "No, Mark. Nobody pushed me. I fell."

"A man seduced you. And your father, your own father, told everyone you were dead—"

"I could have said no." Jessica spoke softly. "He didn't force me."

"You were fourteen—"

"I was fourteen, not a baby. You believe that you were capable of reason at ten, and able to discern right from wrong. I knew what he was doing, and I let him do it." She looked at him and willed him to believe her. If he walked away, she could run. She could vanish before Weston appeared, and Mark's reputation would stay intact. He'd survive, and his family would see him through.

"But—"

She put her hands on her hips. "I don't exonerate him entirely, but I *chose* to fall. I chose to leave with him and go to London. It may have been stupid and it may have been wrong, but you belittle me when you relieve me of the responsibility of making it. You would make everything I've done a collection of events that has happened to me."

He was growing more and more confused. "Jessica. I don't mean that you're incapable of choice, just that—"

"What am I supposed to think, when you imagine me pure as the driven snow? I am not a child. If you strip me of the responsibility for my decisions, you strip me of the capacity to make them, as well. I am not a kitten, to be rescued from the jaws of a wolf. I'm a grown woman. And it is not your place to solve my problems without asking me for my opinion."

She didn't have to pretend her anger. She *was*

angry that this wasn't for her, that once again, happiness had eluded her.

He shook his head in frustration. "Jessica. I want to help you."

He did. If she showed him Weston's letter, he'd undoubtedly spring into action. Just as undoubtedly, Weston would find a way to tell the truth.

"You can't help who I am," she said. "All you can do is make me believe you for a few days—believe that I can be what you want me to be, believe that someone might think of me as something other than a whore. And what will happen when all that is revealed as the illusion it is? I'll be small and powerless again. Only this time, you'll realize it, too, and want to be rid of me."

"Stop." He took her shoulders. "Just *stop* with this. If I could rid myself of you, I'd have done it weeks ago. I have waited all this time to find someone I want to share my life. I've found her. Listen to me. Stop panicking. I love you."

But that just made her want to recoil all the more, to fight harder. If she let herself believe in him, all this goodness would be stripped from her. She could survive her own disappointment. She couldn't survive his.

"You want to love the facsimile of a perfect woman, wronged by society. You don't love *me*. *I* made mistakes. *I* made choices. *I* made myself who I was—not anyone else. And when I'd been brought to this point, *I* was the one who survived them. You admit your own sins, but you won't give me the burden of mine."

"Jessica." Mark took a step toward her.

"I made a living manipulating men into paying me a great deal of money in exchange for something they could get for a few shillings along the docks. If you can't see that in me, you are not looking very hard. You're in love with an illusion."

"You had to survive. I don't blame you for it."

"Why ever not?" she whispered. "I still blame myself."

When she'd first tried to seduce him on that long-ago night, he'd grinned at her and told her that he rather liked himself. And that, more than Weston, more than her reputation and all her fears for the future, seemed a suddenly unbridgeable gulf.

She loved him. But she would never like herself. She couldn't stand to stay long enough to see his fine regard gray and wither. She couldn't risk breaking something so valuable.

"I like you," he said. "I *treasure* you. I want you to let me protect you."

"I don't want a protector!" The words burst out of her, uncaged at last. "And I don't care whether you call yourself a husband or a lover or just the man who offers me money for my favors. I know what it feels like to have all choice stripped from me. To really not have any power over the future. To have someone protect me. I've felt that before."

"You know what I mean," he said. "I'm not going to apologize for wanting good things for you, for caring about your happiness. What on *earth* has got you so worked up? Why are you ripping up at me?"

"Because right now, you put me in mind of George Weston!" she shouted.

It was the worst thing she could have said. She could see it in the sudden lurch of his shoulders, the furious set of his mouth as he turned to her. This, then, was what she had to look forward to for years to come—anger, not affection. Love wouldn't linger, not for her.

Destroy it now, then. It's better for him—and what does another lie matter to you?

And so even though she knew it was wrong, even though she knew it would hurt him, she stabbed her finger into his chest. "You're just like him," she said, "solving my problems without consulting me first. Throwing money at me, without so much as asking my permission. I never asked you to help me. I can't bear it."

"You can't mean that," he said thickly.

"Can't mean what? That you make me feel like I'm nothing? That you make me feel as weak and stripped of my ability to choose my future as he once left me? That you are the last man on earth who will ever make me happy?"

"Jessica," he whispered. "Please."

One last blow, and she would free herself from all future sorrow. "You and Weston are cut from precisely the same cloth. I can't believe it took me this long to see it. I won't marry you—I couldn't bear to live with you."

He had turned utterly white. "I suppose there's nothing else I can say," he said quietly.

"There is this. Get out of my house."

He left. Of course he left. After he'd gone, she flung the contents of her desk to the floor with one sweep of her arm. Pens and paper and ink went flying. But it didn't help, not even when she curled on the floor beside them, her fists clenching, her breath coming in great sobs.

She'd done it. She'd freed herself from all fear of the future.

After that, there was nothing she couldn't survive.

CHAPTER TWENTY-TWO

JESSICA WAS NOT SURE how long she stared at the wreckage she'd made of her desk. The inkwell had cracked when she'd thrown it, and its contents had seeped out to soak into the rug underfoot. She felt like that vessel—cracked and stained and impossible to fix.

It was only when she heard church bells strike midnight that she shook her head and looked up. There was nothing to do now but pick up the pieces.

With a sigh, she reached for the glass. But her hands were shaking, and the shards were slippery with ink. When one slipped from her fingers, she grabbed for it automatically. The glass sliced her skin. Jessica's breath hissed in, and she pressed her finger in pain.

Pain. Just a few months ago, she'd thought herself beyond pain, beyond all feeling. She'd thought herself made of rock. Pain *hurt,* but it was better than emptiness, more desirable than the nothing that had consumed her then.

Yes, she'd lost Mark—but at least she'd found herself.

At that thought, her eyes fell on the letter Weston had sent her. She'd crumpled it into a ball and tossed it into the corner of the room in a fury. Now, she walked over to it, picked it up and smoothed out the paper again.

She'd found herself? What a lie. She'd found nothing, nothing but the cold certainty of more lonely years. She'd walked away from everything good in her life. She had let George Weston make her powerless. Again.

Her hand crept to her belly, stifling the faint echo of cramping.

No. No. Not this time.

A white-hot fury filled her. It was enough anger to wash away her fear, to fill every empty place Weston had left inside her.

Never again.

She looked at the damning letter she held in her hand and then folded it in careful quarters. Strange; her hands had stopped trembling.

"I am never going to be helpless again," she vowed to the paper, and then she slipped the note into her skirt pocket and reached for her cloak.

"Sir Mark."

Mark had retired to his chambers in his eldest brother's house in town. He'd poured himself an inch of brandy—not apple brandy; that he couldn't have borne—but he'd yet to drink. He looked up at those words.

"You have a visitor," the butler said. His mouth thinned briefly. "I've put her in the parlor from earlier."

Her. It was Jessica, then. He wished he could feel happy about that, but mostly he felt wrung out. By the time he'd arrived home, he'd realized that anger and fear, for Jessica, came out to nearly the same thing. He had known she would calm, that she would apologize.

What he didn't know was how to keep it from happening again.

He stood, wearily, and went to meet her.

She had not sat down. Instead, she was pacing a wary circle around the settee. She was so beautiful she nearly stopped his breath, so lovely he might have forgiven her outburst then and there, were it not for the vise clamping about his heart, telling him that this would happen again, this endless cycle of fear and recrimination. He didn't want that. And she—*she* deserved better.

She stopped on the turn as she saw him. "Mark," she whispered.

He wasn't sure what to say, wasn't sure if he should open up his arms for her or turn away. He was tired. He was upset. He'd had a glass to drink and had scarcely had a chance to think of the things she'd told him.

She must have seen the conflict writ in his face because she nodded firmly and reached into her skirt pocket.

"I received this letter early this evening," she told him.

He walked close enough to take the paper from her outstretched fingers. He opened it up, read the contents. Blackmail. Innuendo. Of *course* she'd been afraid; she'd feared for Mark, not herself. She would never stop fearing for him, Mark suspected. Somewhere, he could dimly feel his anger begin to burn.

"I could kill him," Mark said. His voice sounded cold and conversational to his ears. He looked over at her. Her skin was so white, all color washed from it. No; fear and anger weren't so far apart in her. And there had been just that ring of truth in her voice earlier, when she said she felt powerless.

He took a step closer to her. "I *could* kill him," he said more softly, "but then, I'm not sure it would do you any good. I promised you once that I would be your knight, willing to do battle for you. But I don't think that's what you need of me."

She shook her head mutely.

"You've always been your own knight," he said, "riding to your rescue. I'm just the man who came along and saw how brightly your armor shone."

He folded the note again and held it out to her.

"I have never needed to make a romance out of you. But I suspect that you need to make one of yourself."

"I won't let him ruin you." Her chin had a determined cast to it.

"No," Mark said. "You won't. But you were going to let him ruin *you*."

She let out a long breath. "I was," she said softly. "I realized something." And then she raised her chin and looked Mark in the eyes. "I can do better," she said.

And that, Mark realized, was precisely what he'd needed to hear.

George Weston came striding out of the mist at Harford Square early in the morning. The little stretch of green wasn't truly a square; it was more of a park, with a small copse of trees in one corner. He headed toward Jessica with a pompous smile on his face. But his smile was split by red, angry scratches; his cheekbone marred by bruises.

"I knew you'd see it my way," he told her. "Now, give over the account and Sir Mark's ring."

She would never have been rid of him, if she'd done his bidding. He would always have held power over her.

"I don't believe I will," Jessica said.

From behind her she heard more steps. Then:

"I say, Weston, is it your fault I was roused at four in the bloody morning? Not very kind, I tell you. Not very kind."

Weston peered around Jessica. "Godwin?" he said. "Godwin, what the devil are you doing here?"

Mark's voice followed. "What, don't you know? He's your second."

Only Silas Godwin could have done, Mark had explained to her. Mark had chosen him. He was, he'd said, good-humored. More important, he was close-mouthed. When Mark had told him he was needed, he'd come instantly, without asking and without regard to the lateness of the hour.

"Turner?" A gob of spittle flew from Weston's mouth. "*Turner?* You're having me fight a duel? And who else is that you have with you?"

"This is Doctor Agsley." Mark glanced at Weston. "It's customary to have one present at an affair of honor."

Jessica's fingers found the edge of her glove as Mark spoke. She worked the leather off her hand.

"Not enough to beat me to a pulp, is it?" Weston was turning red. "No. You're going to challenge me to a duel. Don't tell me you're going to fight for a whore's honor. Even you couldn't be so—"

Jessica slapped him with the glove she'd removed. "Don't be daft, Weston. *I* am going to fight you for his."

She would never have agreed to this had she

felt herself in the slightest danger. But she knew Weston. She'd watch him shoot before, and she'd every faith in his inability to hit anything at thirty paces.

"You?" He put back his head and laughed. "*You? Oh, that's a remarkable jest. The day I stand before one such as you, and—*"

She smacked him again with her glove, and while he rubbed at his cheek, she reached into her skirt pocket and pulled out a pistol. "You haven't a choice between fighting a duel and walking away. You have a choice between fighting a duel and being shot in cold blood. I told you last time that if you ever intruded on my life again, I was going to shoot you." Her voice was steady; it was only inside that she trembled.

"I can't fight a duel," Weston said with a scoff. "I don't have my dueling pistols."

"Got them here," Silas Godwin said cheerily. He glanced at Weston and frowned. "Is something amiss?"

Godwin's other main qualification, besides his quiet demeanor, was that he was none too bright.

"Of course something's amiss," Weston snapped. "I'm not fighting a woman. It would be…ungentlemanly. Wrong. Jess, really."

"Don't call me Jess." She jerked her pistol at him.

"But, Jess—"

She took a step back from him. "You want to believe that I'm impotent. That I'm helpless. That I am yours to move about as you wish, to comfort you in your life. You want to believe that you own me. And I let you do it for far too long."

"Come now, Jess. You're upset, I see that. But let's be rational about this."

Her voice was shaking. "I am not your victim. And I *am* being rational. The only way to win is to rid myself of you. You look at me and the only thing you can see is a possession, something that you can pick up and use however you want."

"Jess, we both know how poor a shot you are. This is utterly ridiculous, this notion of a duel."

"That's what you want to believe. You're telling yourself that you're safe, that surely a woman couldn't hurt you. You're telling yourself that you have nothing to fear, and that once you're released from this situation, you won't need to be afraid again. But maybe I'm not a poor shot. And maybe, this time, when you try to hurt me and mine, I won't just walk away."

He gave her a flat look. "You just go on and think so, then. Insist on this charade if you must, but when I emerge unscathed, we'll… We'll talk again." He cast a wary glance at Mark. "Assuming I'm allowed to do any talking. *Some* people here have already shown their bad faith and ungentlemanly conduct."

"I didn't box to your rules," Mark said quietly. "Think about what you've done."

"What? What did I do?"

"Weston," Jessica said, "I came within three inches of death because of you. What makes you think I'll let you off?"

He yawned. "Let's get this over with."

Her blood was pounding as they faced away from each other. Their seconds—Godwin, on Weston's part, and Mark, on hers—counted the paces. Each stride seemed interminable. It was unbelievable that this should be happening to her, that she should be taking him on.

They turned. Weston was a shrouded figure, almost disappearing in the mist. He was also a pitiable man; she couldn't believe that she'd believed herself powerless before him. She could feel her whole body trembling. On the sidelines, Godwin held up a handkerchief.

She didn't need to fire first. She braced herself, let her stance still. He wouldn't hit her. In this fog, at this distance—it was entirely out of his capabilities.

The white cloth fluttered down. In that instant, as Jessica stood on the cusp of pulling the trigger, Weston turned toward Mark. It must have happened quickly, because Mark had not even begun to react when Weston raised his gun on him. Still, the space between one beat of her heart and the next seemed to take forever. The barrel trained on Mark with an ominous certainty. Seeing that weapon swerve toward the man she loved—

Jessica fired. The report of his gun sounded, almost atop her shot. Someone shouted. The recoil snapped her arm back; the black powder smoke obscured everything. Jessica was running before the shreds cleared away, running as fast as she could, her heart and hands like ice.

They were both on the ground, Mark and Weston. But Mark was calmly pressing a handkerchief to Weston's shoulder, while Godwin huddled ineffectually in the background.

"My dispute has always been with Sir Mark," Weston was saying. "Any other course would have been foolish."

"This is irregular," Godwin was repeating to himself, as if he had finally noticed. "Most irregular."

"Precisely my point." Weston winced as Mark pressed harder. "There are no rules of honor in an affair like this."

"Should we…should we tell others?" Godwin asked.

"And admit a woman winged me? God, no." He glanced at Jessica. "You missed."

"*You* missed," Mark said. "And you were standing at six paces."

The doctor was coming up behind them. The

man knelt beside Weston, probed the wound. "It's just a flesh wound," he reported. "Straight through the shoulder. But had it been three inches to the side…" The man whistled and pulled a flask from his bag. "Here. You'll be needing this."

"I didn't miss," Jessica said as Weston raised the flask to his lips. "You came within three inches of killing me. I gave you those three inches."

His eyes met hers, and he turned white.

"Next time," she said, "I won't feel so generous. What you did to me—it was a hanging offense. You have nothing on me, Weston. You can embarrass me, but I can do far worse to you. I have the power of life and death over you. This—" she pointed at his wound "—this was so you would know that next time you bother me and mine, I'll not be afraid to use it."

He swallowed.

"But then there won't be a next time. Will there, Weston?"

He shook his head. And this time, *this* time, she believed him.

CHAPTER TWENTY-THREE

MARK BUNDLED Jessica into the waiting coach and then entered himself.

He'd had many sleepless hours to think of the harsh words she'd spoken last night, to hold them up and examine them from all sides. He'd reread the serial she'd published, too. And he'd come to one inevitable conclusion: part of her really *did* hate him. They'd not talked of it much, and it still hung between them unresolved.

She sat awkwardly across from him on the carriage seat, not meeting his eyes.

"I'm sorry." She fixed her gaze on the leather squabs. "I'm so sorry. I shouldn't have said what I did last night."

"Don't apologize." His gaze was steady. "When I first met you, you flinched from my touch. Well, I've realized you didn't stop flinching—at least not inside."

She shut her eyes at those words.

"I think," he said, "you told me the truth of it all the way back in Shepton Mallet. You hate that

I've had it so easy, while you've had to struggle for everything. You despise me because I like myself. And Jessica…I suspect you still think you don't deserve happiness."

She let out a shaky breath. "Happiness leaves. And it hurts so much when it does."

"Try it for a year. I think you'll grow accustomed to it."

"Happy for a whole year?" she said.

"Happy for a whole lifetime," he responded. "Happy and surrounded by people who love you— brothers and sisters, friends and children. Horses, if you wish, and cats and ducks."

"Ducks?"

"Yes," he said obstinately. "Ducks. And a husband."

She lifted her face at that. A faint line of crystal tears had collected in the corner of her eyes. "Today," she said quietly, "I stopped running from my past. Maybe I can stop fleeing husbands and ducks, as well."

He crossed to her side of the coach. He gathered her up in his arms and kissed her, soft and sweet and gentle, as if it were her first kiss and he wanted to savor it. And maybe it *was* something new, because for the first time, she relaxed against him in truth. His hands framed her face, and she kissed him as if he were a future she finally wanted to hold to. She kissed him as if she planned to keep him.

"I love you," she said, taking a deep breath. "Now, about that special license. Maybe we should use it after all."

He kissed her on one cheek. Again on the other. And then he pulled away and looked into her eyes. "No, Jessica," he said gravely. "I think the time for the special license has passed."

Those eyes widened, and her hands clutched his elbows.

"I've been thinking about family," he told her. "And I've decided the special license was a mistake. There's something more important."

MARK DIDN'T THINK he would need any introduction to Alton Carlisle, vicar of Watford, a small town outside of London. Still, he'd come prepared. When he stood on the steps of the vicarage, he handed over the letter of introduction to the woman who was brought to the door, along with his card.

The maid must have passed the card on to Mrs. Carlisle, because she arrived scant seconds later. She ushered him in, her hands fluttering. "Mr. Carlisle is out in the garden," she said, her voice breathy. "I'll go fetch him. At once."

She swept him into a side parlor, lit by morning brilliance. The embroidery was fading, but it felt homey.

"Please be seated."

But instead of leaving immediately, she opened another door. "Ellen!" she called. "You're needed. We've a very important guest. Do come keep him company."

Mark heard a murmur in reply but couldn't make out any words. Mrs. Carlisle's back was turned, and so Mark could not see her expression. But the young lady who walked into the room had her chin set in a rebellious line. She cast one glance at Mark—and then quickly looked away. Mark could guess what her mother had communicated with waggled eyebrows.

Look, here's a splendid catch! Be polite to him.

They were still trying to throw fourteen-year-old girls at him. Ellen Carlisle, however, seemed to have no interest in being thrown. He was, she supposed, pretty. She had too much of Jessica in her not to be. But her long dark hair was still in childish braids. And she folded her arms over her chest, as if daring Mark to flirt with her.

Oh, yes. This was definitely Jessica's sister.

"Do you always appear on so little notice?" she demanded, once her mother was safely out of earshot.

Mark shrugged. "Think of me as John the Baptist. I am of no interest in myself. I come merely to prepare the way."

This got him an exasperated stare. "I'm to think

of you as John the Baptist, am I? Your confidence is simply stunning. And here I am, entirely without silver trays."

Good. He liked her already. Mark took his watch from his pocket and set it on the table. "How sweet. Don't worry. You'll adore me in…oh, six minutes and twenty-two seconds."

She rolled her eyes. "Please don't tell my father that. It will only raise his hopes, and he shall use it as an excuse to utterly ruin my life." She scowled. "As *usual*."

"Don't worry," Mark said. "I've as little interest in marrying you as you do me."

She let out a little huff at that, her eyes cutting toward him. Mark almost wanted to laugh at that petulant conceit. Of course she didn't want to marry him—but she *had* hoped he was interested, so that she might have the fun of turning him down.

"Don't be ridiculous," Mark growled. "You're a very pretty girl, I'm sure, but you're too young for me, and besides, I'm in love with your sister."

Miss Ellen's eyes widened. "Charlotte? But she's *married*."

"Not Charlotte. Jessica."

The color washed from her face. All that haughty indifference fell away. "Jessica?" Each syllable wavered, as if she spoke an impossibility. Her hands fell to her sides, and then she darted across the room, kneeling before him and grabbing for his hand. "You know of Jessica? I'm not to speak of her, not to say her name, never again. But—is she well? How do you know her? Can I see her? I shall do anything you ask, if you just—"

"Ellen!" The sharp tenor sounded like a whip crack from across the room. "What do you *mean* by such forward behavior? Sir Mark—I'm dreadfully sorry for my daughter's conduct."

Mark realized how the scene must look. Ellen Carlisle was on her knees before him, her eyes glittering with tears. Ellen glanced once at her father and bit her lip.

Mr. Carlisle, after all, was the one who had declared Jessica dead. He was the one to whom she addressed the letters she sent—the ones that had gone unanswered. He had banished her and lied about her.

And yet the man in front of him didn't seem like a monster. He had graying hair, a narrow face—and an expression that was exasperated and embarrassed, but not stern. He had Jessica's lips. Surely, that lift of her chin had come from him.

Mark strode forward and offered his hand. "Sir Mark Turner."

The man shook it. "Alton Carlisle. At your service, sir. Your book—it's been a pleasure to be able to quote from it in my services. An even greater honor to have you in my home. You'll stay to dinner? There will be no repeat of that foolishness."

"You'll have to excuse Miss Ellen," Mark said quietly. "She's merely overcome. You see, I have decided to marry your daughter, and Miss Ellen has just discovered it."

"Marry my daughter." Mr. Carlisle stood, his face going slack. Mark could tell precisely when he began to think again—when the advantages presented themselves. The connection to a duke, a son-in-law who had the favor of the Queen. There followed a small, proud smile as he realized that somehow, *his* offspring had landed the most desired bachelor in five counties.

It took only a few seconds before the man was nodding. His breath rushed out. "My permission— of course. You have it."

"I've already settled five thousand pounds on her," Mark said conversationally. "For her separate use, and for our children, should we have any."

"Yes. Of course." Mr. Carlisle shook his head. "Pardon my stupidity—but I am convinced this must be a dream. I had not even known that you were acquainted with my daughter. Certainly, you and I have never been introduced." He scrubbed his hand through his thinning hair. "Next, you will tell me that you wish to marry her by special license, in a grand ceremony held in St. Paul's. This…this can't be happening."

"There your dream ends," Mark said. "I don't want to marry by special license. I want you to call the banns in your church. I want you to tell your entire parish that your daughter is marrying me. I want you to acknowledge her by name."

At Mark's feet, Ellen began to cry softly.

"Of course, of course. It will all be as you wish. Precisely as you wish."

"One last thing," Mark said.

"Whatever you say."

"From now on, when she writes you letters, I want you to answer them. And when she arrives on your doorstep, which she should do in, oh…" Mark peered over his shoulder at the watch on the table. "In two minutes, then I want you to welcome her inside."

Mr. Carlisle swallowed hard. He looked at Mark. He looked at Ellen, where she'd curled her legs about her on the floor. He looked back at Mark.

"You surmise correctly," Mark said. "This is no dream. I'd never met Miss Ellen before today. I mean to marry your eldest daughter, Jessica."

Mr. Carlisle pulled up a chair and sat down heavily. "I can't announce banns for Jessica. Everyone thinks she died."

"Everyone will have to be disillusioned. How you go about it is, quite frankly, not my problem to solve."

"I had to think of my other daughters. They— they wouldn't have been allowed anywhere if it had come out that their sister had been so ruined. I—"

"I do understand," Mark said. "You were frightened. You had to think of your position, your reputation. But as for Miss Ellen's prospects—we rather thought the Duchess of Parford might sponsor her Season. I don't think you understand what I am offering you. I am going to marry your daughter. My brother is going to welcome her into the family with open arms. If you think that the two of us cannot counteract any scandal you can imagine, you are greatly mistaken."

"Sir Mark, perhaps you don't understand—"

"*You* don't understand. I did not come to ask permission to make your daughter my wife. I am asking if you would like to make my wife your daughter once again."

"Yes." He stood up, his voice breaking. "Yes. Yes. You have to ask? You think I didn't read her every letter and hope that I could find a way? Do you think that a single night passed in which I didn't regret what had happened? I didn't know what else to do. And by the time I'd acted, it was too late. Too irrevocable."

For a moment, Mark thought of reminding the man that he'd had seven years to act. That he'd let it all slip away, knowing what his daughter had faced out there. But now was the time for reunion.

"It's not too late now. She's waiting at the door. Come on, now. She's missed you." He glanced at Ellen and gave her a smile. "She's missed *all* of you."

Three weeks later.

THERE WAS NOTHING Jessica could do to calm her nerves on the morning of her wedding.

She tried pacing in the nave. She tried braiding her hair. Her sisters distracted her by fussing with her gown, pinning flowers to the hem of her skirt…and just by being present. It was lovely having sisters again. She'd spent the past weeks with them. At the first service, her father had introduced her to the congregation and announced that he'd told a lie when he said she had passed away, and that he was deeply ashamed—but then he'd said nothing further, not one word against her. When he'd called the banns, everyone had forgotten everything else. And for the remainder of the time, she and her sisters had been free to take calls and talk to one another.

Then there had been Mark. He'd gone on walks with Jessica and her sisters. He'd held her hand chastely through three weeks' worth of afternoon rambles through country lanes. She had dined with

his brothers; he had engaged her father in a philosophical conversation that ended up with the two
of them arguing over texts for hours. And after
dinner last night, she'd scarcely had any time to
see him alone. Still, he'd pressed her against the
back wall of the garden in the few minutes they'd
found and he'd kissed her—soft and sweet, but
with the force of three weeks of pent-up longing.
He'd kissed her until they were both dizzy with anticipation, until she could scarcely stand for wanting him. And then, when he'd finally pulled away,
he'd whispered in her ear: "Tomorrow. Finally."

She didn't think that anyone had noticed their
disappearance, but when Jessica had returned to
the rest of the company, her sister had come up beside her and gently pulled an errant twig from her
hair. "How lucky for you," Ellen had said, with a
sly, sideways look. "It seems that Sir Mark has no
interest in being *practical* about chastity."

It would almost hurt to leave her sisters again.
They hummed about her now, Ellen patting the
bows on her dress into place. It was tomorrow, finally, and a mass of butterflies seemed to attack
her from inside. Charlotte went to join her husband
in the front pew, and Ellen departed to take her
place as maid of honor. Seconds seemed to stretch
into minutes. For this small space of time, Jessica
was utterly alone once more.

And then: "Hello?" A short man popped his

head through the door of the vestry where she waited.

"Mr. Parret. What are you *doing* here?"

"You invited me." He smiled cheerily. "Also, I wanted to give you this."

He handed her a newspaper. Jessica unfolded it—and gasped.

Sir Mark: Married at last! proclaimed the headline.

"By the time the church bells have rung," the man said gleefully, "all the other papers will have copied the details from me."

This morning, she read, *Sir Mark Turner wed Miss Jessica Carlisle, the daughter of Reverend Alton Carlisle of Watford. Our readers will be interested to note that she is the woman whose account appeared first in these pages. Our investigation has uncovered the details of her past, which we hereby recount.*

Her fall, according to the article, was that she'd taken up reporting for a London scandal sheet at a young age and had been cast out by her family as a result. Nothing more. It made her sound... youthfully ambitious. In comparison to the truth, she sounded almost respectable.

"Mr. Parret," Jessica said, shaking her head, "this is a pack of lies."

He shook his head. "Nonsense. You *were* a reporteress—and quite young for one. Fully twenty years younger than me."

"I suppose you couldn't resist the money," she teased.

A faint smile touched the man's face. "This one, I'm distributing for free. Your…your brother-in-law-to-be came by the other day, and told me what you'd done. Mr. Turner—not the duke."

"What did Mr. Smite Turner claim that I did?" she asked, puzzled.

"He told me that you'd insisted upon settling money on my Belinda." Parret's voice cracked. "Enough for her to have a Season. A dowry. For that, I would even tell lies for a reporteress."

"He said that, did he?" Jessica hid a smile. She could already imagine how Smite would have done it—just a little cold in his delivery, and so distant. But Jessica had made no such settlement. Smite must have done it himself.

"You know—" she began.

"There's no time to argue now." Parret reached up and touched her veil, sliding a ribbon into place. "It's already printed, and here comes your father. Even if you don't mind keeping Sir Mark tapping his toes, you shouldn't keep Her Majesty waiting."

"Her Majesty!"

"Oh, yes." Parret set one hand on her shoulder and turned her toward the door. "I had nothing to do with that—but a certain duke that we both know made sure she received an early copy. After she read what I had written, she insisted on attending. You know that she admires a happy marriage. Not one person in all of London will dare look down on you after this."

They hadn't planned on living in London. They probably still wouldn't. But…it was nice to know the possibility was not entirely closed to them.

Mr. Parret suddenly looked down. "You gave my daughter a dowry," he muttered. "The least I can do is give you one, too." His eyes looked suspiciously red. But he gave her a gentle shove toward the door.

She walked out in a daze, let herself be guided to the aisle. The organ music seemed to swell around her. Light played through stained-glass windows, casting patterns on the gray stones that marched up to the front. Fabric swished as guests rose to greet her—a sea of faces, new and terrifying mixed with old and familiar. His brothers. Her mother. Old friends from childhood, who had long thought her dead; new acquaintances whose names even now slipped from her mind.

Her sisters.

And, yes. Her Royal Highness.

Panic struck, blinding. She *couldn't* walk down there, not in front of all these people. She *couldn't.*

Jessica forced her breath to slow, and she looked even farther up the aisle.

Mark stood in front of the church, wearing a white-and-silver dress coat. He smiled at her; she could feel it clear through to her toes. Dukes and queens and all her fears disappeared.

There was nothing in front of her but her future. And she walked toward it with open arms.

* * * * *

AUTHOR'S NOTE

SHEPTON MALLET is a real town, but the people I describe in it are entirely the product of my imagination.

In order to write a story with actual conflict and obstacles to overcome, I had to create some town residents who were less than perfect. My apologies in particular to the rectors of Shepton Mallet, who have absolutely nothing in common with the fictional Mr. Lewis.

Luckily for me, the reality of Shepton Mallet was much, much friendlier. From the Shepton Mallet Tourist Information and Heritage Centre, to the workers at Dungeon Farm who helped me find my way, the people I met were universally kind and helpful. (The only exception to the "kind and friendly" label was a herd of cows who apparently hadn't been informed that they were supposed to be herbivores and attempted to eat me. Bad cows.)

Even though the bones of this story are fiction, it's woven around bits of historical fact. For instance, there was no MCB (as if you couldn't guess that part), but Queen Victoria really did get the silk for her wedding dress from Shepton Mallet. Mark's father never really exploited anyone, but the workers in Shepton Mallet burned factories years in advance of the Luddite movement. The Shambles are, in fact, called Shambles, and the ones that were in the market square in 1841 dated from medieval times. The market is still held around the Market Cross on Friday, and the cheese is delicious. I confess that I exaggerated the potency of the apple brandy, although it was fun to try it in the name of research.

I've done my best to try to capture a little bit of the feel of Shepton Mallet in this book, but there's no substitute for the real thing. Visit, if you have the chance. I highly recommend it.

If you're from Shepton Mallet and you're wondering why I've renamed the River Sheppey, I haven't—it didn't get its current name until the Ordinance Survey conducted in the late nineteenth century.

Finally, I did my best to capture the countryside, but the truth is that Shepton Mallet and Somerset today are very different than they were in early Victorian times. This is because modern machinery has obviated the need to use waterpower, and so the millraces and leats that would have been widespread back then have fallen into disuse. Modern agriculture has also drained most of the bogs, the marshes and the wet places; in 1841, drainage techniques were being applied for the first time. I've done my best to reconstruct what the countryside would have looked like, but the historical accounts I've found are incomplete. I had to use my imagination.

REQUEST YOUR FREE BOOKS!

2 FREE NOVELS
FROM THE ROMANCE COLLECTION
PLUS 2 FREE GIFTS!